TROUBLED BORDER

Books by F. D. Allan

DOCTOR IN BUCKSKIN

TROUBLED BORDER

Books by T. D. Allen:

DOCTOR IN BUCKSKIN

TROUBLED BORDER

Troubled Border

By T. D. Allen, pseud.

 Harper & Brothers, Publishers, New York

ONE

I

John McLoughlin stooped to select another sample from the beaver skins stacked knee-deep around him. Straightening, his head bumped again the slope of Chief Wisagun's lodge. Along with the soot, he brushed from his hair the appetizing odor of smoked deerhide.

Pete Ogden, sitting cross-legged beyond the lodge fire, looked up and grinned. Pete's eyes, meeting John's above the prime beaver, gloated. Given an hour for getting back to the fort, they had, once more, outwitted their Hudson's Bay Company competitors.

Chief Wisagun's skins, stretched flat as parchment, had been aired and brushed. They showed no sign of sand or moths. Examining only two specimens had convinced John that he must have these furs at any price. The trouble was, he had loaded too few bolts of calico and duffels, far too few brass and copper kettles on those five dog sleds outside. Besides, five dog teams would find it mighty dry sledding with this many beaver and no trail back to Rainy Lake House across the night's fresh fall of powder snow.

Still, they could hardly have known what to expect. Their North West Company scouts sent only bare word—band of Crees passing to south and east with autumn take of beaver. No hint of prime pelts garnished the message.

John had first decided not to bother with the usual subterfuge. Then, not so much as a precaution but more because his men hadn't had much excitement lately, he sent young Jamie Douglas the mile down Rainy River to invite the commissioned gentlemen at the Hudson's Bay post to a party.

Sticking around long enough to greet the Britishers when they arrived, John and Pete had then meandered through separate

[3]

doors. Breathing hard when they met at their hidden sleds, they had ordered their drivers to make a run for it. They would trade with the Crees, race the furs home to their warehouse, and drift back into the party half through one of Pete's tall tales as if they had wandered in from the veranda.

In the black eave of the lodge at John's back a child whimpered. The look of concern that Chief Wisagun turned toward the sound brought an inquiry to John's lips but Pete Ogden broke in. "Let's get on with it, Doc."

John could never anticipate that from Pete's rocklike body would come the voice of a hoarse ten-year-old. Now Pete fidgeted and hunched his red blanket capote high on his short neck. He got to his feet. He moved in to stand over Chief Wisagun in spraddle-legged impatience and his fluster pulled his voice higher off its sandy center than usual. He said in Cree, "Chief Wisagun must have fine squaw to take such good care of hides." To John he added in English, "If that party breaks up before we get back to the fort, we'll have a fight on our hands."

"It's always a fight or a race with things the way they are between Hudson's Bay and us Nor'westers," John answered in English. "Fact is, I'm trading closer to the line than I like. A lot closer."

"You can manage," Pete answered. You could say one thing for Pete's voice. It might grate but it was a cheerful, good-natured kind of grating. "I can't say I give you full credit for the way you manage," Pete went on in English while Wisagun opened and shut the folding knife John handed him. "It was God, I reckon, let you keep growing till you can't straighten up without bumping your head on something and he turned your hair white while you were still a kid. These Indians look at you like they were seeing the Great Spirit himself. Every Indian between Red River and the St. Lawrence would rather do business with you than any other trader in Canada. You could get this fellow's beaver for half what you're showing him."

"Except that Hudson's Bay has been paying such exorbitant prices for skins in any condition," John objected. "We all have,

[4]

for that matter. Now that a haul of fine pelts comes along, they ought to command a price and we don't have it. It's not fair."

"We've got two jugs of rum on the dog sled outside," Pete reminded him. "Why not use that and get this over? It's midnight now and we're a full hour away from the fort. I say use the rum and let's be on our way."

"That's hardly my idea of giving Wisagun a fair trade," John answered. He pulled a loop of his blanket tunic from its red worsted sash and said in Cree, "Chief Wisagun like this shirt?"

But even this made him feel guilty. Wisagun's tunic of red deerskin with its fringe of mink was worth fifty of John's even if he threw in his pantaloons.

Wisagun, beginning at his leather boots, lifted his eyes slowly up John's full height. Then he grinned and gave a playful push at John's disarranged tunic. "Put it back," he said. "Big as Cree lodge. Chief Wisagun lose head and arms in such big shirt."

They all laughed at the joke but Pete cut his high cackle short.

Outside, a sled dog bayed at the moon and his driver set the music to French curses.

John told Pete, "I know, I know, we must hurry. But this one trade might be enough to stop some of that talk in Montreal about making a deal with Hudson's Bay." He handed the chief a box containing a gross of shiny steel awls.

"Why not pay in fire-water?" Wisagun asked. "Crees have much need of fire-water to make hearts strong."

Pete Ogden took a step toward the lodge opening but John stopped him with a jerk of his head. "Crees have more need of food to put in bellies," he said. "Northwesters pay in buffalo guns, in scalping knives, in axes. Crees make fine buffalo hunt, eat great feast."

Wisagun looked up and nodded. "You say true. Chief Wisagun know." He nodded again. "Still, young men ask for fire-water. They say, 'King George men pay in fire-water.' They talk of this all time when follow beaver streams. They make squaws stretch hides just so with promise of fire-water."

"Squaws care more for beads than for fire-water." John handed the chief a hide bag filled with blue trade beads. "See, the latest style," he pointed out. "Every squaw wants blue beads this season."

Wisagun ran his spread fingers into the transparent bubbles and laughed at the glassy tinkle they made falling back. But a cough and a cry from the eaves stopped him and he forgot all about beads.

Pete Ogden failed to keep the hurry from his voice. "If you want them, say so," he broke in.

"Take beads." The chief got to his feet. "Take fire-water, too." He moved back into the shadows murmuring to the child.

"For the love of Methuselah," Pete exclaimed. "We won't get home till next month."

"Is the child sick?" John asked.

Chief Wisagun's head came out of the shadows. He grasped his throat and groaned. "Poor son, poor son."

"Bring your son to the light," John told him.

Wisagun carried the boy to the fire. John knelt beside him and turned back the corners of his blanket. Four years old, he guessed, but the sunken cheeks and pointed chin might be pulling him off two years in either direction. He pushed up the child's scraggly bangs with the back of his hand. He turned to Pete.

"My medicine bag—it's on the first sled."

"Sure, Doc. Time and tide have nothing in common with you."

"Show me your tongue, Lad," John said in Cree. Looking around for a depressor, he picked a flat file from the trade goods beside him and peered down the boy's inflamed throat. "Tut, tut, tut," he said.

"Tut, tut, tut," Chief Wisagun repeated on the same note of concern.

When Pete returned with the bag, John made a swab of soft linen and soaked it in turpentine. The boy's gags and yells helped John get to the red blotches in the poor child's throat but they started the dogs growling outside. The treatment over, John said in Cree, "There, Lad, now it should feel better. Shut your eyes and I'll sing you a bonnie song of old Scotland."

Pete Ogden's fists propped on his hips were a loud gesture of protest.

[6]

John had sung only as far as, "By yon bonnie banks," when Chief Wisagun picked up a monotonous humming that coincided with the pitch at infrequent intervals. Soon a will-o'-the-wisp smile twitched a corner of the sleeping boy's mouth.

John replaced his medicines and linen and buckled his bag. Then, afraid to take out his brass watch to see the time, he turned again to the beaver skins and trade goods.

But Chief Wisagun spoke without lifting his eyes from his sleeping son's face. "Take beads. Take gun flints. Take flat files. Take awls. Doctor keep fire-water."

John and Pete heaved the bundles of beaver through the lodge flap. Their French-Canadian drivers flung them onto the sleds. They had no time for slapping each other on the back and speculating on the caliber of the oaths that would emanate from the region of Portage de Chaudière when the gentlemen of Hudson's Bay learned of this night's work.

As always, John had put on his deliberate manner along with gathering up brass thimbles and twist barrel rifles for purposes of Indian trade. Now, outside Wisagun's lodge, he gave his head a shake like the flick of a magician's handkerchief. His unhurried manner vanished on the white billow of his breath. He jerked up the hood of his capote. He called out, "*Lève, lève, lève.*"

Under the whir and snap of the drivers' whips, dogs nipped at their teammates and growled their objections to the loads but they laid into their harness. Sled runners broke from their tracks.

John stepped into his snowshoes and let out his seven-league stride. His only thought now was to make time. He even forgot Pete's low-to-the-ground build and, since Peter Skene Ogden would never be guilty of slowing down a party, they were some twenty minutes nearer home before John noticed the squat shadow huffing along half a pace behind him.

"I should have stuck to my doctoring and left fur trading to you hot-blooded young firebrands who like the hump ribs of a Hudson's Bay factor for breakfast once a week or so." He was making cover talk to keep Pete from resenting a pace slowed to accommodate him.

"You're a great one to be calling somebody else a firebrand!"

[7]

They were skirting International Falls well to the north but, above the scrape of sled runners, John could test his bearings by the distant rumble of the water. From habit he kept going while he cocked his ear to the sound. But this was no trip to try his knowledge of the Rainy Lake trapping district. Tonight, all they needed was speed. The greenest sled dog in the outfit could follow his nose from here and arrive, in time, at the fort. In time—there was the rub. Judging by the three-quarter moon riding high to the left of their single-file brigade, it must be past one. Sometimes a fort party could hold its guests that late but not always and James Douglas was only a kid and new at this game.

Once more John found himself out in front with Pete bobbing along like a Scottish terrier at his heels. They were entering the grove of pines where they had found it necessary to chop out a few seedlings on the way down to clear a track for the sleds. And now, although he could feel no wind, John saw a clod of snow fall from the crotch of a tree. He stopped. Coming up, Pete said nothing but John could feel him searching the way ahead. Both men set down their snowshoes, when they moved, as if they were walking on tiptoe, trying not to step on the tree shadows striping their trail.

A dog whined and his French-Canadian driver, instead of swearing, scolded in a tone he might use with a frightened child.

There was something then.

Before John had actually seen any movement ahead or had heard anything that could not be laid to frost and the low-pitched hum of dry snow beneath loaded sleds, he worked his pistol forward in his belt and shook off his deerskin mitten.

A branch snapped. Instantly then a rifle sang out and a shower of snow cut off the view in front.

John kept his voice low but threw all his weight behind it. "Bunch the sleds," he ordered. "Draw but hold fire."

He and Pete crouched to see under the trees and try to separate the shadows that moved from those rooted in the ground.

Two pistol shots came on each other's heels. Staccato yelps suddenly peopled the emptiness on both sides of the trail ahead.

Pete asked, "Injuns or Britishers?"

"Both, I'm guessing," John answered, "and all well oiled with rum."

"Our rum," Pete pointed out.

"They don't get this load," John vowed more to himself than to Pete.

Still, men's lives were worth more than furs. John didn't want his men killed or even hurt. He couldn't estimate numbers from those wild animal yaps. The gamble was all against him on that score though. No Hudson's Bay man ever left a thing like that to chance. It was always easy enough to attach another fifty Indians to a foray simply by baiting the enterprise with rum and arming it with British-made pistols.

Those pistols set up an argument now that required an immediate answer. Just how five drivers plus Pete and John could send back a telling rebuttal was the question. Certainly they could not do it with seven pistols. They'd have to add their wits.

John lowered his head and listened again. Still scattered, their attackers' range was short but they were making corrections with each pull of a trigger.

A spot like this always hit Pete Ogden with the force of a dare. John saw him stand, black against the snow, and ease on his mitten. "Well, Doc," he said, as if he were ready to go home from a tea, "let's be on our way."

John caught his leg. "Down with you, Lad. They're feeling for a range finder just your size. By the auld Cloots, down!"

"The devil you say!"

"That's what I just said. You'll make a run for it," John told him, "as soon as I've pulled them off side."

Pete objected. "I'll pull them off. You run."

A fountain of snow erupted near enough to spray their faces when it fell.

John whispered, "Don't argue. I'll work off to the left. When you hear my new Collier speak twice, let out your legs. Fire if you must but, mostly, run!"

A rifle shot cut across the spasmodic pistol fire. It snapped a high limb from the pine under which they lay.

[9]

"I won't be long," John promised. He wormed his way back to the first driver. "You're going through," he said in French. "Follow Pete Ogden."

"*Oui*. M'sieu Pete take us through," came the confident answer.

On elbows and knees John plowed the snow at an angle to the trail and forward into range of the pistol fire. Startled by a barrage of shots, he jerked up and saw through the trees to the right spatters of snow well aligned on the trail. He pulled off farther to the left. Catching his pantaloons on a snag, he tore himself loose and lunged on. Every yard he could put between him and his party would give them that much advantage, but lead thudded into the snow all around him now. He weighed the risk of not being able to give the signal, if he waited, and aimed into the treetops still farther off to the left.

But just then the pistol shots slowed and stopped. The animal yelps and yaps died out.

Perhaps, John decided, he could wallow his way a bit farther off side. But before he could move again a voice too near for quibbling called out, "I say, Doctor, you're surrounded. You may jolly well surrender or we're coming in with our knives to finish you off."

John raised his arm and fired once, turned the cylinder on his five-shot Collier, and fired again.

He heard Pete Ogden's "Hi-yi," then the drivers' whips snap in the cold air. The dogs wrangled and growled and John could hear the sound moving up even with him, passing, and then growing dim with no wind to carry it back along the trail. Good! The furs were on their way.

Yelps and shots filled the night. John, too, although he aimed high, kept his pistol and his mouth going full blast. He shouted first in French, then in Cree, then in English, hoping he sounded like an international platoon. The moon shone too bright for the ruse to fool many of the Indians, though. He could see them milling into the trail and giving chase to the sleds. But several Britishers were trampling down the undergrowth, converging on him.

If they had any horse sense—John couldn't help thinking of

Hudson's Bay men with scorn for their gumption—they'd be tearing off in the opposite direction to spur the Indians on and waylay those furs. A Hudson's Bay man could carry out orders to a T but put him in a spot on his own and he'd pick the densest way out or know the reason why.

A knife stabbed the ground within reach of John's fingers and quivered there, hissing at him.

Well, he didn't want anything that wasn't his. He'd give the knife back fast enough.

Then another knife cut the cold air near his ear but John could not see it strike. He reached for the one at hand but his arm seemed pinned to the hood of his capote. Startled, he tried his fingers and found them, for some silly reason, refusing to unbend. Slowly a shilling-size numb spot below his right shoulder developed a core of pain.

John swung his legs around and sat up. The numbness gave way entirely to pain.

As if it were a log, he lifted his right arm into his lap. With his left hand he could reach around to make out the hilt of a scalping knife protruding from his back. Warm and somehow comforting he felt blood begin to trickle down under his shirt. He had never felt so cold. After he rested a bit, he must see whether he could get his trigger finger to work. Otherwise, those Britishers were almost on him.

He could make them out clearly, now. Their Hudson's Bay cloaks, blue by day, looked black and voluminous against the snow. He could easily pick them off with his pistol but he didn't want that. All he wanted was to keep them off Pete Ogden's neck. Let them swoop down on him like bats, their black wings spread. Black filled in the spaces between the trees. It rested his eyes. The blood soaked through his shirt and turned cold as the night got to it.

Well, he had rested long enough. He struggled to his knees and then stood up. He tried the pistol in his right hand. The Britishers were barely ten yards away. He'd have to make that finger squeeze the trigger. He swiped at the sweat on his forehead. Then the trigger gave way but the sound of the pistol came

[*11*]

to him all mixed up with the rumble of International Falls and the grumbling of sled dogs.

Slowly John sat down and then lay on his side in the snow. The snow felt warm as swansdown. Only his back was cold. Black—that was what he needed—just for a moment to rest his eyes and give Pete time to get through with the furs. Soft as a beaver pelt, the whole night turned to grateful black.

II   Hands moved on his back, offsetting the throb of pain. They stroked up his spine and circled on his neck. They soothed his left shoulder and then his right. The hands felt so sure of themselves that John saw no need to hurry his return to consciousness.

Later he could take in his surroundings and find out how he got here. Soon now he would open his eyes and see who it was who bent over him. Her hair smelled of pine. She crooned as if to a child,

> *Le changement n'est pas défendu,*
> *J'en amerai bien d'autres:*
> *En vous perdant, mon beau monsieur,*
> *Je ne perds pas grand' chose!*
> *C'est pour vous dire encore bien mieux*
> *Que j'aime quand je veux. . . .*

John had only half made up his mind to lift his heavy eyelids when she began to improvise at the end of the verse. Without a break she sang on in French, "You are playing possum and you are not fooling me one shilling's worth." Then he could feel her breath on his forehead. She kissed his temple, his cheek, and finally his lips.

When he opened his eyes, she sat back on her heels beside the bed. The candle on the table at her shoulder had burned down until the wick lay almost flat in a small pond of tallow. Now it sputtered and threw off a shower of sparks that hung for an instant like sapphires in her black hair. She did not bother to brush them off.

John had never seen so much strength and so much beauty mated in one body. She lifted the cape of her hair and laid it back over her shoulder with a hand that might have been modeled in porcelain. And yet he had felt the strength in that hand on his back. An artist might have mixed the color for her eyes but the quality of distant hills that John found in them stirred him more than their special shade of smoky blue.

Quiet lived within her. He could see it in the easy bearing of her head and shoulders, in the tranquil curve of her parted lips. And yet it was the quiet of banked fires. Live flames played in her eyes. John had felt vitality and excitement in the touch of her hands.

He wanted to tell her how the feel and smell of her, how the sound of her voice, had brought him back to consciousness with a song inside him loud enough to drown the drumbeat of his pain. He wanted to tell her how the sight of her warmed the cold ball of anger that had remained in the pit of his stomach through the hours of unconsciousness. Instead he asked, "How did I get here?"

"Chief Wisagun—he brought you to me in his canoe." She spoke with long e's replacing the short i's. In her low-pitched voice the words seemed of no one language but blended from the most pleasing sounds in both French and English. "He said," she went on, " 'Tell him Chief Wisagun come back for pay in brass kettles.' "

John grinned. "That old scoundrel!"

"Chief Wisagun, that old scoundrel, is blood relative of Marguerite's." She paused and her only sign of censure was the slow lowering of her eyelids. "Perhaps Cree chief save your life. Much blood run out."

John laughed and started to turn but the pain stopped him.

"No, no, no!" The girl's hands went under the blankets to rub him back to quietness. "Might be you can turn more on your side to rest. I will help." Gently she laid one hand on the wadding that had been applied to his wound. She held it firm while she eased his left shoulder under until he could push back on the bed and get comfortable.

"You'll stay where I can see you?" he begged.

[*14*]

"I will do more. I will come in bed with you, now that you have made room for me."

"But this is no good," John protested, when she had blown out the candle and climbed in beside him. "I can't put my arm around you. You've strapped it down."

"It is the best way. The cut is back of your right arm. It opens when you move." Then she came close and rubbed her cheek against his. "Johnny, Johnny." She said it with a soft *J* as if it were the French *Jeannie* and the way she said it filled his name with the sound of love. "Johnny, I am sorry to have you so hurt."

He could not move to kiss her.

"What time is it?" he asked at length.

"Soon the sun will get up."

John said, "We put one over on them this night."

"They put one into you," Marguerite reminded him. "I have it for you. It is a Hudson's Bay Company trade knife." She moved away from him.

"*Oui*, I know, I know. But we beat those Hudson's Bay dudes to the fattest load of prime beaver I've seen in all my seventeen years in the fur trade." John smiled his satisfaction into the dark room but it did him as much good as if the honorable Governor and Committee in London could see it. "They'll talk for weeks— behind their hands, of course."

"It will not be the first time." The remembering in Marguerite's voice did not sound elated by his victory.

"No, not the first time," John admitted, hoping she could hear in the words how much he'd like to make up to her for the gossip. If only he had his good arm out from under him so he could reach her. "Come over close and tell me what a clever fur trader I am," he suggested. "Who cares what they say?"

She did not move. "Marguerite cares . . . sometimes."

"They're not worth caring about."

She was silent a long time and still she did not move. At last she said, "Johnny?"

"What's bothering you?"

"I don't like you to have a cut in your back."

[*15*]

John scoffed. "What's a little knife thrust? I'll be as good as new in a week. That is, if you come closer. I'll never get well with you way over there." He expected to hear her giggle in answer to this. Her giggle sounded so childlike that it always seemed to come from someplace outside Marguerite and John often found himself casting for it with little dry flies of nonsense.

But tonight Marguerite did not giggle. "Johnny?"

So, she did have something more than his wound on her mind. "What is it, *ma chérie?*"

"You said there would be talk at the fort?"

"Talk will flow like the water over International Falls. You should hear it."

"I prefer not. I have heard enough." Marguerite never bothered to hide from him what she was thinking. John knew that through this long silence she was reliving the days when she had been the chief subject of gossip around the fort. At the time, she had held her head higher than usual and had insisted that it was nobody's business but theirs. "Johnny," she burst out now, "could we be married?"

"Married?" John reared up on his elbow but the stab of pain jerked him back.

"Now, now, Johnny," she soothed and moved over. Her fingers slid up through his hair behind his ear.

"Where did you get this idea?"

She turned onto her back and clasped her hands under her head. "A minister has come from England to Red River Settlement. He is—" She struggled with his title. "He is the Reverend Mr. West." Once through that, the point of all this poured from her in one breath. "He says all trappers and traders ought to marry their wives."

"Oh he does, does he? Why the auld Clootie!" John felt every muscle in him tighten. A man could not be properly angry while lying in bed with one arm strapped to his side. He should be standing every inch of his six-foot-four with a black satin tie knotted around his highest collar and his best beaver hat set square on his head. That way he could give Hudson's Bay Company to understand that for all their size they were not big enough to send some little pip-squeak across the ocean to tell him what he ought to do. He was a free man and free he'd stay.

"Johnny, you are not angry?" Her fingertips touched his lips.

He chuckled. "I'm angry all right but not with you, *ma chérie*." Ignoring the pain, he screwed his left arm from under him and slipped it around Marguerite. "There now, let me tell you once more. You're my girl, forever and always. Our names are written in the North West Company book at the fort. I'm sorry that we couldn't have written them there right at first. I'm sorry people talked but that's all over."

"But the Reverend Mr. West says—"

"The Reverend Mr. West has been sent to Canada for no other purpose than to stir up trouble for us Nor'westers." John set his jaw. "The way I feel right now, if the honorable Governor of Hudson's Bay Company came from London in person and ordered me to eat three meals a day, I'd cheerfully starve to death and relish every minute of it. Does that ease your mind?"

Before she could reply, a lanky boy of eight appeared in their bedroom door. He clutched a lighted candle. His bare feet protruded from beneath a red nightshirt. "*Papa*, are you all right?" he asked.

Marguerite sat up in bed. "Sh-h-h, Jacques. Go back to bed, *mignonne*. He is wounded. You must not touch your *papa*."

"*Papa!*" the boy screamed.

"Quiet, Son," John answered. "I'm all right. It's just a knife scratch."

The child came to the foot of the bed but did not reach out. "But *Papa*, I dreamed about you." He threw his arm across his eyes. "It was awful."

"There, there," Marguerite soothed. "You will wake up your sister. Come. Your toes are curling up from the cold. Climb in on this side and *Maman* will sing you to sleep."

Marguerite settled back on John's arm and he still had room to gather in with her his son, the child of their first defiant love.

They had named him John Junior and Marguerite's names for her two men sounded so nearly the same that they sometimes

[*17*]

answered in unison when she called. The same soft *J* with the breath of love in it began Johnny and Jacques.

It was on the day that his son was born that John McLoughlin had dressed in his best clothes and made a special trip to the fort to record in the Company book Marguerite's name beside his. Writing, he said to himself, "Till death us do part." For him the ceremony had been solemn and binding. No minion of Hudson's Bay was going to set it aside.

Marguerite lay on his arm and half sang, half whispered to their son:

> *Mignonne, ma mignonne,*
>   *Mon coeur joli,*
> *J'te donn'rai cinq cents livres*
>   *De mon argent*
> *Si tu y veux me rendre*
>   *Le coeur content.*

No other voice could be so exciting and at the same time so calming. In spite of straining to hear each note, in spite of the pain in his back, John felt himself drifting off to sleep.

And then a series of bangs on the front door brought them all awake. Outside, Pete Ogden squealed at the top of his sandpaper lungs. "Doc, open up. Open up, I say. News from Montreal. Confound it, open this door!"

By the misty light of dawn reflected from the snow, John watched Marguerite slip from bed and tuck the blanket around Jacques. Taking her time while Pete kept up his clatter, she exchanged her ruffled nightdress for a beaded antelope tunic.

Finally the racket outside stopped and John heard snatches of Marguerite's explanation at the door. He knew that she was blocking Pete's way but he also knew Pete. If the news was urgent, nothing Marguerite could do would keep him out.

"But I tell you he is cut in the back. You will, perhaps, give him the fever with these news."

Always sure of his ground, Pete answered, "Brew up your best cup of tea, Marguerite. That will cook the fever." And he slammed into the bedroom. "What's the idea, you big grizzly?

You know I would have left those furs at the first hint you had a knife in you!"

"*Oui, oui,* I know. The furs are safe?" John asked.

"Locked up tight in North West's warehouse and the best I ever ran my fingers through. But a whale of a lot of good they'll do us"—he slapped John's blanket with the dispatch in his hand—"once we sell out to Hudson's Bay Company."

In spite of his awkwardness with the strapped-down arm, John managed to slide past Jacques's feet and sit on the side of the bed. "Nobody's going to sell out to Hudson's Bay. Is that dispatch for me?"

Marguerite gave the distinct impression of stamping her moccasins at Pete as she passed him with an angry toss of her head and came over to soothe John's back again with her sure hands.

Pete handed the dispatch to John. He asked Marguerite, "How bad is he hurt?"

"He is hurt too bad for having his door pounded down at dawn," she flung at him.

But John had unfolded the dispatch.

Urgent to Dr. John McLoughlin, Rainy Lake House, Lac la Pluie District, Rupert's Land, Canada. Ready to negotiate coalition with Hudson's Bay Company. Proceed Montreal immediately for conference with officers before sailing for London via *H.M.S. Blossom* from Quebec, November 3, 1820. Officers depending on you to keep terms favorable to North West Company interests. Essential you arrive here early as possible. Signed, Simon M'Gillivray (McTavish, M'Gillivray, and Company, Montreal).

John would have sprung to his feet but Marguerite's hands interfered.

"No, no, no," she whispered, her breath warm on his cheek.

John struck his knee with his left hand. "Ready to negotiate, ready to negotiate with the auld Cloots! What's the meaning of this flimflam? Speak up, Ogden. Speak up, man. What do you know about this?"

Pete said, "I know that you yourself are sick of the way our Montreal agents are treating us field partners. You've been the loudest one to talk of finding a fairer way to dispose of our furs."

John felt Marguerite's hands lengthen out their rhythm on his back. It was a trick, he knew, to help him regain control of his temper. And he found his words coming now in single file instead of piling up as they did when he was angry and excited. "You're right," he told Pete. He stared at the dispatch in his hand. "Negotiate," he mused. "Negotiate is not 'sell out' in my language. If a fair coalition could be worked out, it might be the answer. At least," he reminded himself, "it would put an end, once and for all, to Hudson's Bay men cocking their pistols behind every tree."

"And that would put an end to most of the fun," Pete said with a wink.

"It is perhaps fun for you, M'sieu Pete," Marguerite snapped. "For my Johnny, it is a big cut behind his arm."

"You want me to send to Red River Settlement for the doctor from there?" Pete asked her.

"Certainly not," John snapped. "You know Marguerite can tend a knife wound better than any doctor. As soon as she lets my writing arm out of this strap, I'm going to sign over my medical license to her."

"You're able to travel then?" Pete asked. "To London?"

John looked up. "You going with me, Pete?"

"Not me. Seems I talk too much. My orders are to keep my trap shut on what I think about Hudson's Bay or prepare to set up a one-man trading company."

Marguerite's hands stopped. She said nothing but John could feel, in the almost imperceptible pressure of her body against him, her dismay at his leaving.

He reached up and took her hand. "I'll bring you a silk chiné dress and a hat with a plume from Paris."

"You've got a brother in Paris, haven't you? A doctor," Pete said. "He can look after you."

John scoffed. "A lot of looking after I'll need when I get to David in Paris. It's London where the honorable vultures are circling."

"You'd best practice on the ship saying that word 'honorable' so it sounds a mite less like cussing."

"The honorable Governor and Committee had best practice saying 'please' before I get to Fenchurch Street. Otherwise, I'll teach them the literal meaning of that 'Skin for a Skin' motto they keep flying in our faces."

"I'd like to think you could." Pete shook his head. "Still, we may as well face it. They're mighty big."

"Big? Tut, tut!" John could not remember hearing Peter Skene Ogden admit that an impossible undertaking might prove anything but easy. "They're men, aren't they, the same as us? Well, no man's bigger than any other man, in my code. If they haven't heard that at Hudson's Bay House, then it's time they did."

Jacques sat up rubbing his eyes. "My *papa's* bigger than anybody."

"Mighty nigh," Pete agreed, reaching over to tousle the boy's dark curls. "At least, they have to gang up on him to be bigger." He started for the door. "The trouble is, they've been ganging up for a hundred and fifty years."

III   John McLoughlin stooped to grasp the brass knob that
would admit him for the first time to Hudson's Bay House at No.
3 Fenchurch Street. But the shortened ligament in his back gave
a tug that reminded him of recent weeks in Paris with his brother
David. Along with doctoring that stubborn-healing slice in his
back, David had gone to great pains to give his brother from the
wilds of Canada a refresher course in dress and the social graces.

In his west-end London hotel John had dressed this morning
with a care that would have delighted both David and the Bond
Street tailor who had been so elated at finding a chest broad
enough to carry satin lapels as wide as the latest trend. But on the
steps of Hudson's Bay House he instinctively shoved his hand
under his ulster and missed the bulge of a pistol in his belt.
Silly, he scolded himself. He tapped the crown of his beaver hat
and reached, this time with his left hand, for the doorknob.

The astonished blink and slow recovery on the face of the
uniformed attendant inside convinced John far beyond any
argument that David had been right. Clothes could make an
immediate impression on Hudson's Bay dignitaries and gain him
an advantage for the Northwesters he represented.

"You . . . your name, sir," stammered the attendant, holding
out his hand as if he expected John to drop his name into his
palm, "and . . . your hat."

"I'm Dr. John McLoughlin." He gave it all the Scotch it would
stand with a slight burr on "doctor" and a good strong guttural
in the center of "McLoughlin" so it sounded close kin to Loch
Lomond. "And the name of my hat," he added, using both hands
to remove it, "is Northwester. See that you show it the proper
respect."

The attendant held the hat at arm's length, gave it a wide stare, and then a solemn bow. When he recovered enough to take John's ulster and to say, "Yes, sir. This way, sir," John could permit himself a small grin behind his hand.

His hat, actually, meant something very special to John. He knew that the whole business had been merely a belligerent kind of gesture but he had felt compelled to make it. He agreed with David that he would be able to maneuver a better deal if he played the game of dress and manners along with these British financiers and merchants. And he liked the new finesse in conversation and society that he had caught in Paris as easily as he might have caught smallpox in Canada. Besides, he liked dressing up and looking his best. And he admired the skill with which the Bond Street tailor had fitted and sewed his half-dozen black broadcloth suits in the latest style. But when it came to a hat, something would not let him rest until he knew for sure that his hat was made, not of Hudson's Bay beaver, but of North West Company fur.

To satisfy himself on this point he had gone, the first day he arrived in London, directly to Dunnage, Hatters, with ten of Chief Wisagun's prime beaver skins rolled in a strip of scarlet blanket just as he had brought them on the ship all the way from Quebec.

The clerk's turtle-like head screwed from his shell-like collar and he gasped for the plant foreman. The foreman removed his green eyeshade, scratched his gray sideburns, and left the counter to bring back Mr. Dunnage.

"But my good sir," the founder and president of the company explained, "we can't very well separate the wool from ten beaver skins and use only that to nap your particular hats, sir. Besides, sir, I fail to see what possible difference it could make if just a teeny bit—"

John slapped the counter. "You fail to see!" He snatched up his beaver skins. "Well, then, I'm sure that Overbury and Jepsin will be able to see perfectly. Good day!"

But Mr. Dunnage could see quite readily what difference it made as soon as he heard John mention the names of his chief competitors. And John, by hanging around the steamy hat plant

[23]

off and on for three days, left with an aversion to the smell of hot fur and with the conviction that his new hats were the silkiest in London. At least, not one barbed hair of Hudson's Bay beaver defiled his head.

"Dr. John McLoughlin," the attendant intoned to a long, dark room which, at John's first glance, appeared inhabited by carved mahogany figures.

Two of the figures—one medium tall and one definitely short—started toward him down the left side of the endless table that divided the room. In time, these two developed pale faces and then the taller one extended his hand.

"I am Andrew Colvile," he said. "As Governor of our honorable Company I welcome you to Hudson's Bay House."

When John took Colvile's waxen hand he remembered barely in time that it would never do for him to break any bones in his first greeting to the Governor. He checked his grasp and let go.

"And this," Colvile turned to the man with him, "is one of our most able young officers, George Simpson. He has just returned from a year in Canada. The two of you will have much in common, I am sure."

George Simpson's handshake did not require any special consideration from John. They both hung on and pumped while each sized up the other. Simpson's head came to the top button on John's coat and yet, looking into his steel-gray eyes, John did not feel particularly tall. Simpson's mouth, cut in precise curves, waited to smile until he had made up his mind and John liked that. Perhaps Simpson, too, was sensing some bond between them and was as curious as John to know whether they were to be friends or enemies.

Then Simpson smiled and gripped John's elbow with his left hand. "Dr. John McLoughlin, a name to conjure with! Doctor, your fame had traveled as far as Fort Wedderburn where I was stationed last year in Canada."

Simpson turned to Governor Colvile. "Governor, we gentlemen of Hudson's Bay must keep our wits about us during these negotiations. The North West Company has sent us their smartest trader and the quickest pair of fists in the fur business. The tales

[24]

they tell of this man McLoughlin in Canada are enough to lift the wig right off your head."

Simpson kept this playful but it was play in the sense that his toy gun was loaded with lead shot. His suave voice was loaded with little barbs of irony. John felt his hackles bristle under Simpson's probing eyes. He dismissed, once and for all, his first careless transfer of notions from Simpson's short stature to his size as a power in the Company. Friends or enemies, whichever they were to be, the relationship, John knew in that moment, would be intense. They'd be friends against all comers or enemies to the death.

John kept his mouth shut and his ears cocked during the meeting that morning. He probed through the smooth surface of a half-dozen speeches and came up with the solid fact that Hudson's Bay Company had paid no dividends during the years the Northwesters had been giving them a run for their furs. The stockholders would appreciate—in fact, were demanding—a change.

Then John Henry Pelly, one of the big nabobs, spoke regarding the British Parliament's interest in a settlement of the undeclared war between fur companies operating in the Canadian provinces.

Tongue in cheek, John listened to Pelly's pompous references to Hudson's Bay charter, dated 1670, signed by the illustrious King Charles II, and granting exclusive trade privileges throughout Rupert's Land. John happened to know that Rupert's Land had not been Charles' to bestow until some hundred years after he signed the charter. He knew, too, that Parliament had outlawed monopolies more than forty years before these exclusive trade rights had been granted Hudson's Bay.

But now John shut out everything else and sat tall in his chair. Pelly had come to the point. "Parliament is tired of these backyard fist fights that are keeping things upset in Canada," he said. "In return for a complete union of the warring parties, Parliament has promised to license the new unified company for twenty-one years to trade exclusively with the Indians throughout the vast territory in North America beyond Rupert's Land."

The gentlemen of Hudson's Bay could no longer contain their approval. "Hear, hear!" they burst forth.

Governor Colvile gave his reins a sharp tug. "Gentlemen, I feel that I should point out one restriction, namely the agreement reached between Great Britain and the United States three years ago—the 1818 Treaty of Joint Occupancy. This treaty, as you know, grants to citizens of the United States equal rights to trade within the Pacific Slope." He stopped long enough for several at the table to agree with sober nods. "However, gentlemen, by virtue of this treaty we have seven more years in which to take furs from that same territory. True, the Americans may compete with us there, but we are an old established company, wise in the ways of the fur trade. We have resources at our command that no green company of Americans can hope to duplicate. As a case in point, I cite you John Jacob Astor and his miserable failure at Astoria. The seven years left may not be long for our purposes but, if we race against the running out of this treaty, who knows but we can skim all profit off the trade in that area during the time at our disposal?"

John squirmed. Surely these men knew that conservation was as much a part of the fur trade as trapping. Even the Indians in Canada were forward-looking enough to set a limit on their take of spawning salmon. He cleared his throat to ask for the floor but Governor Colvile had not finished.

"There is one more aspect to this matter. It has to do with the western boundary between our Canadian provinces and the United States. Just when that question will be settled, we cannot tell. When it is settled, the holdings of Hudson's Bay Company on the continent of North America will, undoubtedly, influence the placement of that boundary line. While this matter has never actually been put into words between us, our Parliament is vitally interested, I can assure you."

"You mean we should colonize that Oregon Country?" Simon M'Gillivray, known for his bluntness, spoke without asking for recognition. "And all the time I thought we was in the fur business." But M'Gillivray was not the man to worry about rights except M'Gillivray's. Relieved of his little joke, he planted

[26]

his palms on the table. "Well, if you boys have talked yourselves out, let's get down to figures."

"Precisely," the Governor agreed.

Getting the figures down consumed the afternoon session, including a social recess during which the arguments flowed hotter than the tea. Both companies had set face-saving evaluations on their assets, and getting them to the point of unmasking took time.

Fog settled in with the dusk. The attendant lighted the candles in the pewter chandeliers. Finally, John asked for the floor.

"Dr. John McLoughlin." Governor Colvile recognized him in his most formal voice but added with a smile, "We've waited all day to hear from you, Doctor."

"Gentlemen, this matter of Company assets is not my strong field," John began. "I've been listening and learning. As you know, I'm a wintering partner—an outdoor man. When it comes to buying furs from Indians, I seem to get along pretty well." He paused to assure himself that the honorable gentlemen would listen to an outdoor man.

Their solemn nods urged him on.

"I've been doing some figuring. After fighting each other for fifteen years, it looks to me like we've reached the point where we make up or give up. I suggest, gentlemen, that the North West Company and Hudson's Bay Company each declare assets at two hundred thousand pounds—that we leave the starting line together."

Groans of pain and wounded pride went up from both sides. John gathered his coattails and sank into his chair. Waiting and undisturbed, he propped his elbow on the table, pushed his chair back, and twisted his left ear. Marguerite teased him about that ear when they were alone. She claimed that he twisted his ear instead of laughing when he was amused. Well, perhaps he did.

Still protesting about their sacrifices, both factions gave in at five minutes before nine and the meeting adjourned until morning.

Once the two companies had made a standing start from the

line, they appeared to work in harmony toward a new administrative setup. But, during the third day's break for tea, John happened into the middle of a conversation not intended for him.

"It's bad business for one man to get his way too much," he overheard.

George Simpson, more direct, handed John a cup of tea. "Doctor, we may have to borrow Delilah's shears and trim those white locks before we're through with you."

John tasted his tea and found it too sweet. "Come now, Mr. Simpson. We all know that both companies have assets worth far more than warehouses, forts, and beaver traps. Hudson's Bay has its charter and the backing of Parliament. North West Company, on the other hand, has men with guts enough to buck weather and Blackfeet and grizzlies to peel the hides off those beaver out there in the wilds and start them on their way to market. If we dovetail all our assets, we'll have a fur trade second to none and I'll be for the new organization whatever we call it."

They called it Hudson's Bay Company and that was hard to swallow. John slept little that night. He kept hearing the scorn in Peter Skene Ogden's falsetto epithets. Half a dozen times he dozed off only to come awake to the crack and rustle of silk in the wind. Before his eyes, flapped the red and blue banner of Hudson's Bay with its trapped beavers and its *Pro Pelle Cutem*," a motto they had to disguise in Latin for fear its victims might resent the Company's deliberate policy of "A Skin for a Skin."

But things looked different by daylight. After all, the Hudson's Bay name was an asset and John could learn to wear it with his head up. He had won his fight for partnership for field officers and wintering partners. These commissioned gentlemen were to be given contracts, an annual division of profits, and a retiring fund. With all these wins to his credit, he could learn to accept the Hudson's Bay name. And now he had only one more fight in him. Today he'd win that one, too.

Governor Colvile nodded assent to John's bid for the floor soon after the meeting opened. "The chair recognizes the young doctor from Canada. I am sure we are all agreed that, in John McLoughlin, Hudson's Bay Company has acquired an able man."

Confident in the rightness of his cause, John began with no possibility in his mind of losing his last skirmish. "Gentlemen, I have contended here for better terms for factors, traders, and field officers. You have been generous in your acceptance both of me and of my suggestions. The point on which I feel most strongly, I have left till last. I am sure that you will agree with me and take some just action."

The room got too still. John went on, however, not really noticing.

"Gentlemen, this is about our voyageurs. On a pittance of seventeen pounds a year they wade icy waters, cordelle canoes through rocky currents, transform themselves into beasts of burden at every portage. They work eighteen hours of every twenty-four—all this that the profits of their muscles may pour wealth into the coffers of this trade."

Now he had gone too far. The storm broke around him.

"We're in no condition to raise anybody's wages," someone shouted and shook his fist. "What we need is to cut, cut, cut!"

Governor Colvile lifted both arms and patted the air before him. "Gentlemen, gentlemen!"

George Simpson stood to ask for the floor. Colvile nodded in his direction but could not restore order.

Back in Canada with the roar of International Falls in his ears and the sting of wind off Rainy Lake on his cheeks, John would have held the floor by raising his voice or raising his fists, whichever the occasion demanded. Here in this mahogany-padded room he settled back in his chair to wait out the fracas his words had set off. Let the gentlemen of Hudson's Bay beat their manly chests in defense of their pocketbooks, he decided. Back at his post, he'd find a way to ease things a bit for his own voyageurs. He'd shorten their hours, assign them lighter loads on portages, manage to let them have goods at a smaller mark-up. *Oui, oui*, he'd find a way. . . . Given time, he'd see that all voyageurs got a living wage.

The argument simmered down, finally, to an occasional bubble and eruption like a pot of porridge removed from the fire. The fist-shakers cooled into table-thumpers. At last the Governor could make himself heard.

"Gentlemen, I am sure that no assemblage of men in the British Empire would be more sympathetic toward the plight of the common laborer than we are here. And, it may be that, in time, we shall be in a position to reconsider this matter of the voyageurs. At present, of course, it is out of the question." He bowed toward the far end of the table. "The chair recognizes Mr. Simpson."

"Honorable Governor and gentlemen." Simpson appeared unruffled by all the hullabaloo. John liked that in him. "Gentlemen, we are agreed, of course, that it would be pleasant if we could afford to humor our voyageurs a little more. However, from what I've seen, most of them could carry heavier packs and all of them can work faster than they generally do. I've proved this several times in Canada where I've invariably broken speed records on every route I've traveled."

He drew from his inside pocket a folded sheet of paper. "With your permission, Governor and gentlemen, I should like to make a proposal which I consider both sane and feasible."

The Governor nodded and draped his arm over the back of his chair.

Simpson unfolded his paper and tossed a sidewise glance toward John. "I've been over the figures rather extensively, gentlemen, and I've decided that by next year we may be able to decrease our expenses by some fifteen thousand pounds."

A gasp eddied around the table.

"Furthermore," Simpson went on, "we can effect this saving without the smallest embarrassment to our affairs."

Stunned, the treasurer asked, "But how?"

With an airy lift of his hand Simpson said, "It's perfectly simple. We shall dispense with the service of two hundred and fifty men next season."

John made no more speeches during the London meetings. Some speeches were made about him. He listened with one ear while he twisted the other in amusement. They had come to respect him, he was sure. They had also decided to watch him.

On the last day, when they were sorting the personnel of the two companies so as to man the unified business, Simpson stood. "Gentlemen, as you know, I am an impatient man but I realize it will require two, three . . . maybe four years before we can complete a full merger and deploy all our men. Still, I would like to propose that, as soon as feasible, we send Doctor McLoughlin to the Columbia Department." The others chorused, "Perfect."

Simpson used his pointer to mark out the Columbia district on the wall map, stressing the indefinite nature of the boundary between Canada and the United States along the Columbia River. "A most strategic location right now," he reminded the gentlemen. "A spot where time may prove our most valuable commodity. Returns from this department are small, at present, but," he went on with a knowing smile, "who can tell what the returns may be, politically as well as economically, if affairs are properly handled here during the time allotted us by the Joint Occupation Treaty?"

The gentlemen agreed with pleased nods and little flames of ambition in their eyes.

John twisted his ear. If they thought they were fooling him, they weren't. He knew that the preliminary session for this meeting today had been held around a dinner table at London Coffee House on Ludgate Hill last night. He could come mighty close to hearing the plot, word for word.

"He's too strong in Canada, wields too much power with the Indians and with the Northwesters for us to make an enemy of him. The thing to do is take him in, but where can we put him so he won't make trouble?"

Somebody was bound to think of the Columbia Department after that. The Columbia was the problem child of the fur trade provinces. It was always in a tug-of-war with poaching Americans, or Russians, or Mexicans from California. Indians on the lower Columbia had no ambition to trap furs in order to better their conditions by acquiring trade goods.

But the big advantage of sticking John way off there on the Columbia was the distance from London. That far away, the young doctor would find little opportunity to needle the honorable Committee about paying exorbitant wages to common laborers.

John sat at the table while they discussed him in the most glowing terms and he could hear beneath their words those other words that they had said the night before. "The perfect solution," they must have agreed. "We'll get his lavish fingers out of our exchequer and keep him quiet."

Now they called on him. Taking his time about it, John got to his feet. "Gentlemen, it will be a pleasure for me to go to the Columbia," he began. "I appreciate the honor you have bestowed upon me and the responsibility you have seen fit to thrust upon me. It will require some time for me to wind up my affairs at Rainy Lake House but I think I can promise that very soon after I arrive at Fort George, the Columbia Department will begin to show a profit."

He sat down and wriggled his shoe off his bunion. He had maneuvered the best deal possible for the North West Company. For himself, he had drawn exile. But Pete Ogden used to talk about that Columbia River Country with a special shine in his eyes. "It's wide open, Doc, for whatever a man could make of it," Pete used to say. And Marguerite, John remembered, never tired of prodding Pete Ogden to talk about Oregon. He slid his foot back into his shoe and now it felt almost as soft as one of Marguerite's moccasins. So, they'd send him and his prodigal ideas into a far country, would they? Then he might just show them what a man could make of it!

IV John wanted to travel another hour before they stopped for breakfast but Jacques was begging for food. John's watch said only seven o'clock and they had covered far too little ground in three hours this morning. Rivière la Biche had turned up considerably more *biche* than water and the going was slow.

Six of the voyageurs had carried the two North canoes light on their shoulders most of the way the last three days. The other eight voyageurs had each slung two "pieces" on a leather strap and plodded along without complaining. But a hundred and eighty pounds made a mighty heavy load for a man to carry strapped across his forehead even for a short portage. Three days—that was too much! Besides, complaints or not, John hated to see men turn themselves into beasts of burden.

"*Papa*, before eight o'clock I will starve to death and you will have to bury me in this stinking country."

Marguerite, walking behind, led Eloise by the hand. "Quiet, Jacques. Your *papa* will stop when the time comes. See, not even Eloise, a girl, is making a fuss."

"She's walking in her sleep," Jacques came back. "I'm awake and starving."

"You're right, Son. Everybody must be hungry by now. We'll stop as soon as we come to a meadow clean enough for breakfast," John promised.

A fire had run along both sides of this so-called river. Since then a rain had soaked the charcoal and ashes and the party was wading, had been wading for three days, through a black morass.

To keep the children's minds off the slop underfoot, John lured them with the intriguing names that lay ahead. "Athabaska River, Slave Lake, Five Islands, Fort Assiniboine."

Actually, for a short way now, the river had run wet enough

[33]

that the canoes might be launched. It would certainly be a relief to everyone if they could ride for a change—that is, if they could ride without snagging too many holes in the canoes. John heard a real current running midstream. But, he decided, they might as well wait until after breakfast to try the canoes again.

Talk and laughter picked up among the voyageurs, however, so they too were eying the water and looking forward to riding their paddles once more.

"Monique!" John called.

Before him appeared the half-breed Iroquois who was, more in name than in fact, the leader of the party. His salute, a mere flap of his hand in John's direction, tinkled the bells that adorned his fringes and gave him an excuse to grin. Monique's grin was John's best reason for keeping him along. The lines in his brown face ran perpetually out and around. Even his gray braids lay on his red-blanketed chest in a bowed pattern. Now Monique, along with all the others, was black from his moccasins to the center part in his hair. This made his white grin all the more captivating, somehow.

"Take a look at that clearing ahead to the right," John told him in French. "If we can tell the food from the soot there, we'll eat."

"*Oui, M'sieu le docteur.*" With his two "pieces" on the leather strap pulling his head high, Monique trotted on ahead of the party.

"Pierre!"

The cook's answer never came at once. John had learned to wait for it like waiting for an echo in the mountains. Always when he was about to give up and call again, Pierre answered.

"*Oui, M'sieu le docteur.*" A month's growth of black beard muffled his voice.

"Breakfast early this morning," John ordered. "My son threatens to starve on our hands."

After the usual delay, "*Oui, m'sieu*" sifted through the beard.

"Follow Monique. If that meadow will do, get your fires going."

[34]

Pierre shrugged a sooty shoulder and flicked his once crimson sash. *"À la bonne heure, M'sieu le docteur."*

The clearing provided an irregular patch of soggy but unburned grass back from the river and the breakfast fires were all hiss and smoke when the main party arrived.

Marguerite found a large boulder from which to direct her children's face washings. John stood behind her, watching their leggy son bound from stone to stone to reach the middle of the stream. Only there would Jacques deign to splash water on his face and over the black tumble of his hair.

"That son of yours!" John exploded and pushed aside Marguerite's once red, calico skirt to sit on the boulder beside her. "Why must he always be smack in the middle of the stream before he can wash his face?"

Marguerite leaned back, brushing his cheek with her hair. "That son of yours, Johnny, why must he get so wet his new deerskin tunic when he can leave so dry his ears?"

They laughed but Marguerite sobered at once. "He is a beautiful boy, our Jacques. He must be in the middle of the stream, *oui*. But he will never fall. Our Marie Eloise sits down on a rock where are a million fleas. But not our Jacques."

"He is his mother all over again." John held her to him for a moment. Then he stood up. "The worst of it is, Jacques gets around me. Now that we have water in this would-be river, we should paddle, paddle, paddle."

"The water will stay while we eat."

"Tut, tut," John said.

But Marguerite was teasing. "I know, Johnny," she soothed, "it means much to you that you should arrive at Fort George on the Pacific ahead of this George Simpson." She settled back and hooped her arms around her knees. "All I do not know is, why?" When John started in impatience and opened his mouth, she would not allow him to speak. "*Oui, oui*, I know." She spoke in a singsong, wagging her head from side to side. "He is your new boss. He is a big man in Hudson's Bay Company. He is Deputy Governor of Rupert's Land. And you admire him very much."

Hearing his words parroted back at him in this fashion, John chuckled and sat down again beside her. "All right, all right. Maybe I'm overanxious but I do admire George Simpson and, so far, he thinks pretty well of me. I'd like to show him that I can make good time and still not kill off my voyageurs. Also, his orders were not to slow down my party by traveling with my family. I intend to show him on that score, too. If we can arrive at Fort George early enough to prepart a welcome for him I'll prove my points. Is that too much to ask?"

"Is it too much to ask that you do not growl at everyone like a mad *maman* grizzly? This George Simpson, if you do not arrive at Fort George before him, let him prepare the welcome for you. You, too, are a big man in Hudson's Bay Company. And I admire you very much. But"—she sprang up and tossed her head—"do not be cross with our Jacques because of this George Simpson."

John followed Marguerite to breakfast. Maybe he had been pushing a wee bit too hard. After all, his party had left York Factory with twenty days' head start on Simpson. Surely they'd get to the coast with time to spare in preparing for the Governor's arrival. Beyond the burned area, John stamped off some of the soot. Then, twisting his ear, he moved into the breakfast circle. It was a funny thing the way Marguerite, with her longest *e* in the middle of "this," invariably referred to "This George Simpson" as if he had three names.

John gulped down two scalding cupfuls of bitter tea. But the pemmican they had bought from that last party of Blackfeet was hairier than the buffalo from which it had been made. Giving the others time to down what they could of it, John walked off then and called, "*Lève, lève, lève.*"

Jacques skimmed his tin plate onto the growing stack in front of Pierre. "*Papa,* the steersman wants me to ride with him today."

"No, no. You ride with me. I must hear you and Eloise say your lessons while we travel. Get on your moccasins and help your mother."

"Johnny," Marguerite reproved under her breath, without looking up from her brush and Eloise's soft brown hair.

"See, *Papa*"—Eloise lifted a strand of her hair into the sunlight—"why don't you tell me what a beautiful lady I shall be, the way you used to?"

John stopped to give her a playful spank. "You'll look like young Charlefoux if you don't stop growing. And you'll be only half as smart as that chipmunk there if you don't work harder on your lessons. Think of a girl past ten who still makes mistakes in her 'times nines.'" Marguerite was right, he admitted to himself. He hadn't taken enough time for the children.

Suddenly all activity at the breakfast camp froze. From upstream came a wisp of stray notes that sounded suspiciously like singing. They all turned, transfixed. Their eyes strained through the matted spruce boughs. The notes closed ranks and became:

> *En roulant, ma boule roulant,*
> *Rouli, roulant ma boule roulant,*
> *En roulant, ma boule . . .*

"Simpson!" John swore but not aloud. He could feel the blood stain his face. "No, no, no, of course not." It wasn't possible that Simpson could have caught them.

And then, painted in red and black on the high-riding bow of a North canoe, gaudy spirit guardians of speed appeared in the river.

John found that he had been holding his breath.

Eight voyageurs, clean and ribbon-decked, singing for all they were worth, paddled the canoe. From the stern flapped the triangular pennant of Hudson's Bay Company with its rampant deer and four beavers caged on a shield. On the passenger's seat rode a gentleman in Hudson's Bay blue and high beaver hat. He was, beyond all hope, George Simpson.

John felt Marguerite at his side. She said nothing but that was one of the thousand reasons he loved her. She knew when words only cluttered the understanding between them.

"It isn't possible. How could human beings make such time?"

"This George Simpson, he is perhaps one who whips his voyageurs like dogs."

John strode to the river bank and folded his arms on his chest.

The *boutes* in the bow and stern brought the canoe around

[37]

midstream and held her while an immaculate voyageur, disregarding his beaded and ribbon-decked leggings, came over the side. He lifted George Simpson from the craft and, feeling his way to shore through the slippery boulders, deposited the Deputy Governor, dry-shod, at John's feet.

Simpson's tilted gaze had a disturbing way of cutting John's six-foot-four down to the Governor's own five-foot-six so their eyes met now, as they had at Hudson's Bay House, on the level. John resented and, at the same time, respected Simpson for this knack he possessed. Each waited for the other to make some move toward shaking hands.

Deliberate as cold molasses, Simpson folded his arms on his chest and stared. Finally, he said, "Well, well, upon my word it's John McLoughlin and, judging by the wool on his face, he has taken to growing his own fur for the trade." His eyes traveled downward and flicked the butt of John's pistol in his belt. "And the latest fashion in these parts seems to be armory and ammunition." He backed away to stare some more and then suddenly he laughed. Beginning with a chuckle, he kept on until he doubled up laughing.

John's arms dropped to his sides. If Simpson was merely having fun, all right. But his laugh was hard to read.

When the Governor could control himself enough to speak, he said, "Your chin would do honor to the jaw of a grizzly bear, Doctor. And your . . . your"—his arm made an upward sweep that included the full vertical expanse of John McLoughlin—"your clothes! This was obviously once a Bond Street suit but what hit it?"

"My wife likes bright-colored patches," John said and felt like a schoolboy caught drawing pictures of teacher.

Simpson sobered. "Your what?"

"My wife," John repeated. "I want you to meet her."

Simpson drew himself as tall as a deep breath could lift him. "Your wife," he said, "as you so euphoniously refer to her, was supposed to follow later. I believe you had orders to that effect before leaving York House."

John bristled. "*Oui, oui*, I did. But—"

[38]

"As sound a reason for bringing her as any, Doctor." Simpson's mouth pulled to the side. "When no explanation is adequate, a dignified silence often suffices. Remember that, McLoughlin." Dismissing this subject with a shrug, Simpson slapped his hands together and massaged his palms. He sized up the situation with a brisk glance at John's men lounging beside their breakfast fires. "I'll have a talk with your voyageurs. It's partly your family slowing you down, I know. But I have a way of getting men to throw themselves into a job. You're new in Hudson's Bay Company, McLoughlin. You'll do well to study my methods and learn how to get things done. You easy going Nor'westers—"

"It's your method of traveling Rivière la Biche and keeping yourself so confounded clean that I'd like to study," John said. "I confess you have me baffled."

Simpson tossed his head to the right. "Remember your breakfast stop yesterday? We camped there last night. Thought we'd do you the honor of dressing up to overtake you." The Governor gave John's elbow a friendly squeeze. "It's all right, Doctor. We've been as black as you are the last two days. We've walked the same as you through this charred hell. The difference is, we've made better time."

Under the Governor's genial tone, John loosened up.

"*Papa!*" Jacques came tearing down the slope, Marie Eloise in his wake. "*Papa!* Is it that confounded Governor we've been trying to beat to Fort George?"

"Jacques!" Marguerite's tone was the one the children never disregarded.

Off balance, Jacques stopped and turned. Eloise wavered in her tracks.

As if she had all the time in the world, Marguerite swung down the slope, gathering children like daisies.

John saw Simpson's eyes follow each move of this small drama and continue to gaze toward the willows beyond which Marguerite and the children disappeared. Then without comment, he strode into the cluster of voyageurs on the meadow. "Monique! Come forward!"

For the first time that John could remember, Monique's braids lay stiff and lifeless on his chest.

"Charlefoux!" Simpson barked.

The lanky French-Canadian who saw to the packing for the McLoughlin party stepped up, nothing cowed about him. Charlefoux was his own man and not even the Governor could take that from him. John knew now why he liked the brazen young reprobate and kept him around. Actually, he swore and drank too much and boasted of a squaw in every Indian village between here and Rainy Lake. But he never failed to stand up for his rights as if they'd been born in him. John respected the respect Charlefoux had for himself.

Once he'd called the leaders forward, Simpson began with a playful pot shot at the leathery crew, claiming he'd seen turtles that could make better time on the trail. But soon he came to his main point. He had broken the speed record between York House and here, covering the distance in forty-two days—eight days better than the record. The McLoughlin party had dallied along for two months.

"Hudson's Bay Company will tolerate no more of this idling. I'm sure you can make better time from now on. All you have to do is put your backs into it. It's partly for your own good that I urge speed. You'll be caught in blizzards in the mountains ahead, if you continue to drag your feet. Here it is, September twenty-sixth. Heavy snows could come any day now. But partly I urge speed for the sake of the Company. You are servants of the honorable Hudson's Bay Company and you owe her your best."

John breathed easier. The uncertainty about whether he could beat the Governor to Fort George had gnawed at him night and day since leaving York House. Now for the price of a lecture, his party could travel at a comfortable pace with Simpson out ahead.

Suddenly Simpson became all charm. "There now," he concluded, "no great harm done that you can't correct on the rest of the journey." Dismissing the circle with a wave of his hand, he turned back to John.

[*40*]

Appearing from nowhere, Marguerite stepped between them. Her eyes downcast, she offered Simpson a steaming cup of tea.

John stepped forward to introduce them but something about the ceremony of Simpson's taking the cup and turning it slowly while he peered into its depths caused him to wait before speaking. The Governor seemed on the verge of making some graceful acceptance of Marguerite's hospitality.

"Tea," he murmured as if tasting it on his tongue. Then he stiffened. "Tea," he sneered, "presented by a squaw in the middle of the morning when travel, travel, travel ought to be our only order of the day." His eyes narrowed and his mouth pulled to the side. He flung the tea out on the meadow and turned on his heel.

John gripped his arm and spun him around so violently that the Governor had to scramble for a footing. Tightening his noose of fingers, John spoke in cold, deliberate fury. "This is Mrs. McLoughlin. Marguerite, may I present Governor George Simpson?"

Marguerite gave John a look from beneath her dark lashes that reminded him he had his superior officer in his grip but, superior or not, the man was going to recognize this introduction in a manner to wipe out that insulting word "squaw" as he had spat it at Marguerite.

Marguerite caught her red calico skirt and dipped in a curtsy that seemed to John a shade too elaborate for the circumstances. "*M'sieu*," she murmured.

When Simpson said nothing, John tightened his grip until the Governor finally muttered, "How do you do?"

"How do you do, Mrs. McLoughlin," John prompted through tight lips and gave the Governor's arm a wrench.

Trapped, Simpson repeated the words by rote and with a distinct tongue-in-cheek slur.

Instead of letting him go as he had intended, John held him while he summoned the two children.

"This is my daughter, Marie Eloise, Governor Simpson," he said when the children ran to him.

Eloise glanced at her mother who took a surreptitious pinch of her own skirt to remind the child of her manners. Instantly Eloise curtsied and then bounced to her feet to come over and hug John's free arm.

"Governor Simpson," John went on doggedly, "I would like to present my son, Jacques."

Jacques stepped forward, his outstretched hand insisting on a shake. "It is a pleasure to meet you, sir," the boy said. "We've been talking about you all the way from Rainy Lake. We've been saying—"

He shook Jacques's hand and then tousled his hair. "I'm sure you have," the Governor himself interrupted. The tension gave way to sheepish grins all around.

"A fine boy," Simpson said.

John released his grip on the Governor's arm. So things were going to be all right between them after all. Perhaps Simpson had used the word "squaw" from habit and without intending to belittle. This incident could be forgotten in the interval before their next meeting at Fort George.

"Doctor!" Simpson was facing John on the level again. "From now on, your party will travel with mine. Your men need a lesson in covering ground." He slapped his hands together. "Monique! Charlefoux! Ready to travel!" He brushed a speck from his wool cape. "My traveling clothes," he barked at his servant. He struck off toward a clump of brush. His manner aloof, his tone playful enough to dull the edge of his words, he tossed over his shoulder at John, "And see to it that your precious bits of brown don't come poking their noses through the willows while I change my clothes. I'll have my privacy from squaws and their litters even on the trail."

This time it was Marguerite who caught John's arm. She held him by force for a moment and then by the gentle reminder in her voice. "Johnny."

"I'll wring his snobbish neck. I'll—"

"No, no, Johnny. This you will not do. It is his kind of joke."

"But I won't let him talk that way even as a joke."

"Johnny!" Marguerite stamped her foot. "This George Simpson, he is your superior officer, as you say, and we must, it appears, travel with him. This we will do. But I will not have you sloping your shoulders down. I will not have it!" She turned on the toe of her moccasin, flung her head high, and swinging her hips until her deerskin fringes fairly bristled with spirit, she set off toward the trail.

V For three weeks the two parties raced upgrade under the lash of George Simpson's tongue. Regardless of whether he spiced his "*Lève, lève, lève,*" with sarcasm or charm, men and animals responded to the Governor's demand for speed.

For six days now, since taking on pack animals at Jasper House, they had traveled the impossible Athabaska Portage along a maze of mountain trails all leading nowhere except up. For the last three days of the ascent, they had clung to the backs of Company horses, one leg scraping the mountainside, the other dangling in space. Whenever they began to feel secure on a ridge, some devil spirit whisked away the ribbons of mist that had padded the tortuous death lying in wait for one misstep.

But, thanks to George Simpson's drive, drive, drive, they now stood on Height of Land. A cloud, wet and heavy on the barren rocks, obscured the prospect wherever John looked. Still, it was Sunday noon. And even the Governor agreed they should rest men and horses half a day.

John swung from his saddle and gave his black stallion a pat. "If I'm stiff, you must be ready to fall apart at the joints with my weight on you."

He hurried back along the string of horses to Marguerite. She skimmed her blue-beaded legging over the saddle horn and slid down so lightly that John shuddered. "When you can come off a horse as easily as that, how have you managed to stay on these three days?"

She was wearing, over her leggings and deerhide tunic, an old capote left from John's Nor'wester days. Its red hood draped to frame her fair skin and black hair, and set against this vast wilderness, John knew he would never forget. His desperate sense of

[44]

thankfulness that they had all reached this place in safety would fix the picture forever.

"Danger makes you glow, *ma chérie*. You never have been so beautiful." He had taken far too little time to look at her the last three weeks. But, here from Height of Land, the end of the drive felt suddenly just off there to the west and south. This afternoon and night were theirs and before them lay their new country.

Marguerite unfastened the bulky cloak. "I'll be warm enough without your capote," she said. "Why should it be suddenly warmer on top of the world, Johnny?"

"Because you smiled on it, I think," he told her.

Around them voyageurs, able to handle a canoe with a dancer's grace, lumbered off horses as if their legs and arms had been bound in splints.

Marguerite's hand slid into John's. "Could we perhaps take a small walk to see where we are?" When John kept straining to see beyond the cloud to the west, she added with a tug, "Now?"

"*Oui, oui*, of course, but what's your hurry?" John chuckled. "Don't tell me you've caught Governor Simpson's speed bug!"

"From this George Simpson I have caught nothing." Marguerite's head came up and she turned her back on the Governor's arrival. "Shall you walk with me?"

John tightened the grip on her hand. "Watch your footing. Looks like we're on a moraine." He turned to lead her off to the right and along a milky stream searching its way through the moraine's tumble of granite.

Marguerite stopped and pointed. "Johnny, look! The cloud is melting." Her grip and breathless "Oh!" startled him.

"What—?" he began but he saw it too. Before them appeared a jade and emerald lake. Round as a cut gem, its color defied belief in this world of granite and glaciers.

"Oh Johnny, quick! I must touch it before it isn't really there!" She dropped from the crag on which they stood, pulling him along.

But George Simpson's servant dashed up. "Dr. McLoughlin, the Governor wishes to see you at once."

John opened his mouth to ask for time.

[45]

"He said, 'At once,' sir," the boy emphasized.

"*Oui, oui.*" John turned to Marguerite. "There will be a moon this night," he whispered, "and so much the better for a walk beside the lake."

She smiled without hiding the disappointment in her eyes and moved away.

Exploring was the thing Simpson had in mind, too. He, instead of Marguerite, led John to the lake. Soon they were both engrossed, not in the color, but in the currents. The stream they had followed to the lake shore flowed to the east. But the confused ripples on the lake's surface lured them around until they came to another stream, emptying to the west and inevitably making its devious way down the intertwining mountains to become the Columbia.

John wanted Marguerite by his side. Squatting on his heels to let the glacial water wash through his fingers, he felt already half carried away to that new country waiting out there for him to make what he could of it. But the rite lacked validity without Marguerite.

Simpson, unable to contain his excitement, talked too much and fidgeted to move on too soon. But first, he must give an appropriate name to this round pitcher of a lake with its two lips, spilling to the east and to the west.

"A name," he mused. And then in an instant, "'I have it! The Committee's Punch Bowl."

"Excellent," John agreed. What a brilliant man Simpson was! Even a name for a lake came to him in a flash. "*Oui, oui.* Perfect."

Simpson pulled on his gloves. "Now then, the men should have our camp set up. I sent Charlefoux and two of our voyageurs out hunting. Cadotte and Lesperance have gone down for wood. With luck, our Sunday dinner should sport more meat and less hair than we're used to."

John was just getting away to look for Marguerite and the children when the hunters dragged in a mountain goat and a sheep. Simpson insisted that John examine the skins to see whether they might have commercial value in the fur trade.

Charlefoux breathed down John's neck while he supervised the skinning. "Better save the time, *M'sieu le docteur*. If it is good, if it is bad"—he shrugged the whole weight of his body—"still nobody hunt him."

Jabbering wild tales, the other hunters joined in. They had tried for a dozen goats but each one raced up the mountainside and kicked stones down in a steady avalanche. They were favored of the gods to return with their skulls uncracked.

When John looked up from the goat hide, the clouds had escaped to the east. The sun, content with his rout, had stopped to rest on a peak to the left of the westward roving stream. Through a ledge of ice, light glinted the color of Marguerite's eyes when she was especially happy.

John stood up. He simply would not stay away from his family another minute. But Simpson wanted him for first one job and then six. He escaped to his own lodge only when Pierre called him for dinner. By that time, the sun had set. A haunch of the mountain goat crackled beside the fire. The light air had cooled. On it hung the odor of roasting meat plus a musky scent that John hoped did not belong to their dinner.

Marguerite, her hair gleaming from the brush and tied at her neck with the red satin ribbon he had brought her from Paris, came from the lodge and wrapped her arms around his waist. "Johnny, Johnny, it was two weeks—this afternoon without you in this place so close to heaven."

John kissed the top of her head but when he expected her to loosen her arms, she held on and would not let him turn.

"It is a surprise," she explained. "Pull shut your eyelids and I will lead you by the hand."

He felt the warmth of the fire on his shins when she told him to sit down. He heard Jacques and then Eloise giggle.

"Now open your mouth," Marguerite ordered and into it she popped a morsel so light, so sweet and rich in flavor, that John had chewed and swallowed before he could think what it was.

"Hot bread with real butter! But, *chérie*, how could you? The flour—where did it come from? And butter!"

John's eyes were open now. Before him, Eloise and Jacques jumped up and down, clapping and laughing their delight.

[47]

Marguerite, holding a flat pan of steaming bread before her, allowed the children time to enjoy the fun. Then, she gave John a surprise even greater than the first.

"This bread is too much," she said. "You would like, perhaps, to send it to this George Simpson?" Before John could collect himself to answer, she added, "*Oui*, I have also butter. Pierre is waiting to carry this bread and butter to the Governor's lodge when you say he should."

John got up and draped an arm around each child's shoulders. "First let me see how much you have left for us before I give any away." The three of them inspected the bread still browning between the sheet of tin and the fire.

"Pierre," John called, "be sure to tell the Governor it is from my wife."

"*Oui, oui, M'sieu le docteur.*"

Marguerite had hoarded the flour, guarding it at each loading along the way. The butter, packed in its hide bag, she had managed to trail in the water over the side of the canoe when the going was hot. The mountain goat, true to its odor, tasted of musk. And, trying to chew it, John put more credence in the hunters' stories. This animal had been kicking stones, all right, and any man strong enough to bite through his sinews and stomach his stench could have him. As for John, he had Marguerite's hot bread on his tongue and her hand in his.

"Before the dark comes, Johnny, could we begin our walk beside the lake?" She sighed. "The color is like the blue-winged teal."

"We went this afternoon," Eloise said, "after *Maman* heard our lessons."

"*Maman* told us stories about the people way up there in the ice," Jacques added.

Eloise asked, "Did you see the hunchback, *Papa?* And the beautiful lady who made him well?"

The children had finished eating and, chins propped on their hands, were gazing, half asleep, into the fire. John questioned Marguerite with a lift of his eyebrows. She answered, with a lift of her shoulders—just a story.

To the children she said, "The blankets are waiting. Say your prayers and dream of the people up there in the ice."

"Will you need the red capote to keep you warm?" John asked Marguerite when the children were tucked into their pallets.

"Your arms will be my red capote tonight," she answered. "My skirt is wool and my deerskin tunic soft and warmer than most."

They had to walk by the Governor's lodge or else wet their feet in crossing a wide cascade that fell into the lake beyond their own skin dwelling.

Simpson, cordial and gracious except that he did not greet nor seem to see Marguerite, intercepted them. "Doctor, I've learned from the hunters who went out today that there's been a fire on the trail ahead. You know what this means—fallen trees to be cleared and, with the horses, that's slow work. There will be a moon tonight. I want you to take a dozen of the best men and go ahead, clearing the trail. Move as fast as you can. You may save us a full day's travel and put us that much sooner at Boat Encampment."

"I, I—" John stopped and started again. "I can't leave Marguerite."

Simpson stepped back and folded his arms on his chest. "Doctor McLoughlin, for three weeks I have been willing to let my fondness for you outweigh your unfortunate tendency toward insubordination." He paused to lift himself taller with a deep breath and to pull his mouth off side into his belittling kind of smile. "I can be a patient man," he went on, "until that patience begins to interfere with Company business. At that point, orders are orders, McLoughlin, or else you are no longer in our employ."

"*Oui, oui*," John stormed, "and that suits me!"

"Johnny." Marguerite stood between them. "Is it not a small matter tonight to be perhaps a big regret when the sun is high?" She tossed her head. "We do not walk beside this lake so we may walk sooner beside the great river of the West." She shrugged. "It is no thing for deciding to be no more the employee of the Company." She snapped her fingers. "It is no thing for giving two thoughts."

[*49*]

Marguerite's manner, as aloof as George Simpson's, made insignificant and ridiculous the Governor's insistence on exerting his authority. John felt anger sweat out through his pores and evaporate. A flat refusal in the face of the way Marguerite had managed to turn the matter, would give Simpson the satisfaction of standing tall on his prerogatives. Going ahead to clear trail now made nothing of it, one way or the other. John's hands closed on Marguerite's shoulders. "You'll be all right?"

"I'll be here." Simpson's tone was cool. "The men are waiting," he prodded. "Here is Charlefoux to carry for you. You'll reach fallen timber by the time the moon is high enough to light your work."

John pulled Marguerite close for a moment. She was the only one who could have sent him off this night. His longing for her filled his throat. He wanted to tell her how he felt but what words could he say with Simpson listening? Abruptly he dropped his arms and struck off with Charlefoux.

Marguerite swallowed as she watched John's broad back, shoulders less erect than they should be, disappear beyond a granite boulder. Her moccasins turned toward their lodge but an amber arc of moon floated from behind the ice ledge and stopped her.

Lured by the moon, she moved idly at first, along the tumbling, noisy stream that flowed from the lake. The sound of the water took her again to Lac la Pluie and the stream where she first met John. Such a free, devil-may-care young man he had been. She had loved the big easy swing of his walk, not for itself, but for the thing inside him that made him walk so.

Perhaps she had been wrong to interfere tonight between John and this George Simpson. Perhaps a man should always be free to say, "I will," or "I won't," and to prove it with his fists, if need be. And yet a man with a wife and a family could not say, without stopping to think, *"Oui, oui,* it suits me to be no longer the employee of the Company." Especially, if that man wanted more than anything else to reach the Columbia Country and to show the gentlemen in London what he could make of it.

"Still, a man perhaps should be free," she repeated in a whisper.

[50]

These words never failed to chill her. She knew that hers and John's was different from the usual alliance between a Company man and a half-breed girl. When they defied the gossips and began living together, they had more reason than that John was under contract to stay in the wilds of Canada, cut off from female society of a class to be married. He had convinced her that he wanted her for better reasons than that she was convenient. She had a million ways of knowing beyond all questions that their marriage of consent was not for-the-time-being-only. Still, if John would ask a minister to say the proper words, perhaps she would not shiver always to think that he might like it better to be free. Perhaps if she wore on her finger a circle of gold such as those worn by ladies who had been married by a minister, it could be that this George Simpson might not so often say "squaw," and she might not so many times surprise him standing to one side staring at her with his eyes narrowed down to hide where they were looking.

A shaft of light swung across her way like a gate closed before her and Marguerite came up with a start. She had been unaware of walking hard, climbing over boulders, splashing through rivulets that cascaded into the lake. Now her palms felt raw from clutching at loose granite. Her breath lay heavy on the top of her lungs. Muscles throbbed in her legs.

Over her left shoulder the peaks beyond the lake cradled the moon like an opal in a wine glass. She had been walking a long time then. No wonder her breath came fast, burning her throat with its dryness. She must rest a moment and turn back.

She leaned against a wall of rock and then remembered her Paris ribbon. Loving its crispness, she untied the bow and shook her hair free. Now, she must hurry.

But it was a night for loitering, for stopping at each cove to listen to the water tumbling the sharp-edged gravel. She found herself stepping softly that she might not disturb the small night creatures intent on foraging for food or love. But soon, she had another reason for stepping softly.

It was not a reason with a sound of its own and certainly she could not see it. It was that vague sense of being watched. She thought little of it. Marguerite knew nothing of fear. John had tried to convince her that she needed, on occasion, to be afraid. But her mother's people were Crees, a tribe which had fought and defeated its enemies so often that they now wore tranquillity on their faces in place of war paint. Her Swiss father had taken her, when she was a child, on many long trading expeditions. He had always taught her that she was more than a match for man or beast or the forces of nature.

Now, under these unseen eyes, she felt curiosity but not fear. Perhaps her passing had disturbed a bear. But she could outrun any bear fattened for his winter's sleep and after he showed himself would be soon enough to start.

Her senses alert to detect any sound of actual footsteps, Marguerite moved on, taking her time. Instead of feeling afraid, she was excited a little by this game of hide and seek. Whatever or whoever he might be, her opponent was skillful in keeping his whereabouts secret and yet she knew he was near.

One moment the rim of the lake curved before her with only here and there the black geometric shadow of a boulder cutting across her path. The next moment a man stood before her no more than ten steps away. No taller than Marguerite herself, he made, against the moonlight, a figure as well embedded and unyielding as the great slabs of granite beside the lake. Marguerite kept her gasp inaudible and did not stop until they were face to face. Then she waited for him to speak.

"Good evening," George Simpson said, stiff as pine gum in winter.

"*Bon soir*," she answered without committing herself. If he had some purpose in tagging her, let him state his case.

Simpson cleared his throat. "It is a pleasant evening for a walk," he commented.

"*Oui*." Once more, she did not commit herself.

"I took the liberty of watching you to . . . to . . . see that you were safe."

Marguerite's head lifted. "Safe?" Skeptical, she added, "And am I?"

He turned to the lake. She heard him breathe in one long breath

[52]

and let it out with a rush. "I'll see you back to camp," he said and stepped aside as if he would have her lead the way.

But Marguerite remembered this man's stares through narrowed eyes. "*Merci, m'sieu*," she said. "But you shall walk ahead."

"Have you seen so much of men refusing to ride in front of other men in the wilds of Canada that you expect me to shoot you in the back?" His words were teasing but his voice sounded angry.

"I expect only that you will walk in front. I do not wish longer to have the night made watchful by being stalked like an animal." She held her ground until, with another of his hard-to-read laughs, he wheeled and struck out ahead.

Most laughs, Marguerite thought, were catching as yawns and drew others into the fun. But this George Simpson, his laugh shut others out.

The moon poured down enough light to let Marguerite move in and out and over the boulders with a sure step and still watch the ghostly play of iridescence on the ice ledge towering against the sky. Soon she was listening for the separate currents in the lake. Was it real—or did she make it so by wishing—that the westward moving water sang a quicker, brighter song? She stopped, then moved out until the water lapped at the toes of her moccasins. Across the lake the moon turned to gold the jumble of shale and rock that had marred the triangular head of a glacier. Beyond, the red moon sent out flames licking up the wall of ice.

Marguerite forgot George Simpson. She stood, drinking in her fill of the night and then strolled on entranced. Coming to a table rock extending over the water, she stepped out and, instinctively, lifted her arms, spreading them wide and upward. "*Merci,*" she whispered.

It was just something she did, not exactly a prayer. Prayers, she said on her knees. Also a prayer asked for more and, at these moments, Marguerite would never think of asking for more. And yet the Great Spirit was in this rite of hers. He heard her, she knew. He was out there, listening, and he knew that within her outspread arms she was including, as of a piece with all this beauty, her children and her Johnny. He knew that she was saying thank you and feeling a little guilty because she possessed more than her share of love and goodness.

And the way she knew he was there was that, whenever she stopped like this, night or day, just to be glad for things as they were and to murmur, "*Merci*," the Great Spirit answered.

"*Merci*," he whispered back and when she heard it the moon grew brighter for an instant and made her warm.

Her arms fell to her sides and she added "*Merci* also for off there beyond the mountains." She dropped cross-legged onto the rock to watch the shimmer of light on the current that flowed to the west.

"Marguerite."

To hear this George Simpson call her by name startled her far more than to be reminded that he was there. She sprang to her feet. "*Pardon, m'sieu*. For one moment I forgot."

He blocked her way. "Marguerite," he repeated, "that cup of tea you offered me there on Rivière la Biche—I know I should have taken it. I had so much on my mind. I acted like a cad."

"When I have much on my mind, I often act like what I am," she said and added, with a toss of her head toward the mountaintops, "as I did just now, forgetting you were here, forgetting everything—"

"You can forgive me, then?"

Was this George Simpson whom her Johnny admired for his quick brain so simple that he did not know she had called him a cad? She hesitated long enough to tell herself that she must not hurt Johnny by what she said to this little man, his superior officer. But surely not even Johnny would see so hungry a fish in the pool and keep his hook in his pocket. She straightened and flung back her hair. "I can forgive you, *m'sieu*. But what do you yourself think of a man who insults a woman in public and then comes in the night to ask, 'Forgive me'?"

He took one step toward her. "Why you—!"

She heard something more than anger in his voice. She stood tall. "I must go see about my children, if you will kindly step aside, *m'sieu*."

He touched her arm. "Come. Your children are sleeping." He

[54]

walked out on the overhanging rock and sat down. "Your young Junior is a quick one on the trigger."

"Jacques?" Marguerite could not refuse to listen to a man who spoke so warmly of her son. "I hope he has not been under your feet."

"Certainly not. On the contrary—" He stopped himself. "Come now. Sit down." He offered her the rock beside him.

Marguerite stepped aside and stood with the river at her back. Her moon shadow lay on the rock between them. "Jacques wishes always to learn," she said. "It makes of him sometimes a nuisance but you can send him to his father when your tongue grows lame from answering questions. He is like his father."

"So he is," Simpson agreed. "One of these days he'll make a fine fur trader. We'll keep that in mind."

"One of these days, he will make a fine doctor," Marguerite corrected.

Simpson raised one shoulder. "Quarter-breeds! Bits of brown! McLoughlin will do well to remember the sordid facts before he builds up too many ambitions for his offspring."

Marguerite bristled. "You will please not to say 'bits of brown' when you speak of my children. And it is Jacques himself who has decided he will be a doctor. His father believes a child should decide for himself."

"Quarter-breed!" A sneer edged Simpson's voice. He boosted himself to his feet and stood confronting Marguerite. "What do you 'breeds' think you are anyway—putting on airs, telling me what I am not to say, setting yourselves up as somebody!" He made his voice mocking. "Your son will be a doctor. Your daughter will be a fine lady, no doubt." His laugh belittled everything Marguerite had just embraced in her "*Merci.*" "As for you—"

Marguerite watched his chest lift and fall, lift and fall. She longed to strike him but that was Johnny's fiery, quick-tempered way, not hers. Her way was to turn to the lake and wait for a quiet to come within her that would let her speak with a dignity cold enough to chill a man's bones.

But then she heard his heavy breathing and, before she could whip around, his lips were hot on her neck, his outspread hands pressed her ribs and moved upward.

"Marguerite, Marguerite!" he whispered. "You're irresistible. No man could bear it."

Every muscle in her tightened. Wrapped in fury, she jerked away and waited for him to compose himself. Then, head up, she started past him.

But Simpson caught her arms. His grip had steel in it.

She beat his chest and butted him with her head but still he hung on.

"Marguerite, I want you. Don't you understand?"

She kicked his shins and clawed at his face.

"Easy there." His tone changed from hot to cold. "A show of fight, yes, but squaws don't leave scars on white men, you know." He locked an arm around her and grabbed both her hands. "Come, come, who do you think you're saving yourself for? Not John McLoughlin! He's a big man. He'll have him a real wife, one of these days."

She strained against him.

He lifted her hands to the moonlight. "Look. McLoughlin didn't even give you a wedding ring." Simpson's voice turned syrupy. "Isn't this as long as you usually struggle, my fine she-wolf?"

Her fingernails tore into his hand on her breast. A twist and she was free from his arms but he still blocked her way. Turning, she dived into the lake.

She would never again be warm. Rigid with cold, she lay through the night, staring into the cone of her lodge. As a great dark cave in her breast she felt the shame of being stalked in the night and expected to respond like an animal.

When she had first reached the lodge and stirred up the coals to dry her tunic and leggings, she felt sure that she could never bear it until she could talk with Johnny. She must warn him that this man he looked up to, this man whose orders he must carry out, was a beast of prey. When she slipped under the blankets beside Eloise to borrow warmth from the child, she thought of

[56]

Johnny's anger and shuddered. Then she remembered the light in her Johnny's eyes when he spoke of the Columbia and what it would mean to a man to take an unspoiled country and shape it into something new. By dawn, when she stood before the lodge in the red capote and looked up to the snow-ledged peaks, she could say aloud what she had known all along, "I must never tell Johnny."

Johnny, if he knew, would kill this George Simpson, quick, with his fists. And so Johnny would kill also the big dream burned in his heart—his dream for the new country off there to the west, for the new life to be won for his family in a land where labels of "half-breed" or "quarter-breed" had no power to rob a man's son of his chance.

If, on the other hand, Johnny did not know about last night, she could handle this George Simpson herself, in a slow way with a poisoned word here and a small bullet of doubt fired from nowhere. This George Simpson—with his one set of rules for daytime and another for dark, with his aristocratic manners and his slimy hands—in time, she could snare him like a beaver into a trap he had baited with his own castoreum.

VI John had fidgeted in the stern of the North canoe the whole hundred miles upriver from Fort George. Beyond the sweating voyageurs, dipping and lifting their paddles, he could almost see written in black ink on Simpson's blue wool back the big question that had stood between the two of them since their first meeting in London—were they to be friends or enemies?

Through the winter at Fort George neither man had been willing to tilt the thing by making an open play for friendship. John had felt that the question must not be settled on any false basis such as politeness or deference for Simpson's position and, for that reason, had deliberately and sometimes belligerently stood up for his rights and opinions. Perhaps Simpson had done the same. And yet they had not become enemies.

But today, John was in a mood to make overtures, if need be. He wanted Simpson to fall head-over-heels for the new Columbia Department headquarters. He wanted him to carry a report to London so glowing that the gentlemen there could not consider withdrawing their support until they'd given this Department time to show a profit under John's direction.

Before he actually arrived at the Columbia, the idea of a new country, waiting to be shaped one way or another by his hands had intrigued John in the way that an unquarried mountain of marble might intrigue a sculptor. But from the moment he felt the power of this unharnessed river beneath his canoe, from the moment his eyes first climbed the majestic cone of Mount Hood, he had been a sculptor with a masterpiece in him. It clamored to be let out.

This country had been land-marked by the Creator as a place where a man could stand as tall and independent as her mountains and John had to see it shaped to that mold. As a Chief Factor of Hudson's Bay Company, he could develop the resources of these rivers and mountains and meadows, he could civilize the natives, he could see his son grow up and take his rightful place in a land where a man's birth meant nothing and his true worth was a matter for proving.

A scowl from Simpson this morning or one of his belittling sniffs could mean grudging and inadequate support from the gentlemen in London and, eventually, transfer back to Canada. No, no! This day must enlist Simpson's full backing for John and this Oregon Country.

John kept trying to put out of his mind that evening last fall when they approached Fort George at sunset. Simpson had liked nothing about the whole setup. He had taken one step inside the fort's twenty-foot-high stockade and pronounced, "Altogether too pompous for an Indian trading post." At the entrance to the main building, he had stopped to stare at first one and then the other eighteen-pounder mounted there and trained on the stockade gate. "Everything on the Columbia appears too imposing except the trade!" he scoffed.

The buildings they had been able to throw together at the new site were nothing to curl the Governor's lip by their grandeur, John was sure. And the stands of fir so nearly balanced by tillable acres surrounding the new post, the great shipping thoroughfare of the Columbia within a stone's throw of their door could—unless they were blotted out by fog or, worse, by a gray March rain—win the Governor over. But all the way upriver Simpson had said no word to commit himself one way or the other and now the time had come for the voyageurs to turn midstream, head for the raw new dock, and strike up their song:

> Sing, nightingale, keep singing,
> Thou hast a heart so gay,
> Thou hast a heart so merry,
> While mine is sorrow's play.
> Long it is, I have loved thee:
> Thee, shall I love alway.

As the canoe came around, the white tip of Mount Hood poked

through a billow of cloud. The voyageurs' vermilion paddles threw out a wake of tinted spray and the canoe skimmed like a flat stone across the water. Before them, blue-carpeted by the flowers of the wapato, lay the mile-wide prairie where John had longed to set his buildings except for the chance of spring floods.

On shore, Company men, natives, children, and dogs made for the dock in a bedlam of squeals and barks. John noticed a great many Chinook Indians in the crowd. They must have raced up here from the mouth of the Columbia after one of their number had eavesdropped around Fort George to learn of this affair. Even the horses, waiting to carry John and the Governor across the blue meadow and up to the compound, joined in the gaiety and commotion.

The sun on the bare planks filled the air with the perfume of fresh-sawed fir. Without a word, George Simpson stepped from the canoe and onto the dock. His slow about-face of inspection ended in a gasp. "By the great Jehoshaphat, no peer's holdings in England can match this!" he exclaimed.

John enjoyed the astonishment in the Governor's tone and dismissed without a second thought its hint of envy. He wished Pete Ogden were here this day instead of out there on the Snake somewhere trapping beaver. Pete ought to be here. And, confound it, where was Marguerite? She had come up from Fort George a week ago to make the half-finished Chief Factor's house livable but he could not pick her out in this crowd. If the Governor was going to be as pleased as all this, it was an occasion requiring Marguerite by his side. But before John could pull away to look for her, the Governor had changed his tune.

He turned, as John had hoped he would, to let his eyes drink in the blue Columbia flowing at their feet, the green scallops promising rich pasture and plowed fields along the Willamette across the way and, for climax, the mighty thrust of Mount Hood on to the east. "I'll have to give it a name," he said.

"I've picked a name," John blurted.

"You?" Simpson's gaze relegated John to a position in the Company well beneath the level required for naming a post.

Then, his voice became indulgent. "Very well. What's your choice?"

"Columbia. Columbia House, I think. For the river."

"For the river, be damned! For that upstart American's ship, you mean. Never! Not in a million years. Not for Gray nor his ship nor for anything or anybody else American. Let's get that clear."

John made an effort to keep his words coming in single file. "So far, this river is as British as she is American and I happen to like her, name and all."

Simpson's eyes narrowed. His nostrils flared. "Fort Vancouver this post will be christened at sunrise tomorrow before I leave here. And Fort Vancouver she'll remain. Let the Americans stick that one in their saucy caps and wear it. George Vancouver discovered this coast and this river on behalf of Great Britain and may you never forget it, Doctor."

John had been reminding himself all morning that he must not lose his temper on this of all days. The big thing was that Simpson liked the site. It was even worth something that he cared enough about it to make an issue of the name. "Very well, Governor," he said.

Simpson turned on his most skeptical and one-sided smile. "What's this? Are you giving in without a fight?"

"I want you to like the place—name and all," John told him. "The name means little to me compared with that. And," he added, "I've never wanted to fight with you, Governor. I'm hoping we can be friends for the good of the Columbia Department."

"Friends?" Simpson's eyes looked just past John. "Of course we're friends. Remember that always. Remember, too, that any suggestions I make are for your own good. You're new in Hudson's Bay Company and I can help you get ahead, if you'll learn to act on my orders without quibbling. I suppose I need not remind you that I can help you in the other direction just as readily."

"I know, I know."

"I like to see a man think for himself, Doctor, but you'll save yourself trouble and get further in the Company, if you can learn

[61]

to think more nearly in line with your superior officers." He touched John's arm. "Come. I want to see your buildings."

But first, Simpson had something more impressive than buildings to inspect.

The daughter of Chief Comcomly—a buxom and influential matron called the Princess of Wales—had tried since they arrived at Fort George last fall to press her eighteen-year-old offspring upon the Governor. She had begun bargaining with a dowry of a hundred beaver skins. To that she had added daily some new attempt at trickery or inducement. She was hell-bent for building up her personal prestige by securing a prominent King George man for son-in-law.

Simpson could have squelched her at first by being firm. But the Princess of Wales was valuable to the Company. She wielded as much or more power than her father, Chief Comcomly. And she was an incurable gossip. From her, Simpson was able to learn all kinds of intelligence regarding affairs both inside and outside the fort. Several times during the winter she had actually saved Fort George from serious losses by running to Simpson with tales of thieving raids planned by the Indians. So, Simpson owed her something and he needed her. Her friendship could, on some dark night, mean the difference between having trade goods on hand or going out of business.

For four months the Governor had encouraged the Princess just enough to keep the gossip lines open but not enough to become actually involved with her daughter. Another day and he would be off for the East, out of danger. At the moment, however, escape looked unlikely. The Princess of Wales and her plump daughter had planted themselves at the end of the dock.

The Princess, every inch an aristocrat by the standards of her people, stood square on her archless feet, her flattened forehead held at an arrogant slope. The usual shredded bark skirt, its drawstring low on her hips, hung to her knees. For this special occasion she wore, also, a bib made from the bellies of wood rats. Obviously intended to enhance rather than obscure, the fur bib covered the flat part of her chest. From beneath and around it, her pendulous breasts swung free.

[62]

John twisted his ear and glanced down at Simpson. "Never knew for certain what 'best bib and tucker' meant until right now," he said.

The daughter of the Princess, known among Company men as the Filly, wore the uniform shredded skirt and, from the perforations around her ears dangled a small fortune in hyaqua shells. But the Princess of Wales had made one lavish, irretractible gesture to obtain the Governor for son-in-law. This, she brandished before him on her daughter's still reddened skin.

There, tattooed in blue and red, were the rampant deer—one on each breast—the shield with four beavers in the spaces marked by the red cross, and the alert fox at the top. The Hudson's Bay coat-of-arms! The banner of the emblem flew across the girl's abdomen with its never more appropriate motto, PRO PELLE CUTEM.

Hoping to learn from the Governor how to handle these delicate situations that had a way of cropping up among the Chinook Indians, John stepped in closer.

The Princess intercepted him. "No, no. Not for you. For the Governor," she specified in French.

Simpson stared at the Filly. Then his mouth pulled to the side and, with an exaggerated show of obeisance, he bowed before the tattooed symbol of his highest loyalty. Coming up, he remained suave and unperturbed. He leaned toward the Princess, grasped one of the tubular white trade beads suspended from her ear, and whispered half a dozen words.

The Princess pulled back. "But when do I see this one you promise?"

"Tomorrow," Simpson answered. "Tomorrow for certain."

She nodded but set her jaw. "Tomorrow it will be then or my people make much trouble," she threatened. "Come," she said to her daughter and they flounced through the crowd.

Only now did Simpson permit himself an amused and disparaging shrug. He pulled off his beaver hat and waved it before him to clear the meadow. "Out of our way, here," he said but he kept it good-natured.

Dogs, Flatheads, Company servants, French-Canadian free

[63]

trappers, and voyageurs all fell back, opening a path before the Governor.

John wagged his head for the stableman to bring up the horses. "Or would you rather walk?" he asked, hoping for a chance to stretch his legs and draw a deep breath of this spring-scented air.

"No, no," Simpson objected. He grasped John's elbow and, in a comradely tone, advised, "Never slight the ritual, Doctor, and whenever you can, pour it on a little. Serves to keep the Company's servants on their mettle and, especially, pomp and feathers impress the natives. It's a thing you're inclined to be lax in. Why, man, with your physique"—he socked John's shoulder on the old wound— "with your physique, you could have every Indian between here and Hudson Bay scared of your shadow."

"*Oui, oui*, perhaps." John swung into his saddle. Confound it, where was Marguerite?

Simpson laid the quirt to his mare and raced her across the blue meadow and up the bluff to the compound gates. When John came up, he gave vent to his impatience by jerking his mare to the left toward the flank of buildings along the west side of the fort yard. "I'll take a look at the storerooms first, if you think your nag can amble over there."

John kept his eyes on the windows as they moved past the dwelling house in the center of the open court but Marguerite was nowhere in sight.

And now, Simpson could not be hurried. He must dismount and inspect every inch of fur storage space to see that it was tight enough to keep out varmints, dry enough to prevent fur damage from moisture.

At the warehouse where they would store trade goods and supplies as soon as they could move them upriver, he had to express himself once more on the extravagance of items imported from England to Fort George. "Ostrich plumes, steel armor, shelf after shelf of mustard! You'd think mustard was an item for Indian trade! Well, never again. I'll see to that. And"—he swung around on John—"you see to it, too. Don't let me ever lay my eyes on another requisition for mustard from the Columbia Department. And sell that suit of steel armor to somebody. Did you get those seed potatoes planted?"

"We did. Just to the north of the compound. I've never seen such soil. It's my guess this soil will grow any crop we plant."

"It had better be good, for your sake," Simpson threatened, "for I'll have no more shipments from England such as this post has stuffed its belly on. From now on, the men stationed here will eat salmon and potatoes until they forget the existence of flour and tinned beef imported from England."

The Governor's brusque manner might have rubbed John's bristles the wrong way any day but this. Now, it meant only that Simpson was leaving no stone unturned to put the Columbia Department on a paying basis. He inspected it all, from potato field to temporary quarters for the men and finally commented, "Fine, fine!" He even gave John his hand. "Now, let's get things lined up in the office. I want to give you every benefit of my years with the Company and there's not much time left before I must leave."

They handed their reins to John's big Scotsman, Bruce, who waited in kilt and sporran at the steps to the factor's residence. John stopped on the top step for his usual look out across the stockade toward Mount Hood but George Simpson strode across the portico and into the office. He seated himself at John's desk with his routine bustle of arranging coattails and smoothing wrist ruffles back off his hands. "Now then, get me some paper," he ordered. "Fill this inkwell."

When John reached in a drawer for black ink powder, Simpson brought from his pocket and thrust at him two sheets of foolscap filled with names.

"The employees in the Columbia Department are to be reduced from one hundred and fifty-one to eighty-three. Ship the sixty-eight men on this list off to Canada by this summer's Express." The Governor leaned back and dismissed the men on the list with a wave of his hand. "There alone is a saving of well over two thousand pounds a year. This one move will set you well up on the ladder with their honors in London."

[65]

"But Governor Simpson," John objected, "what will these men do for a living? What will happen to their families?"

"Families?" Simpson shrugged. "Let their squaws and litters go back to their Indian tribes and all the better for them. As for the men, the employees in this Department must be brought into reasonable relationship to the volume of its business. Otherwise, you'll find yourself without a department to run. The Governor and Committee in London are in no mood to subsidize the Columbia much longer. That was understood when you were appointed. I'm doing my best to give you the benefit of my experience so you can make this Department pay."

"*Oui, oui,* but you say 'employees,'" John persisted, "as if they were names on the books." He glanced at the top sheet in his hand. "I see here Gervais who has been with the Company since 1808. Seventeen years of faithful service and we cut him off with no way to feed his wife and five children." He lifted the first sheet. "You say 'employees' and here is Étienne Lucier who saved our lives last fall when we left Fort George for Cape Disappointment and our canoe began to come apart at the seams." His eyes went back to the first sheet and he began to read through the list, name by name. He looked up. "Charlefoux, you have here. No, no, that can't be."

"That young reprobate!" Simpson scoffed. "And what possible reason can we have for keeping him on? He's a troublemaker, the most independent man in the lot. He keeps all the others on the brink of mutiny half the time."

"But he's just taken a Chinook girl and vows this time it's different, that he's going to stay with her. I'd like to see him have a chance. If we cut him off now and send him back to Canada, what will happen to her?"

"She'll be right where she started and a jump ahead if she doesn't have to put up with Charlefoux."

"But she's expecting his child. She isn't the highest type," John admitted, "but Charlefoux seems genuinely smitten by her charms. Already he's built a little shack to the west of the compound and Marguerite has started to teach the girl how to cook and keep house in civilized ways."

[*66*]

"Doctor, I have little patience and no time for arguments. Send the men on that list back to Canada by this summer's Express. They can do as they please about their families. In addition, you will warn all commissioned gentlemen to cut costs in every branch of the business. They must disregard little domestic comforts. You can't remind the men under you too often that the fur trade is no tea party." Simpson got up and began to pace.

John sat down in the leather winged chair that faced the window. He stared at the list in his hand, worrying, first about the men and what would become of them, and second about how he could with a handful of commissioned gentlemen man a half-dozen trading posts, keep two or three big trapping expeditions in the field, explore his vast new territory and study the possibilities of its resources, keep a hundred little tribes of Indians in line, finish his building and planting program, and on and on and on.

Simpson paused long enough to say, "About that Snake River Country . . ." and then went on with his pacing.

"There's our best chance to make the Columbia Department pay, it seems to me," John volunteered. "And if any man can bring out furs against weather and Blackfeet and starvation, Peter Skene Ogden is that man. I look for him to trail into our post on the Walla Walla with four thousand prime skins before long."

"A fur desert," Simpson mused.

John knew that the Governor had heard none of what he said.

"What's to prevent it?" Simpson wheeled and whammed his fist into his palm. "We've almost four years left under the Joint Occupation Treaty with the United States. It's a race but we can win it. Pour every available trapper into the Snake Country before the boundary question comes up for settlement. Leave all that land from the Blues to the Tetons barren of furs and American trappers will stop on the other side of the Stony Mountains. King George would knight a man for a job like that."

John sat forward. "But you can't mean what you're saying, Governor. The North West Company always followed a strict policy of conservation in the fur trade. Otherwise, we slit our own throats."

[67]

Simpson perched on the corner of the desk and tented his hands on his black satin waistcoat. "But in this case, conservation is all wrong, don't you see? That Ashley sitting over there in St. Louis with his high prices for furs and his short supply line for trade goods and ammunition—he makes our lot too hard in the Snake Country."

"But by terms of the Joint Occupation treaty, the American Fur Company has as much right in there as Hudson's Bay," John pointed out.

"As much right, but no more. That's the point until the boundary question is settled. And how is that question going to be settled?" Simpson came over to wag his finger in John's face. "You know as well as I do, Doctor. All this Oregon Country will go to whichever government has the most colonists here when the boundary line is drawn. Already Americans are beginning to traipse across the mountains. But, if we stop their traipsing, the British Parliament will have time to bring colonists by sea or herd them in from Canada and we can claim this land for King George. So!" Simpson sat down at the desk. "As soon as Mr. Ogden gets into Walla Walla, give his men a week-long regale while the horses rest and send them out again."

"But our regales for men off the Snake are usually two weeks with an extra ration of rum."

"A week of carousing is long enough, even for men off the Snake. I want trappers on the Snake summer and winter."

"But summer pelts are no good."

"Take them anyway."

"Our policy has always been to save the young."

"Now we take anything—young or old, prime or poorly." When John opened his mouth to protest, Simpson stopped him. "This is not merely for the sake of the Company and bringing in a profit from this Department. It is, even more, for the sake of your king. Surely you can't hesitate when it's a matter of patriotism. We're first in line and playing for big stakes, Doctor. You yourself have been singing the praises of the Oregon Country from the minute we landed here last fall. Surely you'd like to have a hand in claiming this land for the Crown." Simpson tipped the desk chair against the wall. He linked his fingers across his waistcoat and, slowly nodding his head, confirmed each word as he spoke. "Yes sir, what better monument could a man erect for himself than the winning of a territory so rich in so many resources? Add the Oregon Country to Canada and you can greatly increase the value of Great Britain's holdings on this continent and, at the same time, make a place for yourself in history, John McLoughlin."

"True," John agreed. A place for himself in history meant little to him, one way or the other, but a place for his son to grow up as good as the next man meant a great deal. So, too, did a guarantee that this country would be developed and civilized. He very much wanted a hand in that. It was his idea to start with the Indians. They'd been unspoiled, so far, and John felt sure they could be elevated and taught civilized ways all as a part of his day's work for the Company. "I'm wondering how soon we can provide a school and church services at this establishment," he said. "The Company is obligated to enlighten the Indians, as I read our charter."

"I've always remarked that an enlightened Indian is good for nothing." Simpson let his chair back to the floor with a jar. "They're already too much enlightened and more of it will do harm instead of good to the fur trade."

"But the country! What about good to the country? Hudson's Bay charter makes us responsible for the moral training and education of natives and the children of Company men in areas where we trade."

"All right!" Simpson gave in but with too much vehemence. "The Company is obligated to educate natives and children and you have your own bits of brown that you make so much of. You want a formal school for them. Very well. I shall see to it. You'll have a chaplain who can also serve as school teacher. It will be attended with little good other than to fill the belly of some hungry missionary and rear the Indians in habits of indolence. Still, you'll get your chaplain. I'll pick him myself." Simpson pulled up to the desk and dipped a quill. "I'll also attend to that Snake River Country myself. I'll write out orders for Pete Ogden and carry them to Walla Walla tomorrow. You'll have your hands full nearer at home for a while."

And so it went, into the night and on through the night. Simpson figured and wrote instructions and gave verbal orders and paced the floor.

John listened and argued. He gave in at points where little seemed at stake. He decided to bide his time and work things out with regard to such big issues as what to do about the men Simpson ordered dropped from the Company's books.

An hour before dawn the office door banged open and Bruce announced in his rolling burr, "Mrs. McLoughlin says to tell you, sir, your breakfast is cooked and ready to serve."

George Simpson reared back from the desk and snorted something that sounded to John like, "Mrs. McLoughlin, indeed!" But then he stood and smoothed his shirt ruffles into place. "Breakfast is an excellent idea. I've wanted a cup of tea for hours." He stretched off his business manner and became his affable social self. He bowed John through the office door ahead of him and strolled beside him through the hall.

Two Indian servants in rush skirts—one with a huge platter and the other bearing a basket the size of a washbowl—entered the far end of the hall from the covered passageway to the kitchen at the back. They followed the men into the candle-lighted dining hall.

Simpson took the chair at the end of the table near the iron stove. "It's an odd thing," he said, "but in four short months I've come to look down on the unflattened heads of servants the same as the Chinooks themselves do."

"*Papa*, I've come to eat breakfast with you." Jacques, in the doorway, raked his fingers through his tousled curls. "Good morning, Governor Simpson." He finished pulling into place his thrown-on deerskin tunic and marched to the table. "I caught a fish yesterday," he announced.

John grinned and nodded permission for the boy to stay. Then, as the servants arranged the food on the table, he noticed that they had no tea. "Confound it," he said, "Marguerite has forgotten the tea." He summoned a servant with a jerk of his thumb.

"Tea, tea, tea," he sputtered. What had gotten into Marguerite?

The Indian woman shrugged.

John's blessing sounded a bit impatient even in his own ears.

Jacques helped himself to a potato from the basket, stabbed it with a knife, and lifted it to his mouth. "I don't think you'll get the tea," he stated flatly.

"Young man, put that potato down and cut it up."

Jacques obeyed.

"And why won't we have tea?" Simpson asked the boy.

"Well, you see," he answered, speaking slowly, giving his opinion its full weight, "tea is imported. And *Maman* said that you, Governor Simpson, had given orders that this post was to live on salmon and potatoes, salmon and potatoes. She heard," he glanced toward John but did not let him interrupt, "that you said salmon and potatoes were good enough for an Indian trader."

Before John could trust himself to speak, Simpson laughed. Grateful, John joined him. You couldn't help liking a man who could laugh when the joke was on him. This day had really seen the Governor's friendship won, then, and John glimpsed the way ahead for this country lying shorter and smoother because of this. But he preferred not to give Jacques too many opportunities for tossing monkey wrenches. "Son, the ceremonies are at sunrise," he pointed out. "You'll want to wash your face and brush your hair."

"Be glad you don't have to shave, as I do," Simpson said.

"Yes, sir." Jacques bowed to Governor Simpson. "Excuse me, please."

"A fine boy," Simpson commented. "He'll make a good Company man, given another five years."

"He'll make a good doctor."

Simpson pushed back from the table and donned his business manner once more. "Unless you take some decisive step to keep Comcomly in line, you'll find him a powerful enemy"—he picked up where they had been interrupted by Bruce's announcement of breakfast. "As you saw last fall, Comcomly virtually controls all trade in this area. So far, our men at Fort George haven't been able to cut into his hold over the chiefs of neighboring tribes.

They've traded through Comcomly's grandfather, through his father, and now through his one-eyed majesty himself and they won't listen to anything else."

"I know," John agreed. "Sometimes these Indians seem as civilized as any London dowager. Her grandmother and her mother before her bought their buttons from the little merchant on Bond Street and she will, too, or know the reason why."

"These Indians know one sound reason why they trade through Comcomly," Simpson pointed out. "They're afraid of his British-made rifles."

"Maybe we should have thought of this before we let him acquire these rifles," John said.

"We thought of it but Comcomly, due to his power over the other chiefs, is always the man with the furs and we're in the fur business, remember. You'll find it to your advantage not to interfere too much with the natives and their ways. Don't get any noble ideas of reforming them overnight. You'll need to enlist Comcomly on your side by whatever means the situation requires."

"You have any suggestions?"

"I have." Simpson got up and, locking his hands behind him, rocked on his heels. "I want you to form an alliance with that daughter of the Princess of Wales. Comcomly sets great store both by his daughter and by that particular granddaughter."

John heard but could not comprehend. If he had heard rightly, the thing was beyond taking in. Dully he said, "But, but, but—"

"I know." The Governor lifted a calming hand. "This is a new idea and you'll need time to get used to it. But it's merely our usual plan as practiced at all our posts. These so-called marriages wield more influence with Indians than anything else we've been able to think of and a man does need a squaw for various reasons. The Princess is interested in prestige. A big Company man for son-in-law, that's what she wants." Simpson paced the length of the table and back again. "After I've gone East, you'll be the biggest man around. Besides, the Indians like the way you treat your woman. You carry a basket instead of loading it on Marguerite, you open doors and let her go first—these are subjects of much talk among the Chinooks." Simpson slapped his palms together. "Well, so that's that. The Princess will agree, I'm sure. In fact, I've been promising her I'd get her the top man as soon as I left. She'll agree fast enough and it's the kind of arrangement the Company has needed for years with Comcomly."

John found himself towering above the Governor. Still, the enormity of this suggestion held his anger below the surface and kept him from striking out. His words came slower than usual and in rigid single file. "You can't mean that the Company requires me to set aside my marriage and contract another simply because we need a hold on Comcomly." He hoped with everything in him that Simpson's answer would not release the fury in his fists.

Simpson backed up one step but his lifted shoulder and tilted head denied the presence of any dynamite in this situation. "No-o-o-o, I wouldn't say the Company requires it. But you, as a good Company man, must see how sensible my suggestion is. It's merely good business and with the Columbia Department consistently riding the wrong side of the ledger, you can't afford to pass up any guarantees of trade with Comcomly."

"But man, man! There's Marguerite. Surely—"

"Yes, yes," Simpson soothed. "I've thought of that. But you know the usual procedure. Make up a small dowry and we can find someone to take Marguerite off your hands. As you know, I have a squaw at Red River, but I'd be willing—for the good of the trade here on the Columbia—to set that one aside and assume responsibility for Marguerite myself. In fact, I'll take Marguerite back East with me at once and you'll be free to negotiate for the Filly before the Princess has time to stir up trouble over this."

The old pain stabbed John's back. He sprang forward and caught Simpson's shoulders. "No, no, no!" He shook his quarry until he could see nothing but the aloof smile on the Governor's face.

Still unruffled, still with an air of being above all this, Simpson tossed his head and attempted to break from the hold by pressing his elbows into John's chest.

[73]

John pushed him off and shook him again and then his hands moved in toward Simpson's throat. He forgot that this was his superior officer. He forgot that he wanted and needed above everything else the Governor's friendship. He saw only that insolent smile and he kept hearing the way Simpson had spoken Marguerite's name, as if she were a piece of trade goods to be used and resold. His hands dug through starched shirt ruffles and caught up a fistful of flesh and tendons at each side of Simpson's neck. He heard a low growl and could not be sure whether it came from his own or the Governor's throat.

Not until that one-sided smile gave way and terror came into Simpson's eyes did John regain his senses enough to know what he was doing. Then, the horror of it released his hands and made him shake his head in disbelief.

Simpson's knees buckled and he fell sideways against the iron stove.

John caught his arm to help him but the Governor jerked away and managed to edge himself onto a chair.

Dazed, John pressed the back of his hand across his eyes. When he looked up, Marguerite stood in the doorway.

A great quietness had come into the room with her. She stood like a figure in wax—her red calico skirt hiding her moccasins, a red sash holding her beaded antelope tunic small at her waist. A pulse beat in her temple. That was the only movement about her. Her voice barely brushed the word, "Johnny," not in censure but more as if she wanted him to know that she was here.

John's eyes fell to his hands and, as his fingers slowly opened, he watched the color return to his knuckles.

Marguerite stepped between the two men. Head high, she faced Simpson who sat slumped in his chair, squinting into space. "M'sieu, I regret but I have heard this your generous offer to burden yourself with me. Can it be, I wonder, that you have forgotten my last so short 'No'? Or is it that you make this gentlemanly offer of so-called marriage because you do not find enough animals by stalking in the woods to satisfy your appetites?"

[74]

The Governor's fingers caressed his Adam's apple and with both hands he massaged the sides and then the back of his neck. His aloof manner returned along with his breath. Tugging his lapels into place and avoiding Marguerite's gaze, he pushed himself to his feet. "Squaws! Squaws running everything," he muttered. Standing tall, he fixed John's eyes. "Very well, Doctor, I will not force you."

"Force me? Force me?" John's fists tightened again. "You will not force me and that is a fact!"

The Governor could use even an interruption, by his manner of ignoring it, to bolster his dignity. "A Company man who deliberately places his squaw above the best interests of the fur trade will bear watching," he said smoothly. "Such a stand will need to be defended with a handsome show of profits and some highly politic handling of the Indians." Plucking to straighten the ruffles at his wrists, he moved to the door. "While the honorable Governor and Committee in London are straining their eyes to find the profits on your ledger," he added, "I'd advise you to keep one eye on Comcomly and the other on the Princess. They won't like this, I can assure you. They won't readily forget my promises." He disappeared down the hall.

John dropped into his chair. His whole body trembled.

Marguerite's hand moved across his shoulder and along the old wound in his back. "Rub it out, *mon chéri*, and forget," she whispered. "This George Simpson, he cannot know to understand regarding you and me."

"But if you were here, if you heard it all, why did you let me make such a fool of myself? I might have killed him."

"I would not let you make such a fool of yourself as to kill him," she answered. "As for making the blood run out from his face and fear dart into his eyes, this is not to make a fool of yourself."

"I should be able to control my temper," John insisted. "And I was trying so hard to win the Governor to my side. By rights, he ought to report this to the honorable Committee and ask to have me dismissed. They'd do it in a minute."

Marguerite's hand stopped on his shoulder. "But I think it is perhaps not the way of a so-small man to make one big fight and then it is finished," she mused. "Is it not more to be expected that this George Simpson would choose that you stay with the Company? In such case he can then try to make you pay with a small knife thrust tomorrow and a slap of insult next year." Her hands began again on John's back. "Some men seem given to pulling the wings from flies," she said lightly, "until they catch by mistake a bumblebee."

"I don't feel like a bumblebee," John objected. "That was a cheap display of temper I put on. I must go and apologize. That's the least I can do."

Marguerite stepped in front of him and tossed her head. "It is the least you can do that you do not slope your shoulders down before this George Simpson. Is it not time for the flag raising? A flag is so proud a thing! Do you not think so, Johnny?"

Pink from his shave, Governor Simpson stood in front of the house at the flagstaff.

Through the big double gates gentlemen, servants, chiefs, lesser Indians, and squaws streamed into the compound. A colorful lot they made and John stopped on the last step to drink in the sight. And then his eyes lifted and the sun, still below the horizon, began to outline in gold the icy tip of Mount Hood. He felt, once more, like a man in control of himself.

"Gentlemen and servants of the honorable Company and all those here assembled," Simpson intoned, "you will stand at attention while the flags are raised for the first time on this sturdy staff."

A clerk pulled the ropes. Slowly the Union Jack climbed the fir mast. Beneath it rode the pennant of Hudson's Bay.

Then Simpson drew from under his cape a bottle of rum. His arm came back and, as a wistful "ah-h" escaped from the Indians, he struck the staff. The sacred scent of rum filled the air. "In behalf of the honorable Hudson's Bay Company," the Governor proclaimed, "I hereby name this establishment Fort Vancouver.

God save King George the Fourth." He dropped the neck of the rum bottle. "Now then, three cheers." He spread and lifted his arms to conduct the mighty yell. "Hooray. Hooray. Hooray!"

The celebration broke loose in noisy order. Simpson's men served Company employees and Indians alike each with a couple of drams. With what the Indians were able to steal, they had swigged themselves into fine fettle by the time for the Governor's four canoes to set their prows into the current.

And Simpson, John knew, was using the general hullabaloo to cover his leave-taking. His good-bys, he called to the crowd. He did not shake hands. He stepped into his canoe and gave his attention to arranging his blue cape across his knees.

His voyageurs, oars ready, laughed at private jokes among themselves, cheerful as if they were looking forward to a pleasure jaunt in place of steady paddling and portaging eighteen hours a day for three months. An Indian baby cried and his mother tested with her finger the flattening board on his forehead. A dog fight simmered, cooled off, and then boiled over on the dock. Simpson raised his gray beaver and held it high as the Express put out for York House on Hudson Bay. Voyageurs found their pace and picked up the song of the oar:

> *Dans mon chemin j'ai rencontre*
> *Deux cavaliers, très bien montés,*
> *L'on ton larridon danae,*
> *L'on ton larridon dai;*
> *Deux cavaliers, très bien montés,*
> *L'un a cheval, l'autre a pied.*

John waved at first and then settled his hat and lifted his shoulders. Simpson's canoe made the turn into the current. John was in charge. The questions between them had not been answered. Still, John was in charge.

He strode halfway up the dock and raised his arms. "Gentlemen of the honorable Company, I declare this Fort Vancouver's first legal holiday."

"Hooray! Hooray!"

So far, so good—for the men. As for John, he must lighter the bulk of the Company's possessions up here from Fort George before the Indians discovered that the post there was still stocked with goods but shorthanded. When men as able as John Jacob Astor had found the mouth of the Columbia to be their Waterloo, a newcomer who had, in one day, spurned the hand of Comcomly's granddaughter and come close to strangling his superior officer would do well to move fast and double his guard.

TWO

TWO

VII

A new country, waiting for a man to make what he could of it—that was the Columbia Department in the summer of 1825 and John McLoughlin was the man.

But, thanks to the Governor's maneuvers with the Princess of Wales and her tattooed daughter, John had his hands full for a time.

The eight men left at Fort George to move the Company goods to Fort Vancouver sent a frantic appeal: "Chinooks stealing supplies. Can't load bateaux for their pilfering. Need guards and gunpowder."

John gathered up every man he could spare from building and planting. These were mostly on George Simpson's list—slated for dismissal and return to Canada. John had delayed telling them of the Governor's order and now, with this emergency at Fort George, he could delay a little longer. He took the men himself to the mouth of the Columbia.

He doubled the guard his first night at Fort George and sat down in the dining hall to a bare plank table loaded with roast venison, plenty of imported mustard, and baskets heaped with pilot bread.

Through the log walls of the fort, the roll of breakers on the sand bar sounded far away and peaceful. The venison had been roasted to a juicy turn. Tales grew taller and hairier as the men palmed grease from their beards and downed an extra ration of rum. Good feeling—Company feeling, John liked to think of it—pervaded the room along with the odor of browned game meat and tobacco smoke.

John leaned back in his chair and eased off his boots. He put his mind on figuring out some way to keep all these men on the books without actually defying Simpson's order. Heaven knew

[81]

he needed this many men and more to carry out his plans for the country. Still—

Three rifle shots brought the men to their feet.

While they held their breath, the peaceful sound of distant breakers gave way to yells, spasmodic volleys of gunfire, and running feet.

"The cannons. Man the cannons!" someone roared.

Knocking over his chair, John rushed from the hall and into the fort yard. An arrow lopped over the stockade and droned past his ear.

Men ran from their guard stations to mill in crowded confusion around the two eighteen-pounders trained on the palisade gates.

"No, no, not the cannons," John ordered. "That's what they want. Once you open the gates, Indians will storm the place. Back to your posts. Into the bastions."

Men scattered and John, standing alone between the cannons, pulled his pistol from his belt.

"Down with you, Gov'nor," he heard from the bastion loophole above him. "We're thinkin' one Injun come over the wall. We're tryin' to nail him."

John dropped to his knee and jostled his pistol to get the right feel of the butt in his hand. His eyes searched through the dark from log to log the length of the stockade before him. The Indians had probably upended a canoe against the wall to serve as ladder. But if they thought their man could drop inside unmolested, he'd give him more than broken legs to worry about.

The yells had died out now. Head low, John inched toward the compound gates. He had barely decided that his men were mistaken about an Indian scaling the wall and that the Chinooks had given up for tonight when a scrappy animal, swearing in French and English, landed on his back. The two of them rolled and tangled in the dust.

This naked Indian was as slippery as a greased salmon. John still managed to grip the butt of his pistol and he used it to batter at whatever shadow promised to be head or shoulder or any part of his clawing, snapping assailant. But most of John's blows missed and the few that landed brought forth new spurts of hair-pulling and kicks and bites.

"You confounded eel you, I'll get a hold on you one way or another!" Flaying the air with his pistol, John managed to back off and scramble to his feet.

The shadow on the ground struck blindly at an opponent who wasn't there and then made a headlong dive into the dust at the gate.

John had no intention of letting him escape, but when he clutched for him, the Indian had found his weapon.

John made a grab for the tomahawk that came at him out of the darkness. Cold steel grazed his forehead. He grabbed again and the Indian butted him below the belt. They grappled and rolled in the choking dust. The Indian yelled.

John saw it coming and shunted the blow aside but the tomahawk nicked his thigh. He seized and got a grip on the handle.

The Indian's teeth tore into his hand.

John nabbed a fistful of matted hair and hung on. A quick twist of his body and he held the tomahawk in one hand, the Indian by his greasy scalp in the other.

Men milled into the fort yard. Someone ran up with a lighted torch.

"What do you want?" John asked the Chinook in jargon.

"Hungry. People hungry. This one open gates." The Indian's jargon used more gestures than words. "People run through gates, take flour, take rifles."

"Come inside." John towed him by the hair toward the hall. "Make talk."

In the light, it was easy enough to see why this Indian had been able to put up such a struggle. Far from being hungry, he looked uncommonly well fed. Since his head had not been flattened, he had come by his muscles, no doubt, in the honest work of paddling canoes for his master.

"Who owns you?" John asked.

"Comcomly," the fellow grunted. "Princess, too. Princess of Wales promise new squaw for open gates, take rifles. New squaw

[83]

much pretty." His face clouded at the prospect of losing the squaw promised him for this night's raid on Fort George. "You take now?" he asked. "You big strong. You capture."

"No, no. I don't want you nor your squaw. I do want to make peace talk with your people. If I keep you here, will Comcomly or the Princess come to get you back?"

The Indian spread his legs and clasped his hands behind him. His head lifted. "Comcomly come. You capture chief's best servant," he boasted in jargon. Then he rocked his head up and down and added in English, "He come get, sure thing."

For some reason, the men picked this up. "How about something to eat, Sure Thing?" someone called.

The interpreter dug from a chest in the corner a cutaway coat. He offered the garment to the naked Indian. "Here you are, Sure Thing. You can't eat at the Company table without a coat."

"Sure Thing. Sure Thing," the Chinook chanted, pulling with all his might to get into the coat. Once he got it on, the sleeves came no more than an inch below his elbows. The buttons lacked a generous foot of meeting the buttonholes in front. But these shortcomings did not lessen Sure Thing's pride. He strutted around the room, naked as a turtle walking on his hind legs, and strong men in acute pain from laughter had to be supported on other gasping men's shoulders and taken from the room. Recovering their breath, they'd come back to start all over again.

No captive ever provided more hilarity for his guards. And Sure Thing enjoyed the center of the stage so much that John began to wonder whether they might have to drive him out by force when Comcomly came to claim him.

But Comcomly did not come to claim his servant. Instead, he sent at sunrise a cedar dugout with twenty oarsmen and a gift of fifteen salmon. He sent, too, a formal message by interpreter.

"The great *tyee* of the Chinooks desires to bid the King George man welcome to his village. *Tyee* Comcomly desires the King George man to smoke in the *tyee's* house."

Pleased for Comcomly to make the first move toward a council of peace, John hurried to gather up gifts and let himself be paddled across the river by the *tyee's* oarsmen.

Comcomly's servants, waiting for him at the village, led him to the chief's long plank dwelling. They indicated that he should seat himself on the mat beside the fire. While he waited for his one-eyed majesty's entrance, John laid out before him an extra loud declaration of good will in the form of knives and tobacco. He hoped that he had not brought so many gifts that Comcomly could see at a glance how very eager he was to establish a truce. Fortunately, he and Comcomly had kept on friendly terms during John's early months on the Columbia. Surely now they could stay friends for each other's benefit in trade, in spite of the Princess and her personal grudges.

John glanced up to find Comcomly in the doorway. Behind him trailed his usual retinue of servants and relatives. Most prominent among these this morning was Sure Thing in his cutaway coat.

Although the day was warm, Comcomly had dressed for this state occasion. From his shoulders hung an otterskin robe that made John's mouth water. His high flattened forehead gave Comcomly's one good eye a studious appearance and, in growing shut, his left eye had pulled the corner of his mouth awry so that he seemed always about to say something particularly profound. So pronounced was this impression on John each time he saw the chief that he was invariably taken by surprise when the expected profundity came forth in Chinook jargon with its *l* sound for *r* and *p* for *f*, and its helter-skelter combinations of Indian dialects with French and English words sprinkled in at random.

John got to his feet out of respect for the chief's position and out of downright, open-mouthed admiration for that otterskin robe.

Impassive, Comcomly made his speech of welcome through his interpreter.

John acknowledged the welcome and extended his hand.

With no change of expression, Comcomly shook hands a full minute. Then, cocking his good eye toward the gifts, he motioned John back to a seat on the mat.

[85]

The chief sat beside him while his retinue filled in around the edges.

John took his time about speaking and even more time before presenting the gifts. He meant to buy as much peace as he could stretch from these twists of tobacco.

"It is unfortunate," he began, "that some misunderstanding has arisen concerning the *tyee's* favorite granddaughter."

John saw Comcomly's eyelid droop to screen a covert glance toward the laid-out knives.

"Our Governor Simpson intended no insult, I assure you," John went on slowly, giving Comcomly's interpreter plenty of time. "It was only that he could not conveniently take as wife the daughter of the Princess of Wales since he has a woman at Red River Settlement."

Comcomly's index finger jabbed John's chest. "You, you! You take Comcomly's granddaughter," he shouted in jargon. "That Simpson!" He shrugged and, imitating the Governor's most superior expression, wagged his head from side to side. "No, no, not him." He jabbed John's chest again. "We take you. You big strong."

John scooted back on the mat. "No, no, no! I have a wife as you know. For me to take your granddaughter is out of the question."

Comcomly shrugged. "Why?"

John blurted, "I just told you. I have a wife. I don't want to change. I don't want your granddaughter." He could not afford to make the chief angry but neither could he afford to leave any question about this.

But the chief, instead of becoming angry, turned on a grin. "Your wife upriver. You take wife here also. You big strong. Look at Comcomly." He flung back his arms so John could see his scrawny chest. "Comcomly not much big. Still, he take one, two, three wives. Wives much good. You see. You take Comcomly's granddaughter."

John scooped up the twists of tobacco as if he would leave. "No, no! Once and for all, no!"

Comcomly reached out and pressed John's arm. The old chief

did not intend to risk losing the gifts of knives and tobacco. Suddenly he became put-upon and ill-treated. His lips trembled when he spoke. A tear swam in his one good eye. "Very well, then. Big King George man say 'no' with no thought turned on his friend Comcomly. Princess not like. Princess call Comcomly poor weak squaw that he cannot arrange this so small favor." He leaned close to plead, "You take granddaughter one sun, two suns, only. Granddaughter maybe get King George man-child. Princess proud then. Princess tell it in villages up and down river. Princess not angry with Comcomly then."

In spite of himself, John felt sorry for the old chief. In his most patient tone he explained, "It is our custom to take but one wife. This you can understand as your people, also, observe many customs that you refuse to change when we ask it."

When the interpreter stopped, Comcomly sat considering this for some time. Then he said, "It is our custom to make gifts to our friends and to smoke."

"*Oui, oui,*" John agreed quickly. "This is our custom also. But first, we like to know which people are friends. Perhaps out of gratitude for the gifts I bring you today, you will persuade your daughter, the Princess, not to steal goods from Fort George. Perhaps you will not send your servant over our stockade. Perhaps you will not turn on us the rifles we have traded to you."

"Perhaps," Comcomly answered in English.

John sensed that he had nothing to gain by pressing the matter further now. He presented the gifts and Comcomly prepared his pipe for their smoke.

But one smoke did not satisfy Comcomly. John must return to smoke tomorrow. The next day, he must smoke with Comcomly's guest, the chief from the village of Neacoxy. And then he must return to smoke with Comcomly's friend, Chief Schachanaway from the Cowlitz.

Chiefs from villages on the coast and the Cowlitz and as far away as the Nisqually straggled in to fondle the pipestem in their scabby lips.

John knew, through all this, that he had become a kind of unofficial hostage. Comcomly had sent out runners. He was using this situation to strengthen his power over the nearby tribes. They came. They saw with their own eyes the great King George man sitting cross-legged in the plank house of Comcomly. They smelled with their own noses the prestige billowing from the chief's carved stone pipe as the King George man puffed. Because of this, they bowed low before Comcomly. Leaving, they promised to bring their dried salmon and their furs to trade, not with the King George man, but with Comcomly.

Still, John played this game with the Chinooks because, while it went on, his men, unmolested, were clearing out the storerooms at Fort George.

When the last load of trade goods was ready to shove off from the Company dock, John wrote the game off as finished. The time had come to be firm about additional smoking bouts with visiting chiefs.

He gathered up a respectful farewell gift of tobacco and had his men paddle him across to Comcomly's village. To his relief, he saw no outsiders' cedar dugouts pulled up on the sand. Perhaps Comcomly had run out of chiefs he wanted to impress. John's departure, in that case, could be on a friendly basis and this whole expedition might prove quite a boon to Company business. John whistled "Annie Laurie" as he climbed the slope to Comcomly's plank house.

But the Princess of Wales in her wood rat bib stood in the open doorway. When John asked for Comcomly, she shrugged and stood aside. He stepped in and found the chief sitting cross-legged beside the fire. But this was a cowed Comcomly with no spunk in the lift of his head and no dignity borrowed from an otterskin robe.

He glanced up in answer to John's greeting but he said nothing and his good eye turned, at once, to follow the Princess.

She said, "Come," and led the way to the opening cut through to the connecting room in the series that made up the long house.

John turned again to Comcomly, waiting for but not really expecting a show of authority. Chinook chiefs could be tough men to meet in a trade but their women ruled the domestic roof. Now,

Comcomly sat staring at his bare belly and refused to lift his eyes under John's gaze.

"Come!" the Princess commanded.

John followed her.

The Princess backed through the opening and into the next room. Then, as John ducked through the low doorway, she turned with a sweeping flourish and stood aside.

A small fire in the center of the room provided a romantic light and sent off the faint perfume of pine gum that John always associated with Marguerite. Beyond the fire, arranged in a dozen opulent layers, was a huge bed of prime beaver skins. On top of the beaver, smooth as any coverlet, the Princess had arranged Comcomly's otterskin robe.

On this bed reclined the Filly and she, too, had been arranged by her mother's crafty hands. With her arms flung back on the bed, the Hudson's Bay coat of arms was given its most advantageous spread on her breast. The shredded bark of her skirt had been parted and bunched on its drawstring so as to show off the girl's thighs and her vermilion decorated navel.

Apparently delighted by John's reaction, the Princess turned on a rare smile. "All for King George man," she said in English. "Take daughter, take beaver skins, take otterskin robe." She side-stepped toward the doorway. "Princess of Wales go now. Big King George man take."

John's longing for that otterskin robe brought a salty taste to his mouth and a twitching into his hands. And these beaver skins alone would practically assure him a balance on the profit side of the ledger for his first year on the Columbia. As for the Filly, she had been bathed in the river and rubbed with sand until her skin glowed. Perhaps because he felt his pulses quicken, John strode to the bed and caught the girl by both wrists. He jerked her off the bed and onto her feet.

He whipped around to find the Princess, a pleased smirk on her face, peeking at him from the adjoining room. She wailed when he flung the Filly away from him and caught up the otterskin robe. But she made no attempt to block his way as he stormed from the would-be bridal chamber. He slammed the otterskin robe down on top of Comcomly as he still sat staring at his belly. "Hang onto that now," John roared. "Next time, I'll take it. What kind of chief are you to let this squaw rob you of your robe?"

Aghast, the Princess stood in the outer doorway, shaking her fists. "It is the insult! King George man pay. The Princess is friend toward King George man many moons. Now this insult!"

John turned on her and caught her fists. "As for you, you— Shut up" he finished in disgust and threw her aside.

His long legs slashed down the incline and through the water to his canoe. The Princess would, no doubt, find some way to make him pay for this insult. Obviously, friendship with the Chinooks must be purchased each time it was needed, the same as a dose of quinine. And yet George Simpson expected him to manage this Department with half its present number of employees and no allowance for emergencies inspired by disgruntled Indians.

His voyageurs leaned into their oars.

John fitted the oilskin cover on his beaver hat and settled himself for the hundred-mile pull upriver. Perhaps, he mused, he might be able to dismiss the men on Simpson's list, fulfill the charter requirements by offering them return passage to Canada but do it in such a way that they'd fight to stay on in this country.

Freemen who hung around a Company post, hiring on for an occasional trapping expedition, were usually far below the caliber of these men on Simpson's list. But the deal the Company gave them—making them buy their horses and gear at a high markup and allowing them a niggardly profit on their catch—could hardly be expected to attract men of guts and gumption. If they could manage a respectable profit on work they did for the Company, these men might be turned into solid citizens to help balance the unpredictable Chinooks. Still, George Simpson had ordered, "Discharge them and send them back to Canada."

John tipped his hat low on his eyes to shut out the light. He tried to picture the honorable Committee, meeting in London, considering his situation here and his need for dependable men.

The answer to his question came before he asked it: "No, no, decidedly not. Settlers destroy virgin forests, frighten beaver from the streams. No, no, Doctor, by all means, by any means, keep the land undeveloped."

John flung back his cape with the scrappy air of a schoolboy rolling up his sleeves. Beneath him the mighty Columbia squandered her power against the prow of a flimsy canoe. On shore, towering firs beckoned for saws, fertile meadows waited for seeds. And Simpson himself insisted that, along with taking furs, they raise potatoes to feed Fort Vancouver. Well then, John concluded, he'd have to use his own judgment about men and about developing the land. He'd reckon later with the Company and with George Simpson.

VIII

Simpson's list stared up at John from his desk. Charlefoux, arms crossed on his chest, stood wide-legged against the office window. "What you wish, M'sieu Factor? Out with it."

John stood up. Blunt as he could make it, he said, "You're dismissed from the service of the Company."

Charlefoux took a startled step forward. "Why is this? Who says so?"

"I say so," John answered. "And I don't have to say why. I'm in charge here, remember."

Charlefoux tilted forward from his waist. His fists drove into his pantaloon pockets showing like rocks through the buckskin. His blue stocking cap, which he had not bothered to remove, wagged in defiance. "I demand to know why is this. Nobody can say to me I am dismissed without he say also why."

John stood his ground and kept his voice steady. "The Company will send you back to Canada by the first opportunity this summer."

"The Company, *mon Dieu!*" Charlefoux spat out. "Nobody sends me back to Canada. I like it here. I stay. My son will grow up here."

"Your son?" John asked.

"*Oui, oui*, my son. You hear right. Only just this morning my woman wake me. Hand over to me my son. Like damn fool, I name him for you. Now the Company will cut me off. *Bien!* This Company I do not need but so, also, do I not go back to Canada, you hear! I stay on the Columbia."

"You know the rules, Charlefoux. The Company discharges no men in fur country."

"The Company! The Company! The sound of it is a roaring

[92]

in my ears. So I am finished with the Company and good riddance. Still, you are not so strong with all your bigness as to make me go back to Canada." He jarred the house with each furious step toward the door.

"One moment," John said quietly and reached for an inscribed sheet of foolscap on his desk. "You've made up your mind? You're sure?"

A disgusted flap of Charlefoux's hand answered and dismissed the matter.

"Then you wouldn't object to setting your mark on this paper, would you?" John held it toward him. "It merely says that I tried to send you back and you refused."

Charlefoux grabbed the sheet. "To such a writing I will set my mark with the greatest pleasure." He slammed the paper onto the desk and held it down with both hands while he waited for John to dip the quill. Then he made an X that filled half the sheet. "*Bien* and damn the Company!"

"Thank you." John gave Charlefoux's hand a vigorous pumping. "You say you named your new son John?"

Charlefoux backed off. "No, no, no. I name him Petit Chief Factor."

John laughed. "He may be Big Chief Factor someday, too."

"Maybe, *mon Dieu*. He will be!" Charlefoux corrected.

"I'll help you all I can to make that happen, Charlefoux," John promised. "How'd you like to trap the Snake with Pete Ogden's next party?"

Charlefoux shrugged. "Perhaps, *oui*. This I will decide when the time comes. For now, my house is here. My son is born here. My woman likes this country. We stay here."

When he left, John folded the foolscap with care and tucked it into the drawer with his personal papers. If he ever needed to use it, there it would be. Then he took another sheet and wrote out the same statement: "I, the undersigned, being offered passage back to Canada, have refused same and do hereby declare myself a free agent, the honorable Hudson's Bay Company having dismissed me from service before the expiration of my contract."

Next, he'd send for Lucier—a good steady man, an asset to the

[93]

country. If Etienne Lucier, too, could be egged into defying Company orders—and Joseph Gervais and Xavier Ladouroute and a dozen more—he might not be left so short-handed after all. To-morrow, he'd offer Charlefoux a plot of ground and a peck of seed peas.

As for the other men on Simpson's list, he'd see to it they had a way to take their families with them to Canada. He could guarantee them that much on his own authority and with some he could send letters that would help them find work.

With that list off his desk, John could get on with the hundred jobs waiting his personal attention. The Indian store had to be roofed and shelves built. Goods lightered up from Fort George waited to be inventoried and sorted into warehouses or packed and sent out to the other posts in the Department for use in the trade. Fort St. James on Stuart Lake needed more dried salmon. Fort Colvile had run short on flour. From Kamloops on Thompson River came a demand for materials for gunlocks. Then the cows at Fort Vancouver began to calve.

Determined to start everything off under his personal direction, John rushed from desk to potato field to blacksmith shop to warehouse to pasture.

"Those sheep have scab. Get them washed with tobacco juice at once" . . .

"Plow a straight furrow there, man. Always a straight furrow" . . .

"By the auld Clootie, you might have let the Chinooks pilfer that suit of steel armor," he protested when a clerk set the bulky thing in the Indian store.

"Here's a requisition from Mr. Ogden," the clerk greeted him when he went by the office before breakfast one misty morning in June. "It came by runner in the night. Must be important."

"*Oui, oui.*" John unfolded the sheet. "Requisition!" he gasped. "Grand larceny, you'd better call it. Seventy-five horses and another two hundred beaver traps! What's got into Pete Ogden? He's usually as saving of Company goods as the Governor himself."

Receiving such a requisition from any other Chief Trader in his employ, John would have marked him down for discharge. From Pete, it meant trouble on the Snake. And the Snake was no place to tolerate trouble. They needed those furs.

John sent a runner to Fort Colvile at Kettle Falls on the Columbia with an order that all spare horses and traps be despatched at once to Fort Walla Walla. He sent another runner with the same message to Fort Okanogan. He put off, again, the trip he'd planned and put off before to the Falls of the Willamette. He'd have to hurry upriver himself to meet Pete Ogden at Fort Walla Walla and straighten out this business.

"I'll go with you, *Papa*," Jacques stated at the dock. John could see him searching for an excuse. "Then we can keep on with my lessons."

"No, no, no. I've too much on my mind and no time to be bothered."

If, like most boys of twelve, his son had begged or pouted, that would have finished the matter for John. Instead, Jacques caught his lower lip behind his teeth and that was all.

"I am too busy right now," John argued against the hurt in his son's eyes when it stayed with him into the afternoon. "Launching a new country is particular work. Once things are under way, I'll have more time for Marguerite and the children. I must find time soon to play and read and explore the land with them. Their training must not suffer simply because we don't yet have schools. "I'll find more time for them," he promised himself, "once this beginning rush is past."

Over a glass of wine in the office at Fort Walla Walla, John probed through Pete Ogden's fury and disgust for a report on his winter's expedition to the Snake.

"Americans! Thieving, conniving Americans!" Pete paced the sod floor from desk to window and back again. "I tell you, Doc, they're loud-mouthed barbarians. They've got no morals and no decency. All they've got are guts and go."

"Come now, Americans are no different from anybody else." John tipped his chair against the wall and a shower of crumbled chinking dusted his hair. He swept idly at the top of his head. "Americans are just human beings, trying to make a living the same as we are," he soothed.

"How they can make a living at the prices they pay for beaver beats me."

"Why don't you set yourself down, drink your wine, and then tell me what happened?" John suggested.

Pete gulped the wine and slammed his glass on the desk. He stood over John. "I'd have you know they pay three dollars for hides—full-grown or cub, coarse or fine, however they come."

His chin on his black satin stock, John pondered this and kept his voice calm to hold Pete steady. "As much as that," he mused. "As much as that!"

"And that man Ashley sits back there in St. Louis, it seems, sending out calls for trappers and word that he supplies long guns and traps and all the necessaries." Pete paced again to the window. "I tell you, Doc, their men put out for Snake not owing the American Fur Company one farthing and then in St. Louis— some say they haul them only as far as the Spanish Country to a place called Taos but wherever they unload—Ashley pays three dollars for every hide no matter what shape it's in. I tell you, it's not fair."

"Not fair? Not fair?"

"Of course it's not fair! It's an insult to Hudson's Bay Company. We can't pay prices like that. And we've got to pack our furs three times as far as they do. Besides, our trappers, whether Company men or freemen, are carried on the books for their gear. Hudson's Bay can't hand out horses and guns and traps for free the way that Ashley does and you know it."

"You going to tell me what happened?"

"Aw, you've probably heard a dozen versions already." But Pete did sit down, at last, and his voice slid up the scale a bit into its normal sandy channel. "You know what I think of Americans. Well, hoist them all up by their topknots and shove under the lot a varmint named Johnson Gardner, lowest of the pack. He had a batch of trappers with him and they'd been cleaning out every beaver stream ahead of us for three weeks. Then, they camped not a hundred yards away, ran up the U. S. flag big as life, and he started spieling."

" 'This are U. S. Territory,' he yelled. 'Everybody here's all free. We ain't indebted or engaged,' he bleated."

Pete slapped the arms of his chair and squirmed. "Well, it got night and that stopped him but next morning, here they came, bright and early."

" 'You know whose country you're in?' Gardner asked, pushing bold as you please into my tent."

" 'I'm in anybody's country,' I told him, 'under treaty. And do you know whose tent you're in?' "

" 'I know all right,' he came back and just then some Iroquois shoved through my tent flap, cocking his gun. He held his pistol on me, making threats all the time, while Gardner rounded up men and their traps and the furs they'd taken through the winter. Grabbing horses and blankets and traps, off they went down wind —old Pierre and Montain and Patrick Prudhommes and—" Pete shrugged. "Twenty-three men in all, not to mention their plunder. The horses were the worst loss of course and I was left with only seven freemen and them none too settled in their minds they shouldn't have gone along."

"Company men—they stuck by you?" John asked.

"They stuck—the ones I had left. Louis Kanitogan's woman had accidentally pulled the trigger on his rifle and killed him some time before. Blackfeet got Benoit. Took sixteen beaver, three horses, and the poor man's scalp. Of course, you can't expect much from freemen. They're might' nigh as low as Americans to start with."

Mr. Dease, Chief Trader in charge at Walla Walla, threw open the office door. He waved John back when he offered him his desk chair but he gulped down two glasses of wine. He smacked his lips and raked through his brush of black hair.

Not much addicted to clean shirts, Dease nevertheless gave John the same kind of easiness that he got from working off his boots. "Sit down, Dease," he insisted. "I don't see you often enough."

"I'll be called to Chief Hasumtooks' lodge any minute," Dease said. "Might as well stand."

"We were talking about the free trappers sent into the Snake," John explained. "Pete Ogden's opinion of them is something less than high."

"Scum of the earth," Dease commented.

"*Oui, oui,* they've mostly been dismissed from the Service for some crime or other, but what would we do without them? We need trappers, if we're to take the furs from these waterways in this Department."

"Scum of the earth," Dease repeated and reached across the desk to refill his wine glass.

"I don't know," John demurred. "In general, I find it not a good idea to melt down an entire body of men in one pot and call the whole of what you get 'scum.'"

"You haven't spent a winter in that pot, Doc." Pete stirred in his chair.

A Nez Perce youngster came in to call Mr. Dease.

"Sorry, but I'll have to go. The chief lost his younger boy two months ago," Dease explained, "and now his favorite son has the same sickness."

John reached for his medicine bag. "I'll go with you."

Dease waved him back. "It's too late for that. Too late and too risky. The *te-wat* has been there for days with his drums and rattles and his body streaked in black. The son will die. Let the *te-wat* take the blame."

John started anyway but, as he stooped to pick up his bag, they heard from across the river the piercing wails of the squaws. The chief's son was dead and Mr. Dease insisted on going alone to Hasumtooks' lodge.

John and Pete sat for a long time saying nothing. They could not shut their ears against the squaws' shrill mourning.

"About those freemen who deserted," John said at last, "maybe the Governor shaved our payments too close to the line, or figured the advance too high on equipment we supply them."

"Nonsense! Not at all," Pete objected. "They knew the terms when they went out. They signed on for the season."

"But, if the terms were unfair—"

"It's the men were unfair," Pete cut in. "Scum, that's what they are, and good riddance. Except that the Governor ordered, 'One week's regale and out you go again.' The question is, where do I get trappers with any loyalty? The men we take out aren't worth the powder to blow them to hell."

John stood up. "Get me your records. Bring everything here. I want to figure. Bring all your books on the men's indebtedness to the Company, number of beavers taken day by day—everything."

"Sure, but—" Pete stopped astride the threshold.

"Well, well, what is it? You're wasting time."

"But Governor Simpson, won't he—"

Mr. Dease, returning from Chief Hasumtooks' lodge, stopped at the office door. "The chief wants you both to attend the funeral," he said, his voice heavy. "At dawn, on that rise of land yonder. It's important. The chief is taking this son's death mighty hard. He's always counted on this boy filling his moccasins someday."

John thought of Jacques and saw him again on the dock, his lower lip caught back to stop its trembling. "We'll be glad to attend the funeral. Of course, of course."

John worked far into the night on Ogden's books. He twisted, manipulated, and maneuvered but he could find no escape from the figures. The Company required a fixed percentage of profit on goods shipped out from London, on furs shipped in. He could not pay trappers halfpenny more and still maintain that margin. But he kept checking and shifting his columns and working in more products that could be grown at Fort Vancouver and still the final answer came out the same. No need to figure his way around the rutted course again.

He tossed his pencil onto the desk and moved to the window. A faint gray blurred the eastern horizon. He remembered that he had promised to go at sunrise to the funeral of Chief Hasumtooks' son.

Pete Ogden joined him at the compound gate. With no more

greeting than a nod, they strode to the knoll beyond the fort. Nez Perce and Cayuse Indians, awed and silent, filled in around them. At their backs the Walla Walla River flung itself headlong down its rocky bed to join the Columbia. An earthworm writhed from its prison in the wall of the open grave at their feet. Beyond the Blue Mountains, a shimmer of light played on the sky.

Suddenly the groans and wails of women filled the morning.

The dead boy's father stepped to the brink of the grave. Erect, he shed no tears. No sound came from his lips.

John had never seen a finer specimen of manly form and features. Until this moment, he had never seen a grief too deep to find some outlet.

At length the father gave an order with his upraised hand. His son's body, shrouded in blankets, was lowered into the grave.

And then the wails and moans subsided. The tone of the Walla Walla deepened.

Chief Hasumtooks lifted his arms in his blanket and folded them across his chest. "Long have my feet walked this land," he said, "and many are my riches." In a tranquil voice he spoke of his hundred horses that set him apart, wealthy above all others of his tribe. He praised his married daughters and his faithful woman who, through the winters, had filled his lodge with fires and laughter. Then he reviewed the past few months—the tragic death of his younger child that left him but one stalwart son, a vessel into which he had poured all his hopes and all his desires.

"And now," he said, "the string of my bow is broken. The last hope of my declining days has been snatched from me. Seek not to dissuade me from the resolution I have adopted. All you can urge will be as the wind. The days have no more to offer me in trade for my life. I was once a hunter but I am no longer so. I was once a warrior but I now have no heart for fighting. I was once the proud father of two noble sons, but, alas, where are they? Wherefore shall I continue to cumber this earth with my useless presence?"

The very river stood still. No man dared breathe.

John could see the blanket tighten on the chief's folded arms. The carved face softened as he turned, first to the fields and then to the river. And now, he stepped into the pit and laid himself upon the corpse of his son. "Fill up the grave," he ordered. "Cover my last earthly residence. Do not hesitate, for I am resolved to die."

Screams of horror, the tender pleadings of his woman could not touch Chief Hasumtooks' resolve.

Helpless, John watched the black clods fall in on father and son. He heard the rumble of their falling and it seemed that he would never be rid of the sound.

Back in the office, John stood with his hands gripping the edge of the desk, his heart pounding. As if those clods that he had just heard rumble down to fill up that grave were pressing on his chest, his breath came short and dry with an alkaline, burning dryness.

Pete Ogden clenched and unclenched his blunt fingers at his back as he stood peering through the window. "We ought to grab those shovels and do something." Pete's voice, for once, had no high-pitched roughness in it.

"It's too late." John had been figuring the time and wondering whether they might undo this thing. "Besides, it was never in our province to interfere," he went on. "Even a savage is born with rights a man must respect."

"Then let's forget it." Pete brushed his hand across his eyes. "Let's not keep hearing his voice, going through the whole thing over and over. What's it got to do with us, anyway?"

Through the office door, the rise of land with its crown of fresh-turned clods held John's gaze against his will. He rubbed his arms but the morning chill stayed in him and, as the damp spade-marked clods of earth refused to let him turn away, he shivered with cold. "It has to do with me, Pete Ogden. Of that I am sure," he murmured.

"No, no, of course it hasn't." Pete came to the end of the desk. His voice had climbed back to its old falsetto. "You're reading something into it that isn't there. You're telling yourself it's you and your son but it's not. What's one Indian chief more or less in this country and one chief's son? It's nothing more than that."

A shaft of sunlight poured through a break in the clouds to pick out the mounds of clods. Chief Hasumtooks' voice sounded in John's ears. "The string of my bow is broken."

John turned on Pete. "You're wrong, Pete Ogden. I don't know yet in what way, but this thing that happened this morning has to do with me and my son. Of that, I am sure. And it has to do also with here and now, with me and those men out there in the yard. In that one awful gesture that savage broke open a shell to show me the size of a human being. 'Scum' you labeled those trappers of yours in this same room a few short hours ago." John shook his head. "No, no! No man is scum. There's bigness in him. You were wrong, Pete Ogden." He gazed at the sheets of figures on the desk. To himself he added, "The Company, too, could be wrong."

What a commotion he had stirred up back there in the mahogany confines on Fenchurch Street with his suggestion of humane hours and a living wage for voyageurs! If only those fine-frocked gentlemen could have stood with him this morning beside that grave, they'd know beyond all room for argument that the stuff in a man—any man—is too big for beating down or starving out. Somehow, he'd make the Company see it.

One by one he wadded the sheets of foolscap. These figures had proved through the night that he could not pay trappers an extra penny for furs.

When the crumpled sheets lay in a gray mound, he moved around the desk and summoned Pete Ogden to follow him into the fort yard. There a dozen freemen, unshaven and slack-jawed, propped themselves against the adobe wall in the shade or lolled among the mangy dogs in the dust.

Scum, scurvy, the rag-tag ends of morality and civilization they were generally called. And yet these men lived on the brink of a grave every day they spent on the Snake. Each time they ducked their heads into a stream for a drink of water, a Blackfoot arrow could topple them into that grave. Each day they camped in the snow on Salmon River, their bones showing through their hides, could mark the end of their body's strength to hold out. Any Piegan behind any shrub, any break in the ice when they

[*102*]

cleared out their traps, any mouthful of maggoty meat, could thrust them from the brink of that grave to its depths.

"Gentlemen," John said, his voice and his feeling for them respectful, "I have something to say."

The freemen barely lifted their eyelids.

"As of today," John went on, "you will receive ten shillings in trade for large beaver, five for cubs. Also, you will find that our prices on trade goods and equipment for trapping have been lowered."

Every freeman in the compound got to his feet, stood tall, and crossed his arms on his chest.

John's eyes moved slowly from face to face. He had to give himself time to take in the change. He knew what they had been. He knew that, in all likelihood, these men would never be much different. Still, they had that in them—and he could see it when they stood like this—that made it intolerable for any man to heap burdens on their shoulders they could not hope to straighten under.

"Brigade makes up for Snake in two weeks," he told them. "Peter Skene Ogden, leader. Spread the word. We need men. Regale ten miles up the Walla Walla. Meanwhile sleep, eat all you can, and enjoy yourselves. The fort bids you welcome in the name of Hudson's Bay Company."

Mutterings of astonishment and even a weak cheer floated back as the freemen strode off.

"Governor Simpson won't allow this change in rates," Pete blurted. "You don't have that kind of authority."

"Governor Simpson wants beaver brought out of the Snake Country, Mr. Ogden. He's racing the calendar along with those same Americans who lured off your trappers. So far, the only way we have of getting beaver out of there is with men."

"The Company wants furs. You're right about that," Pete agreed. "And George Simpson is hell-bent for cleaning out the Snake while that Joint Occupation Treaty still goes. Just the same, much as he wants furs, he wants them at a profit."

"I'll get them at a profit."

"But shaving it down that close . . . you're asking for

[*103*]

trouble." Pete shook his head. "You'll get yourself dismissed from the Service, cut off without a penny, and what more can you expect? The Governor won't like this one bit. I don't think he'll see it."

"I think he will see it," Marguerite decided when John got home and explained to her that he might be discharged as soon as word got to London that he had taken it on himself to change rates.

"It's an impertinent step to take," he admitted, "but we can't have the honorable Company treating men like slaves."

"You know what I think?" Marguerite stood at their parlor window looking out on Mount Hood. "This George Simpson will see it, providing you explain it is the only way to get furs and providing you do not explain, as you say, 'We cannot have the honorable Company treating men like slaves.'" She turned. "This George Simpson must keep always his eyes on the beaver, my Johnny, while you must see always the man with the trap."

IX John reached for the perpetual calendar that George Simpson had brought him from London. He slipped out February and slid March into its cardboard window. Monday, March 2, 1829. It seemed he was always shuffling the months in his calendar with no time between—particularly since the end of October when George Simpson arrived.

He replaced the calendar above the pigeonholes of his desk and sat staring at it. He recalled the trip from Rainy Lake and felt again that tense kind of flutter in his chest that had ridden him across the continent. Actually, during these five years on the Columbia he had raced, the same as on that trip, to keep ahead of George Simpson.

In the old Nor'wester days, time had been cut up into hours and even minutes. Here on the Columbia, time had lumped itself into seasons—each one too short for the jobs to be done. It was the season to plant or harvest. Or the time was upon him to send out trapping expeditions or welcome them in and sort their furs. Or it was the time of year when the Indians came to trade. Or, unless he hurried to stake claims at the Falls of the Willamette and on the Cowlitz and on the Umpqua, he'd lose his choicest sites to newcomers arriving during the travel season from the Sandwich Islands. Or it was spring and time to receive and unload the annual supply ship from England or it was fall and time to load her with furs and send her back again. Or it was fall and the season to watch for the Montreal Express or spring and time to see the Express off for the East.

Recent months had been the time of rebuilding, moving the post from the bluff down here to the meadow where they need not haul water, where supplies could be stored directly from the dock without an expensive loading, hauling, and unloading added to their cost.

Marguerite had almost stopped reminding John that he spent too little time with the children or that he was too short with them when they asked him questions, and yet it was true. He was missing the best years of their lives. Governor Simpson would be downriver any minute from his inspection of the sawmill but John left his desk and hurried along the hall to the parlor. He hadn't seen Marguerite all day.

He found her sitting cross-legged on the floor with her mouth full of pins. Before her stood Eloise, tacked into the cream silk chiné with the tiny red rosebuds that John had brought Marguerite from Paris.

Eloise ran to him and John pricked his thumb when he wrapped his arms around the child to swing her in a circle.

"*Papa*, when am I ever to have new silk for a dress? This old thing of *Maman's* is all yellow. For all I know, it may fall to shreds the first time I dance with one of those handsome officers off the *William and Ann*."

John pulled his punctured thumb from his mouth to answer. "You're not old enough to dance with an officer anyway." He bent himself double to kiss the top of Marguerite's head. He caught her hand that came up to caress his cheek and sat on the floor beside her.

"Oh *Papa*," Eloise objected, "you're interfering with my dress."

Marguerite took the pins from her mouth. "You are tired?"

"Lonesome," John answered. "I haven't seen you all day."

"We do need some new silk, Johnny. You have, perhaps, something at the store?"

"I have less than nothing at the store except one suit of steel armor. This I will sell you dirt cheap, *madame*, and I can think of nothing better for my daughter's first dance."

"Oh, *Papa!*"

Marguerite's mouth twitched at the corner, but instead of giggling, she said, "It is a long time to fifteen and your first dance. To Eloise it is no thing for making a joke. You have still, perhaps, that gold brocade?"

"The Princess of Wales traded otter skins for that some time ago. For the Filly, I believe."

Marguerite giggled then. "So we make do what we have. The Filly has more need of brocade than our Eloise."

Eloise stamped her foot. "*Maman*, then the Filly will look prettier at the party than I do. You'd think she was the Chief Factor's daughter." She came over, stood above John, and twisted a strand of his hair around her finger. "*Papa*, you're the boss of this country. Why don't we ever get any China silks? Surely, if you'd just order them—"

"Eloise! You will not say to your *papa* what to order!"

"It's all right, *ma chérie*, if she is big enough to go to a dance, she is big enough to understand about the business." He wondered when it had happened that little Eloise had become a grown young lady with her hair in a bright twist on her neck and her head full of opinions regarding China silks and the business. To his surprise he found himself giving her question the kind of answer he'd give to an adult. "It's the East Indian Company, not Hudson's Bay, that holds the exclusive trade charter with China, my bonnie lass. If I were to send direct for China silks, I'd have Parliament on my back."

The parlor door was kicked open with a clatter. Jacques, a squirming, dripping bundle of pale curls and buckskin in his arms, came in and backed against the door to shut it. "*Maman*, have we an oven warm for drying out one Petit Chief Factor?" Jacques' grin took his family into the joke but he kept his voice serious for Charlefoux's boy in his arms.

John was struck by the grown-up look of his handsome son. "What happened?"

Jacques upended the boy and set him on his squashy moccasins. He squatted down to unlace the child's tunic at the neck and peel it over the tangle of wet curls. "He went swimming a mite before he learned how."

"I can so swim!" Petit Chief Factor's lower lip defied anybody to deny it. "But only not in water," he added, "because I am going on four and *Papa* says swimming in water is for six years old."

Marguerite got up to help with his pantaloons.

"Isn't he sweet?" Eloise cried.

"I am not so!" Petit Chief Factor kicked out of his clinging pantaloons and his moccasins came off with them.

"Better give him a good hard rub," John suggested and went into the bedroom to bring a towel from the washstand. "It's a little early in the season for a swim—in water, that is."

"I'll get a blanket," Eloise offered.

Jacques reached up for the yellow-bordered towel John dangled above him. "His *papa* is always using a willow switch on him for nothing at all so I thought I'd better dry him out here before Charlefoux found out about this."

"*Oui, oui,*" John agreed. "Charlefoux is mighty strict with the boy but he has great hopes for him and the child's *maman* doesn't take very fast to civilized ways."

Marguerite sighed and picked up the wet clothes to begin working water from them. "I have tried these so many years to teach her even to make bread." Her hands lifted and fell, giving up Charlefoux's Chinook woman as hopeless. "She knows always that the Chinook food is best, that a long plank house is much to be preferred as against the square house of Charlefoux, that Petit Chief Factor will grow up to be a nobody because Charlefoux would not allow her to flatten his head."

"But flattening his pretty head would be horrible," Eloise exclaimed, coming in with a scarlet blanket. When Jacques stopped with the towel, she wrapped the blanket around the boy, giving him a hug in the process.

Petit Chief Factor broke out and darted for the door.

They all tried to nab him and Jacques barely managed to capture one pudgy arm. "No, no, you can't go yet," he tried to explain. "Wait till your clothes dry."

"Can't wait." The boy started to prance and squirm.

"So that's the trouble," John said, taking over. "In here, then. You may use the chamber."

"No, no, no! Must put in little fence or *Maman* switch." The boy began to cry.

"You can't get that far, if I'm any judge," John said in his most

[*108*]

matter-of-fact voice. "Come in here this time. Your *maman* won't switch you. I promise."

The boy squirmed and twisted but he refused to take a step toward the bedroom until he asked, "Can I take it home with me?"

John answered, *"Oui, oui,"* as the quickest means of putting the child out of his misery. But when Marguerite had dried his clothes as much as she dared without getting them too near the stove, Petit Chief Factor insisted on emptying the chamber's contents into a tin cup before he would dress and leave. He kept repeating in a kind of frightened singsong, "Must put inside little fence, must put inside little fence . . ."

"I'll walk to the village with him," Jacques volunteered, "and find out what this is all about."

Eloise took a dainty pinch in each side of her skirt and dipped in a graceful curtsy. But her, *"Au revoir,"* ended in a squeal of dismay as her knee pressed the tender silk. *"Maman!"* she wailed. "Now look! *Papa!* See how it split. I shall simply have to get some new silk somewhere. The Princess of Wales' daughter will have a new gown and the Chief Factor's daughter will be in this raggedy old thing."

Jacques said, "It's not her clothes that give the Filly an advantage over you, Sister, it's—"

"Jacques!"

Eloise tossed her head. "Aw, he thinks he's so smart now that he's going to Paris."

"I've always been going to Paris as soon as I was seventeen." Jacques offered to carry Petit Chief Factor's tin cup for him.

The child drew back. "No, no. You might spill it."

So Jacques, with a hand in Petit Chief Factor's curls, herded him from the room.

"Maman! What will I do?" Eloise was on the verge of tears.

"Sh-h. One moment." Marguerite's pins went back into the corner of her mouth. *"Oui, oui.* Come close. Now we turn the skirt around." She shifted the split to the center back. "Now we gather the tear up so and add here a bit of lace from the chest and a red velvet bow to match the rosebuds." She pinned it all as

[*109*]

she spoke and then gave Eloise a slap such as she usually reserved for her pony when she turned him out to pasture. "You will dance like a lady, with short steps, for which I nod my head to approve. So!" She got up from the floor, surveyed the effect with her dark head tipped first to one side and then to the other. "Go to your room and take it off gently so not to disturb the pins." Satisfied, she turned to John. "So you at last come to see your family. And where is this George Simpson?" she asked.

John locked his hands at the back of her wide beaded belt. "When you hear my news, you may decide that the time has come for you to refer to 'this George Simpson' as 'the Governor.'" He reached inside his coat and brought out the letter from their honors in London that Governor Simpson had delivered just this morning at the breakfast table. "From the honorable Governor and Committee in London," John said. "They like me. They think I have made a fine beginning with the Indians. They like not importing flour for us any more. They like my new saw-mill and approve my plan to sell lumber in California and the Sandwich Islands. And, at last, they agree that I was right about paying freemen enough to keep them trapping for us."

"They said all this on one letter sheet?"

"All this and more. Said it, signed their names, and raised my salary."

"And why did this George Simpson wait from October until the month of his leaving to hand you this letter?"

"I asked that, too. 'Orders from London,' he said."

"And is this George Simpson also pleased with all these ways that you win praises from the gentlemen in London?"

"*Oui, oui,*" John answered without stopping to consider. "He is also pleased." But then he did consider. "That is, I think he's pleased. He even seems a little envious of our fine living here and of the large crops we raise and the way the furs are coming in."

"*Oui?*" The lift of Marguerite's eyebrows gave too much importance to the vague hint of envy John had felt in Simpson's manner.

"That's foolish, of course. How could he possibly envy what we're doing? He thinks always of the Company and its good."

"I wonder." Marguerite pulled away from John and turned to the window. "Does he not think, also, that he has been born with no proper wedding for his *maman* and that he will climb up in the Company to show everyone what a big man he is in spite of this?"

"Where did you pick up this gossip about George Simpson's birth?"

"It is a thing that is often talked of. Some do not think he is a proper one to put on airs regarding who is a person's *maman*."

"Such airs become no one," John answered. "All that matters is what a man is, not where he came from. I hope you do not discuss the Governor's parents with the women around the post."

Standing tall, Marguerite faced him. "I do not discuss, Johnny, but my ears happen sometimes to hear. Also, I agree with you. I do not care where he came from. But where is it he plans to go in the Company? And who is it he will stand on to make himself so tall? On these matters, I do care, *mon chéri*." She came over then and stood on tiptoe to reach John's lips. Then she stepped back and smiled. "These praises from London are of much good since they make you to lift up your shoulders so."

"Doctor! Doctor!"

"*Oui, oui*, Bruce," John called through the door. "What is it?"

"Governor Simpson, sir. He's in the office."

"Right away, Bruce. Tell him, right away."

George Simpson did not bother with a greeting nor even break the rhythm of his pacing when John entered the office. "I want you to build two ships—two hundred tons and equipped to ply the coast," he blurted. "Your sawmill is quite adequate to turn out lumber for ships. There'll be a carpenter on the *William and Ann* when she gets in. We'll spare you him."

John stood in the middle of the office. He was never quite comfortable sitting at his desk while Simpson paced and Simpson had paced a great deal these last four months.

"With two ships on the coast we can cut into Comcomly's bloody monopoly over those little tribes and freeze out the Americans at the same time," the Governor went on.

"But Comcomly won't have a chance to make a living, if we

beat him to the little tribes around. We can't just cut him off after all these years."

"Don't be ridiculous. We're not running a charity."

"And yet the honorable Company does want natives well treated. If we undercut the few chiefs who make it their sole business to trade, the Chinooks will starve."

"They'll learn to hunt and fish, if they find their trade stopped. They'll be better off in the long run. But, getting back to the coastal trade"—Simpson looked up for the first time—"you'd better write this."

John sat down and dipped his quill.

"I'm putting Pete Ogden in charge of the coastal trade."

His quill in mid-air, John looked up. "You mean pull Pete Ogden off the Snake?"

"Yes, yes, of course. We're doing damn well against the Americans on the Snake. Now, let's clear out their bloody ships. They're draining off too many furs from the Indian villages along the coast. Those New England traders are cagey ones and you've been too easy on them by far. We'll put Pete Ogden in charge at once of all coasters. That's an order. Make copies for London."

His surprise well mixed with relief, John wrote the order. "Perhaps this is best," he said. "I can't say I'm too proud of the job we've been doing on the Snake. I've always stood for conservation. Pete has been pretty ruthless in carrying out your suggestions for that territory. Still, we can't be blamed for all the damage. Americans are trapping in there as hard and fast as we are."

"Americans never have sense enough to see which side of their bread is buttered. By helping us create our fur desert on the Snake, they're playing right into our plan for keeping Yankee colonists from coming across that way."

"But we'll soon begin to miss revenue from that quarter," John persisted. "It's starting to level off already. What would you say to pulling our parties off the Snake for two or three years? Now that you're shifting Pete Ogden to the coast seems like the ideal

[*112*]

time. If we'd do it immediately, there are still enough beavers left to restock the streams."

"And let those Americans gain a fresh impetus? Not on your life!" Simpson lapped his arms across his white satin waistcoat and staked all this territory with his heels. "The way the Joint Occupation Treaty has been renewed, either side can call it off on a year's notice. If the Americans I've seen traipse across the mountains are any sample, they'll shoot first and ask whose country they're in afterwards. No! We don't for one minute let that section recoup. Freeze out the Americans and you'll have furs enough to show a ruddy profit for the rest of your life and what do you care after that?"

"You're dead wrong there," John snapped. "Wrong about furs holding out and wrong about my caring beyond my lifetime. I do care. I care about this country. Given another five years at our present rate, our men won't find enough furs on the Snake to pay for their traps."

Simpson pursed his lips and hung his thumbs in the pockets of his waistcoat. "Then we'll take more furs from the south," he decided. "The Umpqua section, for example—our parties haven't scratched the surface in there."

"But we've tried to hold our take to grown beaver and winter skins only."

"Nonsense. Clean them out. And after that, send trappers on south. There's all that Sacramento River area we've barely tapped."

"But we'll have a dozen Indian uprisings on our hands," John pointed out. "We're in pretty deep right now with the Indians on the Umpqua."

Simpson dismissed this subject with a brusque "There's another thing! About the Willamette—"

"What a valley!" John broke in. "Power going to waste this very minute in the Falls of the Willamette, enough to change the face of this whole land! I've staked a claim to the island there and to a couple of sections of land along the east bank of the river. We've put two small houses on the island and hauled in squared timbers for a sawmill and gristmill. That valley is one big wheat

[*113*]

field fifty miles wide. There's no end to the grain we can raise, once we get a few people in there to work that rich loam."

"It was 'people in there' that I was talking about when you interrupted," the Governor reproved. "That man Lucier and Joseph Gervais and Xavier Ladouroute and that reprobate Charlefoux, living here in the village. You know that, according to charter, Hudson's Bay Company discharges no employees in Indian country. You were under orders to return all these men to Canada."

"I know, I know," John admitted. He reached into his personal papers and brought out the signed refusals of these men to return to Canada.

Simpson took the sheaf and read the form statement. His covert glance, as he lifted the sheets one by one, seemed to weigh John against the papers in his hand.

They had managed to keep their relationship on such an even keel through the winter that John felt it worth while to explain. "Most of these men, as you can see, refused to go back to Canada. Lucier went but he turned up again on his own. And . . . well, take Etienne Lucier, for example. He happens to be the kind this country needs—a wide-awake worker with a love of the land and a will to be his own man." Suddenly a stronger argument struck him with such force that he had to speak slowly to keep his words from piling up. "After all, these men are all British subjects. If you're so sure the boundary question will be tipped one way or the other depending on who's occupying the land at the time it's decided, I'd think you'd be begging me to settle French-Canadians all over this country."

Simpson did not answer. Instead, he turned and paced from desk to window and back again. Then, he tore the sheaf of papers through the center.

Too late, John reached out to stop him. "But I wanted those for London," he protested.

"You won't need them," Simpson promised. "I'll tell the gentlemen in London it was my idea. You won't be blamed."

"Nor credited?" John asked, remembering Marguerite's hint

that this George Simpson might stand on him to climb up in the Company.

"You disobeyed orders," Simpson snapped and turned at once to new business. "Send an officer and a half-dozen Company servants to man the old buildings at Fort George."

"But that's on the south side of the Columbia. I thought we didn't see much point in keeping up that post for Americans to come in and take over whenever they happen to feel like it."

Simpson's grin was one-sided. "We won't keep it up too much. But in case of trouble, Indian or American, a handful of men there with a couple of well-aimed cannons might make quite a difference."

"I can spare a few men for Fort George, if you say so," John admitted.

"I say so."

"*Docteur, Docteur!*" The house shuddered with a furious pounding in the hallway. "Comcomly comes to trade."

John excused himself and hurried back to the parlor. "Marguerite! Eloise! Come. It's Comcomly."

The Columbia, usually so broad, seemed filled with canoes when John returned to the portico. He mounted the horse Bruce held at the steps and rode through the stockade gate. He would have preferred walking to the dock but he could not afford to show Comcomly such disrespect.

Riding to the river, he counted fifteen canoes, twenty-five or thirty feet long, each with a high rising bow and stern. Behind these came a procession of ten or twelve half-size canoes, made on the same pattern but less highly ornamented. Comcomly's collection of furs would be loaded in these smaller craft and John made a quick estimate of their worth in strong black figures on the ledger.

In the lead canoe with the great thunderbird carved on its prow and shells edging its gunwales, Comcomly rode with his three wives and twenty servants. Behind him, the Princess of Wales presided over her own canoe with its prow carved to represent a fish leaping from the water. Behind her, rode servants and children.

John reined in beside Jacques and dismounted.

"Some show," Jacques commented. "You told *Maman* and Eloise?"

"*Oui, oui.* They'll be along. What was that business with Charlefoux's Petit Chief Factor?"

Jacques shook his head. "I'm still as puzzled as ever. Charlefoux has a place about a yard square marked off with little stakes no more than knee high."

"*Oui, oui,* I remember Charlefoux digging a hole by his front door. He borrowed a spade."

"That's where it is—beside his front door—and that 'little fence' as the kid calls it, doesn't make it very private but this time it was all right. Petit Chief Factor led his *maman* from the house so she could see him empty the cup in the center of the plot and here's your cup." He laughed when John frowned. "I washed it in the river."

"Maybe some of our efforts haven't fallen on deaf ears then," John said. "Your *maman* and I have tried since Charlefoux married that Chinook girl to get her to observe some of the proprieties. Charlefoux could be quite a man, given a few boosts along the way. I hope this means that his woman is becoming civilized— even if the fence is too low for privacy and even though beside the front door is hardly the place I'd pick for a privy."

Jacques shook his head. "I don't know. It may be that but I have a feeling there's more to it than a bow to civilization. That kid is really scared. I think they switch him every time he doesn't go inside the little fence."

Suddenly John knew what it was all about. Stupid of him not to have remembered sooner. "*Oui, oui,* of course," he said aloud and wished he hadn't. There was no need to go into the matter with Jacques since he'd be leaving so soon. But he must remember to call in Charlefoux and put a stop to it. It was part of his dream for this country that the Indians could be taught civilized ways and he did not intend to let that one Chinook girl of Charlefoux's spoil his whole barrel of apples. The Chinooks' filthy practices

[*116*]

were certainly not to be carried outside their villages. To lure Jacques off the subject, John said, "Charlefoux is a good example of a fellow who broke all the rules himself so he bends over backward being strict with his son."

Jacques grinned. "The same as you, *Papa?*"

"*Oui, oui*, the same," John bantered. He liked this grown-up son of his.

George Simpson galloped up and jerked his mount to a halt.

John watched Jacques reach out and ease the bit in the big mare's mouth. He was glad the boy had a real feeling for animals. He'd be a better doctor for it.

By now, every gentleman and Company servant, every freeman and voyageur around the post, the blacksmith, the butcher, the coopers, and bakers, and all the women, children, and dogs had collected in the meadow to see the Chinooks arrive. But Comcomly could more than match the Britishers for numbers. His servants, shoulder to shoulder, railed the dock on both sides. Between their ranks, Comcomly marched in all his dignity.

When the old chief passed Governor Simpson and got up the official line to shake John's hand, he turned slowly to sweep the thickly populated meadow with his one-eyed gaze. Wearing his most profound expression, he said in jargon, "Big crowd," and grinned his pleasure at this attention.

Simpson took care of the welcome to the chief from the honorable Governor and Committee in London, from the British Parliament, and from King George IV.

John, when his turn came, said merely, "It is good to see you again. We have been too long without the company of the great *tyee* of the Chinooks. This meadow is yours wherever you choose to set up your plank houses except inside the new stockade and planted fields." He made a special point of shaking hands with the Princess of Wales and then with the Filly. "Your daughter looks pale," he told the Princess. "Has she been sick?"

For some reason the Princess was insulted by his question. "She is unsick as bear cub," she snapped and turned her back.

John waved forward the servants carrying his gifts of tobacco and knives for Comcomly.

[*117*]

John would have allowed the Company men to stand around for an hour or two, watching Comcomly's servants drive pairs of poles into which they could slide the heavy planks they had brought along for the chief's house. But George Simpson swung onto his horse and gave the "Back to work" command. John knew that Comcomly would have preferred an audience. To ease the slight, he sent Jacques back to the meadow at once with a bottle of rum to be delivered to Comcomly in person.

Fifty of Comcomly's servants, their arms piled with loose furs, stood waiting to be let into the compound before John finished his breakfast the next morning.

"All right, all right," John told his big kilted gateman, "you know how we do it. Let them in, three at a time. Send Bruce when the chief is ready to trade."

John waited to see his men open the gates to admit the first three servants. He watched them begin at the steps to spread the carpet of beaver skins on which Comcomly would walk the hundred yards from the compound gates when he came to trade. Then John went inside and began a letter to his brother David. Jacques would carry it with him when he went East with the Montreal Express and finally on to Paris.

David was not to spoil the boy, John wrote, and yet Jacques must have the best that Paris offered in training for medical practice and, also, in training for social life and civilized society, spare no expense. He became engrossed in the letter and in his dreams for Jacques. His son, with his quick understanding and sympathy, with his natural charm, would return a full-fledged doctor and a gentleman. In this country no one could point a finger and take anything from the boy with a derogatory "Quarter-breed." There would be no stopping Jacques when he got back.

But suddenly the quill fell from John's fingers. He brushed his hand across his eyes. Still, the face of Chief Hasumtooks gazed back at him from the letter sheet. No, no, no, Chief Hasumtooks could have nothing to do with him and his son. Jacques would return from Paris, win a place of leadership for himself in this country and live out his days here. But John had to push back

[*118*]

from his desk and move to the window to rid himself of that haunting burial at Walla Walla. And he could not entirely escape until Bruce announced that Comcomly had started up the beaver skin path to the office.

John hurried out to the portico. Comcomly would not relish arriving without an audience.

Dressed in his fabulous otterskin robe, the Chinook chief made his usual entrance on the carpet of beaver laid by his servants from the big folding gate, past the Indian store, along the full length of the officers' barracks, and to the Chief Factor's front steps.

In the office, the usual battle of wits began. In spite of George Simpson's sitting on the edge of his chair as if he would wind this up in thirty minutes, John knew that he must skip none of the usual time-consuming flimflam. He asked Comcomly in jargon, "Have you any new children since you last came to trade?"

Two of the chief's wives had presented him with sons. "And how is the great medicine man's fine son who will someday take his place among his people?" Comcomly asked through his interpreter.

John told him that Jacques was about to leave to cross the great waters where he would learn to be a bigger medicine man than his father. Some day he would take a position of leadership in this rich country. And had Comcomly done much hunting through the season of the snows?

Simpson sprang from his chair. "By the great Jehoshaphat, Doctor! Find out what condition his furs are in and how many he's brought. You're wasting time."

"Tut, tut, Governor. We have to trade time as well as furs in this country."

"Not my time, you don't. Get on, man, get on."

"Well, I'll try," John agreed, "but we haven't reached that point yet, not by a long shot."

Comcomly untied the beaded leather strings from beneath his chin and removed his cone-shaped hat. Giving his scalp a thorough scratching, he trapped a louse behind his right ear,

[*119*]

examined him closely with his one good eye and, satisfied, popped him into his mouth. Settling himself for the day, he looked up at John with that wise look of his and asked in one word of jargon, "Well, what now?"

John waved Simpson down and settled himself, too, in his chair. "How big are your new sons?" he asked.

The chief measured out their respective lengths with his hands.

"I hope they are both in good health and that they grow to be brave men with strong arms for the paddles and far-seeing eyes for the bow and arrows," John told him.

Comcomly shrugged and grinned. "*Cly, cly, cly!*"

"Small babies need to cry some," John excused his sons' weakness for the chief. "And how is your beautiful granddaughter, the one called the Filly?"

"She has sometimes a shaking and fever," the chief said in English.

"I'm sorry to hear it. And your daughter, the Princess of Wales—how is she?" John asked to round out his duty.

Comcomly's eye narrowed. His head moved slowly from side to side. "Do not know how to tell it. She is not sick with shaking and fever, still . . ." He touched his chest. "She buries a sickness in here. I cannot know it is safe to walk away when she holds a gun."

"Oh come now, she's your daughter. You can trust her," John assured him. "It is only the King George men who have insulted the Princess."

Simpson bustled to his feet once more. "I can't take all day for this. Let's have a look at the condition of his hides. If they're prime, let him pick his goods."

Now Comcomly, too, got to his feet. "*Alkekh,*" he said, giving it a strong guttural rebuke on the end.

Simpson turned to John instead of the interpreter. "What does he mean by that growl?"

"Hold on—not so fast."

"Not so fast, indeed!" Simpson jerked at his watch and the stem caught on his waistcoat pulling a thread in the silk. "Bloody

[*120*]

nuisance, he is," he railed. "Bloody niusance." He looked up from his watch. "Do you know we've spent a full half hour and still haven't started?"

"*Oui, oui*, Governor. I know. I know, too, that we may not have started after we spend a full day."

Startled into sitting, Simpson gripped the arms of his chair and leaned forward as if he could hurry things by tightening his muscles and setting his jaw.

Now Comcomly had changed his mind about trading. He might decide to go back to his village, taking his furs along with him, the interpreter told them.

"Everybody around here in too damn big hurry," Comcomly explained in English.

Simpson spluttered and swore.

John frowned. With dwindling returns from the Snake and Indian trouble on the Umpqua, he could not make up a full shipment for London unless he managed somehow to get the furs that Comcomly had accumulated through his monopoly over his neighboring villages.

"But he can't out-and-out refuse to sell," Simpson told John in a bristling whisper. "We'll force him to let us have his furs. After all, who's he as against the Company?"

John sat back and twisted his ear. "That's a funny thing, Governor. A civilized man, bucking a company with the power of Hudson's Bay, would back down. He'd know he couldn't win a fight so one-sided. But my friend here doesn't know he can't win and he succeeds quite often in getting the long end of the deal even against Hudson's Bay."

"Don't spout nonsense at me, John McLoughlin. We'll force him to trade."

"How?"

"Get him to go on talking about his family. I'll think of a way."

But the Chinook chief, always quick to seize an advantage, would not stay even to discuss his new sons. He could not be pressed into telling his threadbare hunting and fishing tales. No, he was through for today. He was probably through for to-

morrow and the next day. But, since the King George men insisted with so much smiling, he would agree to live in his house
on the meadow until time for the Express to paddle upriver. This
was a thing he liked to see. But he did not wish to be bothered
with talk of trading furs for beads and vermilion. No, not even
for a suit made of steel.

John could not stifle a grin of admiration. "As I said," he
reminded Simpson when Comcomly left, "it's quite amazing what
one lone man can do when he doesn't know in advance that he
can't win."

Simpson came up short in the middle of the office. "I told you
I'd think of a way," he exclaimed. "Send Jacques to me and leave
us alone." When John hesitated, the Governor fumed, "Well,
well, get Jacques, I said."

John found the boy in the parlor, trying on a spencer jacket
Marguerite had made for his going away to school. "Governor
Simpson wants to see you, Son. In the office."

"Governor Simpson?" Jacques asked in surprise.

"*Oui, oui.* Better hurry. He's never long on patience." John
waited for Marguerite to help Jacques from the new jacket without misplacing the pins that marked the buttonholes. He'd get a
few minutes, at least, with her while Simpson talked to the boy.

But Marguerite became very busy the moment Jacques slammed
the parlor door. She had no time for a kiss. No, no, she must
sweep the hallway.

"But surely that can wait," John objected. "I never get to see
you when the Governor is on hand."

"It cannot wait, Johnny." She pulled away and, catching up
the broom as if she must use it for beating out a fire, she went
through the parlor door and then took her time to close it without a trace of sound.

Breathing hard, Marguerite stood in the hallway with her ear
against the parlor door. "*Bon.* Johnny does not follow, then," she
said to herself and, taking care that her moccasins did not whisper
on the plank floor, she hurried down the hall.

Outside the office door, she grasped her broom in the position for sweeping but she held it slightly above the floor and went through the motions only while she listened.

She heard Jacques's eager voice first. "Certainly, Governor Simpson. I'll be glad to do you a favor. And if, as you say, it will also help *Papa* to make up his full shipment of furs for London, so much the better."

Simpson's oily voice sounded so close that he must be standing with his back against the door. "It's nothing hard. You'll have good sport, in fact. It's the Filly—old Comcomly sets great store by her. I want you to form an alliance with the Filly."

"You mean marry her?" Jacques gasped.

"Yes, yes, go through the usual Chinook ceremony and feast. Play around with her a week or so—until our Express is ready to start East. That will satisfy Comcomly and the Princess and give us time to get their furs. Then, you travel to Montreal with me and on to Paris."

"But Governor Simpson—"

Marguerite threw open the door and gave George Simpson a jolt. "Jacques, you will go to your room," she said in the tone her children most respected. She waited while Jacques bowed to her and to Simpson to excuse himself before he went out. Then she pulled the door shut and stood confronting Simpson.

His gaze faltered first. He moved to the desk. "Well, well, if you've come to sweep, get on with it."

Marguerite flung the broom on the floor between them. Her words came out cold as blocks of ice cut from the sawmill pond. "One word of this thing I have heard and my Johnny would finish the choking of you that he once started."

Simpson's mouth pulled to the side. "Squaws!" he sneered. "Squaws behind every door."

"But I do not tell what I have heard and so, also, will our Jacques not tell," Marguerite went on as if he had not spoken. "My Johnny would kill you. But my Johnny must not be hurt by the thing he must do to you. It can, I am sure, be done a better way." Pondering, she gazed at her broom on the floor. "No, no, this is not a thing so easy as to choke a man and go to prison for it. This is a thing of . . . of . . . as we say in French, *finesse*." She picked up her broom. "When we find this better way, it will be, I think, to cut off from you whatever it is that you most want."

John had to hurry to the sawmill the next day and lay out plans for Simpson's two ships. When he got back a week later, he heard much talk of sending across the river for the medicine man living on Sauvies Island at the village of Cathlacomatup. The Filly was dying.

John convinced the Princess that he would care for her daughter and, because a certain amount of distinction would thus rub off on her from the personal attention of the Chief Factor, she let him have his way. But, while the girl did not die, she got better so slowly that Comcomly used this as another excuse for refusing to trade until the day arrived for the Express to leave.

The Governor issued frenzied last-minute instructions that did not include a way to trade Comcomly out of his furs. They merely added up to hurry, hurry, hurry. Hurry those ships. Hurry the farms. Hurry a handful of men with ample gunpowder to Fort George. Most of all, hurry those trappers. Don't leave bait enough on the Snake to lure even a handful of Americans across the Stony Mountains. Get furs off the Umpqua. Get furs off the coast. Send trappers on south.

Marguerite had no time for rubbing the lines from John's troubled forehead nor the pains from his shoulder. She was sewing and packing and giving last-minute instructions herself. She was sending her son off to school.

The wapato vines on the meadow burst into blue. Loaded with letters to be delivered along the line, with a short shipment of furs that did not include Comcomly's, with consignments of home-grown wheat to be dropped at the Flathead post, Fort Walla Walla, and Spokan House, the sleek North canoes lay in the river.

Looking suddenly too young and somewhat frightened, Jacques stood on the dock and took his father's hand. "*Au revoir*." He caught his lip to stop its trembling.

John had to throw his arms around him and hold him close for an instant even though he was seventeen and almost as tall as John himself.

George Simpson took John's hand then and gave it a squeeze.

John was reminded of that first time they gripped each other's hands at Hudson's Bay House on Fenchurch Street. Then, he wasn't sure whether they were to be friends or enemies. Now he said, "Take care of yourself, Governor. The Company will never find a man to fill your shoes."

"If they ever need to, I'll have the shoes stretched to your size, Doctor," Simpson promised. Then he went into one of his quick changes back to business. "Remember what I said about manning Fort George? The *William and Ann* should come over the bar any day now. She's carrying an extra load of rifles and ammunition. We can't take a chance on some hot-blooded American patriots starting something in this country. I've given the ship's captain orders to run in behind Clatsop Spit and unload all the guns and powder there at the fort—save hauling them up here and back. Get men down there at once. That ship may sail in tomorrow or the next day."

"*Oui, oui,* Governor."

Soon the passengers were loaded and the scarlet paddles lifted and fell.

> *Dans mon chemin j'ai rencontre*
> *Deux cavaliers, très bien montés. . . .*

The breeze from the sea caught and fanned up the voyageurs' ribbon-anchored plumes and, with a sharp turn and a flourish of paddles, each canoe cut into the current.

John fixed his gaze on Jacques's beaver hat lifted high in salute. Confound it, he'd spent too little time with the boy. Five years had slipped through his fingers. He felt cheated. When he turned, Marguerite stood at his side but her eyes were not on Jacques. Instead, they were fixed on George Simpson. A look that John had never seen before on his wife's face narrowed her eyes and pulled her lips into a fixed line.

The *William and Ann* did not arrive "tomorrow" nor the

[*125*]

"next day" but Comcomly and his retinue must hurry to the mouth of the Columbia. They would not consider missing the arrival of Hudson's Bay Company's annual supply ship from England.

When it came to packing up, however, Comcomly decided to trade off his furs. John was furious at the thought of having to brush and air and store all these furs through the summer. But, he needed skins on any terms and, all at once, Comcomly was no longer fussy about terms. He traded so open-handedly that John felt the entire transaction, when it was finished, deserved some kind of memorial. At the last minute, while he kept spectators and Chinooks waiting at the dock, he presented Comcomly with his compliments and a suit of steel armor.

Comcomly's delight sparkled in his good eye and, with his most profound expression he exclaimed, "Bloody nuisance!" in perfect imitation of George Simpson.

But Comcomly's pleasure in the gift only served to point up the fact that John had made no comparable presentation to the Princess of Wales. She was insulted. John reminded her that he had taken care of the Filly all spring and that now she was better. He had made no charge for this service nor for his medicines, he pointed out.

The Princess was still insulted.

John kept the crowd waiting while he hurried to his medical office for a full bottle of quinine crystals. The size of his supply did not justify his being so generous, but the *William and Ann* would be in soon with a fresh stock and the Filly still suffered from intermittent chills and fever. To placate the Princess and, at the same time, speed the Filly's recovery he could afford to run a bit low on quinine.

The Princess accepted the gift and listened to his minute instructions regarding size of dose and one dose at a time. Then she said, "The Governor Simpson has insulted the Princess. The Chief Factor McLoughlin has insulted the Princess. Such insults are bigger than any glass bottle with bitter powder." She clapped her hands and, at this signal, her servants pulled her canoe from the dock. Then, defiance in every move, the Princess stood up and flipped her fur bib around to the back. She worked the stopper from the square glass bottle and emptied its contents into the Columbia.

John swore under his breath and Marguerite's hand slid into his.

"The old insult is, perhaps, a soreness in the Princess that keeps swelling when no man takes the Filly for his woman," Marguerite said with a special tone of understanding in her voice. "A *maman* does not give up a wedding for her daughter as a thing finished and forget it."

"You may be right," John murmured.

"Johnny, it is a big soreness that the Princess keeps inside her. It is so big, perhaps, that you will please not trade to her ever a rifle."

X The *William and Ann* did finally arrive at the mouth of the Columbia and in some mysterious way she broke up off Clatsop Spit. Not a crewman was left to tell the tale. Not one bead nor button remained of her cargo.

Rumors rode the wet Chinook wind that blew in from the sea. Some said the Princess of Wales had hired Indians to sink posts off Clatsop Point to trap the ship. Some said the drunken captain of the *William and Ann* had run aground and then killed his crew to keep the story from leaking out. Others said the ship had gone onto the sand and when the seamen made their way to shore the Indians had murdered them and burned their bodies. All rumors leaned heavy on talk that the Indians had appropriated the cargo.

Disturbed as much by the tone of the rumors as by the loss of the ship and all his trade goods for this year, John sent a message to the chiefs of the villages near the mouth of the river. They must restore to the Company everything taken from the wrecked *William and Ann.*

His runners returned with an old brush and a rusty scoop. The Great *Tyee* of the Sky had dropped gifts at their very doors, the Indians said. They had no intention of insulting the Great *Tyee* by ingratitude. Furthermore, since the Great *Tyee's* gifts included many British-made rifles, they assumed that these were meant to be turned on anyone who made talk of sending these gifts to Fort Vancouver.

John could not afford, on any count, to let the Indians get away with this. He rounded up fifty-four men—every last one available—from the fort and village. Loading a howitzer on the only schooner at hand, they hurried downriver to Clatsop Point.

When John sighted against the afternoon glare the twisted bow of the *William and Ann* sprawled helpless on the spit of sand, he dropped the glass from his eye and let his shoulders sag. Until this moment, he knew now, he'd been telling himself that the rumors could be exaggerated.

Now, the worst reports were true. And, with a cold mist closing like a curtain between him and the battered ship's hull, the whispers became true also. Broken masts made grotesque elbows clothed in a witch's tatters of shredded sails. The ship was mysteriously dead, murdered.

This feeling persisted while John went off in the tender to board and examine the denuded *William and Ann*. Nothing was left—no cargo, no bodies, no ship's papers, no litter of any kind. The sea alone was never so thorough a housekeeper.

Back aboard the schooner, John ordered, "Lay starboard off Comcomly's village. He's behind this or knows who is."

Through the glass as they approached the shore John could see Indians by the hundreds with fishing nets and baskets for their catch. But gradually the naked figures and their gear dissolved into the trees. When the schooner's anchor went over the side, John could not pick up one Indian in the glass.

Through the night he saw no fires on shore, heard no activity. Curtains of mist enclosed the deck of the schooner like a four-poster bed but John slept in fits and starts in a short-backed chair. Toward dawn he went below to pack a basket with twists of tobacco and knives. He'd go ashore and put a stop to this weird silence.

When he ducked into the galley for a cup of tea, he found most of the schooner's crew. No one had been able to sleep. They, too, wanted an end to this night but they protested in chorus to John's, "I'm going ashore."

"There's a Chinook with a rifle behind every bloody one of them trees," the skipper warned.

"If they've got the cargo, they'll fight like blue devils to keep it. A few white men's lives won't mean scat to them Injuns." The mate sounded in a mood to run.

"If they've got the cargo, I'm out of business," John countered. "I'm going in. Man the tender."

[*129*]

The sun, when it came up, made no more difference in the day than a dinner plate hung against the gray sky.

John refused to risk the lives of officers who volunteered to go with him. The six Sandwich Islanders on the tender's oars were expert swimmers and, before they pulled away from the schooner, John gave them instructions, in case of attack, to go over the side and no questions asked.

The lap of the current against the schooner's hull, the squeak and dip of paddles sounded loud in John's ears while his eyes strained to catch any sign of life on shore. As the distance narrowed he felt, rather than saw, movement in the shrubby willows near the water's edge. He eased off his hat and held it on his knees. His white hair would tell Comcomly beyond all chance of mistake who it was approaching the village.

Then, in the clearing at the far end of Comcomly's plank house, John's eye caught the gleam of polished steel. The old familiar suit of armor came lumbering along the side of the house, made a military turn into the clearing, and goose-stepped toward the beach.

John settled back with a grin. That suit of armor must be destined to hound him the rest of his days. But, if Comcomly considered it appropriate garb for an official welcome, this might imply some spark of gratitude in the old reprobate. Gratitude in large measure John could use to tip this precarious mission in his favor. Even this small hint of it relieved, somewhat, the strain of the unknown behind the mist and silence of this morning.

Then, with no warning of any kind, the clatter of concerted rifle fire ripped away the morning's silence. At first, only the noise got through to John in his lulled state of resting back on Comcomly's gratitude. For a long moment, he watched in disbelief the rain of bullets in the water around the tender.

Not one Sandwich Islander obeyed orders. Their paddles caught and held at the crest of a stroke and the craft came around. Like a spring shower before the wind, the patter of bullets followed along as the little boat cut cross-current for her schooner.

John looked around to see the man behind him grab his shoulder, make a pained attempt to pick up the stroke, and slump forward.

John slid back to his place and recovered the oar.

They made the lee of the schooner barely in time to keep the gunmen on board from committing wholesale massacre.

"Keep that howitzer up," John yelled. "Aim high—at their houses."

A fusillade from the cannon splintered and sent planks flying into the trees. Rifle fire gave way on shore to screams and wails. Where there had been no Indians, now they darted everywhere along the beach and helter-skelter up the sandy slope. Then, once more, there were no Indians. Even their screams faded and died. The mists veiled again Comcomly's village and blotted up all sound.

John called for his medicine bag off the schooner. He probed in the oarsman's bloody shoulder until he could find and hack out the bullet.

"What now?" the skipper called over.

"Give us a hand with this wounded man and let me have a replacement," John answered. "I'm going in."

"Not again!"

"*Oui, oui*, again. Keep the nose of that howitzer up and cover us, if need be."

Expecting any minute a salvo of bullets, they pulled into better and better rifle range of the shore. Stroke by stroke the waiting lengthened out until, finally, the only thing left was to beach the boat and invade that dead quiet on foot.

From the sandy edge of the clearing they strained to see through the mist any rifle barrel trained on them, to hear any whisper of sound denoting Indians at hand.

His fingers ready on the pistol in his belt, John took one step, searched ahead and to each side, and dared another step. Behind him crept his huddled oarsmen.

They climbed the slope and ventured, inch by inch, around the pile of rubble that had been Comcomly's house. John convinced himself that the Indians had taken to the woods out of respect for that howitzer. All he had to do now was to locate the cargo off the *William and Ann* and take it on board the schooner.

A sharp wail at hand brought his pistol from his belt. His Sandwich Islanders flung themselves on the ground.

Clearing the way ahead with his eyes and covering each move with his pistol, John followed the sound to the next pile of rubble. At his feet lay the suit of steel armor.

Remembering the Trojan's horse, he stooped and somewhat gingerly raised the helmet's visor. Comcomly's good eye peered up at him. A flicker of recognition burned out too quickly but the old chief's expression was still capable of holding John in expectation of some profound comment. Comcomly's obvious effort to speak added significance to his one word of jargon. He asked, "Well, what now?"

"You're hurt. What is it?" John fumbled at the shoulder pieces of his armor to release the helmet. A beam must have fallen on the chief and knocked him senseless. Perhaps his people thought him dead and left him here when they fled or, more likely, went into ambush.

"Could be a trap." One of the oarsmen crept nearer for a cautious look.

"Where does it hurt?" John asked the chief in jargon. Confound this awkward armor. Every joint in the thing was wedged.

"Make no mind. Too late. Too late," Comcomly muttered. "Hole in back. Steel suit hold much blood."

"A hole in your back? No, no, of course not." To humor the chief John reached around and let his hand slide down the twisted backplate. But he came up with a start when the tip of his index finger fitted itself into a clean round role in the cold steel. "But how? Who did it?" The chief was dying. His listlessness was real and not from shock nor from a blow on the head as John had diagnosed. "Here now. Let me straighten your legs, get you out of this armor, and bandage your wound."

"Too late, too late," Comcomly repeated. "Princess want all goods off ship. Princess take. You make peace with Princess."

Sensing the need to hurry, John asked, "That cargo off the ship—where is it?"

"Take goods first," Comcomly murmured, "make peace with Princess after."

[132]

"Where is it? Where is it?"

"House." Comcomly tried to raise his arm but managed the fingers only. "You find. Find also granddaughter. She much sick."

"*Oui, oui,* I'll find her." John got the helmet loose and lifted it gently off Comcomly's head.

"No, no. Put back. Fine suit in burial canoe. Put back. Put back."

Nothing would quiet him until John replaced the helmet.

"Servants. Tell servants."

"*Oui, oui,* I'll tell them to leave the steel suit on."

"No, no. Send servants. Servant called Sure Thing go with *tyee.* Help *tyee* walk in spirit world."

John could not argue with Comcomly now about the Chinooks' custom of killing servants to accompany them to the other world. Then, he had no need to argue. The old chief was dead.

John lowered the visor and stood up. Comcomly had been a devil in his day—perverse and grasping, and his hold on the other chiefs nearby had cost the Company much. But now, John reached for his handkerchief to blow his nose before he could take out his pistol again to guard the way as he moved on through the tumbled village to search for the stolen cargo.

They found it in the last plank house of the village, well back from the shore. None but the rifle crates and kegs of powder had been opened. John saw no marks of water. The Indians, from the look of things, had taken the cargo well before the *William and Ann* had met with trouble. But no one could say this for sure.

John poked through the stacks of "pieces" trying to estimate how many trips the tender must make to load all this in the schooner's hold. As long as the tide held, they could tack in close to shore and save time. But the work would be slow. They'd need to keep men on guard against Indians sneaking back, against Indians secreted with their new rifles among the litter of goods and knocked-down houses.

A cough near at hand brought the Sandwich Islanders up wide-eyed but they stood fast. Behind his pistol again, John closed in on the sound. He came on the rifle barrel first. It lay, however, on the sod and across it sprawled an arm.

[*133*]

The Filly, on a pallet of beaver skins behind a wall of trade goods, opened her eyes but her expression did not change at sight of John. She made no move to ward him off.

He pushed the rifle aside and squatted to lay his hand on her forehead. She burned with fever.

"I'll take you on board our schooner," John said.

"*Oui*," she answered.

"This could be a trap," an oarsman again reminded him.

"*Oui*, it could be," John admitted. "Give me a hand."

They wrapped the Filly in a blanket and, aboard the schooner, gave her tea and a bunk and went about their business.

Slowed in their work all day by the necessity of keeping men on guard, they did not actually see one Chinook. But, even with the goods secure in the hold of the schooner by low tide, John knew that he dared not leave without making a real peace. If he did, he could expect thieving and attacks from ambush and wrecked ships as long as he stayed in the country. Still, negotiating a peace against those new British-made rifles and on the heels of this day's confiscation would require a large helping of finesse.

John had no question about the identity of his opponent. Comcomly had specified that he must make peace with the Princess. He needed someone acceptable to both sides to send ashore with gifts and a message of peace. All he had on deck were Canadians and Sandwich Islanders and a few Iroquois half-breeds. So, he would have to go himself. He wished they could weigh anchor at once and head those trade goods safely upstream toward Fort Vancouver. Instead, he must wait for morning and get this thing settled, one way or another, with the Chinooks.

Before propping himself in his chair on deck for the night, he laid out the supply of beads and pewter buttons that he would take ashore in the morning as a peace offering. Normally, beads and buttons were items of trade and not to be used as gifts. But negotiations with the Princess of Wales, secure behind her new rifles, would require something more spectacular than the usual formality of knives and tobacco.

When John wakened an hour before dawn, his gifts for the Princess were gone. Gone, too, was the Filly.

XI Angry at first, John reminded himself that he should have known not to expect gratitude from the Filly nor from any other Indian. They ate the lice from their heads and argued that they would seem ungrateful to the *Tyee* of the Sky who sent these tidbits, if they abandoned the practice. But they expected medical care from the *tyee* of Fort Vancouver as their due.

Having told himself, while he combed his hair and poked his shirttail into his pantaloons, that Indians were not to be judged by civilized standards, he had to swallow every word of his reasoning with his first gulp of tea in the schooner's crowded galley.

They heard a commotion on deck and, running out, looked down on a frantic splashing in the river.

"Must be a crewman went over the side afore he remembered he couldn't swim," someone suggested.

"That one can swim," John pointed out. "He's swimming but—"

"But he ain't happy about it."

"Looks plumb wore out."

John went himself for the rope ladder and wondered at finding it over the side. "This way. Here," he called to the struggling swimmer. Then he saw who it was.

Naked except for her tattoo, she came up the ladder.

John threw his coat around her and felt her racking shudder. He hurried her to the cabin and piled on her every blanket he could find. He had the cook heat pans of salt which he folded into squares of blanket and kept changing on her chest. An hour passed before she could speak through her chattering teeth.

Her story came out at last, half in English, half in jargon. She had seen the gifts laid out and guessed that the *tyee* planned to go ashore with a message of peace. But she knew her people and their present mood. In possession of the goods off the *William and Ann*, they had gone crazy in their heads. They had talked far into the darkness of paddling up the river and killing the King George *tyee* so they could steal all the trade goods stored at Fort Vancouver and become the most honored people on the earth. So, she took his beads and pewter buttons and swam ashore. She delivered the gifts to her mother, the Princess, in the name of the great *tyee* of Fort Vancouver. She delivered also his message of peace.

"But how could you know that I wished to talk peace?" John asked.

"Big people talk peace," she explained. "Little people make talk with rifles. The Princess promise she will talk peace."

"Helluva lot her promise is worth," the skipper growled.

"Many chiefs pay great honor to *Tyee* Comcomly," the Filly stated almost as if she talked to herself. "Princess make peace, sure thing, so other chiefs do not hear what I see."

John stepped close to the bunk. "You saw her shoot Comcomly in the back?"

"I see. She knows I see. She will talk peace."

As John and the Filly approached the shore, the Princess stood alone on the beach. She wore a token of Comcomly's fortune in hyaqua shells on a dozen fathom-long strings around her neck. The mists had drifted to sea and, back among the trees, John glimpsed Indians carrying on a kind of frenzied rushing in and out around the rubble of their village.

He helped the Filly over the side of the tender and motioned an oarsman to follow with the basket of knives and tobacco.

The Princess stood her ground. Neither mother nor daughter spoke when they met.

John bowed. "I have come to sit in council with you and the important men of your village. I bring with me gifts of knives and tobacco for the men. The Princess has received her own gifts."

"We make talk here," the Princess countered. "Men of village hollow out burial canoe for Comcomly," she explained. "Also burial canoes for servants. Men do not find time for talk."

"Servants? Burial canoes for servants?" John stormed. "What's going on here?"

The Princess stepped back. John saw her eyes harden. "Many servants sick. Some die. They go with Comcomly."

"The one called Sure Thing—is he one who happened to die at this convenient time?" John asked.

The Princess turned her aristocratic head away from his questioning. "He happen to die," she admitted, "and two more but we do not talk now of servants. We talk of goods you steal from our village. We wish pay."

John considered just how far he should press the dictates of civilized justice in this case. After all, he was the law in this country and the Princess had defied all the laws of humanity and decency. Still, George Simpson had cautioned him against interfering too soon with the Indians' customs. As to murder, the question had not come up but Simpson, John felt sure, would rule that it was outside the Company's realm unless the victims were white men and, more specifically, British subjects. Soon now, John decided however, he certainly would put a stop to this barbarous custom of killing servants to wait on their dead master in the spirit world. For now, he must of necessity concentrate on recovering his cargo. "You have many rifles that belong to us," he said. "I want them back."

"How much you pay for rifles?"

The Filly spoke up before John could answer. "Give back rifles," she ordered in a tone that left no room for argument.

John could see the Princess weighing the worth of the rifles against her lowered prestige, if the Filly should tell neighboring chiefs that their friend, Comcomly, had died at his daughter's hand. Finally, in her most scornful voice she said, "If King George man so poor he must steal from Indians, the Princess will bring rifles to ship tonight at sunset."

The delay in getting started back to Fort Vancouver annoyed John but he felt that he had won a victory and that he should not press for a total rout. The Princess had her face to save and he could allow her that.

Well before sundown, they put the tender over to wait for the Princess and her promised load of rifles. As soon as they could make the transfer, they'd set their sails and head for Fort Vancouver, dark or no dark. This business had wasted too much time.

The Princess, true to her word, manned a long canoe with servants and pushed out from shore even earlier than she had promised.

John, from his seat in the tender, watched through the glass. Her canoe rode low in the water. Those rifles were heavy. But, though the breakers had begun to pile themselves high in the mouth of the river, the current inside could be run by these paddle-wise Chinooks in spite of the load.

The canoe moved out, making for the schooner. Then, it turned into the current and the paddlers doubled their stroke. Before John could believe his eyes, the Princess and her servants skimmed downstream past the tilted prow of the *William and Ann,* and toward the breakers rolling across the bar.

No one but Indians would attempt to paddle that heavy load through the battling currents where the river met the sea and on to some place of hiding on the shore. And no one but Indians would stand a chance of running those breakers in safety. Even so, their chances were slim. Still, they did have a chance and were attempting, once more, to steal those rifles.

John ordered his men to row after them but he knew they could not intercept that runaway canoe. The best they could do would be to get near enough with a few well-placed bullets to frighten the Princess into turning back.

Aided by the current, they gained fast on the weighted canoe. John lowered the glass and reached for a rifle. A few more strokes of the Sandwich Islander's oars and he could give the tricky Princess a small but alarming dose of her own medicine.

But suddenly the Princess stood tall in her canoe. She swung a gleaming new rifle to her shoulder and sighted along its barrel toward the men in the tender.

[*138*]

"Down!" John called to his men and he dropped forward to his knees. But when he sighted along his own rifle barrel, he saw a commotion and scramble among the Indians in the canoe. The Princess had fallen or she had fired and the recoil of the weapon had knocked her off balance. A scream sliced through the sound of the surf. John watched for a long moment while the Chinooks' paddles flayed the air. Then he sat frozen as the canoe turned slowly broadside and a wave turned in a graceful curve and slid down over the flimsy craft like the cover of a roll-top desk.

He could do nothing except to wait for the Indians to fight their way to the surface and then order his oarsmen to risk their own safety in that mountainous surf to save the Chinooks' conniving lives. The rifles were gone, thanks to the Princess' own stupidity, but these Indians who lived as much in the water as on land would bob to the surface like fishing corks. John made up his mind to give the Princess of Wales a taste of white man's justice, once he laid his hands on her.

But the Princess got her justice in a larger dose than he, even then at the peak of his fury, would have meted out. The canoe itself did not appear again nor did one Indian.

John sat staring into the receding wake of a breaker. Perhaps the captain of the *William and Ann*, unable to clear the sand bar, had ordered his men over the side when the ship began to break up. Perhaps the same fiendish current beneath this innocent surface had caught and held that crew the same as it had these Indians. If so, the Chinooks' guilt in the mysterious affair of the *William and Ann* stood only at salvage level and not at murder as he had been inclined to assume.

With a weary backward pull of his head, John ordered his oarsmen upstream. Comcomly and the Princess, both gone! He felt sure now that, given time, he could have lifted them from their primitive ways. With their prestige to go on, they could have been developed into valuable assets for the Company and for the country. If the Company had only sent him teachers and a chaplain! The Governor continued to promise help but promises did not turn savages into civilized beings. And savages could not be expected to turn a raw country into a homeland.

[*139*]

When they reached the schooner, John climbed aboard and went at once to her prow where he could stand at the rail undisturbed. The Sandwich Islanders could pass on the news. The men could discuss it, making quick judgments against the Princess. As for John, he felt a heavy guilt. True, it was the Company at fault, not John personally. But the Company had bought the Indians' furs for as little as possible and lived with their daughters as long as convenient. It had beat them to the fish in their rivers, pacified them with rum to rob them of their guts, and had set them an all-round example of dog eat dog. And yet the Company charter provided for the education and moral training of natives. The honorable gentlemen in London, John felt sure, had every intention of living up to the high demands of the charter. "Certainly I came here expecting and wanting to better the lives of the natives," he said aloud into the night.

But what had happened? Surely Governor Simpson had not planned to walk over the natives in this ruthless fashion and yet his very promises of a chaplain and teacher had kept John from sending his request directly to London.

John straightened and opened his cape. Sometimes he liked to see its bright Frazer tartan lining instead of its Hudson's Bay blue surface. His weight of guilt lifted as the cape blew back from his shoulders. He'd take matters into his own hands now and see to it that the natives received their due. He'd give them a chance at something finer than they'd known and both the Company and the country would be the better for it.

But an unwelcome visitor came to the Columbia that summer. Some said that he arrived on the *William and Ann*, that he was her lone survivor. Others said that he came by the overland trail across the mountains. Still others claimed that he rode in on the wet Chinook wind from the southwest. His name was Death.

The Filly, ripe for the taking, became his first mistress.

Death moved through the Indians' long plank hutches, visiting each family's compartment and then hurrying on to the next and the next. Up the river he traveled, touching each new acquaintance with a clammy hand and then blowing out his hot breath until every village upstream and down and those along the Willa-mette knew him on sight and knew, too, their unlikely chances of escape.

John used his year's supply of quinine in one month.

Word came that the *Sultana*, an out-of-season ship, had sailed, well-stocked, from Boston. She'd be carrying quinine then and John would gladly trade, even with an American, for medicine. He dipped into his allotment for next year.

Bewildered, desperate Indians arrived by tens and then by fifties to camp outside the palisade at Fort Vancouver. Bewildered and desperate, too, John had to go out each morning to insist that they move on.

"But if we die here, you will make us to sleep safe in ground where wolves cannot eat," they pleaded.

"Here is medicine." He was far into next year's supply. Before it disappeared, surely the *Sultana* would sail across the bar. "Take this. Perhaps you will not die. For your sake and ours, you must not bunch yourselves here."

They would die, he knew. Entire families, entire villages would die. They would place their dead in burial canoes and hang them in trees or set them on platforms that would defy only a few of the less cunning animals. But his men were sick, too. They did not have the strength to dig graves and bury the Indians.

"What can I do? What more do I know to do?" John asked himself a hundred times a day and kept repeating his questions through the night. Even when he slept, he tossed and talked to himself until Marguerite would have to waken him.

"You must not fret day and night, my Johnny," she insisted at two o'clock one damp morning in late August. "Soon you will be as sick as Mr. Ogden and then who will give to the Indians the quinine?"

"I'd better go see about Pete." He'd rather be up and doing something, no matter how futile.

He told Marguerite later that morning, "I think I'll send for James Douglas. With so many men down, I need more help and Jamie is a fine lad. He has no doubt learned much about the business and Company ways since he was a novice Nor'wester back at Rainy Lake. *Oui, oui*, I must send for Jamie at once."

Marguerite, sitting up in bed, her arms around her knees, nodded. "*Oui*, you need more help. Also, you miss our Jacques. The black-haired young Mr. Douglas will be a son to you, Johnny."

John wrote that day to Governor Simpson, requesting James Douglas' transfer from Stuart Lake to Fort Vancouver. To young Douglas he wrote, "You will be a son to me, lad. I need you."

And still the Indians came down with intermitting fever. So did John's dairymen, farmers, clerks, and interpreters. Day and night John examined patients, dosed with quinine in smaller and smaller pinches as his supply vanished and the disease showed no signs of wearing itself out. And then word arrived by way of the Sandwich Islands that the *Sultana* had gone down in the South Seas, leaving no hope of trading for quinine from the Americans. The Company ship from England could not reach the Columbia before March.

Pete Ogden's fever burned away his flesh and left him nothing but bones with a falsetto voice that finally grew too weak to rasp out the one word, "Water."

John, with no medicine, could do no more for him than to keep Marguerite and Eloise taking turns at bathing his face and arms with river water.

"There's power in our river, Pete Ogden," John kept telling him. "You're going to get well."

When Pete grew able to spend his time between chills reading the Bible, John himself began to believe in his assurances. When Pete started reading Shakespeare more than the Bible, his doctor knew that the worst was over as far as Pete was concerned.

But deaths among the Indians mounted. By late fall, John estimated with a shudder that fully half the Indian population on the Columbia had died off.

Figuring his annual returns far into New Year's Eve, John remembered the near war over the *William and Ann* and got up from his desk to gaze through the window into the black night. He had felt uneasy at the time of that trouble, picturing the way things might turn with the Indians. Now the Indians on the Columbia had been so reduced in number and so deadened in spirit that no uprising among them could prove more than a nuisance to the well-fortified Company. And now somehow he must find ways to recoup the Department's heavy losses in trade caused by the epidemic.

George Simpson in his shoes, John knew, would find a dozen ways to balance the loss of trade with the Indians. "Freeze out the Americans. Quit dividing the business with Americans and you'll have furs enough to show a ruddy profit the rest of your life and what do you care after that," the Governor had preached.

In the meantime, an American had anchored a brig eighty-five miles up the Columbia, at The Dalles. John went back to his desk and held the candle over for a look at his wall map. Perhaps he could open a small post just beyond the lava beds there to cut into this American's trade with The Dalles Indians. He'd better show the fellow straight off that no Yankee could turn profits in Hudson's Bay country.

His eyes moved up the map to the lower Fraser where two years ago he'd written in the name, Fort Langley. This post was old enough now to begin fattening up returns from that quarter.

The office door opened and Pete Ogden scuffed in. He gathered up the tail of his red and green plaid dressing gown to keep it from catching in the door when he closed it. "You pick a solitary way to ring in the new year, Factor," Pete said.

"Come in, come in, Pete Ogden." John set the candlestick on the desk and went to him. "Sit over here on the sofa, Lad, and put your feet up."

Pete pulled away but he did settle himself on the sofa. "You've fussed over me long enough, Doc. I'm ready to stand on my own two feet again—on the deck of a coaster."

John swung a leather chair around and sat facing Pete. "You had a close call. As your doctor, I think you'd better wait awhile before taking up your duties."

"I've waited too long. Those blasted Yankees probably started to swarm the minute I turned my back."

"No, no, they didn't. You'd made a mighty good start against their trade on the coast before you got sick."

"But we had to slash our prices to the bone to do it. That's no way to carry on a business. If I hadn't come down with this blasted fever, I'd have my prices up again by now."

"Yes, I know. But you're more important than the prices."

"Governor Simpson would hardly agree with you, Doc."

"Of course he would, Pete Ogden. Of course he would. He knows your value to the Company, in spite of the fact that he drove you so hard we almost lost you with the fever."

"Nobody's of any value to the Company unless he's on his feet and packing in furs," Pete answered. "And here you pace in the New Year, figuring every which way to hoist up profits for the Department."

"*Oui, oui,* so I must. I'm thinking I may set up a small post at The Dalles. Rumor has it that the American brig anchored there is cleaning the Indians out of furs."

Pete nodded. "Freeze out the Americans," he quoted, trying to pull his voice down to George Simpson's register.

John leaned back. "I'm not thinking about Americans as much as I am about furs and revenue. We need furs, Pete. We need friends among the Indians who were spared the epidemic. Also, I want to help them. We failed the Chinooks. Somehow I was always racing so."

Pete flapped his hand in disgust. "Factor, Americans are your big worry. You'd best forget everything else. You've heard George Simpson say a hundred times, 'Get rid of the Americans. Don't let one American get a foothold in the country.'"

"I've heard it until it's a ringing in my ears," John admitted. "But to me, the important thing is to get in furs."

"That's where you're off your base, from Simpson's point of view."

"Their honors in London want furs," John argued.

"Simpson wants Americans out of here," Pete insisted.

"All right, all right"—John tried to keep his voice patient— "but if Simpson would hurry up with that scheme of his to lease a strip of the Alaskan coast from Russia, we could dot posts at the best trading sites up that way and far outstrip the Americans when it comes to getting furs. That's the point, as I see it— increase the volume of Hudson's Bay trade until our bigness discourages Americans and anyone else seeking to cut into the fur business."

Pete swung his feet to the floor and leaned forward. "If that's how you see it, you see it all wrong. George Simpson is playing for bigger game than furs." He shrugged. "Furs, yes, he wants those. But mostly he wants this country for Great Britain. When he says, 'Freeze out Americans,' he means just that. He's never said, 'Freeze out Russians' or 'Freeze out Chinamen,' you notice. It's Americans who threaten Great Britain's claim to this land."

"Yes, yes, I've known this since our coalition meeting in London, of course. But it's a question I've always figured would be settled by governments or by history, perhaps, not by one man who decides it must be as he says."

Pete leaned back and crossed his legs. "It's my guess that down through the ages a lone man decides more of these big questions than we ever suspect. But it may be you yourself who decides this one, not George Simpson. The thing is, are you going to keep out the Americans or aren't you?"

John did not hesitate. "I'm under orders from my superior officer."

"Spoken like a true Company man," Pete approved. "Sometimes I confess you have me a mite worried on that score."

"Also," John went on, "my job is to get in furs. I don't expect many Americans to buck for long the competition I can give them. Yes, Pete, I'm under orders but my method of freezing out Americans will be to let them freeze themselves out while they sit on Hudson's Bay Company's doorstep. I believe that's as far as the gentlemen in London would ask me to go."

"Possibly." Pete nodded his agreement. "The gentlemen in London don't have George Simpson's personal reasons for crowning themselves with distinction. He'd swap his seat in the canoe to heaven for a chance to be dubbed 'Sir George.' Their titles have mostly been bestowed before this and I'd be willing to wager there's not one man on the honorable Committee who can't tell you who his mother was."

"What's this?" John had never heard Pete Ogden skirt so near the edge of gossip.

"It's common knowledge," Pete said, "that Simpson is an ambitious man. And ambition in him is made of sterner stuff than most. A title bestowed by His Royal Highness could well blot out the 'bastard' bestowed on George Simpson by his mother."

John stood up. "As you said, this is common knowledge but it makes no difference in my opinion of George Simpson. Why do you bring it up now?"

"I just want you to know that the Governor will tolerate no monkey business. When he says, 'Get rid of the Americans,' he means exactly that. Keep out Americans and the land is ours. Let them in and George Simpson will never forgive you."

"No, no, you're talking nonsense, Pete Ogden. I want no such responsibility and I think you do George Simpson a dishonor."

"Not at all. I'm for him—lock, stock, and ramrod." Pete supported himself on the arm of the sofa and got to his feet. "Now that the Indians are no longer our major problem, we've been freed to concentrate on grabbing this land for Great Britain. We'd be stupid to leave such a prize to chance. I'm with Simpson. Let's get rid of the Americans and a happy New Year to you, John McLoughlin." Pete hitched up the rope on his dressing gown and scuffed through the door.

John snuffed out the candle on his desk and stood for a moment in the dark. He had the odd feeling that he'd been handed an ultimatum and yet he hadn't. He didn't even have a choice to make. The Americans who had come out here, two and three at a time, representing lone Boston merchants for the most part, had no organization to back them up. They had no system. They didn't seem to realize, even, that they needed to set up bases on land where they could raise their own food and saw their own lumber and make friends with the Indians. No, no, the Americans were no match for him. George Simpson need not worry. The Americans would get rid of themselves, once they came up against Hudson's Bay. If the geography of nations hung on such a thing, let it. He was going to bed.

XII   Hoping for news of a beaver catch that would re-suscitate his ledger before the Company ship put out for London, John had hurried to Fort Walla Walla to welcome his trapping expedition off the Snake. Now, keyed up and impatient, he stood on the bank of the river with Pete Ogden at his side. Together they stepped back from the trail a bit so they could see the length of the Snake Brigade as it dragged itself toward the fort.

John's eyes passed over loose horses, children playing tag, and dogs darting in and out trying to join the game. He picked out, riding in the usual fixed order, clerks, postmaster, two interpreters, engaged trappers next, free trappers, and finally pack horses and families and dogs. But, behind all these, he counted twelve men, plodding up on the poorest looking nags he'd ever seen.

"How'd you make out?" he asked the leader when his lean mount ambled up.

"So-so, Factor. Mountains infested with Americans. Freemen infested with fleas in their pantaloons till I never knew was they stayin' or goin'. But we made a fair catch. Beaver jest ain't plentiful like when old Pete here led the Brigade."

John had his eye on those men at the rear. "What's that tail you're wagging back there?" he asked.

"Tail is right!" The plump, good-natured Trader dropped his voice. "They're Americans, Factor, and I'm waggin' 'em because I couldn't figure out what else to do. They was too near here when they come up with my party for me to shoo 'em back to the States. And they was gettin' theirselves scalped so fast in Blackfoot Country I just didn't have the heart to lose 'em out there. Still, I sure as shootin' know you don't want 'em." He ran a pudgy hand under his gray beaver. "Pesky mosquitoes sure take to my sparse patches of hair." He settled his hat again. "Factor,

[*147*]

you're standin' there yankin' on your ear like you're thinkin' them Americans ain't no prize package. I'm beggin' your pardon for bringin' 'em in to dump on your doorstep but what could I do?"

"Just what you did do," John assured him, "and I'll go make them welcome." Thinking he must find out at once what brought these young Americans here, he strode back along the line.

"Welcome to the Columbia Country," he said, extending his hand to the leader of the twelve.

He was a skinny blond young man, dressed in leather pantaloons and tunic and weighted with small armor—a long rifle across his saddle, two pistols and a knife in his belt, and two more rifles protruding from his saddlebag. But, his blue gaze steady, he leaned down to grip John's hand. "Just a minute, sir," he said. "I'll dismount and rest my poor horse." He came down and offered his hand once more. "Now then, you're Doctor McLoughlin and I've been hearing about you all the way from St. Louis. I'm Nathaniel Wyeth of Boston." He turned with a wave of his long arm to introduce the others. "These, sir, are my companions—as many as are left from the twenty-four who started from the States. John Ball, Calvin Tibbetts, Solomon Smith . . ."

"It's a long journey, gentlemen, and you are welcome. Come inside, come inside. A wee bit of rum will ease your aches."

Making conversation about the kind of trip they'd had while he walked with them to the compound gate, John kept wondering just what a party of twenty-five strapping young Americans could have had in mind when they loaded themselves with all that artillery and started for the Columbia.

Officers, traders, and clerks showed up at the dining hall that night decked out in their best. Decked considerably more than normal himself, John stood at the end of the long table in his black stock and white ruffled shirt. There might be, he conceded, just a nip of showing-these-Americans in his clothes tonight. The Americans, of course, wore their well-greased leather. Still, John asked Nathaniel Wyeth to sit at his right. Company officers he arranged by rank as usual but interspersed Americans among them.

While they stood, John lifted his head and closed his eyes. "Our Father, we thank you for bringing back our old friends from that hell on the Snake. *Oui, oui,* you have been good to us, too, in sending new friends who will soon be moving on. *Merci,* for all this. Amen."

They ate venison and home-grown potatoes and salmon roasted and salmon boiled. Wine flowed from glass decanters. Servants replenished the platters. Men of the Brigade told of Indian exploits to make the hair stand on end. Bruce in his Highlander's kilt and sporran promenaded round and round the table, playing the pibroch of Doniel Dhu on his bagpipes.

When the servants cleared the food away and brought in coffee, the room filled with pipe smoke, tall tales, and wit.

Finally, Pete Ogden grabbed the fire tongs, John got the shovel, and another half-dozen men caught up whatever instruments they could lay their hands on. Arranging themselves on the floor in the order of voyageurs in a canoe, they wielded their make-believe paddles in time to their lusty singing:

> *Sing nightingale, keep singing,*
> *Thou hast a heart so gay,*
> *Thou hast a heart so merry,*
> *While mine is sorrow's play.*
> *Long it is, I have loved thee:*
> *Thee, shall I love alway.*

Toward morning the men drifted off. One by one, they joined the freemen and voyageurs in their carousing in the compound. Or they ambled off to the Indian camps outside the stockade to watch the eternal gambling games and, finally, to look for stray squaws. At last, John was left before the fireplace with Pete Ogden and Nathaniel Wyeth for company.

He had been waiting for this. Now he would get at this American. If rumors he was hearing from the men were true, he needed the facts. If the rumors were true, he'd have to get rid of this Wyeth at once.

He called for Bruce and took a pinch of snuff. "Are you a

family man, Mr. Wyeth?" he asked. After all, he couldn't pin a guest against the wall and ask him what his business was in this country.

"Yes, indeed. I have the sweetest, most beautiful wife in the world."

"I challenge that statement, Mr. Wyeth. You must be speaking of my wife. Isn't that so, Mr. Ogden?"

"Could be," Pete agreed, "but now my wife—"

This tournament broke up in laughter.

"One of my men has told me you are a merchant, Mr. Wyeth," John prodded gently. "In Boston, I believe."

"Formerly in Boston, Doctor."

John asked his question with his eyebrows.

"From now on, I'm to be a merchant in Oregon, sir. Already I've fallen in love with the place. Once I get my trade under way, I intend to go back to Boston for Mrs. Wyeth. Our children will be born in this great country."

"Trade? Trade?" John stopped himself to control those confounded words that came out double.

Pete Ogden, accustomed to helping him out at these times, said, "It's a big dream you've had for yourself, Mr. Wyeth. You know about Mr. Astor, of course."

"Very well, but my plans are carefully laid. I've studied the needs of trappers and settlers. My beaver traps are all American-made, to my specifications. They weigh five pounds, have double springs, jaws without teeth, and a six-foot chain with two swivels. They're the best to be had."

"The modest American!" Pete said it with a twinkle in his eye.

John waited, still not trusting himself to speak.

"I know, gentlemen," Wyeth went on, "that Hudson's Bay Company happens to be in an enviable trade position, at the moment. And I've been told by every trapper between the Missouri and the Snake: 'Doc McLoughlin will give ye a spree and welcome ye to the Columbia like ye waar his long-lost brother. Then he'll skin the hide clean offen yer back and ship it to London afore ye can find out which way yer stick floats.' "

They had a good laugh on that.

"It's just that the first man to fire has the advantage in a duel," Pete explained. "Especially, if he happens to be a good shot. Hudson's Bay started firing a good many years ahead of you, remember."

"I'm prepared to make a place for myself," Wyeth persisted. "In time, I believe, both Indians and Whites in the Oregon Country will appreciate the opportunity to pick and choose between your goods and mine, between your prices and mine."

John felt his composure return. There should be nothing very upsetting in one young merchant trying to lug a few packs of trade goods across the mountains. "Mr. Wyeth, you have my admiration. More than that, I am inclined to agree with your theory. A bit of competition would, no doubt, help Hudson's Bay to keep her standards up and her prices down." He paused to ponder just what he had said and then nodded. Yes, he did agree with this American in theory. Still, he could not afford to agree to the point of jeopardizing the Company. "But you are a young man, Mr. Wyeth. Do you have the capital necessary to weather the starting period and carry this fight to a finish? You know, of course, that it will mean a fight—a duel, as Pete Ogden puts it."

"How in tarnation do you expect to cart enough goods across the Rocky Mountains to make even a dent in our trade?" Pete blurted.

Wyeth chose to answer John. "I have capital, Doctor. You see, there is a growing sentiment in the States against your exclusive holding of this country. As soon as I made my plans known, the money made its appearance."

"*Oui, oui, oui*"—John took a deep breath—"but we do not use pounds sterling nor even American dollars in this country. Your dollars will come off second best to hyaqua shells for hanging in the Indians' ears. The transport of trade goods is a bulky business. Mountains and vast sections of the country well nigh denuded of game stand between you and our exclusive trade in this country, Mr. Wyeth. This you will do well to consider before risking the money of your ready backers."

Wyeth stood up and hung his elbow on the mantel. "You

[*151*]

underestimate me, gentlemen. My goods are on their way by ship around the Horn. They may very well arrive at the mouth of the Columbia before I do."

"By ship?" This was different. George Simpson would not like this at all. His "Freeze out the Americans!" rang in John's ears.

Wyeth was saying, "I talked with every returning trapper I could find. I wrote letters all over the country. For instance, I happen to know that the Indians right now want green beads. Every other color is out of fashion. You know it now, of course, but you didn't know in time to have green beads shipped from England two years ago, I'll wager." His smile made this all man-to-man. "Or, take shirts. I have two hundred figured calico shirts in my ship's cargo. In spite of the demand for bright colors, Hudson's Bay Company must still try to unload its stock of drab striped shirts."

John and Pete exchanged glances that they hoped this American could not translate into the trouble they'd had, trying to dump blue and white beads this season—not to mention striped shirts.

"That's just the beginning," Wyeth went on. "That ship is carrying Spanish knives with five-and-a-half-inch blades and sets to keep them from shutting. She's carrying red cloth and oval looking-glasses and scarlet gartering and playing cards. Don't worry about me nor my backers, Doctor. When the *Sultana* sails into the Columbia, the market will be wide open."

"The *Sultana!*" Pete squeaked.

"No, no, Mr. Wyeth. Not the *Sultana!*"

Both men, on their feet now, turned away.

John simply did not have the heart to tell him. When he turned back, Pete had the young man against the fireplace.

"Your ship went down in the South Seas," he blurted.

John hurried over to grasp Wyeth's hand. "It's a confounded, low-down shame, my lad. We can't make up your loss, either in goods or expectation, but you must be my guest at Fort Vancouver until the next East-bound Express. It will be a pleasure to entertain you and your men. You shall make our post your home for as long as you like."

Gracious and well-mannered even under this crushing blow, Wyeth thanked them and said he would like to walk for a time, alone.

"What will the Governor say to your entertaining Americans at the post?" Pete wanted to know.

"That poor young man," John answered.

"Poor is right," Ogden agreed, "but he's a smart one, too. Look out you don't feel so sorry for him you give him a foothold in the country or there'll be the Governor to settle with."

"I can buy up whatever goods Wyeth brought overland," John mused.

"At his price," Pete pointed out. "And the Governor says, 'Freeze out the Americans. Whatever you do, don't let them get a foothold.' You know as well as I do, Doc, whichever government holds this country when that boundary is decided will get the lion's share. George Simpson is dead right about that."

"Suppose I admit that the Governor is right, from one point of view?"

"There's no point of view that concerns us except the Company's," Pete insisted.

"Maybe not, maybe not. But, Company man or not, I'm still a human being and I feel sorry for young Wyeth."

" 'Sorry' is a luxury the same as imported mustard, Doc."

Frowning, John stepped to the hearth and dropped a hand on Pete's shoulder. "You've changed, Pete Ogden, since our Nor'wester days together. You've changed."

"Sure I've changed," Pete agreed. "I'm smarter. I used to talk too much and think too little. Now I don't need to think. I just do as I'm told."

"I have a feeling a man's obligated to think things through for himself."

"Me, I'm obligated to the Company," Pete answered. "I get farther that way."

John decided to follow Wyeth's example and take a walk. He angled over to the river and struck off upstream. He wished he were at Fort Vancouver. He'd like to see the sun come up to touch the face of Mount Hood with a rim of silver. He had to think.

Only last week Eloise had met him at the parlor door and flung her arms around him.

"*Papa*, it's time for the trapping brigades to be coming in. There'll be dances and parties. I simply must have a new silk gown."

"But, my bonnie lass, I simply do not have faille at the store nor in the warehouse in next year's goods. You'll have to do without or decide on striped calico."

Eloise had dropped her arms from around him and moved to the window. "*Papa?*"

"*Oui?*"

"Why couldn't it be that there would be two stores or maybe three in this country? Then when Hudson's Bay didn't have silk, I could perhaps row across the river and take a beaver skin or two with me so I could buy what I wanted at one of the other stores. Why couldn't it be like that, *Papa?*"

At the time he had put her off with an answer that answered nothing and he was well aware of that because now he, too, wanted to know. Why couldn't it be? Why shouldn't it be, for that matter? This was open country until the boundary was settled. And yet here he was under orders to "Get rid of the Americans."

Before, he had accepted Simpson's order as an impersonal Company policy. It was something decided at the mahogany table on Fenchurch Street and carried out in the Columbia Department against a few vaguely lumped Yankees. But now, here was this fine young man who had fallen in love with the country, a man who wanted his children to be born in Oregon, a man with horse sense. And he happened to be an American. Carrying out that order against Nathaniel Wyeth rubbed against the grain.

"Confound it!" John said aloud. "No American has a right to put me in such a predicament."

THREE

XIII

Standing on the dock at Fort Vancouver, John settled his beaver to shade his eyes against the September noonday sun. "As good as his word, confound his American hide!"

"Whose hide, sir?" James Douglas asked.

"Nathaniel Wyeth's." John pointed to the lead canoe in the long express brigade. "There he is, big as life, in spite of all my warnings. You remember him, Jamie, that stubborn Yankee trader whose goods went down with the *Sultana*."

Jamie removed his beaver to hold it against the shimmer of the sun on the water. "Yes, sir, I remember although I was off on inspection trips and building new forts most of his stay here." His black eyes narrowed. "I thought you warned him when he left that Hudson's Bay would not tolerate a rival trader in this country."

"So I did. So I did. I told him in no uncertain terms that if he came back it would be my unpleasant duty to break him. Now, he has left me no choice."

When Wyeth docked and took John's hand he said, "You'll never guess what I've brought you this time, Doctor."

"If I were a gambling man, I'd take you there, Nathaniel Wyeth. What you have brought me is trouble, trouble, trouble, I'll be bound. I dare you to deny it."

Wyeth grinned and nodded. "Trouble, sure. That goes without saying. But trouble dressed in buckskin or trouble in woven cloth? Which do you guess?"

"Either way, I win," John said, "but, looking at you, I pick you for business rival and trouble both. I take buckskin."

"You lose, Doctor, and I take this as an omen for my future in the Oregon Country. Those five Americans out there on the dock in woven cloth are missionaries."

[*157*]

"Missionaries!"

"Methodists," Wyeth said. "They've heard the Indians out this way are ripe for religion."

"Missionaries! Imagine that! Well, well, Mr. Wyeth, bring them here, bring them here." John turned to Jamie as soon as Wyeth got lost in the clutter of people and dogs. "Trouble, perhaps, but what trouble can five missionaries stir up compared with fifty bustling Americans bent on cutting into our trade? Mark my word, Jamie, that Wyeth means trading."

"Yes, sir, I'm afraid he does."

When Jason Lee held back from the general invitation to the dining hall for a regale of rum, John invited the five Methodists and Nathaniel Wyeth to join him and James Douglas in his office over a cup of tea. Now that his guests had been served, John scraped his chair back from his desk and tilted it against the wall.

The Reverend Jason Lee wore such a quantity of hair on his head and face that John found it difficult to size him up as readily as he could a clean-shaven man. Jason Lee's brows marched straight as a palisade guarding his deep-set eyes, but his eyes had a trick of wandering off as if the man had forgotten what was going on around him and was contemplating the hereafter. Sometimes, when this happened, John had the feeling that Lee was particularly spiritual. At other times, he seemed merely preoccupied.

Lee's nephew, Daniel, clearly worshiped his uncle even to the point of parting his hair on the right and bobbing it off, straight and bushy, halfway down his ears. Given time, Daniel's hedge of beard would conceal as much as his uncle's.

The other three Americans John could not help comparing with his own assistant. Jamie, straight as a square-rigged mast, his black hair brushed and gleaming, sat on a bench in the background now; but he spoke to the servants in their own dialect whenever necessary to fill each guest's desires. The Americans, by comparison, fidgeted and crossed their legs and ran their fingers through their hair. And their clothes did not fit.

Travelers coming in from the overland trip were always so

filled with tales of short rations and long droughts that John had learned to turn them over and empty them of these before he tried to pump from them intelligence regarding American markets, or the temper of political feeling in the East. But these men had ridden harder, walked farther, gotten up earlier, and made more of the trip without a guide than any John had ever welcomed off the trail.

"But Mr. Wyeth, here, had been over the mountains," John protested. "He should be as trail-wise as any scout."

"When he stopped to build his fort on the Snake," Jason Lee explained, "that's when we came ahead by horseback to Fort Walla Walla."

"What's this, what's this?" John turned to Wyeth. "Come, Nathaniel. Out with it, out with it."

"You have built a trading post on the Snake, Mr. Wyeth?" Jamie's voice, slow and easy, gave the whole business the kind of slight that it deserved and that John's excitement would not permit.

"A clear case of necessity being the mother of a trading post," Wyeth answered. "We started out with a consignment of goods and a contract with the American Fur Company to deliver the stuff to them in the mountains. When we got there, the Company had new management and I had the goods." He turned to John. "Surely, not even you, Factor, would have me pack rifles and beaver traps and bolts of calico across a hundred river fords and through that volcanic wilderness between Farewell Bend and the Blues."

"No, no, no. Certainly not. But—" John stopped and said more to himself than to Wyeth, "you'd be better off if the desert had swallowed them—as the sea swallowed your trade goods two years ago."

Douglas inquired, "Where on the Snake did you locate, Mr. Wyeth?"

"At the junction of the Portneuf—a drier, more desolate spot you'd never find. But we concocted a flag from unbleached sheeting, some bits of red flannel, and a few blue patches. It makes quite a show."

"Quite a show, quite a show, no doubt! If anyone happens along to see it." John could hear Simpson's voice: "Freeze him out. Starve him out. By hook or crook, get rid of him." Well, no two ways about it, he'd have to buy Wyeth out on the Snake.

Douglas said, "Then the *May Dacre* lying off Sauvies Island is loaded with your goods, Mr. Wyeth. Can it be that you did not learn how difficult it is to compete with Hudson's Bay Company when you were here last?"

"Come now, gentlemen. You wouldn't call that competing, would you?" Wyeth smiled as he spoke and John could not find it in him to dislike the man.

Life would be so much simpler, John concluded, if the people he liked would stay out of the enterprises he was forced to fight.

"I hope you don't plan to enter the fur trade," Douglas persisted.

"That I do. But I also plan to pack and ship salmon. Surely there's room for two of us in that business, Mr. Douglas. My records show that Hudson's Bay Company hasn't done too well on Columbia River salmon. Am I right?"

John thumped the front legs of his chair to the floor, got up slowly, and walked over to stand above his guest. "Nathaniel, let's not be foolhardy."

The Bostonian suddenly bristled. "It's open country, Doctor."

"Open country but a closed fight," John soothed. "My Company won't tolerate your venture."

Wyeth sprang up and strode to the window. He blurted, "Tolerate be damned! You blasted Britons forget you tried to dictate to Yankees in Boston harbor—and failed. Your cutthroat Company will find my men just as independent as the Yankees from Bunker Hill to Yorktown."

John felt his temples throb but he admired Wyeth's spunk. He went to stand beside him at the window and pointed toward the *May Dacre*. "Let's talk cold facts," he said, "about your stock of goods down there. I'm willing to take over your plunder and include you in the deal to run a post we can build up the Willamette. That's the smart way out of this for you. As I told you two years ago, I'm under orders to undersell and overbid competitors in the fur trade."

"I also have orders from my backers, McLoughlin." Wyeth stood tall. His eyes held John's. "Straight out, I intend to anchor the *May Dacre* right where she is and build a post across there on Sauvies Island. The first year we'll catch and salt salmon. We'll ship to Yerba Buena and Monterey as a beginning. Later, we'll win the Russians from caviar to salmon and lick the pantaloons right off you beaver trappers."

John's nails dug into his clenched fists. Then slowly he relaxed. "Well now, my cocksure friend, just how do you propose to ship salmon without barrels? Before I take you to the wharf to inspect the stores of my salmon house, it becomes my unpleasant duty to point out to you that the Company coopers can turn out all the barrels we need. But the honorable Company will not be able to supply you with hoops—nor with iron to make your own."

Wyeth's gray gaze did not falter.

The man had guts, then. "Perhaps," John said with a grin, "you are salesman enough to sell me your post on the Snake."

"Thank you, sir," Wyeth said with a touch of scorn, "but you don't need to pity me nor protect me. I'll make out on my own." He gathered up his hat and coat. Abruptly, he turned to Jason Lee. "Reverend, let me warn you against this monstrous system. It—and the good Doctor—will be hospitable. But in the end they will gobble you up or try to buy you out body and soul."

Jason Lee, a little pale behind his black beard, cleared his throat. "It appears to me, Mr. Wyeth, that my party is in a better position than yours. Hudson's Bay Company can hardly claim to be in opposition to us Methodists."

When the general laugh died down John said, "I wouldn't be too sure on that score, Mr. Lee. I've had to tutor my own children since we came to this country and I've been conducting two services each Sunday. The Company has intended to send us a chaplain and teacher but, so far, he hasn't arrived. So, I'm your competition, too, as well as Mr. Wyeth's."

[*161*]

"What did I tell you?" Wyeth said. "There's nothing the Company won't set a trap for."

John dropped into the chair at his desk and laced his fingers into a hammock for the back of his head. He watched Wyeth's face but went on talking to Jason Lee. "Sunday mornings, I read the Anglican service and a sermon from some book or, occasionally, I give a feeble talk of my own concoction. I get all the Scotch Presbyterians, the Sandwich Islanders, and a good number who are nothing much in particular. Sunday afternoons, I read Catholic prayers for the French-Canadians. You Methodists may find your theology more consistent than mine but I dare you to find it more persistent."

Even while he talked, John knew that Jason Lee had hit upon a point. As head of the Columbia Department, he must uphold Hudson's Bay Company against any and all traders. But missionaries were different. His own Company had failed the Chinooks. Suddenly these five bearded Americans in their long black coats and boiled shirts seemed sent just now for the express purpose of giving his conscience an out. By the nature of things, he must hand Wyeth or any other trader a good trouncing. But a missionary was a horse of a different color.

"Just where do you plan to locate, Mr. Lee?" James Douglas asked.

"We'll find him a place," John volunteered. "I hope you plan to open a school, Mr. Lee. This country needs schools."

Eloise knocked and then flung open the door and came in before Nathaniel Wyeth could quite get out of the way.

"Pardon, *m'sieu,*" she said with a smile as sunny as her ruffled yellow calico. "I hope I have not hurt you. I am the awkward one in our family."

John went to her to make the introductions but Eloise whirled and opened the door again. "One moment, *Papa,* here is Petit Chief Factor, too. I got so excited at having visitors and a message to deliver that I almost forgot."

Charlefoux's boy swiped at the blond curls flopping over his forehead and stood chewing on something in his jaw that gave him the appearance of a chipmunk with his cheeks full of nuts.

"Come in, come in, Laddie," John said. "I can make all the introductions at once." He laid one arm around Eloise's shoulders. "This, gentlemen, is my daughter, Marie Eloise." He dropped his free hand on the boy's head. "And this is Petit Chief Factor, a young friend of ours." He named each of the gentlemen and felt a real glow of pride as Eloise, who had few chances to practice company manners, curtsied and repeated the names after him with all the poise of any young lady of Paris. He must remember to commend Marguerite on the fine training she had given their daughter.

Petit Chief Factor had his mouth too full to speak. Instead, he made a slow turn in the middle of the office, inspecting each strange-looking man in sequence. Then, he rammed his hand into his pantaloon pocket, made a beeline for Jason Lee, pulled out his hand, and with a fat-cheeked smile, offered a gift to seal this new friendship.

"How do you do, young man," Jason Lee said and extended his hand for a shake.

Petit Chief Factor laid in it his gift.

"What's this?" Jason Lee asked and then suggested tentatively, "An acorn?"

The boy, evidently fascinated by Lee's beard, kept watching his mouth. When Jason Lee did not eat his offering, Petit Chief Factor took out the thing he had been chewing on and held it for his new friend to see.

"Oh, it is to eat. Is that it?" Lee raised the acorn to his mouth, chewed down on it, and John saw his lips pucker for an instant before he turned on a smile for the boy.

"*Bon, bon,*" Petit Chief Factor approved with a delighted grin.

John, thinking he had judged his man well—even through the beard—if children liked him, woke up almost too late to the fact that Jason Lee had said, "Acorn." He lunged over and walloped Lee on the back. The acorn plopped from his mouth and across the room.

Eyes blazing, Jason Lee sprang from his chair.

Nathaniel Wyeth came in ready to fight.

"I'm sorry, Mr. Lee," John apologized. He wanted to explain but not before Eloise.

Coldly Wyeth said, "I think Mr. Lee deserves an apology and an explanation."

"*Oui, oui*, he does."

Petit Chief Factor scampered across the room, found the acorn, and hurried back to Jason Lee, offering it again.

"No, no!" John took the boy by the shoulders and turned him toward the door. "Eloise, it is time for Petit Chief Factor to go," he said pointedly.

The boy burst into loud wails.

"*Oui, oui, Papa.*" Eloise had to shout to make herself heard. "And I came to say—" She squatted and put her arm around Charlefoux's boy. "There, there, don't cry, *chéri*. I have a message and no one will be able to hear it, if you cry so."

He screamed all the louder.

John clamped a hand over the boy's mouth. "*Oui, oui*, you came to say what?"

"That the gentlemen's luggage has been taken to their rooms and *Maman* says you should give them time to freshen up before they eat."

"Of course, of course." John crowded Eloise and the child through the door. He turned back to his visitors. "Bruce is waiting in the hall to show you to your rooms. We want you to make this your home for as long as you like."

"One moment." Wyeth took up a stand with his back against the office door. "What was that business about the acorn? It strikes me you were pretty high-handed both with the child and with Mr. Lee."

"*Oui, oui*, I was, Mr. Wyeth, but I had my reasons. You'll enjoy your dinner more, if I explain later."

Jason Lee said, "I've chewed on many a bitter acorn in my day, Doctor. I'd chew on many more to please a child and win a friend."

"Not that kind," John said. "That was a Chinook olive."

Wyeth held his place against the door. "It looked like an acorn to me," he insisted.

John turned on him. "Mr. Wyeth, it was an acorn. An acorn pickled in urine, if you must know. I bungled the whole thing and scared Mr. Lee half out of his beard, I know. But Chinook olives are a sore point with me. They stand in my mind for all the filth and degradation in which Chinook Indians have lived through the ages. They're a sore point with me because I should have been able to lift these people to a better way of living and I haven't. I've tried but I've been short-handed and, yes, I admit it, short-tempered. I've failed." He swung around to Jason Lee. "It's for that reason that I'm delighted to welcome you and your associates, Mr. Lee."

"Thank you, Doctor, but—"

"This country needs you. Our people need schools and churches. They need an example of clean, decent living. They need standards. Yes, yes, Mr. Lee, I'll see that you find the best location for your work. I'll provide you with seeds and farming equipment. I'll let you have bateaux to transport yourselves and your goods." John saw Jamie's black brows lift in a reprimand for these extravagant promises.

"Perhaps we should let the gentlemen freshen up," Jamie murmured and Wyeth stood away when he moved to the door.

Jason Lee said nothing but he gave John his hand.

John watched them follow Bruce up the hall. *Oui, oui,* he'd like living with himself far better if he could stake the Methodists to seed and cattle and plows to make up, in a way, for what he must do to Nathaniel Wyeth. Wyeth must fail in his attempt to set up a rival trading establishment. But, in spite of everything, the Methodists would succeed in this country. He'd send them to the Willamette.

He went back to his desk to glance through the mail. Perhaps a letter from Jacques had arrived with the travelers. There would be, naturally, further orders from George Simpson. He never missed a mail opportunity.

Ready for bed two nights later, John stood by the window looking out over the palisade and toward the shifting billows of cloud that never quite separated enough for him to see Mount

[*165*]

Hood in the moonlight. He heard the rope lacings squeak and rub as Marguerite climbed into the fourposter. But the old wound in his back was tightening up on him and no amount of working his shoulder in its socket seemed to help.

What did Governor Simpson expect anyway? His letter, arriving with the same caravan as the Methodists, sounded half irrational with its rantings against Americans: "I hear they're crossing the mountains in spite of our fur desert on the Snake. Americans! Always on the go whether there's anything to go for or not. See that your men at Fort George have sufficient ammunition for whatever emergencies might arise. Above all, don't let Americans settle north of the river. No, not even south of the river. I'm working on plans for that country."

John had plans of his own for that country, if only the Governor would let up a little and give him a chance to see them through. He'd been trying for five years to get his mills under way at the Falls of the Willamette. The Methodists, once they started building and plowing, would plant the beginnings of civilization in that valley and John wanted that above all else.

This was his country. It presented a chance granted few men—a chance to shape a way of life. In that rich valley with its excess of power in soil and water, every human being could make a good living for himself—yes, even the Indians, once they were taught. Any man's son could make his own way and grow up as good as the next one, if he proved it. Surely Simpson must have been sick or worked up about something else when he wrote that letter.

"The Methodist, Mr. Lee, seems very pleasant," Marguerite commented from the bed. "He spoke tonight of how good were the melons we gave them for their first meal here. We talked together on other matters, also. It was kind of him to remember about the melons."

"I'm sending them to the Willamette," John told her. "A good thing, too, getting them south of the river, considering Governor Simpson's latest bombast against Americans."

"This George Simpson is having trouble closer at hand than any Americans, according to the rumor."

"Rumor? About Governor Simpson?"

"The air is full of it."

If the Governor was having trouble, that could explain it. John crossed the splintered floor and stood above Marguerite. "What trouble?"

"About his new wife," Marguerite answered, "and his old one. The Company men at Red River Settlement are saying that this George Simpson is too swelled up for his pantaloons when he must set aside his half-breed wife and bring to Red River a young English girl. The Company men say it is a slap in their face. They do not invite this new English girl to their parties. They do not even speak."

"This must be very hard on all of them," John said. "I'm sorry it has happened this way."

"They say that he takes this English girl because he expects to become Sir George. They say that this George Simpson's half-breed wife from the Provinces made him pay a big dowry and find her a good husband before she would leave." Marguerite paused. "Does this not serve him right, Johnny?"

"I don't know, I don't know. Perhaps it does, in a way. But who am I to decide?"

"And who is he to decide whether you do right or wrong?"

"He is the Governor, *ma chérie*, and I felt sure, when I read his tirade about keeping Americans to the south, that he must be half out of his mind over something. This rumor might help to explain it." John untied his dressing gown. Perhaps he could go to sleep now.

"Johnny."

"*Oui.*"

"Now that we have a minister here—our much hairy Mr. Lee—perhaps we could be married."

"By the auld Cloots!" John climbed into bed. "How many times do I have to tell you that we are married?" But when he reached across to draw Marguerite to him, she had scrambled over the blankets and off the foot of the bed. "Marguerite, what's got into you?"

She stood by the window. "I think I prefer not to live in sin," she said.

"Damn that Jason Lee's chin whiskers!" John exploded.

[*167*]

XIV True to his promise, George Simpson sent his hand-picked chaplain to Fort Vancouver. John was annoyed that the Company should let the Methodists beat it to the draw. Still, the Lees were building near the Falls of the Willamette. Simpson's chaplain, on the other hand, would find plenty of pupils to teach and sinners to preach to within Vancouver's stockade. Relieved at having help at last, John ignored his first impression of the strait-laced little chaplain. He made him superintendent of the school and turned over all religious duties to him.

But the chaplain had been in charge of the school only one week when Pete Ogden, his face red from held-back laughter, stomped into the office. "Well, well, there you are, you heathen you."

John looked up from his letter to the Trader at Fort Simpson on the Nass and laid the quill across it. "All right, out with it, before you explode," he prompted.

Pete made his face stern. "I've just been teaching one of the schoolboys to saw a straight line."

John picked up his quill. He knew this wasn't what Pete had come to say. "*Oui, oui,* so you're a big help in these parts," he gibed. "When you can teach the schoolgirls to sew a straight seam, I'll recommend you for a chief factorship."

With a glance around for eavesdroppers, Pete leaned close to whisper behind his hand, "Doc, I hear that you're opposed to the inculcation of female chastity. That schoolboy is asking everybody what it means."

With the quill already in his hand, John wrote out the chaplain's dismissal from his teaching duties.

John tried through the summer and fall to disregard his own eyes and Marguerite's hints that this George Simpson had, perhaps, hand-picked this chaplain for some private purpose. Then he read his delayed copy of a report the chaplain had sent to London months before:

"The tyrant at the head of affairs here is leading a most immoral life in open defiance of the laws of God and man. He altogether discourages marriage and keeps as a mistress a squaw called Marguerite—a female of notoriously loose character."

John sent the chaplain packing. Simpson could like it or not.

Simpson would like his getting rid of Nathaniel Wyeth, no question about that. John stood in the center of Wyeth's warehouse on Sauvies Island with the American's inventory sheets in his hand and asked, "But where are the plows you list here? So far, I have not seen one plow."

Wyeth came over, jerked a pencil from behind his ear, and scratched "plows" off the list.

John waited for an explanation, but when Wyeth offered none, he went on. "Seed corn, twenty bushels; seed peas, thirty-two bushels; melon seed, three pecks; wheat—"

"No, no, that's all gone," Wyeth interrupted. He pulled out the drawer of a long work-table and produced another set of inventory sheets. "Here. This is the list you should have."

John stepped back. "What's going on here, Wyeth? This thing looks a wee bit crooked and yet I'd stake my soul on your integrity. I've had to fight you, my lad, but there's never been anything personal in it. We've been the best of friends and I'll miss you like a brother when you're gone. I'm sure you can explain this business of two different inventories."

"I can, of course." Wyeth pointed out the date on the list he held—March 30, 1836.

John's inventory was dated two weeks before. "But what happened?"

"A good many of my men have decided to stay in the Oregon Country," Wyeth said. "Those and a few I brought out my first trip—Solomon Smith, Cal Tibbetts, John Ball—needed plows and seed and livestock. They've loaded up and gone to the Willamette, Doctor."

John pushed back his beaver. "Gone to the Willamette, have they?" He crossed his arms and propped himself against a packing box. He could see George Simpson's aloof smile, hear his, "Get rid of the Americans." He said, "Good, Nathaniel. Good, Lad. Your men will make steady, hard-working farmers. I'll do what I can to help them. Now if you yourself would send for Mrs. Wyeth—"

"I'm a merchant, Doctor, and merchants don't have a chance in this country right now. But I warn you, this state of affairs will not go on forever. For the moment, Hudson's Bay can beat down any trade opposition. You've proved it at the price of my hide." He grinned. *"Pro Pelle Cutem,"* he added under his breath.

"I'm paying you well for your goods, Nathaniel. I was under no obligation to buy you out here nor on the Snake and yet I've made you generous offers for both posts."

"True. Hudson's Bay insists on its monopoly—in the most civilized way, of course. So, I'm a trader and you're buying me out. But I suggest that you don't try to buy out men who are building homes here."

"You're wrong about me, if you think I'll oppose settlers, Nathaniel. I'm for them. I helped Jason Lee get located on the Willamette and made him a loan of livestock. I'm helping the latest shipment of Methodists to set up homes and clear the land. I'll do the same for your men."

"Doctor, you're helping settlers, all right, but you're not seeing this thing big enough. You're seeing the country colonized like any number of Great Britain's tributaries." Wyeth shook his head. "That's not it at all. What you're getting here are free men, building homes. First thing you know they'll be telling you what price you'll pay for their wheat and, if you don't, they'll dump it in the Willamette. How long do you think your all-powerful trade monopoly will hold out, King John, once they start munching on their own wheat straws and quoting Thomas Jefferson behind their own barns?"

John straightened and settled his hat square on his head. "Nathaniel, you're full of big talk about Americans this morning but may I remind you that your Boston backers sat with their hands in their pockets when you needed additional men and money to make your way in this country. Somehow, their example and your big talk don't disturb me much."

"These men who are settling out here are not dependent on Boston backers," Wyeth answered. "They're dependent on God and their plows. I wouldn't underestimate a combination like that, once it digs into this rich Oregon soil."

"Come, come, Nathaniel. We both love this country and believe in her future." John waved toward the lists. "Decide which inventory we're dealing with," he said with a grin, "and I'll draw you a draft on London to cover this and Fort Hall on the Snake."

Wyeth selected the March 30 inventory and handed it to John. "I hear there's another party of missionaries due any day now off the overland trail."

"*Oui, oui.*" John sighed. "A doctor and a preacher with their assorted wives. A runner from Fort Walla Walla brought the news."

"And women coming overland don't worry a fur trader whose business depends on keeping the country wild?" Wyeth asked.

John ducked through the warehouse door and waited for Wyeth to secure the lock. "I confess I've been thinking of some excuse for sending them on to the Sandwich Islands. Soon we'll have one missionary for every farmer in this country, like a Welsh rabbit—one rabbit to one Welshman."

"A minister and a doctor, this time," John reported to Marguerite in the parlor, "and their wives. Sent across the mountains by some American missionary society."

When a groan escaped him, Marguerite laid down her knitting to suggest a wee glass of wine.

"But what will I do with them? When Jason Lee came I saw a chance to get on with my dreams for the Willamette without waiting till I could go there myself and start developing that soil and water power."

"Well then, if you can send also these newcomers to the Willa-

[*171*]

mette, will it not mean two more houses and more fenced fields without waiting?" Marguerite asked.

"I don't know. Perhaps." John felt better. But at the cry, "Brigade! Brigade is coming," he rounded up Jamie and his other officers with a reluctant "We'll have to give these new missionaries an official welcome, no more."

Expecting the worst, they trudged to the dock.

John recognized, all right, the Fort Walla Walla Indians and half-breeds who manned the first canoe. But there must be some mistake about the identity of the passengers.

The first man onto the dock was a clean-faced young giant who crushed John's hand and turned to assist a young lady who could never, by any stretch of the imagination, be a missionary.

John managed his usual, "I'm John McLoughlin. Welcome to Fort Vancouver," but he himself could hear more astonishment than greeting in it.

"I'm Marcus Whitman," the young man said, "and this is Mrs. Whitman."

"We've heard of you, Doctor McLoughlin, all the way from the States." The young lady's voice did not belong to John's pre-conceived missionary any more than her flame-touched hair and her lively blue eyes.

The other young lady who stepped from the canoe could be a missionary, he decided, plain but of the most kindly and under-standing sort. And her husband, Henry Spalding, wore almost as many dark whiskers as Jason Lee, so he could be a minister. "A minister with muscles," John revised the conclusion when Mr. Spalding gripped his hand.

The Whitmans and the Spaldings so disarmed John that he led them to the house by way of an animated tour through his orchard and gardens. Doctor Whitman asked a hundred knowing questions about crops and soil and seasons. Henry Spalding praised the lumber in their buildings and the trees he'd watched day after day as they had come downriver. Narcissa Whitman caught her breath at the view of Mount Hood from the portico. There was wonder and a beauty that John had missed at first in

[*172*]

Eliza Spalding when her pale hand reached out to touch a cluster of grapes.

John had to tell Marguerite about all this at once. Sending Bruce to show the guests to their rooms, he hurried up the hall.

He burst into the parlor. "Marguerite, where are you, where are you?"

He found her with Eloise in the bedroom. Billows of white twill made it hard to separate them so he hugged them both.

"*Papa*, be careful." Eloise rescued the silk and piled it on the bed. "You're mighty disrespectful toward my wedding gown," she chided and then wrapped her arms around him. "*Papa*, we haven't seen you all day."

John gave her a spank. "A lot you care. You've probably spent all afternoon keeping that clerk, William Rae, from his work the same as you did yesterday."

"Why, *Papa!* How can you say such a thing? I barely saw Billy all day yesterday."

"You're the excuse he gave me for his unfinished letters," John persisted but without conviction. He had little respect for a young man who blamed someone other than himself for his shortcomings. John turned to Marguerite. "You didn't come down to the dock to see the new missionaries," he said.

"I have seen missionaries before," she answered with more than a wisp of innuendo in her tilted glance.

"I don't think you have," he said. "Not until you've seen Mrs. Whitman." He could hold back his elation no longer. "Do you know, those two women rode sidesaddle across the continent. There's guts and gumption in these people—men and women both. You can tell it by the way they talk about this country. Imagine two women riding horseback all that way! But you may see for yourself. I won't spoil it by telling you how they look."

"Like Indian scouts?" Marguerite ventured.

John guffawed.

"Well, why not, with all that riding in the dust and sun?" Eloise argued.

"You'll see," John promised. "I've sent them to their rooms to freshen up now, but tomorrow we'll all put on our best bibs and

[*173*]

tuckers and mount our highest stepping horses for a ride up the Willamette. I can't wait to show the Whitmans and Spaldings where they'll make their new home."

"They have turned you to hoping once again for houses and plowed fields beside the Falls of the Willamette," Marguerite murmured. "Is it that the Methodists are too slow to suit you?"

"These newcomers love this country the way we do, *chérie*. They see it both for what it is and for what it can become."

"This George Simpson will not object to these Americans?"

"He may object on the ground that they're Americans. But I'll keep them south of the Columbia and everything will be all right."

John found Narcissa Whitman on the portico when he went out the next morning. She stood alone beside a pillar festooned with purple grapes and her eyes were fixed on Mount Hood in its morning wrapper of lavender mist. Mrs. Whitman wore a green poplin riding habit. Her bonnet hung from its streamers looped around her arm. A special ray of sunlight turned to spun copper the heavy chignon on her neck. Struck by the fairness of her skin, John found it hard to make himself believe that she had ridden through the sun and dust across a continent.

"Good morning, Doctor." Her voice fairly sang. "I'm as bad as the Indians you were telling us about at dinner yesterday. Already I've purloined this view of your mountain and I'm thinking strongly of pilfering a bunch of grapes."

John cut the vine's largest cluster of grapes and presented it with a flourish and a bow. "I hope you rested well, *madame*. If so, however, you may be the only one at Fort Vancouver who could sleep last night. Your coming has brought us more excitement than we've had in many a moon."

"Excitement?"

"*Oui, oui*, excitement. The men in Bachelor's Hall forgot their pipes to spruce themselves with bear grease and razors. As for my wife and daughter, they can scarcely wait to meet you."

"And I am just as eager to meet your family," Narcissa Whitman assured him. "I had hoped to see them in the dining hall."

"That, for some reason, is not our custom, Mrs. Whitman."

"Oh?"

John puzzled on that a moment. "Don't know just why, come to think of it, but Company men and any outside guests have always eaten together in the dining hall while our families eat in their private quarters."

"I see," Mrs. Whitman murmured and it sounded very much as if she didn't see at all. "But Mrs. McLoughlin and your daughter will ride with us today?"

"Yes, yes, of course. I hear them now."

Marguerite's moccasins, as stiff from their blue and white beads as a man's leather boots, barely made a whisper in the hallway but John could always feel it in his pulses when she came near. He stepped to the door and held out his hand.

Marguerite wore for riding a full shirt of fine blue broadcloth and a deerskin tunic. When she sat astride her pony John felt sure he'd see, for this momentous occasion, the new deerskin leggings that his wife had spent weeks embroidering in every shade of silk. Even her eyes wore a special excited gleam this morning.

"Mrs. Whitman, may I present my wife?"

Narcissa Whitman extended her hand. "Mrs. McLoughlin, how nice to meet you. I hope we can ride side by side so we can get acquainted."

"*Merci.*" Marguerite sounded diffident but John saw her delighted sideways glance confirm his judgment of Mrs. Whitman.

"And this, even though we find it hard to believe ourselves, is our grown-up daughter, Eloise."

John and Marguerite both had grave doubts about their daughter's impending marriage but the excitement of a wedding had touched Eloise with sheen and glimmer. Her black merino habit should have toned her down but, somehow, served to make her airy as milkweed on a slender stem.

She cut her curtsy short to cry, "Mrs. Whitman! What a lovely wedding ring. I hope mine is as wide as yours for everybody in the whole world to see."

Narcissa Whitman's laugh tripped up the scale. "Wide is all

[*175*]

right," she said, "but my wedding band has become too big around since we left the States. I live in fear of losing it."

At the sound of steps in the hallway, John said, "Good. Here is Mrs. Spalding." He made the introductions and cut another bunch of grapes. "Nothing like topping off a three-thousand-mile horseback ride with an all-day canter, ladies." He led the way down the steps and across the fort yard where Henry Spalding and Marcus Whitman stood inspecting a pair of millstones he had been saving to send to the Willamette.

When they started for the river, Eloise held back. "Billy feels abused because you wouldn't let him go along, *Papa*. I'm staying with him."

"Stay then," John snapped and got a reprimanding glance from Marguerite. But, paddling across the river, he put aside his worry about Eloise and her choice for a husband. He kept noticing how Marguerite and Narcissa Whitman and Eliza Spalding chatted and laughed as easily as if they'd all grown up together back in New York State.

When they mounted the waiting horses and rode the Indian trail up the east bank of the Willamette, the men discussed the soil and dismounted now and then to sift it through their fingers; the women planned wedding cakes and petticoats and "something borrowed, something blue."

John saw Marguerite's heightened color and heard her laughter follow Mrs. Whitman's up the scale. It struck him that Marguerite had possibly been lonesome all these years in this man's country. The idea had never occurred to him before. But today, Marguerite had made two friends and John saw a difference in her.

John, too, had found a pair of kindred spirits. He and Marcus Whitman compared notes on medical advances in the States and on the Continent as Jacques had written of them from Paris. At the Falls, both Spalding and Whitman agreed with John regarding the future of this country.

"Hardly seems possible you'd find an island ready-made at the crest of the falls to set your mills on," Marcus Whitman said. "Almost too perfect."

Henry Spalding pointed with a bony middle finger. "Looks like a millrace yonder."

"I had that blasted out some years ago," John told them. "Keep thinking every summer I'll get the time to go ahead with my plans here. Those squared timbers there are for my gristmill, once I get at it."

As usual, scattered bands of Indians fished and loafed beside the Falls and played their game of "hand." Their incessant gambling song: "He hah ha," wailed on and on to the accompaniment of monotonous drumming on a hollow log.

"Someday—" John's wave took in his two claimed sections. He seldom talked to anyone about what he had in mind. He'd never mentioned it to the Methodists. But these men, somehow, seemed the very ones to get things started in the way he wanted. Sane men they were with gumption and they both had wives equal to founding a cultured, civilized community. "Someday," he repeated, "there'll be a city here beside these Falls. I'm saving land to donate for schools and churches and a library—"

The Chief of the Chamifus who lived between the forks of the Yamhill River interrupted then. He brought his youngest wife to John and pointed out the sores on her head. Together, John and Marcus Whitman drained out pus and applied spirits of turpentine.

Before the chief led his wife away, five of the Chemeketas who lived above the Falls came to greet their old friend, the King George man, and ask for counsel. What did the King George man consider proper punishment for a young blade of their village caught in the act of wife stealing? they wanted to know.

The idea of hobbling him like a horse each night had not occurred to them and they would try it.

"You see," John said when they had gone, "this location for your mission station offers every kind of opportunity. Indians enough for you to serve and, in addition, you can be the founders of a way of life. This can be a land of food enough and freedom and each man's soul his own."

Excited as three schoolgirls, the women climbed the river bank. They'd been finding agates and carnelians among the pebbles

[*177*]

below the Falls. The men must hold each stone against the sun at once and praise its color.

John heard a strangled gasp from Marguerite. Her eyes were wide in horror on Mrs. Whitman. "Your ring!"

The color drained from Narcissa Whitman's face. "Marcus, my ring!"

Doctor Whitman laid his arm around her shoulders. "We'll find it."

They ran and slipped and slid down the embankment in their frantic rush to keep the river from discovering the wide gold wedding band ahead of them.

Confident, at first, they searched among the pebbles where the women pointed out and retraced their steps. When they found nothing, John and Marcus Whitman pulled off their shoes and waded. Finally, several Indians offered to help them look and then the idea came to John.

He didn't want to get the others' hopes up until he knew for certain, so he climbed the bank alone. He thought no one had noticed when he slipped away but then Marguerite hurried up behind him.

"The Indians gambling," she said, breathing hard, "you will look there for the wedding band?"

John made room for her on the path beside him and took her hand. "Should have thought of that first thing," he said. "It may be too late, now."

"No, no, it must not be too late," she whispered.

John squeezed her hand. "Come, *ma chérie*, we'll find it, one place or another. You're not to worry. You like our new friends, don't you? When they get their homes built in this valley, we'll ride here often to visit them. I'll find the time for that, somehow."

The gambling game broke up when they approached. The Indians, sprawled on grass mats, got to their haunches and sat idly tossing their gambling sticks in their hands while John asked about the ring.

They knew nothing of it. They would like to hear about this ring. How wide did he say it was? Yes, they would be glad to watch for the ring in the river.

[*178*]

Then Marguerite screamed and pointed.

The ring gleamed on a young buck's finger.

He tried to run but John nabbed him. The other Indians gathered round.

"It won't come off," the culprit said in jargon.

"I'll get it off all right," John threatened.

"No, no, I try. The ring is stuck."

"Stuck is it?" John yelled. "Then I'll cut off your finger. One way or another, I'll have that ring." He pulled his folding knife from his pocket and opened the blade.

"Johnny," Marguerite reproved and stepped in front of him. Quietly she told the Indian in jargon, "It is the custom among our people for a man to take a woman with a special ceremony held in a holy place. This ring is one put on a woman's finger so all may see that she is belonged to someone." She stooped and quickly unlaced her embroidered leggings. "See, these leggings are of much more beauty. The ring is a thing of meaning only. So, we will trade."

The Indian took the leggings without a word.

The ring lay in Marguerite's palm. John watched her barely slide the tip of her third finger through the gold band and then instantly withdraw it. "Please, Johnny, may I carry the ring? Then you will give it back to the beautiful Mrs. Whitman."

"*Oui, oui,* of course," John answered. He was thinking that if a band of gold were so significant to Marguerite, he might get her one someday. When they met the others, they had given up the search and climbed the bank. Narcissa Whitman's joy at sight of her ring confirmed John's notion that a ring might please Marguerite. Thinking of Marguerite, he started to slip the ring on Mrs. Whitman's finger.

But she drew back. "No, no!" Then her laugh apologized. "I'm sorry, Doctor McLoughlin. But this happens to be an anniversary of our wedding in the little church back home. Seven months ago tonight, Marcus placed this ring on my finger. You understand, I'm sure."

"Of course, of course."

Henry Spalding cleared his throat.

Marcus Whitman took the ring and turned to Narcissa. "With this ring, I thee wed," he said out bold and clear, "and unto thee, I pledge my love and loyalty, in the name of the Father, and of the Son, and of the Holy Spirit."

"Amen," Henry Spalding murmured.

Then Marcus took Narcissa in his arms and kissed her.

They all laughed and chatted until John called them back to the business at hand. "Now then," he said, "it's time to select the spot you want for your mission station. Take your pick and as much as you need. Soon now, I hope to get these two sections surveyed and laid off in lots. But, even though we may need to make a few adjustments when the lines are fixed, I promise we won't disturb you much. The land is yours. I'll send you timbers."

"But, I thought you knew," Marcus Whitman gasped.

"Har-r-ump"—Henry Spalding folded his arms across his chest—"we must have two stations instead of one, Doctor Mc-Loughlin. And we promised at Rendezvous on the Green to go to the Nez Perces. Seems Doctor Whitman has decided he can put his medical knowledge to best use among the Cayuses somewhere near your Fort Walla Walla."

"No, no, no," John objected.

Marguerite's hand slid into his.

"That is, I wouldn't advise locations in that country," John said, trying to keep his words in single file. "I want you here—on the Willamette. We need you here."

"But the Indians, Doctor, we came across the mountains to heal and teach the Indians and the Nez Perces want us," Eliza Spalding argued. "We have given them our promise."

"The Indians in that country are not to be trusted," John objected. "It isn't safe. Certainly it isn't safe unless all four of you stick together."

"Never!" Henry Spalding cleared his throat.

"But we wanted you for neighbors. Here at the Falls, you would be near enough for visits now and someday, after I retire from the Company, Marguerite and I will make our home here. We dream about it on misty nights."

Narcissa laid her hand on Marguerite's arm. "That would be

wonderful, Mrs. McLoughlin. We would like nothing better. It's just that we feel called to go to the Cayuses and we have to do what we feel is right."

Marguerite touched with her index finger Narcissa's ring. "Of course," she murmured. "It is good that you do what you feel is right."

"Keep them south of the river, south of the river!" John kept hearing Simpson's words in the rhythm of his stallion's hoofs all the way home. By the auld Cloots, these Americans who must always make up their own minds would be the death of him yet. Simpson wouldn't like it. Their honors in London wouldn't even like this. And just when he had done so well against Nathaniel Wyeth, too.

Maybe Wyeth was right about American settlers. Maybe they would be hard to handle, once they put down roots in Oregon soil. If so, he'd better tighten up his reins. Perhaps, if he invited Mrs. Whitman and Mrs. Spalding to be his guests at Fort Vancouver while their husbands went looking for locations, he could influence the ladies in favor of the Willamette. He simply could not have these hard-headed Americans scattered in territory bound to be declared Great Britain's in a short time now. That sort of thing could make for trouble and bloodshed when the boundary was settled. No, no, he'd have to manipulate things and settle these Americans where they belonged.

XV   John learned all over again that Americans couldn't exactly be told. They accepted plows and hoes on credit, listened to his advice, and did as they pleased.

The Spaldings settled with the Nez Perces a hundred miles north of the line where the boundary might be drawn. The Whitmans went to the Cayuses. And on the Willamette, the Methodists multiplied like seed peas and rooted themselves in John's own land claim whenever it suited their fancy.

Directing the affairs of his twenty-two land bases and six trading vessels, John was a king. Dosing Indians with quinine and rhubarb, he was a medicine man. Reading prayers in French on Sundays, he was a priest. Breaking out black loam on the Cowlitz, he was a farmer. Doctor, lawyer, merchant, chief . . .

Under George Simpson's prodding it was always hurry, hurry, hurry—before the boundary comes up for settlement, before the Joint Occupation Treaty is called off. Clean out the furs, turn out your own food, eke out a profit, and, always, keep out Americans.

Importing rope and rice and Peruvian bark from the Sandwich Islands, creating a market for salt salmon in Monterey and in Sitka, John manipulated international trade. Settling retired Company men on the land, providing them with a start in tools and cattle, he dabbled in colonization and thus in world politics. Throughout the Columbia Department—the size now of a small empire since Simpson had completed his negotiations with the Russians and leased the coast of southeastern Alaska—the largest and smallest affairs turned on John's word.

Mr. Black, I trust to your best endeavors to manure ground as much as possible as we require manured ground in spring for peas,

[*182*]

and if possible for a little barley and after that for potatoes and turnips.

I send you with this a receipt to make bread, made with milk by the Trader's wife at Fort Colvile. I never tasted better bread. With the receipt I send two iron pans in which to bake the bread.

Pete Ogden, in recognition of your excellent work toward breaking the back of the American coastal trade it is my pleasure to inform you that the honorable Governor and Committee in London have made you a Chief Factor. You are assigned to command the New Caledonia District with headquarters at Fort St. James on Stuart Lake. I'm proud of you, my lad, but we'll miss seeing you so often. Be sure you get here each spring with your Express and plan to stay as long as possible.

Dear Sir, my man left a pair of suspenders and a shirt of mine at Nisqually. Will you please return them by your first opportunity?

I send you by brig *Lama* two small wooden houses, made of inch boards and mounted on wheels, but all taken to pieces for the convenience of transporting. They are marked so as to be put together easily on arriving. They will answer well as houses for the shepherds both in winter and summer.

"I'm sorry, Mr. La Bonte, but it is against Company rules for you to settle on the Willamette. You must return to Canada now that you have retired. How's that? What if you don't? Tut, tut, Mr. La Bonte, if you don't, why then . . . why then, you're a free man and God bless you."

Yes, John was doctor, lawyer, merchant, chief to everyone except Americans.

But then Jacques came home and John was a proud father, nothing more, until this American thing reared its head again to needle him.

For Marguerite's sake as well as his own, he insisted, Jacques's first night home, on a family dinner. *Oui, oui,* this bucked tradition but Narcissa Whitman had set him thinking. Tonight, Jacques would eat with both his parents.

Tonight, too, John would learn the answer to a question he'd never quite dared put—even to himself.

[*183*]

Through the years he'd longed above all else for Jacques to grow up the kind of man who could, on character and gumption, command respect. His son must prove himself of a size to overshadow the slight and derogation that curled George Simpson's lip when he lumped and labeled the children of Company marriages "bits of brown." Home from his years in Paris, Jacques would be the man John hoped, or he would not. Tonight would answer the question.

John went to the kitchen himself early that morning and ordered the food for their dinner. To the butcher he said merely, "Pete Wagner, this is the day. My son has come home."

He told Bruce to set up a special table in their parlor, to bring plates and the largest Staffordshire platters and tureens. Finally, he sent the big Scotsman to the wine cellar beneath the house. This must be a genuine celebration. The boy had seemed subdued and even sad on his return.

Avoiding the matter of provisions and credits for the Whitman station at Waiilatpu on the Walla Walla, John finished off a letter to the Committee in London and dismissed his clerk a full hour early that evening. He moved to the window and stood looking out across the palisade. Yes, yes, he knew that in time he'd have to explain to Simpson about letting the Whitmans and Spaldings settle to the north. For now, he refused to think about it. Tonight he'd get to know his son. He'd find out whether the boy had in him the stuff a leader must have to match this country.

Marguerite opened the parlor door before John, in his best black broadcloth and white satin waistcoat, had time to settle himself in his favorite rocker. She wore her black merino with the red velvet ribbon edging a slashed peplum. John's grandmother's lace lay in creamy folds at her throat. On her breast gleamed the mother-of-pearl cross that Jacques had brought her from Paris.

John skirted the mahogany table set with crested silver and took her hands. He lifted the cross on its barely visible gold chain. "Beautiful," he said.

Marguerite tossed her head. "Almost I am angry with your son."

"Angry?"

"*Oui.* For Eloise who is not even here, he brings a rippling collar of the finest lace made by nuns in France. For me"—she gave the cross a disapproving flip—"this."

Puzzled, John asked, "Well?"

"And what gift does he bring to his *papa?*" Marguerite came back.

Strange but John had not thought of a possible gift for himself until this instant. "I can explain that," he said and touched Marguerite's forehead with his lips. "There is nothing in Paris that could possibly interest a man who has you."

"Unless it might be this?" Jacques swung through the door and, with a flourish, whipped a thin sword from its sheath. He held the blade in a salute before his face.

Growing up had worn the boy-flesh from Jacques's body and brought out the kind of solid keel and ribs John built into his ships for plying the Pacific.

"What's this?" John asked. "Have you taken up dueling?"

"I intended this for a gift but I believe I overheard something about nothing from Paris being of interest to you. In that case . . ." Jacques brought from behind him the sword's sheath and fitted them together. "I suppose this means that you no longer care for a cane." With a grin, Jacques tossed the sword-cane and John caught it.

He moved to the window to examine the gift.

"Look," Marguerite cried, "a man's head on top. He has blue eyes."

"And a white head like *Papa's,*" Jacques pointed out.

John teased, "I hope you refer to color, Son, and not to the hardness of this ivory. "He held the cane out for Marguerite to withdraw the sword.

Jacques, as if he were guiding a child to write his name, took Marguerite's hand on the sword's head. "Like this," he said, whipping the blade to the right and to the left, "and there!" They gave the sword a hard forward thrust. "You got your man,

Maman," Jacques praised. "Right through the heart. Now you do it alone."

Marguerite made the blade cut the air with the zing and polish of a veteran duelist. "And the gold rings!" she sighed, sliding the sword back in place. "One, two, three, four, five," she counted, touching each ring on the cane.

John could scarcely believe that such a thin tube could sheath a sword's blade. Actually, the largest gold ring, at the top, would no more than fit Marguerite's finger. He stopped in the act of withdrawing the sword for the tenth time. "No more than fit Marguerite's finger," he repeated to himself. Half an inch wide and satin gold, the band winked up at him. The business of Mrs. Whitman's wedding ring flashed through his mind. Of all the ridiculous notions! He gave the ivory head a tap with his palm.

Then Jacques produced a square box and this, too, was for John.

"No, no, no," he protested. "Nothing more. The cane in itself is too much."

"Open it, open it, Johnny!"

Jacques wrapped his arms around Marguerite and gave her a whirl. "And you thought I would bring no gift for *Papa!*"

Inside the box lay the gold watch that John had always promised himself for "someday." The chain with its elliptic links seemed too delicate for a man to handle but John picked the gold key from the box.

"Wind it, Johnny." Marguerite's hands, usually so self-possessed, fluttered in her excitement. "You put the key right here. How can you wait?"

"It has the finest chain movement I could buy," Jacques said.

"I'm so glad for the second hand," John commented. "Not that I'll be counting many pulses now that you're a full-fledged doctor." He turned to the table. "This calls for a toast." He took his time with the sealing wax on the bottle, and when he had filled the three Waterford glasses he felt he could trust his voice again, but his usual facility with toasts had deserted him. Lifting his glass he said merely, "To my son and successor." He hoped Jacques knew how proud he felt.

[*186*]

But as he tipped the glass to his lips, there, framed in the delicate crystal circle, he saw the resolute face of Chief Hasumtooks as he spoke from the brink of his son's grave. The glass fell from John's hand and only the musk-ox rug saved it from breaking.

Marguerite was beside him. "Johnny?"

He gripped her hand. "It's all right, *ma chérie*." He even managed to smile. "See, the wine is spilled but I taste it so lightly anyway there's no harm done." He glanced at Jacques's barely touched glass. "You, too, Son? Have you not learend in France to drink wine with more gusto?"

"I like the ceremony but care little for the wine, *Papa*. I take after you in more ways than being a doctor."

"*Oui, oui*." John raised his voice and clapped his hands. "Bruce! Bruce!"

In kilt and sporran the big Scotsman filled the doorway.

"You will serve dinner now," John told him.

"*Oui, oui*." Bruce turned, clapped his hands, and stepped aside into the parlor.

The odor came first. Unfamiliar and yet eagerly recalled, John could almost taste it, brown and juicy, on his tongue. And then the servant appeared, bearing the great half-acre Staffordshire platter with its intertwined blue leaves and flowers. Over and around its matching trivet washed a fragrant sea of red and brown. Flecks of gold on its surface reflected the candlelight from the table. Crowning the platter, a baron of beef still crackled from the oven. John had not known until this moment how much he'd missed cow beef through all these years.

"*Papa*," Jacques exclaimed, "at last, you've butchered a cow!"

"The time had come, my son," John said, making nothing of it.

Once the platter had been placed at the head of the table, other servants scuffed in on their moccasins. One brought the three roasted ducks that John had ordered stuffed with serviceberries. Another bore the tureen of potatoes, sliced thin and glazed with cheese made in the Company dairy on Sauvies Island. Peas in one tureen, turnips in another, hot loaves of bread came wrapped in linen. Stubbornly John had ignored imported luxuries hoarded in the trade store. He limited his menu to Fort Vancouver products.

Surely no shipped-in dainties could add anything of value to the blended potpourri of fragrances from roasted beef and melted cheese and the tang of berries through the crisp brown skin of mallard ducks.

When John had swung back Marguerite's chair, he dropped a kiss on the top of her head and stood with his hand on her shoulder while he asked the blessing.

At his place, he carved the meat. Then Bruce, handling silver with the sweep of a conductor wielding a baton, served the dinner. Finally, Bruce poured more wine from the crystal decanter on the rosewood chest and withdrew to the wall.

"Seems strange as the devil without Eloise," Jacques said, "and stranger still to think of her married to a man I never even saw. What's he like?"

John rather hoped that Marguerite would answer. He would not for the world do William Rae an injustice and yet neither would he lie to his son.

Marguerite said nothing.

"Handsome," John told Jacques. "A dashing, black-haired boy. He swept your sister off her feet. She'd had so little opportunity here to know young men. William Rae does little but bow-wow about his troubles at Fort Stikine. As soon as Governor Simpson can find a man to take his place, he'll be transferred in this direction, I have no doubt."

"Fort Stikine," Jacques mused. "Sounds calm as a glacier."

"It gets monotonous," John told him. "It's a small log fort on a strip of sand that turns into an island at high tide."

Marguerite said, "Eloise writes us that it is all the time raining and she must often dance with Russian officers who wear most heavy boots."

Jacques leaned back and seemed almost to be talking to himself. "A man could take all the books he wanted to read and have time to figure out what life's all about." Suddenly he turned on John. "Does Governor Simpson spend any time up there?"

"He makes inspection visits now and then. I doubt if he stays any longer than his business requires. Only the roughest Company men are there," John told him. "Governor Simpson sends our riffraff to that post. They can't desert from Stikine and get away to tell it."

Jacques, his eyes narrow, seemed to give this a more thorough mulling over than it deserved. At last, he shifted in his chair and asked, "But is it safe there, then, for Eloise?"

Marguerite laid down her fork. "This same question we ask ourselves each morning when we open our eyes and again each night before we go to sleep," she murmured.

"It should be safe enough with her husband there to protect her," John said.

"I wonder, is this William Rae a man for protecting or for hiding himself beneath a table until a danger is past," Marguerite murmured. "And why," she persisted, "should it be that this George Simpson must pick our Eloise's new husband to send to this most riffraff and dangerous post?"

Jacques leaned forward. "I want to know that, too."

"No special reason," John soothed. "It's just the way things happened to work out, I'm sure."

Marguerite said, "Does it not sometimes appear to you, Johnny, that things do not just happen to work out for this George Simpson? More often does it not appear that this George Simpson works people out as if they happened to be things?"

Jacques reached across to touch Marguerite's hand.

John thought, for a moment, that he saw the boy's fingers tremble but the flicker of candlelight had, no doubt, caused the illusion. "I concede that young Rae has his troubles—most of them inside him as is usually the case. And your *maman* and I will be glad to have Eloise return from Russian territory as soon as possible." John sat back and wagged his knife at his son. "But what about you? What are your plans?"

"Suppose there's any chance of getting appointed physician in residence here at Fort Vancouver for a while? Later, after I get more experience, I might like to try my hand at running some half-size post like Stikine."

John sat forward. Jacques was suggesting the thing that he would like most, if he considered his own personal desires. He

[*189*]

said, "Governor Simpson makes our appointments, Son. As for me, I'd like nothing better than for you to doctor here. I've tried various itinerant doctors who move with the ships but, mostly, I've had to keep up my practice, too. You could give me a rest, at least. Still—"

"You could have your old room." A faraway look came into Marguerite's eyes and then John saw it change to concern. "We could, perhaps, look after you, if you lived here."

"Look after me?" Jacques's laugh rang out but he cut it off too short, it seemed to John. "*Maman*, I am grown up, remember. It is now up to me to settle my own problems and, perhaps, to look after you and *Papa*."

"You are sure that you want to come into the Company?" John asked and was surprised by his own question. He had always hoped that Jacques would become a Company doctor but, lately, he'd been wondering a little whether the boy might not like it to try doctoring on his own.

"I'm positive I want to sign up with the Company for a while, at least. I want to be on the inside as long as you're head of the Columbia Department under that George Simpson." Abruptly he confronted John. "*Papa*, do silk hats worry you? They're becoming mighty popular."

"It balances," John answered. "Fur-bearing animals are becoming scarcer, too."

"Governor Simpson's fur desert on the Snake?" Jacques asked with a lift of his dark brows.

"Partly that," John admitted. "And partly—though this may sound like nonsense—one thing leads to another."

Oui, it did sound like nonsense. It might sound like very little more even if he bothered to point out how George Simpson's protests against imported luxuries, that first year on the Columbia, had led them into planting wheat. In time, those protests led to importing cattle and sheep from the Sandwich Islands and California. To handle the grain they raised, they had to build gristmills. They exported lumber to pay for the cattle and sheep. To provide the lumber, they built sawmills. To carry on all these sidelines to the fur trade, they settled men on the land and supplied them with plows. Settlers, in turn, drove out fur-bearing animals.

When Jacques spoke, it was almost as if John had said all this aloud.

"So the big question turns out to be," Jacques said, "how long can the fur trade hold out against us fur traders?"

"Us fur traders," the boy had said. John slid his new gold watch from his waistcoat pocket and cradled it in both hands. "You're not to sign up with the Company because you think I want it, Son. You could, instead, hang your shingle beside the Falls of the Willamette. The Methodists alone would keep you busy. They bring in more farmers and mechanics and millers with every boat from the States. But, added to them, there's Louis La Bonte and his family—you remember old Louis, a carpenter here in the early days. And there's Etienne Lucier and Xavier Ladouroute who married Julia Gervais and that American, Ewing Young, and Charlefoux is talking of taking his family to the Willamette. You could settle down there and make a real place for yourself in the country."

"Do you mean you don't want me in the Company?" Jacques asked. "I always thought—"

"No, no, no, I don't mean that, of course. It's just that lately I've been wondering . . ." John called Bruce and took a pinch of snuff. "Perhaps on the Willamette you could find a nice girl—"

"No!" Jacques's vehemence brought John and Marguerite to attention.

"What is this?" Marguerite asked in a whisper.

Jacques got to his feet and went to the window. When he turned back, he held his shoulders erect but he could not keep the suffering from his eyes. "I suppose I'd better tell you." He came over and his hands gripped the back of his chair at the table. "I'll never marry." His eyes became tender as he studied the candle flame. "I met a girl in Montreal on my way to Paris," he said and stopped.

John saw the boy's knuckles whiten.

"Governor Simpson first took me to her home when he had business with her *papa*."

[*191*]

"But if she was a nice girl, why did you not perhaps—"

"A nice girl?" Jacques interrupted Marguerite. "Susette was beautiful in every way, *Maman*. You would have loved her. Her *grand-père* was Swiss and her *papa* French. Her mother was part Cree like yours, *Maman*. She had gone to convent school and she could sing to melt your very bones."

"But, but—"

"We were in love from the first minute we met in her *papa's* garden," Jacques went on and John could see him live the moment again as he spoke. "We wrote letters all the time I was in Paris. And then we planned it finally—that we'd be married as soon as I got back to Montreal." Jacques's hand covered his eyes. His fingers dug into his forehead. At last, he drew in a long breath. "She died," he said and shuddered.

"Died, died?" John asked. "But how? Why? Had she been ill?"

Jacques sat down and gazed again into the candle flame. Then he reached inside his coat and drew out a folded letter sheet. "It was a man." John could see how much it cost him to say it. "She cut her wrists with a trade knife."

Marguerite's hands covered her face. "No, no!" she cried.

John reached across the corner of the table to grip the boy's arm.

Jacques replaced the letter in his pocket and straightened as if he would lift himself above the memory. "I'm sorry to make your dinner sad, *Papa*, but I wanted you and *Maman* to know. And now, we will not need to speak of it again." He pushed back. "If you will excuse me now, I would like to walk before I go to bed." He bent above Marguerite and touched his lips to her cheek. He came around and took John's hand. "A perfect dinner, *Papa*."

"Our poor Jacques," Marguerite murmured when he had closed the door.

"*Oui*, our poor Jacques." John nodded. "And only time will heal the wound."

"Do you think, Johnny," Marguerite asked, "that this George Simpson will appoint our Jacques to be the doctor here at Fort Vancouver?"

"I hope so." John was thinking that if he could persuade the Governor to station Eloise and William Rae here, also, they could almost go back, pick up the threads of their lives, and become a family again. He'd been feeling more and more uneasy about young Rae. Still, if he had the boy here for a while, he might be able to graft in more gumption. That way, too, he could defeat the years that had rushed by, giving him only glimpses of both Jacques and Eloise. "My son has more than reached my expectations," he said. "He has in him the kind of stuff this country needs. Soon now, George Simpson and the world will see it."

"Perhaps," Marguerite said softly. She stood tall. "As for the world, I cannot say, but this George Simpson—I do believe that he will see it when the time has come."

John turned and reached for his new cane. "Isn't this a beauty?" He balanced it across his palms for Marguerite to admire once more before they went to bed.

"It is a beauty," she agreed and touched the wide gold band beneath the ivory head. "This is, perhaps, a wee bit wider even than Mrs. Whitman's wedding ring."

XVI Jacques and Marguerite both chose to saddle up and ride with John to the sawmill the next day. Jacques seemed intent on touching all his old bases at once and in gulping down everything connected with the business and the country.

Facing into the sunrise, they rode single file along the river trail and their talk ran to exclamations of delight as they watched the play of morning shadows on the long snow-packed ridges down Mount Hood.

Halfway to the sawmill they dismounted to let their horses rest and graze a bit. They stood on a grassy meadow and watched a long canoe, paddled by Indians, fight its way midstream against the current.

"The country changed while I was gone," Jacques said.

"A new country marches forward, Son. A wise man listens for the rhythm, then falls in step. You know what I've always dreamed for Oregon and for my family in it. It's a land whose trees and mountains thrust too high, whose waters run too free and fast for small men. It was destined from its creation to be a land where every human being has a chance to prove his mettle."

Jacques shifted his weight and pushed his beaver to the back of his head. "Did Nathaniel Wyeth have a chance?" he asked.

John gave him a quick glance and turned back to the canoe. "*Oui*, Nathaniel Wyeth had a chance."

"He would have, I know, if you had been free to treat him as you chose," Jacques hurried to agree. "But what real odds could you give on one Boston merchant against the honorable Company? And as long as Hudson's Bay can provide Etienne Lucier with land and seed and a start of cattle but says to Ewing Young, 'You get no provisions from us regardless of price,' how much chance has any man, even in Oregon, to prove his mettle?"

"Jacques!" Marguerite objected. "You will not speak so to your *papa*."

"No, no," John protested, "it is part of my dream for my son that he speak as he thinks and think for himself. Besides," he added with a grin, "doesn't a boy returning from school always sound like a radical to his father?"

"But he should sound also still like a son and not like finding fault."

"I'm thinking, that's all," Jacques defended himself. "Shall we ride on?"

At the edge of the sawmill camp, they let their horses drink and cool themselves in the millstream, while they sat cross-legged in a ferny arcade overhung with cedar. At once, Jacques pulled from his pocket several closely written sheets of foolscap. "I rode over to the village yesterday afternoon," he said. "Just getting acquainted with the place again. I happened to notice a door off its hinge on one of the houses. Chickens were tracking in so I dismounted to see about things. I found the house empty and these pages on the floor."

"Hall Jackson Kelley?" John asked.

"*Oui.*"

"He spent a winter here and has been bombarding the United States Congress ever since with pleas to colonize this country and grab it from Great Britain. You fixed the hinge?"

"*Oui.*" Jacques took off his hat and fitted it down on his bent knee. "*Papa*, Americans are not the only ones who are standing up for their rights. Something has been happening all over the world. I guess people are just made so they don't like being pushed around but suddenly in France they rose up and demolished the Bastille, in Boston they dumped a shipment of tea. The mood still holds. What do you think settlers in the Oregon Country will do? Burn Fort Vancouver or divert the Columbia right about here and wash Fort Vancouver away?"

"Don't talk nonsense, Son. Nobody here is interfering with anyone's rights. I've worked since I came to the Columbia to develop the land and the people in it. At first, I tried with the Indians—"

"But the Company wanted furs from the Indians, nothing more."

"*Oui, oui*, but, given time, the Company would have educated and civilized them. I saw a chance to train them in agriculture and lumbering and—"

"But what happened?"

"The large part of them died off in the epidemics."

"And through all the years before that, Governor Simpson was promising a chaplain and teacher but never sending one until he found a man who did more harm than good. I repeat, the Company wanted furs from the Indians, nothing more."

"Well, Son, it's pretty difficult to make an educated Indian of a dead one," John said. "As for the white men who really want to settle here and develop the land, I help them in every way I can. I've helped some beyond the generosity of the Company, by far. I'm carrying those on my personal account this minute."

"Exactly," Jacques agreed. "And yet yesterday I met a man by the name of Pariseau, up from the Cowlitz."

"*Oui, oui*, one of the colonists Governor Simpson sent to this country from Red River Settlement. They've had a hard winter on the Cowlitz."

"More to the point, they don't like it," Jacques said. "Pariseau didn't know that I was your son so we brushed up our French on each other. The settlers from Red River are talking revolt, *Papa*, and what fair man could blame them?"

John nodded. "They have every right. To persuade them to leave their comfortable homes and come out here, Simpson promised everything he could think of. Then he forgot to notify me. The forts along their trail were not provisioned to take care of their needs. I had no houses and barns and fenced fields for fulfilling the Governor's promises, once they got here. They have every right to talk against us."

"They're talking." Jacques sat watching the river. "*Papa*, did you ever read the Magna Carta?"

John wrinkled his brow. "I don't know, Son. I guess I've read parts of it at least—a long time ago."

[*196*]

"Ever read the French Declaration of the Rights of Man and of the Citizen?"

John grinned. "There again, it seems to me I may have read parts, at least, in school."

"Ever read the Declaration of Independence of the United States?"

"That rabble-rousing tirade against the Crown?" John shrugged. "I don't have time to read things like that. Someday I might get around to it."

Marguerite pointed downstream. "Can it be the same canoe that we saw below?" she asked.

"They've made good time," John said.

Jacques stood up and turned his back on the canoe. "You ought to read it sometime, *Papa*, I think you'd like it—that Declaration of Independence." His eyes lifted to the arch of cedar fronds above him. As if he weighed the words once more before recommending them too highly, he murmured to himself, " 'We hold these truths to be self-evident, that all men are created equal, that they are endowed by their Creator with certain unalienable Rights.' "

"Jacques, I've had a bellyful of Americans around here lately," John exploded. "They're mostly fine folks and I'd give them the shirt off my back but they're so infernally sure of their unalienable rights! Can't tell them anything. Can't budge them. If you've turned American, my lad, I'll thank you not to let it go to your head to make it as hot and hard as the others I come up against almost every day now."

"Their Declaration only preaches what you practice whenever you get the chance."

"Jacques!" Marguerite's tone commanded respect.

"It's all right, *ma chérie*." John took her hand.

Jacques turned and ambled down to the river's edge.

"He is young," John told Marguerite. "He has been reading Rousseau. Best of all, he is thinking. You will see. Someday, he will be a leader in this great country of ours and no man will dare label him quarter-breed or outsider."

They sat for a long time in silence.

[*197*]

Finally, before he knew that he had been thinking of Pariseau, John said, "I'm going to send the Red River families to the Willamette."

Marguerite pulled away. "But this George Simpson has said nine hundred times, it must be, that you are to keep them north of the Columbia. Will he not be so angry as to explode the buttons off his white satin waistcoat?"

John gathered her hand from the folds in her scarlet skirt. "He will be angry, no doubt, but the Red River families must have their chance."

"It is good, Johnny, that you do what you think is right. And what will this George Simpson do?"

"I don't know. Discharge me, perhaps. And explode the buttons off his waistcoat," he added to keep her from hearing his concern. The Red River colonists were a pet project of Simpson's, he knew, and yet they had starved and frozen and died along the trail from Canada and they'd fared no better on the Cowlitz through the winter. It wasn't fair.

When Pierre Pariseau arrived at Fort Vancouver late in March with fire in his eye and a chip on his shoulder, John welcomed him with a two-handed shake and a question that astonished them both.

"Pariseau, how would you like to move to the Willamette Valley—you and your hundred or so neighbors from Red River?"

Pariseau made a frantic scramble for the office cuspidor. "*Oui, oui*, but . . ."

"I know," John told him. "Your orders were to stay north of the river. But you were promised a house and a barn and fenced fields and a dozen other things I can't supply north of the river. To the south, you and your neighbors can win them for yourselves in no time at all. I think you have something better than broken promises coming to you."

"But the Willamette!" Awe and disbelief trembled on Pariseau's voice. "The best farm land in the world, they tell me." He settled back and dismissed this prospect as too fantastic. "No, no, no. The Willamette—it could never come true."

"It can, it can," John assured him. "And I myself will help you build your house and barn—you and every last family of you."

"But for how long will this be?" Pariseau wanted to know. "We hear talk since this American, Ewing Young, die that no one can say what is to become of his farm. His wife—" He shrugged. "No one can say does she own the land or does she take back her children to the Indian village where she is born." Pariseau shook his head. "No, no. With rich land as in the Willamette Valley, I would wish to know before building and planting fields that it is truly mine, that it is for my wife and children."

"Of course." John got up from his desk and moved to the window. Mount Hood, encased in crystal, wore the abiding look of geologic ages. "How this problem will be solved, I cannot tell you, *Monsieur* Pariseau. But it will be solved and on that I stake my own claims on the Willamette. This country was created for free men. You can't look at her upstanding mountains, at her unfettered rivers and not believe that. Never fear, *monsieur*, this problem that bothers you will be solved one day before too long."

John sent him home to the Cowlitz with an order written in French to show to the others. "Be back here in a month," he told him.

"But the *Gros Bourgeois*, the *Monsieur* Simpson, will he not make trouble for us and for you?"

"*Oui, oui, oui.*" John did not intend to sound impatient but it is sometimes hard to be patient with a man who persists in rubbing the salt of truth into a chafed conscience. "Let us say," he went on, explaining as much to himself as to Pierre Pariseau, "that I need more farmers in the Willamette Valley, if we are to hold up our end of the Company's contract with the Russians." Pleased with this explanation so far, he went ahead, making it a kind of dress rehearsal in anticipation of Governor Simpson's cross-examination. "You see, we supply fifteen thousand bushels of wheat a year to the Russians at Sitka. Already three-fourths of this amount comes from the Willamette but, with our own needs increasing, we find it more and more difficult to make up the balance. The Governor cannot afford to disappoint the Russians, *Monsieur* Pariseau."

Indians were beginning to rendezvous on the sandy beach at Champoeg when Company canoes loaded with Red River settlers and building materials pulled for the shore.

John had hoped to trade for salmon to feed his house-raising contingent but the Indians did not like the smell of all these white people coming to their valley. The salmon did not "like themselves to be caught to feed a strange people." Regretting the loss of work hands, John had to send several men beyond the Indians' rendezvous to fish. But work hands presented no real problem. He had greatly underestimated the pull of any goings-on in this country.

They had paddled upriver by moonlight and reached Champoeg well before dawn. The horse train sent overland to meet them here stood stamping at mosquitoes and ready to carry them in to French Prairie.

Riding into the sun as it peeked over the Cascades, John and Marguerite pulled up for a moment. Shining faces of dogwood strained to see into the prairie through the crowd of firs collected around its edge. And no wonder! Such a hodgepodge of activity and excitement and color must astonish the very mountains.

The meadow itself, decked out for the occasion in buttercups and blackeyed Susans, took second place in competition with the striped calico shirts and scarlet sashes of the French-Canadians and with the red and yellow calico on wives and children scattered everywhere. Clean-shaven mountain men in fringed buckskin, woolly adventurers who had pushed west from the States across the mountains in gray homespun shirts and rusted nankeen pantaloons, leftovers from Nathaniel Wyeth's fizzles, tars who had deserted the sea for the soil, cattle drivers fresh from California . . .

"With so many people and dogs," Marguerite said, "we may perhaps find no square of land big enough for setting a house."

"A crazy, mixed-up crowd it is," John answered. "Odd, this started out to be a French-Canadian shindig. Looks to me like

[*200*]

Americans can match them for numbers. They'll never be able to agree whether the roof goes at the top or at the bottom."

Marguerite giggled and John noticed the heightened color in her cheeks. "It is for you to see that they put the roof on the bottom. For me, I shall see that the stones are hot in the pit for cooking potatoes."

"This whole business looks doomed by too many cooks," John answered. "And I was afraid we'd be short-handed."

"It will go well," Marguerite promised. "See how round and pink are the faces." She tapped her mare's flank with her moccasin and rode into the sunrise toward Xavier Laudouroute's frame cabin.

Carpenters John had brought from Fort Vancouver got things under way. Perhaps Marguerite was right and the building would go well, John conceded. Men clapped each other on the back as they passed. Women laughed and hummed snatches of hymns or of *chansons* from the Provinces as they hurried across the prairie intent on whatever needed doing.

Retired Company men surrounded John. They showed off new babies and bragged, all on the same breath, about the offspring of the cattle he had lent them. Solomon Smith of the first Wyeth party brought his new wife, daughter of a Clatsop chief, for John to meet. Joseph Gervais, whose sister Julia had married Xavier Ladouroute as soon as he harvested his first crop off French Prairie, came to ask for credit to buy a plow. James O'Neill, left over from Wyeth's second party, waved as he hurried by with his crosscut saw.

When young Le Breton sprang like a bantam cock onto a pile of fir logs to announce that the ladies had midday dinner ready, John stood blinking in disbelief at his gold watch. For there before him on French Prairie stood the skeleton of a house where only grass and black-eyed Susans had stood at dawn.

Wall plates, tie beams, struts, and rafters cut from John's well-seasoned timbers made a steadfast picture against the cloudless sky. While the others ate their fill of salmon and potatoes, both roasted Indian fashion, John drank tea boiled to the color of molasses and let his eyes play over this framework that would be a home by evening. Why, in no time at all, this whole prairie could be squared off and fenced into little independent states where families plowed and played together and worked out their happiness.

Julia and Xavier Ladouroute, so excited by the prospect of neighbors that they had spread the word from here to the Falls and beyond to get this crowd here, could have neighbors overnight on every side. Soon they could build a school for their children. A church was no problem since a man could hardly turn around these days without bumping into a Methodist. No, no! John stopped himself. These families from Red River should have a chance to bring up their children in their own faith. He must, at once, look into the matter of a Catholic missionary.

Marguerite touched his shoulder and placed in his hand a tin plate on which frosted flakes of salmon, delicate as pink dogwood petals, circled a mound of potato scooped from its shell and topped with butter.

In mid-afternoon when John was lending a hand with the siding, two Methodists showed up. Mr. Waller, he knew from providing him the timbers for his house and, unwillingly, the land to set it on. The other, in the usual chin-whiskers, boiled shirt, and black frock coat, Waller introduced as a Doctor Somebody-or-other.

"We want to talk to you about what's going on here." Waller's voice bristled a little.

But then John's temper bristled more than a little at sight of Mr. Waller since he had not merely borrowed timbers but had decided, at the last minute, to build, not on his own land claim near the Falls, but on John's which joined his. His protestations that he wouldn't think of actually claiming the land for himself had never quite sounded a yard wide to John.

"Well, well, Mr. Waller," he said now, "talk away."

"I suggest that we move to one side," the Doctor Somebody-or-other said in a tone that clearly warned of trouble.

John handed to Lucier his end of the timber he held. "Very well," he agreed and led them off to the right at a pace that made

[*202*]

them scamper. "What is it? What is it, now? We've work to do here."

"It's about this land," Mr. Waller said. "It looks to us like you're putting French-Canadians in here by the score. We question the right of foreigners to hold this land."

"Foreigners! Foreigners! Tut, tut, Mr. Waller. By what authority do you call any man foreign in this country? Well, well, speak up! Tell me and by that same authority I'll call you foreigner."

"But you know the understanding. This country south of the river is to be territory of the United States."

"The boundary is not decided, Mr. Waller."

"True but the time will soon come when it is."

"And suppose it does," John persisted. "Who knows but this will be an independent country then? As for now, these men and women need a chance to prove what they can do. As long as the land is here, unused, I can't see human beings go cold and hungry."

Waller drew himself tall. "Doctor McLoughlin, as a native-born son of the United States—"

"Mr. Waller," John cut in, "in my opinion a man who has nothing more to shoot off about than the place of his birth is running mighty low on ammunition."

The Doctor Somebody-or-other led Waller to their hobbled horses and John hurried back across the meadow to his work. But that Waller, he knew, was a man to watch.

John was thinking more and more these days of founding a town by the Falls of the Willamette. Oregon City, he was thinking he'd call it. And it had already become so real in his mind that he could smell the soaked logs, waiting in the river to be ripped by saws. The town's main street ran along the river with dry-goods stores and blacksmiths' forges and cobblers' shops and every man whistling at his work. Somehow this stiff-shirted Waller kept stomping through the picture and his long face didn't fit there. Maybe, John decided, he'd better buy Waller out—yes, buy back his own timbers set upon his own land claim. It was buy him out or cure him of his high-handed ways. This new town of

John's would have no room in it for men who bragged about the place of their birth and claimed that gave them the right to special privileges.

The rough-sawed boards of the new cabin's floor were pegged down by dusk. Then the slow *screech-screech* of wagon wheels, loose on their axles, sliced through the talk and laughter that filled the house and prairie.

With their long legs propped to keep them off the ground and from between the wheel spokes, two lanky young men rode the framework of a wagon behind two mules who were in constant danger of stepping on their ears.

"Joe Meek and Doc Newell," John exclaimed.

When these boys had first come squeaking into Fort Vancouver, John had listened to their explanation and then stood with his foot on one of his mounted cannons, twisting his ear and thinking of Governor Simpson.

Joe Meek had said, "It are this away, Doc. Beaver plumb played out in the mountains. Warn't even no Rendezvous for tradin' though this child scouted nigh and far along the Green and up Wind River."

Doc Newell butted in. "So I says, 'Joe Meek, us trappers has been our own man too long. We cain't and won't go back to the States. What say, we put out for Oregon? Thar's a country whar any man's as good as the next and so's his woman.' "

"Waal, thar we be, on the Snake," Joe Meek drawled and that's when John had started thinking about George Simpson who had plotted a fur desert on the Snake to turn Americans back and keep them out of the Oregon Country. "We bein' closer to Oregon," Joe Meek went on, "than to somewhar we didn't want to go to nohow, I says, 'It are us for Oregon, Doc,' and hyar we are."

And here they were again on French Prairie—the biggest kind of Americans and set to throw their weight around.

"They've come, they've come!" Julia Ladouroute waved a wet dishcloth and ran back and forth to find a place to hang it. "It's Doc Newell and Joe Meek!" She got to the wagon ahead of John and Marguerite, still looking for a place to hide her flour sacking. "Did you bring your wives? Did you bring your fiddle? Oh, there they are!"

Two oval-faced, bright-eyed Nez Perce girls clung to the back of the wagon frame. Marguerite hurried around with Julia to make them welcome.

John gave his hand to Joe Meek who took full advantage of the shake to boost himself past his mule's heels and onto the ground. "Mr. Joe, Mr. Joe! By the auld Clootie, it's good to see you, Mr. Joe."

"Waal, if it aren't old Doc Long-John!" Joe made a show of standing on tiptoe to see into John's eyes although he wasn't more than a pair of inches the shorter of the two. His handsome face crinkled in a grin that showed real pleasure. "This are some now!"

John thrust his hand around to Newell who had to shift his fiddle case to take it.

"It are good to see ye, Governor," Doc Newell drawled. "When Julia says, 'Be hyar and bring yer fiddle,' we warn't expectin' no sech spree."

Joe Meek looked over the crowd while he writhed and wriggled himself comfortable in his buckskin pantaloons and then smoothed out the fringes on his tunic. "Pretty nigh ever' old hoss and his woman from the whole peraira, I'm thinkin'."

"Pretty nigh," John agreed. Then, because from their first meeting more than a year before, tacit agreement had sprung up between them as to teasing, he added, "I see you didn't show up in time for work, Mr. Joe."

"Aw now, Doc Long-John, you know this old hoss cain't work. But thar aren't a devil as hisses as can shine with this child when thar's playin' to be done. Tonight this child means playin'."

And play he did. They found a chair to set across a corner of the sawdust-scented parlor. Doc Newell claimed he couldn't do nothin' with his fiddle bow 'thout bein' in position to pat his foot. So he sat and bridged his music box across the gully of his elbow and sawed out tunes through the night the same as other men had sawed out rafters through the day.

[205]

"What'll ye have?" Newell called out at first and from that moment the house was filled with laughter and plain old neighborly spizzerinctum. Babies squealed and gurgled and cried in key. Dogs howled outside as if the music broke their hearts. Inside, men and women danced the Reel of Eight to get things started off by couples—the women waggling sideways to keep from being maimed by the men's stiff-kneed goosestep.

Then Le Breton suggested that their neighbors from up north might like the Red River Jig. This was new to John but twelve couples from Red River scrambled and squealed and found their places on the floor. The dance turned out to be an endurance test of clog and crabwise glides. At any sign of weakening, recruits cut in and out for men and women.

John watched their faces. Sent to this country by the Company, they'd found cold and hunger through the winter and, worst of all, no chance to prove themselves. But tonight, they were at home. It sparkled in their eyes. It twinkled in their feet. Tomorrow, they could start to live.

And then someone cried, "Square dance!" and another demanded, "Joe Meek call out."

Well, Joe Meek took up his post beside the fiddler and John had never in all his days in London, in Paris, or in Montreal seen anything to equal this. As Mr. Joe called figures, he whirled and turned and bowed and sashayed—sometimes alone, sometimes with his Nez Perce wife, Virginia, sometimes plucking Marguerite away from John. Always he kept calling out at the top of his voice. His black eyes flashed with fun. His nimble feet and arms beat out the rhythm.

> Lady 'round the lady and a dos-à-dos
> And the lady 'round the hoss and the hoss stands WHOA!

The din and flurry and scramble of mixed up couples raised a choking dust in the room but through the hullabaloo of laughter came Joe's voice:

> Ladies bow low and hosses bow under;
> Couple up close and swing like thunder.

Room for any low bowing had long since disappeared and

already some couples danced on the grass outside the house, finding there, no doubt, more convenient space for swinging like thunder. But bumps and stepped-on feet and pandemonium could not stop Mr. Joe.

> Now swing the gal as bruised your bunions,
> Now swing the one that are plump as onions;
> Now swing the child that are sweet as mush,
> Now swing the one who makes you blush.

John held Marguerite close for this last swing and Mr. Joe wagged a reprimanding finger at him without missing a beat.

> Sashay around in a single file
> Lady in the lead in the Siwash style.
>
> Jump straight up and never come down,
> And whirl that calico 'round and 'round.

On through the night they danced and John knew that, even so, they would build another house tomorrow. And another, and another . . . His dream of families—making the most of this rich land, making the most of themselves while they plowed and sowed and reaped—was coming true before his eyes.

"This is good," he said to Marguerite and she squeezed his hand in answer.

"It would be so good if our Eloise could live safe here with these happy people instead of with those riffraffs at Stikine," she said. Her nose crinkled then. "What is it I smell?"

Before John could answer, he heard a sound like a gust of wind and up the window beside them rolled a sheet of flame.

One moment, he had not been sure that he smelled smoke; the next, smoke billowed through the house. Screams mingled with the music before the fiddler could stop his bow.

In the instant of realizing what was happening, John grabbed Marguerite and flung her through the door. Back he went to help round out the others.

Flames skinned up the rough, dry siding as if the house were built of foolscap. Women screeched. Men cursed and scrambled for their children.

Joe Meek called out, "Hyar's the door, neighbors. Sashay 'round in single file."

They tried at first to quench the blaze but the heat was too intense, buckets too scarce.

John called them off. "No use," he said. "Somebody's sure to get hurt and we can't save the house."

Flames climbed and fell and soared again against the night. They whipped and flapped in the wind and tore off, leaving ragged edges. Timbers groaned and creaked and now and then one splintered loose to thunder down and feed the conflagration.

Shoulders drooping, the settlers listened to the roar and crackle and watched in silence. John saw hope they'd won this day die from their eyes. He saw them give up and quit. And then, in the play of light on their reddened faces, despair burned out and turned to indignation.

"Injuns!" someone exploded.

"More likely fire-eatin' Americans, bound and determined no Canadian will get a foothold here."

"We got as much right to a home as anybody."

"Doc Long-John!" Joe Meek waved his fists around. "Us boys'll git the old hosses as done it. We'll string 'em up and rip out their guts, and you can go your pile on it."

"I say it was Injuns!" Le Breton shouted.

John remembered the Indians' sullen eyes when he tried to trade for salmon at Champoeg.

"No, no," another argued. "We'd a-noticed Injuns sneakin' 'round. Americans it was."

"Americans, you say! Waal this child says, 'No,' and he are half froze for the h'ar of any old hoss as says 'Americans.'" Joe Meek made a pass with his knife at the fellow who spoke.

"Gentlemen," John soothed.

"Nobody's sayin' all Americans are like that. But two or three of them independents come acrost the mountains for no better reason, as I can see, but for makin' trouble all around."

"That are a fact now!" Joe Meek could be as vehement in agreeing with a man as he could in hacking out his liver. "What this hyar country needs are laws and officers to make 'em stick."

"*Oui, oui*, in time," John said. "In time."

"Who's for baitin' another trap?" Joe Meek yelled. "Let's build a house tomorrow, then keep our eyes peeled."

Pariseau pushed in. "This does not frighten me away," he said. "I am for building houses every day until no man is left without one."

"And old Joe Meek are hyar to help."

"And old Doc Newell!"

"Le Breton, too."

"And Lucier."

"They can't scare us no matter who it was as done it."

"I've picked my site," one Canadian called. "We'll build there tomorrow."

"And I'm next," another shouted. "My spot's ready cleared."

A red streaked dawn began to show beyond the Cascade Mountains. John had to leave at once for Fort Vancouver. George Simpson was due there any day. He'd dreaded telling the Governor about moving his Red River colonists to farms south of the Columbia. Now, this night had held a torch to light up bigger problems.

The Indians resented Whites intruding on their streams and valleys. John had hoped they'd welcome neighbors and, in time, contract mild cases, at least, of culture and cleanliness from the example of the Whites. And, now they'd had a taste of home-building, settlers from Canada seemed just as sure of their rights as those from the States. Simpson would still expect that Hudson's Bay Company should tell each man whither he could live and whether. Simpson wouldn't like it when one of his docile Red River colonists rose up on his hind legs and stated, "I've picked my site. We'll build there."

One way or another, when the Governor arrived at Fort Vancouver, John would have this night's fiddler to pay.

XVII John found a stack of letters on his desk when he got home and a whir of excited rumors around the Fort.

"George Simpson arrived on the *Beaver* from London," Jacques told him, "along with that mail. But he high-tailed it out of here again before I got a chance to see him."

John opened his folding knife and, sitting down at his desk, took up the top letter. "Where did Simpson go in such a hurry?"

"To Fort Walla Walla, I understand." Jacques came over from the window. "Here, let me help you with that." He picked up a dozen letters and began breaking seals. "You're getting popular, *Papa*. I never knew you to get so many letters on one mail."

John looked up. "Is it true what I hear about the Governor— that he may soon be knighted by Queen Victoria?"

Jacques shrugged. "That's the rumor." He spread and pressed out the creases of a letter sheet. "You'd better start reading, *Papa*, or we'll be late for dinner."

Hudson's Bay House
No. 3 Fenchurch Street
London, England

Chief Factor John McLoughlin
Hudson's Bay Company
Fort Vancouver on the Columbia

DEAR SIR:

We feel it contingent on our duty to remind you that the boundary settlement between the territories disputed by Great Britain and the United States has not yet been reached. It has been forcibly called to our attention that you may have been somewhat indiscreet in allowing certain citizens of the United States, in particular, missionaries, to settle within the area which most reasonably will fall to Great Britain when the boundary is drawn. We have been informed that you have

[*210*]

been repeatedly warned against such practices. Settlements of aliens to the north of the Columbia River cannot be tolerated. You will discuss this matter with Governor Simpson on his current inspection visit to your Department. You will, of course, defer to his direction.

I am Dear Sir
Yours truly
GOVERNOR JOHN HENRY PELLY

John picked up the second letter that Jacques had flattened. He read:

DEAR SIR:

We direct your attention to the matter of the boundary settlement within the territory known as the Oregon Country. The United States is endeavoring to obtain an agreement to our disadvantage and the subject is now under discussion between the two governments.

We hope that the valuable part will be secured to this country and the actual occupation by traders and colonists will go far to establish the rights of our Empire which is an additional inducement to extend our posts and the range of our trading vessels as far north as may be practicable.

You will be as pleased as we are to learn that, in the event of a boundary settlement favorable to Great Britain, we have every reason to believe that our Governor George Simpson is to be knighted by Queen Victoria. Such an honor will reflect well on the Company and you are urged to do all in your power to effect the desired settlement.

I have the honor to be
Dear Sir
Yours truly
Gov. JOHN HENRY PELLY

The next letter read:

DEAR SIR:

On perusal of your dispatches and after having given the subjects they embraced our due consideration, we must insist, in the best interests of our esteemed Queen, that you will henceforth refuse to allow citizens of the United States to settle to the north of the Columbia. . . .

John threw the letter down in disgust. "Let's go to dinner, Son."

[211]

Jacques spread his hand on the sheaf of flattened letters and leaned across the desk. "Have they been driving you like this all these years?"

John tilted his chair against the wall. "It has been a drive of some kind all the way," he admitted. "The boundary settlement must be drawing near."

"How do you feel about it?" Jacques asked. "I haven't heard you say."

John sighed. "I don't get worked up about it one way or the other," he said. "It will be decided without my say-so."

Jacques straightened and moved to the window. "I wonder." When he turned, his jaw had hardened. Rigid cords stood out in his neck. "So George Simpson will be knighted." He seemed not to be talking to John at all. "When will he be back? Can you find out, *Papa?*"

John got up from his desk. "Perhaps."

"I'd like to know," Jacques said, "as soon as you find out. I want to be here."

Pete Ogden sailed in the next afternoon with word of a fever epidemic on his ships. His crews were in a panic. Jacques must go at once to make the rounds with his medicine bag and reassuring manner.

Pete and Jacques had hardly sailed downriver when the Governor arrived from Fort Walla Walla.

George Simpson wore, this trip, a monocle, less hair, and a new air of authority. He sat at the end of John's desk and his salmon-colored satin waistcoat extended out and down until it rested on the leather seat of the chair. "Funny how often inordinate ambition flowers on a man's belly," John thought idly, intending no dishonor.

"I'm sending James Douglas off for California," Simpson said. "What do you know about this man Sutter? I hear he's agitating for a tariff on the furs we take out of California. How does wheat look on the Willamette? Well, well, speak up. We're wasting time."

Sooner or later, John knew, he'd have to tell him about the

[*212*]

Red River settlers. "You asked about wheat," he began. "Prospects for next year look better than ever."

Suspicion tinged the Governor's voice. "How's that?"

"I've just located twenty-one new families on the best wheat-growing land this side of heaven."

Simpson stood up. "My settlers from Red River!"

"Sorry, but I had no choice. You promised them houses, barns, fenced fields—" John broke off the recital with a sigh. "They can have all that, win it for themselves, on the Willamette. North of the Columbia, no. They suffered there last winter."

"So!" The Governor tapped his palm with the edge of his monocle and walked to the window. Instead of looking at the mountain, however, he stood staring into the fort yard. "Well, well, go on. You have an explanation, I dare say."

John forgot his well-rehearsed and documented excuse of needing more farmers raising wheat in order to fill the Company's contract with the Russians. "It was inhuman to leave those families in a destitute condition after the Company had persuaded them to come here on the basis of such glowing promises." He knew it must sound like lame reasoning to the Governor.

Simpson came back to stand above him. "Inhuman?" He clicked his tongue. "What strong words you use, McLoughlin!" The irony went out of his voice. "And since when has the honorable Company been declaring dividends on humane considerations?"

John got up and his fist struck his desk. "Governor, my contract with the Company does not require me to ignore the fact that I'm dealing with human beings."

Simpson studied John under cover of his eyebrows for a moment. Then, mild as milk, he said, "A body of loyal Britons."

John opened his mouth to argue but the Governor objected.

"No, no, I haven't forgotten that we've made it a policy to keep our people north of the river but some bloody big developments are afoot, Doctor." He sat down and leaned back for a chat. "Sit down, McLoughlin. You know why history so often moves along from bad to worse without direction? Well, I'll tell you. It's because too many people are afraid to strike out for what they want. Men like you, for instance, are afraid of a big, bold gesture.

[*213*]

They're afraid to plot a thing and make it work by whatever means required."

"What's this?" John asked.

Simpson screwed his monocle in place and laced his fingers across the salmon-colored waistcoat. "Doctor, you're looking at a man who is not afraid. It is my belief—and I have convinced a good many of the honorable Committee in London—that we can take for Her Majesty Queen Victoria all of the Oregon Country, the Sandwich Islands, and California. A wonderful woman, the Queen." His eyes wandered off. "That will be the proudest moment of my life, Doctor, when she singles me out for knighthood. Believe me, Doctor, nothing I can do for the Queen would begin to repay—"

"But, but, but—"

"One moment. This is no idle dream. British subjects in the Willamette Valley may be of help. You don't need to worry about placing them there. I'll shoulder the blame."

"Or the credit?" John would have asked but Simpson was wound up and in no mood to yield the floor.

He was saying, "I've just come from Sitka where I learned that the Russian-American Fur Company is eager to sell its post at Fort Ross on the California coast. They want thirty thousand dollars but, by playing it cagey, I can get it for less. In the meantime, James Douglas is on his way to set up a Hudson's Bay post at Yerba Buena. Ostensibly his trip is for the purpose of buying cattle and sheep. But a post there on that bay will serve us well in our political dealings with Governor Alvarado and the Mexicans."

"But, but—"

"One moment, Doctor. I've had my men in the field. The whole population of California is talking release from Mexican rule. When the time is ripe, it will take nothing more than a British man-of-war off the coast of California to induce the people to declare themselves independent of Mexico and under the protection of Great Britain. As to the man-of-war, the British Admiralty stands ready to back me up in this."

"But—"

"Yes, yes, I know, there might arise the necessity for some bloodshed but I have a plan whereby Hudson's Bay Company can supply citizens with guns—in private, of course."

At last, John got in more than a word. "This does not seem outside the realm of fur trading to you?" he asked.

The Governor sat down. "You have one weakness, Doctor. It has lessened your value to the honorable Company from the first but I'm willing to overlook a fault or two in a man I can use. Still, the fact is, you're too much inclined to criticize your superiors. Or, worse yet, to follow your own counsel without reference to me or to the Committee. Take the affair of that chaplain I sent you. Who gave you the authority to pack him off to London three years before the expiration of his contract?"

"God did," John blurted.

"What!"

"That's what I said. I recognize no higher authority."

"But he's back there now, writing magazine articles and stirring up feeling against the Company." Simpson's monocle tapped his thumbnail. "From now on, you will not play fast and loose with the men I pick for posts. I've plotted this thing to the last detail. The Company cannot afford temper tantrums or whims from you or any man." Pushing against the arm of his chair he stretched his waistcoat smooth enough to slide the monocle into its slit pocket. Hands on his knees and elbows akimbo, his heels rapped the floor. "Now then! I suggest that you write this down so there'll be no room for mistake."

John decided against answering but he flipped open his inkwell with a clatter and dipped the quill so deep it made a track like a two-wheeled cart when he tested it on foolscap.

"I'm moving William Rae from Fort Stikine to Yerba Buena in California."

John considered the point of his quill. "To California," he said. "I had hoped for another chance here to make more of a man of William Rae. Still, you're the Governor."

Simpson's laugh disparaged John's concern. "William Rae is man enough. As he is, he's the very man I can use against the Mexicans. His dark good looks will open doors with them. And he's the only Company man we have who can outlast the Mexicans in a drinking bout." Simpson's wink turned Rae's appetite for alcohol into a virtue. "Well, well, write it and don't try to reform William Rae. I need him just as he is."

John's hand trembled as he wrote. They would get a glimpse, at least, of Eloise when the move was made. And it would be a relief to have his daughter away from Fort Stikine. Marguerite would like this item of intelligence when he could get away to tell her. But, if this plot of Simpson's should bring on a war in California as he had hinted, Eloise might be safer at Stikine.

"Well, well, finish writing it." Simpson's mouth pulled to the side. "My next item will surprise you more. Have you no better quill than that? Surely Hudson's Bay Company is not so reduced in circumstance that we can't afford a goosequill for the Chief Factor of the Columbia Department."

Since Simpson meant it for a joke, John played along. "We do what we can to show a profit." He got a new quill from the box and managed to ink his fingers disposing of the old one.

"Perhaps you can write this item with your thumb," Simpson quipped. "For all I know, you may want to."

"I'm ready."

"To Fort Stikine, I'm sending John McLoughlin, Jr."

John dropped the quill. He stood up. "You mean this?"

Simpson leaned back. "You're pleased, I trust. You've wanted the boy to get ahead in the Company."

"*Oui, oui,* he wants to get ahead. Still, Fort Stikine—a rough post for an untried man. The place is filled with ruffians. They require special handling. They'd stop at nothing, if they ever mutinied." But, John reminded himself, this was a moment he had waited for since Simpson's first slurring reference to Jacques and Eloise as "bits of brown." "You'll never know," he said, "how much it pleases me that you have this confidence in my son."

"I saw possibilities in Jacques from the first," Simpson assured him. "You remember I used to say, even against your judgment, 'He'll make a good Company man someday.' I always thought the time would come when I could use him."

[*216*]

Something about his emphasis on "use" disturbed John's pleasure in this praise of Jacques. Still, with so much coming his way he could afford to ignore the Governor's little annoying habits of speech. "You don't intend to put Jacques in full charge at Stikine?"

"Not all at once, of course. There'll be a second in command until the boy learns the ropes. Surely you have no question about your son's ability to handle a post the size of Fort Stikine."

"No." John moved to the window. Jacques must have his chance and he himself had mentioned that he might like it at Fort Stikine. The hardest school was often the best. The only thing was, Simpson seemed to be pushing the boy into this post as if he had some reason that he kept from John.

Suddenly one of the Governor's quick changes turned him from administrator to friend. "Come, come, Doctor. Let's send Bruce for a spot of tea. This day deserves a kind of celebration. You'll see your daughter when her husband is moved to California. Your son has been promoted. What more could you ask for yourself and your bits of brown?"

While Simpson toured the Columbia Department posts and made a visit to the Sandwich Islands, the Montreal Express arrived and then another ship from London. On each mail John received a sheaf of letters from Fenchurch Street.

Chief Factor John McLoughlin
Hudson's Bay Company
Fort Vancouver on the Columbia

DEAR SIR:
The matter of settlers has been called to our attention . . .

DEAR SIR:
Regarding the settlement of colonists to the south of your Department, we have been informed . . .

DEAR SIR:
It has been brought to our attention that you allowed and—as some reports suggest—encouraged settlers to farm the Valley of the Willamette . . .

[217]

The letters all began on that same singsong note of tattling and complaint. Each one ended with a warning.

You will remember that Governor Simpson is in full charge in Rupert's Land and over your Department.

I am Dear Sir
Yours truly
Gov. JOHN HENRY PELLY

As to the final disposition of this problem, you will defer to Governor Simpson.

I am Sir
Respectfully yours
Gov. JOHN HENRY PELLY

I beg to remind you that the honorable Company cannot tolerate any Factor taking matters of grave concern into his own hands in opposition to his Superior Officer.

I have the honor to be
Dear Sir
Yours truly
Gov. JOHN HENRY PELLY

And while the letters poured in, settlers in the Willamette Valley finished their houses and most of them built barns, to boot. Their crops bulged every storage bin and haymow.

True to his promise, John sent Father Blanchet to French Prairie and helped him start a Catholic mission. No happier lot of French-Canadians ever lived. They had bread on the table and a marriage certificate on the clock shelf and, now and then, they raised another barn, calling in Doc Newell to pat out the tunes and Joe Meek to frolic through the turns.

As always happened with Governor Simpson near at hand, the pace at Fort Vancouver shifted into double-quick that spring and summer.

Eloise and William Rae came and hurried on to Yerba Buena —"Saint Francisco," Eloise wrote back, they called it mostly now. "A cold and lonely town," she said. "Billy is away so much of the time and I keep imagining ghosts in the fogs that roll in from the sea."

Jacques, his luggage heavy with the books he'd always wanted to read, went to his post at Fort Stikine and, already, Simpson had withdrawn Rod Finlayson, the second officer there, and left Jacques in sole charge. The boy was proving himself in short order.

John put aside his concern about affairs at that unpredictable post and tried to enjoy, instead, the pride in his son. But when he returned from a quick trip to California, he came with a weight of worry that would not be put aside.

"Johnny," Marguerite broke into his silence at bedtime his first night home. "Is it that you are sick from the waves or has our Eloise perhaps borne a son with two heads?" She sighed. "Since you step onto our dock at noon, you are not here in your thoughts."

John selected from the rack the huck towel with the yellow border and thoroughly dried his hands before he emptied the used water into a slop jar, replaced the bowl and pitcher ornamented with the Hudson's Bay crest, and turned away from the washstand.

Marguerite had twisted around on her three-legged stool and dropped her hairbrush in her lap. She gathered the folds of her pink dressing gown over her bare feet and waited.

John wanted to go to her, perhaps to drop on the floor and rest with her hand soothing his shoulder. He had never been so tired. Instead, he sat on the edge of the bed and his fingers, while he forgot to answer Marguerite's question, began to trace the quilted scrolls in the glazed linen spread.

Marguerite's brush moved again down the length of her hair. Finally, the strokes quickened. "Well," she said on a sigh, "it must be that our grandson wears two heads. I have heard it said that two are better. Still, I can see why you would not like it to bring me these news."

John said, "You have never liked Governor Simpson."

The brush stopped midway in a stroke. "You wish that I should like this George Simpson?"

[219]

"No. I wish to know what I think of him." John's finger traced on the blue spread the same kind of monotonous, unending pattern that had been going on and on in his tired brain. "I tried to question him on the ship coming home but I got few answers. He can think of little else these days except the honors to befall him, once he hands this country over to the Queen."

John got up and paced the length of the room beside the bed. "In California, John Sutter beat him to Fort Ross and he took that hard. But he claims that the settlers there—even though they are four from the States to one from Great Britain—are all afraid of falling into the clutches of the United States." Down to the foot of the bed he paced and back. "I don't know, I don't know. He's plotting, using Eloise's husband, somehow, in his schemes. But I failed to find out what was going on exactly. Young Rae would never leave me alone with Eloise. Our daughter is unhappy, that much I know, but she got no chance to talk to me about it. William Rae has taken to aping George Simpson in everything. He even smiles now on one side of his face."

"Johnny, the bedtime, it is long ago and you stack up too many thoughts for sleeping on. Come, *mon chéri*, and I shall rub your shoulder."

John stopped by the window. "I don't believe that George Simpson has any notion of doing wrong."

"Except, perhaps, to use a man to step upon to make himself more tall?"

"Yes, yes, he would do that—does do that, of course. But this in itself would hardly convict him of working any major crime. Still, if the outcome of what a man does is wrong . . ."

"Johnny, this George Simpson, I will wager, does not fret so through the night. Is not he the one to pace the floor and worry? And yet, listen, we do not hear a footstep in the room across the hallway."

John threw off his dressing gown and piled into bed.

"Johnny, you will turn so now that I can rub your shoulder." Marguerite's hands moved round and round on his back. To the rhythm, John fitted words murmured into his down pillow.

[*220*]

"Eloise had something to tell me. . . . There's something going on behind my back."

"You have read the letter from our Jacques at Fort Stikine?" Marguerite asked.

"I have and, there again, all is not well."

"Did Jacques say it in his letter that all is not well?"

"No, no, not exactly. But I could feel it."

"You feel too much perhaps. Do not stiffen up your back, Johnny." Her hands moved on until she felt the tension leave his muscles and, finally, his breathing slowed and deepened.

Marguerite lay back in bed but all of Johnny's worries had taken up their monotonous rounds in her. What could it be that Eloise should want to tell to her *papa* but her husband would not leave them so she could? If only Eloise could have been not dazzled by William Rae's black curly hair and flashing eyes and could, instead perhaps, have fallen in love with one of Mr. Wyeth's young Americans! As for Jacques, Marguerite had never liked his going to that riffraff post at Fort Stikine. Now if her Johnny also was in a worry about their son, perhaps it was, truly, a thing to consider through the night.

Taking care not to pull the blankets and waken Johnny, she eased herself from the bed and went to the window. Her foot touched Johnny's cane and she caught it barely before it clattered to the planks beyond the bearskin rug. Her hand gripped the ivory head of the cane and nervously pulled up and pushed and pulled again, half unsheathing the sword.

Could it be, she asked herself, that this George Simpson was striking at their children in order to get back at her for that night so long ago at Height of Land? No, no, she did not think so. That had been no big thing to him to remember through the years. She had remembered, *oui*. She had thought that she could find small ways to keep this little man from hurting her Johnny. She could forget to serve his tea and she could save her Jacques from taking the Filly when the Governor ordered it and she could pass on the talk she heard against him and point it out to Johnny when this George Simpson thought up schemes to make himself look big before the gentlemen in London. Still, these little ways had not stopped him from, somehow, making it that their Eloise had fear in her eyes and was not happy and their Jacques, also, because of the girl Susette.

Suddenly Marguerite saw again the letter that Jacques had taken from his pocket when he talked of his Susette. Could it be that the letter held inside its folds the name of the man who had disgraced Susette so that she must cut her wrists and die? Could it be that the man was . . .

Marguerite caught up her dressing gown and, shifting Johnny's cane from one hand to the other as she pushed into the sleeves, she tiptoed to the door. She stopped to listen to Johnny's breathing and then tried the latch. The door came open without a squeak and she was in the hallway.

Her bare feet made no sound on the planks as she moved across the hall to the room where George Simpson slept. A shaft of moonlight marked his door. She laid her ear against it to listen for his breathing. It came as regular as the lapping of the water on a lake shore. Still, she must be sure that this was right before she did this thing.

This George Simpson, she could agree with Johnny, might not intend big wrongs to happen from what he did. But there was no shutting of the eyes against the fact that he would not allow her Johnny to stand too tall because in Johnny's shadow he himself must always show up small. And was not this alone a reason big enough for the thing that she must do? Her Johnny must not be made to slope his shoulders down because a little man wished to kneel before the Queen and be called "Sir George."

She reached for the latch and gently released its hold. The weight of the door began to pull it open. Marguerite stopped to withdraw the sword. The ivory head felt cold in her palm. The ray of moonlight fell on the black cane with its bands of gold. Her gaze refused to leave the gold ring at the top.

"It is so like the wedding band that makes a woman belonged," she thought.

And in that moment she saw that she must not punish this George Simpson. She and her Johnny were one. If she were to do it, the gentlemen in London would consider it the same as

Johnny holding the ivory head in his big hand. Her Johnny would be disgraced and made to suffer. All that he had dreamed and worked for through the years would then be lost. No, no, this must not be.

She hurried back, replaced Johnny's cane beside the window, and, sliding into bed, she lay there shivering. "It would have been most easy," she thought, "but it was a thing not for me to do." No, no, Johnny himself would have to find a better way than she could think of to keep this George Simpson from climbing up on him and on their children. The sword, she knew now, was not the way. This sword of Johnny's wore two edges—one to stop this Simpson, *oui*, but, if it did, its other edge would surely cut out her Johnny's very heart.

No, no, there had to be a better way.

XVIII

When Simpson suddenly issued orders to close down all but a handful of the posts dotted along the Company's leased strip of Russian coastline, John needed to inspect the property and map the withdrawal with Pete Ogden who would be left to carry out the plan.

Now that the *Cowlitz* sailed up the inside passage, John was looking forward to seeing Jacques—Jacques running his own post, Jacques directing Fort Stikine's complement of rough men, Jacques controlling trade and managing the natives. He had pictured all this many times. Now, the pictures were about to be peopled with live Company men—laughing, cursing, tale-telling Scotsmen and Iroquois half-breeds and French-Canadians.

Jacques stood out, of course, in every picture. He used his skill and schooling to doctor the natives. With fairness and understanding, he settled their disputes. He took in furs and kept his accounts in order. He ran his post with the easy grace and high spirit that he used to give to washing his face in the middle of the stream. Soon now, John would see it with his own eyes and sit to the side with his son at the head of the table.

Jacques pushed his plate of fish away and scraped his chair back from the table. Before him, twenty pairs of arms grabbed and snatched for food. From twenty hairy faces poured out curses and raucous laughter. Suddenly the animal-like crunching and slobbers, the odors of greasy fish, were too much to bear. Jacques stood up.

He turned from the dining hall back to the entry and climbed the steps to the inner gallery. He liked to check frequently on the sentries. He usually caught them, their rifles discarded, gambling and drinking stolen rum or Indian hoochinoo.

Tonight he came on one man sprawled in a drunken coma on the gallery floor. His other sentry, a bottle to his lips, groomed himself toward the same position.

Jacques knocked the bottle from his hand and, snatching the sentry's own rifle, turned it on him. "March! Down you go to the cell. You know the rule—no drinking on sentry duty."

"It's damp up here," the button-eyed Iroquois whined. "A man's got to keep warm."

"We'll all keep warm when the natives give us a dose of their burning arrows some night while you're propping yourself up with your rifle. Now march!"

They stepped over the big Canadian on the floor and Jacques saw to the lock on the basement cell while the Iroquois cursed him through the barred door.

Back at the dining hall, Jacques called out the next two sentries on the board. He watched them scuff up the steps, grumbling at going on duty ahead of schedule. Hungry, but still unable to think of food, Jacques turned then and plodded the length of the huge bare hall that always smelled, somehow, of mildewed hides. He never paced the interminable length of this hall—from bearskin rug to rough-hewn planks to bearskin rug and on—without remembering that here Eloise had danced with fish-breathed Russians to keep from dying of boredom during the stormy winter nights while her husband was stationed at Stikine. "As for me," Jacques said to himself, "I won't die of boredom. I have better excuses than that."

He stopped and reached for a taper to light the candles in the massive brass sticks at the end of the hall. But then he changed his mind. Instead, he crossed to the left and went into his room.

Seated at his desk, he pulled toward him the post journal. "April 19, 1842," he wrote and then sat staring at the page, his quill tapping his chin. At last, he filled in the items for the day and reached for the latest inventory of trade goods on hand. His accounts, however, were all in order. He replaced the inventory and brought out, instead, his letter book. He'd write to Rod to pass the time until he must check again on the sentries.

"Dear Friend," he wrote, "I have had enough to attend to

[225]

since your transfer. I trust no one here. The way our affairs are managed is sufficient to make me take a disgust to the Company. The men sent here seem hell-bent on doing me in. Also, the natives are not so troublesome at any other post and yet where else is one officer left alone with no second in command? I am sure that if it were some other gentleman, the Governor would not leave him so destitute as I have been. Can it be that he is deliberately maneuvering me into a dangerous position?"

His quill hesitated above the letter book while Jacques read and reread his last sentence. He had written it in disgust and half in jest. But now, he wondered. George Simpson had his heart set on being knighted. Could it possibly be that the Governor was afraid that Jacques might use Susette's farewell letter to blackmail him with the high nabobs of England? "No, no, I'm letting the rain dampen my spirits." Jacques shook his head and dipped his quill.

He wrote, "Do send by the Indian messenger a few newspapers or books. I do not know what to do in the evenings when I can't sleep and I've read eleven times through each of the books I brought here with me."

He stopped and sat once more, tapping his chin. And then, somehow, his quill carried on, filling the page almost without his knowledge. It made crisscrosses and circles and wrote a half dozen prescriptions in Latin. It drew a young girl's profile.

"Certain unalienable rights," his quill wrote then on a slant. And, "salmon and potatoes, salmon and potatoes." Along the margin appeared the words, "Life, Liberty, and the pursuit of Happiness."

Suddenly Jacques frowned and slashed a black cross to mark out the ruined sheet. He must finish Rod's letter.

"As you can see, my friend, I am still among the living although reports say that I am going to be dispatched to the Sandy Hills. Reports don't trouble me but they keep me on my guard."

He pushed the book aside. His clerk could copy the letter tomorrow.

Startled, he glanced up. From the corner of his eye he had seen, or imagined he saw, his door move inward.

[226]

He laid down his quill and sat staring at the brass doorpull but he was thinking, "It's a funny thing about rights. Born with unalienable rights to life and liberty, was I? And the right to pursue happiness—except that my happiness is dead."

He reached inside his coat and brought out Susette's last letter. He sat with the folded sheet cradled in both hands. George Simpson was, after all, the kind of man who would weigh and then methodically set about erasing any item on his record that could possibly stand between him and his goal.

Susette had written, "I have told George Simpson that I am writing you everything. Don't let him destroy others as he has destroyed us."

If the revelations sealed in this letter and in Jacques's tortured memory could be the cause of the strange maneuvers here at Fort Stikine, perhaps they were, after all, of real import to George Simpson.

Jacques could not bring himself to decide, however, that the letter might save Queen Victoria from an embarrassment and should, therefore, be sent directly to the Prime Minister in London. But his father, he concluded, would know what should be done and, with things as they were at this unhealthy post, it might be just as well for him not to wear this letter constantly in his coat.

Jacques reached for a sheet of paper. "Dear *Papa*," he wrote. "If anything should happen to me, use this letter as you think best to keep the Queen from making a mistake in her judgment of George Simpson." He folded Susette's message inside and sealed it with red wax. He addressed it:

To Dr. John McLoughlin
Fort Vancouver on the Columbia

With a sigh, he slid the letter again into his pocket but he would send it off by the first opportunity. If anything should happen to him, Susette's accusation might, as she suggested, keep George Simpson from hurting others. But nothing could actually happen, of course, Jacques told himself. He was the boss around here. He was at liberty to run things in his own way, in spite of anybody.

"Life, liberty, and the pursuit of happiness," he mused. His gaze caught and held, once more, on the brass doorpull. "Unalienable rights—that's a laugh. The right to life—but what life have I left without Susette? As for liberty, I'm at liberty to get a hole in my chest any minute now, if I don't watch who walks through that door."

Years of living in the gentle mists of Oregon had almost erased from John's memory the kind of downpour dumped on the decks of the *Cowlitz* this afternoon in April as she made her way into the mouth of the Stikine.

Swathed in his rubber cape, he took his cane from the corner and, leaving Pete Ogden and George Simpson in the steamy comfort of the captain's cabin, went alone to the deck. Storm or no storm, he did not intend to miss the first sight of his son.

Torrents of water, swept down from the mountains, turned to white foam on the leaden river. Against a cold slate sky, sea gulls soared and dipped and circled. A kind of frenzied urgency seemed in them. Lower and lower they dropped until, now and then, John's arm came up to ward off a gull that skimmed by his face, screaming in a minor key.

As the ship plowed through the wash of foam and litter toward the dock, John saw that the tide was in and Fort Stikine crouched on an island of sand, her logs sodden black. Here and there a candle marked a small-paned window in the Company's buildings.

John's eyes strained through the mid-afternoon dusk to pick out his son on the dock. The odor of raw fish and salt and rotting viscera assailed him. On shore a campfire flickered, died down, and flickered again in the rain. The smoke smelled rancid. The ship nudged the dock.

Clutching the hood of his capote beneath his chin, George Simpson came out. "Smells jolly well like we get nothing to eat but fish in this hellhole. Here's hoping there's rum enough on hand to drown it."

Head down, Pete slogged along in Simpson's wake.

[228]

John still could catch no glimpse of Jacques but perhaps the boy had staged a welcome inside the fort for such a day as this. *Oui, oui,* that was it. That was it, of course. John's spirits lifted. He tucked his cane under his arm.

The three men made a stiff-legged dash for the gangplank.

Two long-faced Company men, looking more like wet and bedraggled roosters, faced them on the dock. They said nothing but the near one pointed the way to the gate.

John ducked and warded off a screaming gull.

Simpson growled, "Why are your flags out in this rain?" Then he stopped and his arm blocked John's way. "What bloody thing goes on here?"

John saw them then, the Union Jack and, beneath it, the Hudson's Bay pennant, dank and colorless at half-mast.

No one answered Simpson's question.

John lifted his eyes again to the wet log fort. A watchman, flintlock on his shoulder, paced past the window on the inner gallery. All was well, then. John's shoulders lifted.

Perhaps some Russian official had died and courtesy demanded the lowered flags. In the excitement of preparing a welcome Jacques had, no doubt, forgotten to order the colors struck when the rain began. A reprimand from the Governor would fix that fast enough.

For once, the pace set by George Simpson's short legs was too slow for John. This near, he had to see his son without delay.

Up the dock, across a strip of sand, through the gate guarded by a swivel, and into the fort's main building, the Governor remained in front and held John back.

The entry was deserted. A single candle burned on the newel post.

Frowning, Simpson flung off his wet capote and dropped it on a massive chest that stood against the dark wall.

John turned his head to listen. This silence, this dearth of men around, had to be part of Jacques's planned surprise, of course. Otherwise, a post was always filled with talk and flurry. He unhooked his cape and took his time to catch its collar loop on the antler by the door. He even gave Pete Ogden a hand with his

[229]

India rubber coat. John smoothed his hair, then, and flicked the water from his broadcloth pantaloons. The boy must feel pride when he introduced his father to his subordinates. Finally, John picked up his cane and gave it a toss to catch it in the middle.

When he turned, George Simpson and Pete Ogden stood in the open archway off the entry to the right. The welcome would be waiting for them beyond that wall. John lifted his shoulders.

The big reception hall was deserted.

Four candles in towering brass holders marked the center of the great expanse. They stood at the corners of a dark carved table. On the table, the bare new planks of a casket had been casually draped with black.

John closed his eyes. He heard his own steps then, slow and measured on the plank floor, muffled as he crossed the bearskin rug, sharp and jarring again on the planks, and softened once more by a rug. At last, he stood beside the table. The warmth of the candle near him fanned his cheek. His hands gripped his cane. Pete Ogden's shoulder touched his arm.

His men had not bothered to cover the bullet hole through the breast pocket of Jacques's coat.

Rain rumbled and slackened and swelled on the roof like clods of earth shoveled into a grave. Out from the thunder of sounds in his ears, as if it broke step and stood forth alone, John heard a voice.

"The string of my bow is broken," the voice said.

As if he stood again at sunrise on the knoll away from the fort at Walla Walla, John looked into the open grave of Chief Hasumtooks' son. The mound of black clods lay at his feet.

John felt Pete's hand on his shoulder. He heard the pound of rain but through it came Chief Hasumtooks' voice, "Fill up the grave," he ordered. "Cover my last earthly residence. Do not hesitate, for I am resolved to die."

Pete Ogden's hand gripped John's forearm and things began to shift back into place. This was Stikine, not Walla Walla. It was Jacques who was dead, not the son of Chief Hasumtooks. His own son lay dead, murdered. They had not bothered to cover the bullet hole through the breast pocket of Jacques's coat.

It was he, John McLoughlin, who stood beside his dead son. It was his voice that cried within him, "The string of my bow is broken." His vow, however, differed from that other father's.

"I am resolved to die," Chief Hasumtooks had said and stepped down into his son's grave.

John moved back. "I am resolved to live," he said. It was a promise to his son. He turned to Pete. "I am resolved to live, Pete Ogden. I'll live and fight all men who hold another's life as worth no more than beaver skins or trade beads."

George Simpson met them in the entry. "You're upset, naturally," he said to John, "but you'll have to put this accident aside. I'll need your help to get things straightened out. At least half the Company servants here are out of hand. They've been drinking heavily for days. The place is a shambles. I've called in the crew of the *Cowlitz* to help restore discipline."

John's gaze caught and held Simpson's. "I intend to investigate my son's murder. The man responsible will pay for this."

Simpson's mouth pulled to the side. "Naturally," he said, his manner ready to humor John's whim. "I've talked with the men, though, while you stood in there doing nothing. The thing happened in a drunken brawl two or three nights back."

John watched color come into his knuckles as his fingers loosened their grip on his cane. He took a deep breath. "Governor Simpson, I intend to find out who is responsible."

After Jacques was buried, John collected pieces of the puzzle —from the post's accounts, from snatches of conversation, even from the locked cabinet where Jacques kept his personal allowance of spirits, barely sampled.

The daily journal of the fort was written up to the day of the murder. Jacques's books were all in order. His inventory, always a problem since it dealt in furs and trade goods with a discount figured on the London price, revealed a discrepancy of less than ten pounds. In all his years in the trade, examining inventories from more than twenty posts made out by scores of experienced officers, John had never come across a set of records so nearly accurate.

"Let's question the men, one by one," Pete Ogden suggested.

[*231*]

The ship's captain offered, as a place for their investigation, his cabin on the *Cowlitz*.

Bit by bit, sorting and fitting the puzzle pieces, John began to see the picture.

Jacques had been most vigilant, the men agreed. It was his habit to visit the sentries on duty several times each night. He seldom drank and not one witness had ever seen him drunk.

"Now that William Rae," someone volunteered, "when he was here it was much different. *Oui, oui*, young Rae was drinking all the time but not *M'sieu* McLoughlin."

As for Jacques, he read a great deal, the witnesses all reported. Yes, he punished the men at times, usually by locking them in the basement cell. One Iroquois half-breed insisted he had spent the night of the murder in that cell and was, therefore, beyond suspicion.

"That big Canadian, Urbain Heroux—he was more off duty than was I. Still, *M'sieu* McLoughlin leave him on the floor that night, but me, he lock in the cell."

"Call in Heroux," John ordered.

His eyelids drooping, his manner sullen, Urbain Heroux stood before them.

Pete, at the table with his quill, commanded, "Your full name."

"You called my name to get me here." Heroux thrust out his chin. "Heroux," he muttered finally.

Pete wrote it. "Age."

"Thirty"—Heroux shrugged—"or thereabouts."

John pushed himself up from his chair and stood above him. "Were you at the Fort the night of the murder?" he asked.

"Who is given a chance to get away?" Heroux grumbled. He scratched and tugged with first one hand and then the other at the ragged mat of beard on his face. "Company say 'Stay,' you got to stay. Company say, 'Stikine,' you got no chance to get away."

"What was your duty that night?" Pete asked.

"Sentry."

"Tell us what happened," John prompted.

"Can't remember."

They made him remember, in time. But after he had confessed, at last, and signed his name to the statement Pete took down, John still did not feel satisfied. "But why?" he asked.

Heroux shrugged.

"Why? Why? I must know why!" John insisted.

Heroux just stood there. "We got nothin' here to do," he mumbled finally.

"That's not reason enough to kill a man." Pete Ogden swore beneath his breath.

"Maybe so." Heroux shrugged again. "Maybe I do not like him."

John towered above him. "And you think that is reason enough for killing my son?"

Heroux added, "Maybe nobody like him. Maybe I don't like him. Maybe his clerk don't like him. Maybe the Governor don't like him." He spat tobacco juice through the porthole. "Leastwise, the Governor ain't stirrin' up no fuss about a bit of shootin'."

When their prisoner had been led away, John said to Pete, "There's something back of this that we don't know. I won't feel right until we get all the pieces of the puzzle."

"You'll feel better once Heroux is convicted. His reasons will come out at the trial and that will finish the picture for you," Pete promised.

George Simpson had kept too busy around the post to lend a hand with the investigation. But it had not occurred to John that, once the evidence was in, the Governor would hesitate to bring the criminal to trial and speedy punishment.

Simpson read Heroux's confession at the dining table and tossed it, face up, beside his plate. "The fish up here taste a shade better to me than those you take from the Columbia, Factor. I wonder if we shouldn't set up a salting establishment near this place."

Unable to believe his ears, John slapped the sheet of foolscap. "What about a trial for this man?"

"Oh, that!" Simpson glanced at the sheet as if he had forgotten

[233]

its contents for the moment. "Well, I suppose the Russian Government would have to prosecute, if any government were to do it." His manner asked, "Why bother?"

Pete Ogden spoke up, "It's a case for the British courts, I should think."

"It happened on Russian soil." George Simpson gave his full attention to spreading butter on black bread. "Surely, gentlemen, we can find a more propitious place and a less hurried time for discussing this affair. Besides, as you both know, I dislike having my meals salted with business. What do you say to a bit of shooting up the Stikine this afternoon? We can't work all the time, you know."

John brought the matter up again that night when he found Pete Ogden and George Simpson lounging in easy chairs in the great hall.

The Governor leaned back and hung his thumbs in his waistcoat pockets. "Factor, you press too hard." The words fairly hissed. "After all, Jacques was flogging the men unmercifully for any slight offense or breach of discipline. You can't blame them for not liking that but, on the night Heroux got him, he was drunk as usual and he also gave out a gallon and a half of spirits. What could you expect?"

John sat for a moment, gripping the arms of his chair. Then slowly he got to his feet. "Governor Simpson, I had supposed that we were conducting an investigation of what happened. Instead, you appear to be seeking to prove a case against my son's character. Are you, somehow, wishing to justify the conduct of the murderer?" Without waiting for an answer, he turned and went once more to Jacques's room. He had to find out why this thing had happened.

That night he came across the words in Jacques's letter book, "Can it be that he is deliberately maneuvering me into a dangerous position?" John got up from the boy's desk. He'd go now and have a showdown with George Simpson.

He found the great hall empty. Temples throbbing, he moved along the corridor to the room where Simpson slept. He heard no answer to his knock. He tried the door and slowly pushed it open.

Inside, instead of Simpson, he found Pete Ogden.

"Where is he?" John asked.

Pete jerked his head toward the window.

Midstream, John saw the faint lights of the *Cowlitz*, making for the sea. "You let him get away?"

"He thought he'd better take our prisoner out to sea awhile until this business can blow over. Said he couldn't afford, right now, to upset the Russian Government with your demands for a senseless trial." Pete blew his nose. "He's sending the *Cadboro* for us next month, after our work is finished."

John stood at the window. "So he turned tail and ran," he said to himself. He gazed after the retreating *Cowlitz* and in his mind he could see George Simpson's aloof one-sided smile. At last, he turned away. "Pete Ogden, do you know of any letter? I've searched Jacques's desk and haven't found it. It must be somewhere."

"Letter?" Pete frowned. "There was a letter in the boy's pocket, Doc," he said, his tone dismissing it as unimportant. "The Governor came on it when we prepared the body for burial. I remember the bullet had gone through the folded sheet and George Simpson said, 'A letter from his girl, no doubt. Let's be sentimental and permit him to go on wearing it against his heart.' That could hardly be the one you're thinking of, I reckon."

John's fists knotted. "I could kill him," he said. "With my bare hands, I could kill him."

"You could." Pete Ogden nodded. "You could. No doubt of that. But somehow, Doc, I think you'll find a better way."

FOUR

XIX

"Unalienable rights"—the phrase would not leave John alone. It ran through all his thoughts of Jacques like a martial pibroch. It ran through his worry over Eloise's safety. In these words he renewed, each day, his promise to his son—he'd fight all men who held another's life worth no more than trade beads. "Unalienable rights!" The one set of words raised his anger against George Simpson and also stirred up doubts regarding John's own authority to control the destinies of Company men, Indians, and settlers.

When he got home to Marguerite with his awful burden of news regarding Jacques, her suffering brought up the words again. He had loved Marguerite but now the size of her grief filled him with a new kind of respect. He began to question for the first time his right to shape her life to his as he had done through the years.

These wonderings nagged at John through the summer while George Simpson traveled to the Sandwich Islands and to California in order to forestall a trial for Urbain Heroux. The conviction grew in John that no one man was big enough to decide a matter of life or death for any other man. One who willingly accepted such responsibility, he decided, most likely had some personal axe to grind. In George Simpson he'd seen his fill of tyranny. As for himself, he no longer cared to take the chance of robbing any man of his inborn rights.

John wagged his cane toward the new stakes that marked into squares the clearing beside Willamette Falls. "*Oui, oui,* excellent," he praised his big surveyor who hurried across, his roll of plotted lots hugged beneath his arm. "You've laid it out just the way I

[239]

pictured in my mind. Soon now houses and stores will sprout like seedlings into a city—Oregon City."

"Doctor, you've planned it for a long spell, haven't you?"

"Twelve years, nearly thirteen."

"Maybe that thirteen ain't too lucky." The surveyor jerked his head toward the woods. "Our pious claim jumper is busier than a timber wolf at calving time."

John's shoulders sagged. "No, no, not Waller again!"

"On the level." The surveyor pointed upstream. "Joe Meek sauntered by, near a half-hour ago, headed for the plot you've marked down to give his brother, Steve. Waller hiked after him, kicking down stakes in his path. Something's afoot, all right."

"I'd better arbitrate," John said. "Mr. Joe won't take much abuse from an auld Clootie of a hymn singer."

When John reached the lot he'd promised Stephen Meek, Mr. Joe turned to greet him above Waller's black hat. "Doc Long-John! Welcome to this hyar adjourned meetin' of the Oregon City Debatin' Society. Accordin' to your surveyor's chart, this hyar are the lot you promised my brother, Steve. Our Methodist friend hyar argufies it are part of his claim. Reckon we're mought' nigh ready for the jedge's decision."

"This heathen claim jumper!" Waller stepped beyond the range of Joe's fists. "He's threatening to build on my property."

"Must I remind you for the tenth time, Mr. Waller," John said, "that I spotted this site in 'twenty-nine? No Indian or white man disputed my claim until you and Mr. Lee begged me for a mission site a few years back."

"But I took out my claim as a citizen of the United States. You foreigners have no right here," Waller blurted.

Joe Meek snorted. "It 'pears to this hyar old hoss from Virginia that you're pressin' your citizenship a mite far, Waller, seein' no boundary line are settled. From Fort Laramie to Fort George, up to and includin' now, it are fust come fust served. The Factor hyar waar traipsin' this country afore you waar knowin' which di-rection it lay from the States."

Waller shifted his rebuttal. "Look here, now. The Reverend Jason Lee located me here to help the Indians and—"

[240]

"*Oui, oui*, Mr. Waller," John broke in. "My friend Mr. Lee did just that and you started, at once, trying to help yourself. You've helped yourself to the land I gave for the mission, generously offered my town lots to your friends, and built your sawmill on my island in the river. I must say that I respect Jason Lee and many of your mission associates, but if there's one thing I can't abide, it's a claim jumper."

"You salmon-skinned aristocrats of Hudson's Bay will find out who owns this country," Waller stormed.

Joe Meek reached down and took a grizzly's claw full of Waller's lapels. "I oughta dampen your punk by tossin' you in the river. Ownin' this country are got nothin' to do with the case as yit. Meantime, what about that thar 'thou sha'n't covet your neighbor's house, nor his ox, nor his brother's town lots'? Or maybe so you've done ripped all the 'thou sha'n'ts' outen your copy of the Book. If so, we'll soon have civil laws to make you keep your filthy hands outen other folks' pockets. As for now, get your b'iled shirt outen my sight."

Mr. Joe gave his captive a spin and a shove in the direction of his plank house built from John's timbers on John's land claim.

Retreating, Waller did not kick over any stakes.

"Doc Long-John, this country are sure 'nough needin' some laws afore long."

"*Oui, oui*, in time, Mr. Joe. Laws and someone else to enforce them would relieve my mind right now."

John kept wondering and could get no word of what was going on in California. Eloise's letters came less frequently these days and they read, more than ever, as if she wrote them with a hand across her mouth.

Young Johnny is growing. He looks like you, *Papa*. I go out little these days and see few people.

This was not at all like Eloise. Could the child possibly mean, John wondered, that William Rae did not allow her out? No, no, he had no reason sufficient for thinking such a thing. Still, why was it that Eloise never mentioned her husband in her letters?

[*241*]

"I had prayed that Jacques might be transferred to this post," she wrote. "Word of his death was almost more than I could bear. Did you perhaps intend to write more fully of the circumstances at Stikine, *Papa?* I had the feeling that you wanted to tell me more. How good it would be to ride with you and *Maman* again beside the Falls of the Willamette!"

John did not like the tone of Eloise's letters and Marguerite, when he read them to her, listened with her head tilted to the side and often commented, "Our Eloise is still not happy."

When John learned in the fall that Marcus Whitman was riding East on business, he invited Narcissa to spend the winter at Fort Vancouver to be company for Marguerite. On long horseback trips through the countryside, on picnics beside the river, and through rainy evenings before their parlor fire, the two women grew as close as sisters. Marguerite had lost a son. Narcissa had lost a baby daughter. John never heard them speak of this but the weight each carried seemed lightened by the other's nearness.

John, on the other hand, picked up from Narcissa Whitman unintended notes of warning that kept building, in his mind, into a pattern.

They did not sound to him like isolated happenings as Mrs. Whitman seemed to take them—the young Cayuse buck attempting to break into her room her first night alone at Waiilatpu, the war chief's pulling Marcus Whitman's ear and jerking off the doctor's hat to fling it in the mud, repeated instances of fences broken down and Cayuse horses accidentally trampling down the corn.

No, they looked to John like puzzle pieces.

He wrote to the gentlemen in London pointing out the desirability of anchoring an armed vessel or two in the Columbia. "Nothing that looks warlike," he specified. "With some feeling between Indians and Whites and even more distrust between us old hands here and newcomers, a bristling warship could start real trouble. Still, a modest show of strength lined up in the river might well keep one small incident from setting off a foray that could prove costly."

[242]

The next time John saw Joe Meek, he stepped from his office onto the portico and looked down on the lanky mountain man standing with one leg propped on the rusted cannon at the foot of the flagpole. His slouch hat in a wad in his hand shaded Joe's eyes from the afternoon sun while he stared straight up at the Union Jack and, beneath it, the Hudson's Bay pennant. "Mr. Joe. Mr. Joe," John called from the top step. "Are you seeing the light at last?"

Joe Meek did not move except to tilt his eyes toward John as he walked down the right-hand curve of steps. Solemn as the Methodist who beat the cow John lent him because she bawled on Sunday, Joe said, "Doc Long-John, this hyar old hoss are jest waitin' for you to see the light. Now, if you'd haul down them thar rags and run up a purty smart lot of stars and stripes, us boys from up Champoeg way would let you in as a might' nigh charter member of our new Provisional Govermint."

John reached for his friend's hand. "Provisional Government? Provisional Government? What could that be, Mr. Joe?"

"Waal, Factor, we jest concocted us a independent govermint so's to keep Injuns and Whites in order till Uncle Sam and John Bull can git a boundary line laid out. I'm hopin' you'll j'in us and pay your taxes. That way, we'll pretect your property here and up Oregon City way. And if you pay taxes a-plenty the new sheriff—which I have the honor to be in person—might collect his salary."

"I don't know, Mr. Joe. Seems I ought to be able to handle things on my own awhile longer." John was thinking though of the unrest among the Indians whenever new settlers arrived. He couldn't help thinking, too, of the loud talk among a few of the new American immigrants about running British foreigners from their shores. George Simpson had gone directly from the Sandwich Islands back to England without showing himself again at Fort Vancouver. John had heard no word from him and none from his request for vessels to anchor in the river.

"This child aren't out to scare you, Doc," Joe Meek said, "but feelin's runnin' purty high wherever half a dozen men git together these days."

[243]

"*Oui, oui*, so it is, Mr. Joe. And my big concern is that all these problems be ironed out peaceably and every man's inborn rights respected."

"Then you best j'in up with our new govermint, Doc Long-John. It's every man's rights we're settin' ourselves up to pretect, sure as shootin'."

"I'll think it over, Mr. Joe. *Oui, oui*, I'll think it over."

John thought about it as rumblings and rumor kept building. In fairness to the Company, he wrote the honorable gentlemen in London about the new Provisional Government. He urged now that they send him two small vessels to anchor in the river.

When Marcus Whitman arrived upriver, bringing with him from the States a wagon train of settlers, John heard the rumors swell with each new telling. Company men in Bachelor's Hall became hot-blooded patriots each night before they went to bed. They were rabid to clear Americans from the country. Indians gathered in bunches beside the river to discuss or to consider in tight-lipped silence each new item of intelligence regarding Whites on their land.

John knew that a party of immigrants coming across the mountains by wagon was bound to arrive ragged and hungry. He had Jamie Douglas load several bateaux with food and clothing to be distributed as needed and charged to his personal account. It would do no harm to let the Indians see that Hudson's Bay was aiding these white settlers and would frown on thieving raids or murders.

When Jamie Douglas suggested that Governor Simpson might object to selling Company goods to American settlers, John snapped, "In spite of George Simpson, I'm still a human being, Jamie, with human feelings."

Beside the rapids at The Dalles John asked Doc Whitman, "What's the feeling in Washington concerning the boundary?"

"Indifference," Marcus Whitman answered. "You wouldn't believe it. Indifference and ignorance. A couple of Missouri senators seem to know there is such a place as Oregon."

"I have a feeling it's like that in Great Britain, too," John said. "George Simpson was spouting 'boundary, boundary' by the ıunning rod a long time. Now suddenly he won't show up here and I don't seem able to work up any excitement over there about a boundary settlement, one way or another."

Marcus Whitman raked his fingers through the bristles of his hair. "Doctor, it was like pulling teeth to get folks in Washington even to talk about it. Secretary Webster was positive it couldn't be worth the ink to draw a boundary line on his wall map."

"And yet," John put in, "the feeling here is such that any minor incident could be fanned, overnight, into a conflagration."

"I reckon if a war broke out, both governments would work up an interest fast enough," Marcus Whitman said, "but, by the eternal, we'll show them without a war." His long arm swept the clearing where a stack of ripped-off Conestoga covers, a pile of wheels and wagon tongues and splintered tailboards lay in a clutter. "Wagons, Doctor. We made it all the way in wagons where the whole world claimed we couldn't." His pleasure in this feat gave way to a sheepish grin. "Nine hundred settlers from the States must look like a swarm of locusts to you men of Hudson's Bay."

"*Oui, oui*, a little," John admitted.

"And yet you seem amused."

"I should be alarmed, I suppose," John said. "But I was thinking about the Snake River Country—best fur country in the world, that used to be. In those days a few trappers from the States came in there, trapped, carried their takes to St. Louis and came back as far as the Snake to trap some more."

Marcus Whitman's frown was puzzled. "Furs played out soon after I came to this country, Doctor. Joe Meek used to sit cross-legged before our fire and rant and rave against Hudson's Bay for that."

"I know, I know. And where will you find Joe Meek this minute? Smack in the middle of a new independent government they've set up for Oregon. Here's what I'm getting at—a fur desert on the Snake didn't stop trappers on the other side and, certainly, it didn't stop you and your wagonloads of immigrants."

"And this amuses you, somehow?"

John dropped his hand from his ear. "It does and it doesn't,

Doctor. George Simpson had a notion some years back that he could stop Americans beyond the mountains by clearing beaver from that Snake River Country—creating a fur desert on the Snake, he called it."

"Your George Simpson sounds a mite slow in his study of American history, Doc. Mark my word, where wagons go and carry women, civilization and law and order can't be far behind."

"Then there's nothing for it but to fall in step," John answered.

John fitted the key in his watch and, as he turned it, he could almost hear its loud *click-click* mingled with Jacques's voice saying, "It has the finest chain movement I could buy."

Marguerite, judging by the wistful smile on her face, must have heard it, too. She let her knitting fall in a brilliant wad to her lap. "Time to inspect?" she asked.

John replaced his watch and key in the separate pockets and, pushing the rocker back from the parlor window, turned to Pete Ogden. "Want to make the rounds with me?"

"What's got into you?" Pete's sandy voice kept the question offhand but real concern tinged the look he gave John from beneath his eyebrows. "I never knew you to make inspection rounds at night. Thought you always rode out in the morning when you could see what was going on."

"These days I don't know what may be going on at night," John answered. He didn't want to alarm Marguerite but he'd like a chance to talk with Pete Ogden about the unrest plaguing the country right now. "It's nothing. Our stockade is in need of repair. Pickets are down here and there and it's an easy matter to break into the compound, that's all."

"But you've doubled your guard, someone said." Pete grinned. "I had to give six passwords to get my Stuart Lake Express admitted this morning. Fine kettle of fish when a man can't get inside Fort Vancouver's gates with a load of furs."

"*Oui, oui,*" John answered on Pete's same bantering note. It was good to have Pete at the fort again, if only for a month or so. Everybody had grown too sober lately. Actually John hadn't heard Marguerite's giggle since Jacques's death. That made another score to settle with George Simpson. John touched Marguerite's shoulder to let her know he'd be back soon.

Pete followed down the hall. When John stopped at the office and poked his pistol into his belt, Pete asked again, "What's got into you? Somebody after your scalp?"

"Not exactly, but things are unsettled here, Pete. Up there at Stuart Lake you're too cut off to know what's going on in the world." John reached into his desk drawer and brought out another pistol. "You might as well wear this," he said, "like old times when we used to go out from Rainy Lake House."

"There is something going on," Pete exploded. "What is it? If anybody's been threatening you, I'll blow out his guts."

"No, no, nothing of the kind." They crossed the portico and sauntered down the left-hand curve of steps. "People are on edge and jumpy these days, that's all. Nothing like a scalping or a bullet in the back ever happens around here any more."

"No, of course not," Pete scoffed. "This country's getting too civilized. Now up Stuart Lake way, we still live in fur country and fur times. I had to string up an Indian just last month for stealing a white man's cattle."

"You don't consider stringing a little too severe?" John asked.

"You've gone soft, Doc. You used to handle Indians with a mailed fist. Now when I do the same thing, you call it severe. I can't have every Indian who happens along thinking he can get away with a white man's property. You taught me that in the old days. I had to make an example of this one."

John agreed, "An example is necessary sometimes."

They passed Bachelor's Hall and turned to their right at the corner and then John heard a moan and saw a figure writhing on the ground beside the store. "The Indian store!" he shouted and broke into a run.

"There they are," Pete called, "ducking through the stockade." His pistol gave the order to halt before John could stop him.

"No, no, don't shoot," John objected but he saw Pete level his pistol once more at the figures scrambling to crowd through the missing pickets. John lunged over and knocked the pistol from Pete's hand. "Don't shoot, I said." And then, not ten feet before

[247]

him, a shadow moved. He dived and came up with six feet of cursing, kicking French-Canadian.

Pete turned into the gaping store. John followed, pushing his captive in ahead of him. Just then a snaggle-toothed Indian leaped from beneath the counter near the door and got himself trapped between Pete's legs.

"Let's tie them up and find out what this is all about," John said.

When they got them tied, John lighted candles and discovered the store in a shambles. Bolts of silk had been strung out and slashed with hunting knives. Buff nankeen jackets were tied in knots and smeared with red and black ink powder. Tin dishes, bent and twisted and stomped upon, had been hurled into a corner. Bellows were pulled apart, black Barcelona handkerchiefs were wadded and torn, borax powdered the floor, and narrow sarcenet ribbon festooned the room like cobwebs.

"The dirty, low-down—" Pete railed.

"They ought to be horsewhipped," John stormed. "Instead, let's get to the bottom of this."

The French-Canadian shrugged when questioned. "We hate the Company," he said. "We hate all salmon-skinned aristocrats. We show you. Much big plans brewing. Soon now, we drive you from this land."

"But why? Why?" John asked. "What have we done?"

"We don't like the Company," the French-Canadian persisted and would say little else.

John turned to the Indian. "What about you?" he asked in jargon. "Why did you come here? What do you gain by bending our dishes and spilling out our borax?"

"Not like the Company," the Indian answered in jargon.

"Why?"

"Everybody says, 'Don't like the Company.'" His hands lifted and opened. "So, I do not like the Company." His broken teeth made a jagged pattern in his grin.

But the French-Canadian shook his fists. "Other raids there will be," he threatened. "This one only small, so-so. Later you will see. Nobody like the Company. We band together. We drive you from this land."

"Shut up," Pete ordered. "Don't talk that way."

"Everybody's got a right to talk," John answered.

"Let's cut off their hands. Make an example of them," Pete said. "You stopped me when I wanted to shoot down the others. This minute they're out there somewhere telling everybody what they did and got away with. It's an open invitation to all malcontents to try the same thing, come another dark night. We might keep these two until morning and then hang them in plain sight of everybody. That would put a stop to this business fast enough."

John shook his head. "I can't do it, Pete. This is no longer a lawless country with me the only man here to decide what shall or shall not be done. The country has grown beyond that."

"You're still the law around here the same as I am at Stuart Lake. It has to be that way or the Company is in no position to protect its property."

"No, Pete. I can't do it. Things are not like that any longer. The land is becoming civilized. I'll confine these two for safe-keeping. Then, at the first opportunity, I'll take them to Joe Meek. He's the sheriff under the new Provisional Government. These men will have a trial."

"Trial! Silliest thing I ever heard of," Pete scoffed. "This isn't like you, Doc."

"A trial they'll have, regardless," John said and they herded their captives to a cell in the nearby warehouse.

John hurried back to the store then to make sure the guard had not been injured. He untied him and brushed him off and, sending him to bed, took up the fellow's beat himself.

In silence Pete paced along with John from the store to the big folding gates and back again, from the store to the gates and back.

Finally, Pete blurted, "Doc, I think I'd better tell you. A good many Company men are whispering about you behind their hands. Last time I saw George Simpson he asked me point-blank as to your loyalties. This thing you said tonight about turning

[*249*]

over to the Provisional Government men who had destroyed Company property—that wouldn't sound good to the Governor."

John stiffened as he always did these days at mention of George Simpson. "Sound good or not, there's nothing subversive about it. The Provisional Government is independent. It's a buffer state with laws and a few officers to hold things steady until the boundary is settled—that's all."

Pete stopped in his tracks. " 'Independent state' is one thing to say but let's not pull the wool over our own eyes. We all know that this Provisional Government ran up the stars and stripes at Champoeg. To the Governor and Committee in London, this thing you're doing will look like treason." Pete picked up the pace again. "You ought to know that George Simpson, even though he hasn't come around in person lately, is still as set as ever on taking all this country as well as California for Queen Victoria. He's working things out in fine detail. He simply will not tolerate anything that might in any way interfere with his ambition to be knighted."

John came up short. "Pete Ogden, to the Provisional Government these men we caught tonight will go. They'll get a fair trial." He said it as if it were a vow.

Pete took a deep breath and a new tack. "But that little band of independents can't try anybody and make it stick. Provisional Government!" he scoffed. "They don't have any influence."

"No influence?" John pondered this. "Well, maybe not," he admitted. "But they will have. I'll join them."

"Join them! Great Jehoshaphat's ghost! You can't do that, man. You can't!"

More to himself than to Pete, John said, "My mind's made up. I'll protect the Company's property but I'll do it by law, not by tyranny. *Oui, oui*, I'll join the independent government and pay my taxes. Then they'll have influence enough to make themselves felt in this country."

"There'll be the devil to pay," Pete warned. "George Simpson will see to that."

XX The ink had no more than dried on John's signing up with the independent government when, back on the Missouri at the edge of the States, a wagon train hawed-and-geed into line.

Fourteen hundred immigrants arrived in Oregon that summer. Chips on their shoulders, trigger fingers ready on their rifles, they poured down the Columbia. For three months, it had been with them: "Look out for Injuns. Shoot first and find out later who you hit. Otherwise, you might not get the chance to shoot." For three months, too, talk at night around their campfires had roasted the British. "Grab the land before they do. . . . Drive out Hudson's Bay and their cussed corner on our rightful American trade."

No matter how they talked, John could not let men and women starve their first year in the Oregon Country so he gave out seed grain as far as it would go. But he saw the settlers' envious eyes fixed on the porcelains and crystal, the silks and broadcloth of Hudson's Bay even while they signed his credit sheets.

Spring rains and seepage had finished the job of rotting the fir logs in Fort Vancouver's palisade. They must be replaced at once and, while his men were at that job, John decided, they might as well build up a blockhouse in the northwest corner of the compound. Nothing elaborate, but a three story bastion, loopholed in its lower floors and given an octagonal cap that could handle eight three-pounders, should prove an unpretentious plea for peace in case a few firebrands should let their feelings get out of hand. As long as he got no response from London to his plea for ships, he felt he had to take some slight precautions on his own.

While the rebuilding moved along, John kept his blacksmiths

busy, as usual, making up a year's supply of small axes for the Indian trade. Somehow the two jobs, put together, added up to war talk such as the Oregon Country had never heard.

One by one, rumors sifted in to John.

"Look at that blockhouse they're r'arin' up in our faces. These brazen Britishers are fixin' to fight the minute the boundary question comes up again," some said.

"They're fixin' to arm the Injuns and turn them all loose with axes. It'll be bloodier than the War of 1812!"

"We'll keep our eyes peeled. One false step from them and Vancouver goes up in smoke."

Hearing these rumors, John was glad the Company had ignored his requests for ships. Any unwary cannon of John Bull's that dared lift its nose among these settlers now would start a war, sure as shootin'.

And then, Her Majesty's ships and couriers began to descend on Fort Vancouver.

A stale pilot-biscuit of a man, Captain Gordon introduced himself in John's office and the square hanging corners of his jaws wagged in a reprimand. "How's that? You mean you had no word of us? Are fifty-gun frigates so common then in the Strait of Juan de Fuca that they come and go without your knowledge?"

"I'd have heard in time, I have no doubt," John told him. "But things have been somewhat disturbed in these parts lately. I've tried for three years to get a vessel or two in here to let newcomers know that the Queen is not without a navy. Now suddenly you turn up with a fifty-gun frigate. I'm not quite sure what this is all about."

But when he learned that Captain Gordon was the brother of Britain's Foreign Secretary and that the dapper lieutenant with him was the son of the Prime Minister, John could see George Simpson's hand at work behind the scenes.

Lieutenant Peel clicked his heels and bowed when the captain got around to introducing him to John. "Dr. McLoughlin," Peel said in the properly brisk tone for the son of a Prime Minister, "we are here, sir, to maintain the rights of the British Govern-

[252]

ment in this country, come what may. We will not allow our rights to be encroached upon in this or any other part of the world."

Captain Gordon's jaws wagged. "Be damned if I can see why they'd bother about this beastly country, one way or another, but the Pacific Squadron lies in the Strait of Juan de Fuca—fifteen ships carrying four hundred guns."

"Of all the confounded bungling!" John exploded. "Fifteen ships can start a war right now with no other action than to lie there ready. Nobody wants or needs a fleet like that. All we asked three years ago was a sloop or two. With feeling what it is today, any armed ship sailing in here now builds up suspicion and hatred against us."

Captain Gordon snuffled. "You excite yourself for nothing, Factor. Your Governor Simpson waits aboard my flagship for the big moment to make his entrance and direct affairs according to the plan laid out. With the Pacific Squadron at hand and our moves all mapped, we can handle any incident the settlers might incite."

"With bloodshed, yes. But, gentlemen, I've been the law and order in this country for many years. The Indians were our main problem at first and now our big problem has changed to immigrants. We've seen famine and epidemics and good times and bad and yet we've been able to keep the various factions well in line. Only a very few disputes have been settled by tomahawk. So far, none have been settled by two-shoot guns. I'm proud of that record, gentlemen. I do not want it sullied at this late date. Also, I do not want this country scarred by war."

"Come, come, Doctor," Lieutenant Peel said affably. "Aren't you letting sentiment get a mite ahead of your patriotic duty? It's our understanding that colonists from the United States are being raced in here in order to grab this territory away from Great Britain when the boundary is settled."

"Lieutenant, you're off a little in your intelligence. In the first place, they don't call them 'colonists' and they're not being 'sent.' They are settlers—free men and women with the urge to build

[253]

homes and live in a land where their children can have a chance to prove the stuff that's in them."

"Poppycock and sentiment, I call it," Lieutenant Peel scoffed.

"Call it what you will," John told him, "but don't check it off your list of the opposition's assets until you've had a chance to see how big it looms. Spend a few days traveling to the settlements. You'll be made welcome. They'll take you in without so much as asking your name unless you volunteer it. They'll feed you on salmon and pork and potted cheese and strawberries with thick cream. But while you're eating, don't forget to listen to them talk about this country. And, afterwards, wander with them outside their cabins. Get them to show you how they can shoot."

"Poppycock," Captain Gordon grunted.

Next thing John knew, Pete Ogden guided into Fort Vancouver two more English gentlemen. They wore belted jackets of the roughest tweed and made a self-conscious show of being sportsmen off on holiday.

John watched them snoop around a few days and smelled a rat. He cornered Pete Ogden in the office with a glass of wine.

"Pete Ogden, it's good to have you at the post again. We miss you through the winter." John raised his glass. "To Oregon, the finest place in North America for the residence of civilized man."

"To Oregon." Pete drank and settled back in the leather chair.

Hands clasped beneath his coattails, John stood above him. "Now then, Pete, the Company is not so reduced in circumstance that she's sending out Chief Factors to act as guides for visiting sportsmen."

Pete's eyebrows lifted. "No?"

"No."

Pete's high-pitched gravelly chuckle had admiration in it. "Any guesses, Doc? My orders are to guide them and keep my mouth shut. But I've had no instructions about listening while you ask questions."

"I'm not blind nor deaf, Pete Ogden. My guess is, they're spies and from the Army."

"Tut, tut, Doc. 'Spy' is a nasty word. 'British Intelligence' offends our sensibilities less."

"But why? Why send men snooping in this country now?"

Pete shrugged. "In case of war over the boundary."

"War, war, war! Let one word of British spies in here leak out and we'll get war, all right!"

Pete came up in his chair. "Sit down, Doc." His voice dropped down the scale a notch. "For old times' sake, I'm going to let you in on one thing more. They're under orders from George Simpson to investigate your loyalty."

"Under orders to get something on me would be nearer the truth, I have no doubt."

"Doc, I'd like to tell you what these blighters are sending in their report to Parliament."

"Tell away." John sat down and pulled his chair to the desk so he could prop his elbows. "And when you've finished, I'll tell you what I think of Parliament for sitting with folded hands when they could have helped us here. And now, when affairs require finesse and understanding, they dump on me the Pacific Squadron, the brother of the Foreign Secretary, the son of the Prime Minister, and assorted spies and crackpots!"

"In their report they're saying," Pete went on as if John had not spoken, "that without the personal assistance of Dr. John McLoughlin not thirty American families would have settled in Oregon."

John sat back to ponder this. He should, by rights, get mad, he knew. He should spring to his feet and knot his fists. His pulses ought to race and his words come tumbling out in double file. Instead, he thought of Simpson, waiting out there on that flagship for his big moment to be a hero before Great Britain. And he thought of the hundreds of American settlers, waiting on their own plowed fields with their two-shoot guns ready in the nearest fence corner. "'Without the personal assistance of Dr. John McLoughlin not thirty American families would have settled in Oregon,'" he murmured. "Well, well, imagine that."

Pete's brows pulled down. "Doc, you're as hard to handle as you ever were, even back in our old Nor'wester days."

"Pete Ogden, you're not as hard to handle as you were back there. When you trail in here with nothing better to do than play wet nurse to a couple of Simpson's snoopers, I confess I can't see much of the old Nor'wester in you."

Pete shrugged. "Orders."

"Orders from the Governor!" John got up and went to the window. No better Company man ever lived than Pete Ogden, he reminded himself. So what was it about him these days? Somehow, he'd lost his gumption. Maybe he'd been used by George Simpson until he was all used up.

"You'll have to defend yourself when that report reaches the gentlemen in London," Pete said.

John blurted, "Let time defend me as it must defend my son since George Simpson stands in the way of justice."

"But you're risking your position with the Company—your big salary, the honor and respect of the gentlemen—"

"I'm risking nothing that I value above human beings and their rights, Pete Ogden. I will not stoop to defend my actions as long as I'm guilty of nothing more than helping men and women in this country."

John had cut a bunch of grapes for Marguerite at dusk that day when he looked down on what appeared to be an animated toadstool climbing the steps to his portico. He released the catch on his folding knife and waited. When the figure reached the top step, its toadstool topper came off in its hand.

"Petit Chief Factor," John exclaimed. "What are you doing with Joe Meek's hat?"

"Sh-h-h!" Charlefoux's boy gave a guarded glance around. "I'm a spy," he whispered in French. "You are to come with me to the river." He gave John's coat a tug. "We take back Joe Meek's hat."

"Just let me step inside to deliver these grapes and pick up my cane." John glanced at the grapes in his hand and back to the boy. "Better still, you eat the grapes and I'll get my cane."

Petit Chief Factor led him across the meadow to a clump of willows where Joe Meek waited in a half-size canoe.

John leaned across the muddy bank to shake hands. "Mr. Joe! It's good to see you." He straightened and flicked a glance behind him. "Or should I say it in a whisper?"

Joe Meek stepped onto the grass and snatched his hat off Petit Chief Factor's head. He offered the boy his free fist. "Hyar you are, Son—the foldin' knife this child promised. Now you best high-tail it outen hyar afore dark or your *papa* will come scoutin' for you."

The two men stood shoulder to shoulder, watching the boy stretch his skinny legs along the river path.

Joe Meek slapped his battered hat onto the top of his head. "Doc Long-John, thar's trouble afoot." He backed deeper into the screen of willows.

"Mr. Joe, you're behaving more like a criminal than a sheriff," John teased. "Confess. That's my advice. Then I'll use my influence with the Provisional Government to get you off with a light sentence."

"Aren't no jokin' matter, Doc. A band of renegades are gatherin' this minute upriver near the sawmill. They're layin' to burn Fort Vancouver this hyar night."

"Burn Fort Vancouver! That's ridiculous."

"Ridiculous it is and that are a fact," Joe Meek agreed. "Still, they're gatherin' up thar by the score," he insisted.

John found this too far-fetched to take as more than one of Mr. Joe's tall tales. "You're making this up, of course," he scoffed. "There's been some talk against the Company but nothing hot enough to start a blaze. Most of the Americans, even, are friendly toward us."

Joe Meek folded his knees and sat cross-legged on the grass. He loosened the strings in the rawhide bag suspended from his neck and got out his pipe. "That are what puzzles this child," he murmured. "Most folks like you, Doc Long-John, and respect your jedgment. But somethin' are goin' on. Somebody are stirrin' up Injuns and Frenchmen and hot-head Americans all alike. This old beaver's been askin' questions since rumors of a burnin' got 'round more'n a week past. Been hopin' to bring in the ring-leaders afore anythin' busted loose." He screwed his hat another half turn onto his head and dug his pipe into his beaded tobacco pouch. "Cain't figger it no-wise. Cain't figger it and cain't stop it. It are like these hyar firebrands are catchin' their hate di-rect from the air." Joe's fingers foraged for a wad of dry grass into which he could strike his flint for a light.

"If you're serious," John said, "I'll go meet these malcontents. Surely they'll listen to reason."

"They'd kill you," Joe stated flatly.

"Nonsense. I don't know who they are but they're not murderers, of that I'm sure," John told him. "They're nothing but settlers from here and there. I've provided most of them with seed and a start of cattle. I'm not against them. I'm for them. All they need is to be reminded of that. I'll ride upriver and have a talk with their leaders."

Joe Meek lost all interest in his pipe. "Doc Long-John, this child knows you're not ag'in 'em and you may know it. They jest know they're r'iled a-plenty and half froze for the ha'r of Britishers."

"But, Mr. Joe, they'll have to be stopped. A thing of this kind, happening right now with feeling what it is, would set off a war." John sat down on a driftwood log and gripped the ends of his cane across his knees. "I'll tell you a secret, Mr. Joe. The Pacific Squadron of the Queen's Navy is anchored this minute in the Strait of Juan de Fuca. Let one renegade's torch touch off one picket of Fort Vancouver and Captain Gordon will sail that squadron into the Columbia and war is declared. No, no, this can't be. I'll have to ride upriver and stop them."

"How stopped are they goin' to be after one of their hot-heads lines up his hindsights on you and squeezes his trigger? Thar's how it'll be if you try talkin' to that thar mob in their prissint mood."

"You have something better to suggest?"

"This child are for ringin' a guard, shoulder to shoulder, around the stockade. Let 'em come then and we nab 'em. Surprise 'em when they got their hands full of torches 'stead of two-shoot guns and we got a chance to hang onto our ha'r and a place to bring 'em in, one at a time, for questionin'. You got a corral whar we can run in two score fire-eatin' renegades if need be?"

John nodded. "The new bastion." He got up. The whole business seemed unreal. Figured out in cold blood, it made no sense and couldn't happen. Still, the tightness in his chest told him that, impossible or not, the thing he had feared most was on the verge of exploding in his face. He pulled on the ivory head of his cane, half unsheathing the sword inside and then gave it a tap to send it back again. Up and down he worked the slender blade. In the old days he would have handled this business in his own way as he had handled unrest and thieving and threats through the years but, tonight, too much was at stake to risk any accidentally pulled triggers. One misstep tonight and John Bull and Uncle Sam would be at each other's throats. "I'll call in Captain Gordon and Lieutenant Peel," he told Joe Meek. "And Pete Ogden, too. We'll lay our plan as you suggest. You think there's time?"

Joe Meek stood up. "They're fixin' to strike after the moon goes down. That'll be jest afore dawn," he said. "You meander on in. They're watchin' the fort and you can go your pile on it. Give your guard at the business gate word to let me in, come pitch dark. We gotta keep it a surprise that we're trappin' for 'em or we lose our advantage. This way, we got a chanct—not good but a middlin'-fa'r chanct—to stop 'em, previdin' you can rake up enough men from the fort and village and rake 'em up fast."

"The thing can't happen," John vowed and gave Joe Meek his hand. "It simply cannot happen." He drove the sword into its sheath and struck off down the river bank.

John got Lieutenant Peel seated in one leather chair and Captain Gordon in the other. Pete Ogden he put at his desk in the candlelighted office. Personally, he was too worked up to sit. Instead, he stood by the window. One hand gripped the sill. In the other, he clutched his cane. Already the moon had climbed beyond the snowline on Mount Hood.

"Gentlemen, I've called you here because I have just received intelligence of a plot to burn Fort Vancouver." He paused and added, "Tonight, as soon as the moon goes down."

Captain Gordon's fat eyelids folded back slowly and John saw his gaze meet Lieutenant Peel's without excitement or surprise.

Pete Ogden came to his feet.

Captain Gordon cleared his throat. "What was the source of your information, may I ask?"

"It's authentic enough," John assured him. "It came direct from the sheriff of the new Provisional Government. He's known of the plot for some time but he put off telling us because he was hoping to bring in the instigators. So far, the source of the trouble has eluded him."

"Righto!" Lieutenant Peel sat back and crossed his arms on his chest.

Captain Gordon's jowls wagged up and down. "Bully for us," he mumbled and cut a generous two inches off a twist of tobacco he brought from his pocket.

John banged the floor with his cane. "Gentlemen, you must have misunderstood me. I said 'tonight'! We have three or possibly four hours in which to call in every man of the fort and village and assign them to stations surrounding the stockade. I brought you here to plan our strategy."

Captain Gordon shrugged and plopped the cut of tobacco into his mouth. "How much strategy do you want, Factor? We've got our fleet at hand and everything in readiness to fight."

"That's what we can't do," John flared, "and if you had the country's interest at heart you'd know it."

Pete's voice cut in so low-pitched and steady that John was startled by it. "You'd better tell him," Pete said to Gordon, "or I will."

Captain Gordon merely reached with his toe to hook the brass cuspidor nearer.

Pete took a wide stance facing John. "They know all about this plot to burn the fort," he said. "The thing's been brewing for quite some time."

"Know of it? Know of it? And why wasn't I told?"

"They were afraid you might object."

"Object? Of course I object," John stormed. "It can't happen. Can't possibly happen." He turned to Gordon and Peel. "You must help us set up our defenses and leave at once. A fire in itself would be incident enough to start a war. Personal injury to the son of the Prime Minister or to the brother of Britain's Foreign Secretary would set the world ablaze."

Captain Gordon used the cuspidor. "The fire alone should turn the trick with feeling as high as it is."

Lieutenant Peel stood and anchored his thumbs in his pantaloon pockets. He rocked on his shiny heels. "You see, Factor, the whole thing is working just the way George Simpson planned. Simpson assures us that he has seen, personally, to all the details. All we have to do is wait for those renegades to lay their torches to your new stockade. Our horses are saddled and waiting beyond the potato fields for us to escape. Fort Vancouver goes up in smoke and the Queen's Navy steps in to protect British property. So"—he shrugged, his arms outspread—"the war is off to a fine start. Then"—he went to the wall map beside John's desk— "we race to the south, taking as much of the land as we can before the boundary is settled. We fight our way as far down here as California and Governor Simpson has a man at Saint Francisco —name of William Rae, as I recall—and he's been supplying rebels with rifles and lances. Once our troops show up in California, this Rae's men will set Alvarado back in the governor's chair and Alvarado has been fixed to surrender California."

"Stop!" John's cane clattered to the floor. He snatched the map from the wall and ripped it through the center. He wheeled on Pete. "Did you know this, too, Pete Ogden?"

Pete's voice had slipped back up the scale. "I knew it, Doc. It's all on the Governor's orders. Some of it may look hard to you— you're so in love with this land. But that's the way nations and empires are shaped, Doc. We're not big enough to buck it."

John looked into Pete's eyes. "Not big enough?" he asked calmly. "That's where you're wrong, Pete Ogden. You've forgotten the size of a human being." He pushed Pete aside and sat down at his desk. He flung up the cover of his inkwell and snatched a sheet of letter paper from the cubbyhole before him.

"Honorable Governor and Committee, No. 3 Fenchurch Street, London, England," he wrote. "Gentlemen: I hereby tender my resignation . . ."

"You can't do that, Doc," Pete objected over his shoulder. "Think of your salary, your stock in the Company. A few years more and you can retire on a good fat pension, take it easy the rest of your life."

John wrote on and signed his name. Breathing hard, he folded the sheet and sealed it with red wax. He thrust it then at Lieutenant Peel. "Deliver this in person to Governor Pelly," he said.

With an astonished, "Well, well!" the lieutenant accepted the letter.

When John turned to the door, Captain Gordon kicked aside the cuspidor and got to his feet. "You're not going, Dr. McLoughlin. I'm afraid we'll have to ask you to stay here until the attack," he said, making the words bland to cover the note of command in his voice.

"*Oui, oui,* I suppose you have to ask it," John agreed in the same mild tone. He stooped to retrieve his cane from the floor. "But I'm not staying." Unsheathing his sword, he backed to the door.

Gordon ordered, "Stop him! Don't let him get away."

Pete stepped over and, with a jerk of his head, hurried John out. To Gordon he said in his sandy falsetto, "It's his country, Captain. He's due this one more chance to see what he can make of it."

John ran up the hall to get Marguerite.

"Bruce, Bruce!" he called as he passed the dining room. "Come along, man."

Marguerite threw on an old capote and followed John through the passageway to the kitchen without asking an explanation.

"You want horses saddled?" Bruce asked.

"Horses waiting beyond the potato fields," John told him. "We'll take those. Keep to the shadows now," he warned and eased open the kitchen door.

He led the way along the north side of the stockade and to the new bastion. With a backward flap of his hand he kept Marguerite and Bruce in hiding while he went in. "I'll take my prisoners now," he said to the guard. "Sheriff's waiting for them at the business gate. You might tie their hands and let me have the use of a pistol for tonight."

"Yes, sir."

Outside with his captives from the Indian store raid, John took time to explain in French, "You're going with me to meet the rest of your crowd. Any commotion and you'll be shot down here in the fort by one side or the other."

At the business gate he told the big Scotsman on guard, "Sheriff's waiting for these prisoners."

"Yes, sir." The guard made a full turn. "Where, sir?"

John heard a low whistle. "Outside," he said. "Open the gate."

"Yes, sir."

Joe Meek was harder to convince. John made him strike off with the party in search of the saddled horses but Joe argued with each step. "You cain't do it, Doc Long-John. This child aren't doubtin' your word about Britishers baitin' this trap to lure Uncle Sam into a war. You jest give me the only explainin' as makes sense outen the shenanigans goin' on in these hyar parts. All this child are sayin' is, that band of renegades will be full force by time we get upriver. At sign of your white head shinin' out like Mount Hood in the moonlight, they'll shoot and ask their questions later."

"But I've got to explain," John insisted. "They must be told that they're playing into the hands of those bloodthirsty plotters."

"A dead Factor aren't never goin' to make a good story outen that one," Joe Meek persisted.

They could smell the smoke from choked-out campfires and feel the dust in their throats before they drew close enough to the renegades' rendezvous to hear muffled voices.

Joe Meek called back in a whisper to Bruce and Marguerite, "Wait up." Then he pulled around to John's side. "This hyar child rides into that meadow fust," he said, leaning into John's ear. "That are the law."

"We ride in together," John came back. "Bruce has his instruc-

[263]

tions to keep Marguerite out of range. You and I take the captives with us. We can use them for cover, if need be." John touched his mount's flanks with his heels. He turned to see their captives and Joe Meek—pistol drawn—fall in behind.

They rode into the meadow at a gallop.

"It's Doc McLoughlin," someone called.

"It can't be," another scoffed.

"Aren't nobody else that size."

"Doc McLoughlin. Doc McLoughlin!" The name ran through the crowd like wind through fir trees.

"Fan up a fire," John ordered.

Half a dozen shadows scrambled to the job.

John called out, "I'm John McLoughlin. I've brought two of your own men and Joe Meek."

They snatched him off his horse and threw him to the ground.

"Britisher! Kill him," they shouted. "He's the one we're after."

Joe Meek let out a yell to curdle the night air and, in the split second of his attackers' surprise, John scrambled to his feet. He reached back and jerked his tall French-Canadian captive off his horse and nosed his pistol into the fellow's back.

Joe Meek called into the gasp that followed his yell, "Our pistols are cocked and ready on your men. John McLoughlin are sayin' his say or we blow these hyar old hosses to hell. Fan up more light!"

"You can't stop us, Factor. We're burnin' Fort Vancouver this night, regardless of speeches."

"You're free to," John told him, "once you hear what I've come to tell you."

"Let him talk," someone called. "We got nothin' to do till the moon goes down and he ain't got a chance of gittin' away."

"Sure. Let him talk. Then we'll take him in and tie him to the big foldin' gates while we burn 'em."

Fires flared to light the meadow as men fanned them with slouch hats. John transferred his pistol to Joe Meek's free hand.

Joe settled his heels in the grass and held a man with each muzzle while John stepped out between two campfires where all could see him.

[264]

"Gentlemen, let's hear your grievances."

He got an avalanche of epithets and curses.

"Let me tell you," he said and held out his hand. "First . . ." he ticked off his thumb, "you want higher prices for your wheat. Second . . ." he marked it with his index finger, "you want lower prices on plows and seed. Third, you want more credit. Fourth, you want my land claims. Fifth, you want competitive prices."

Their own well-worn chants filtering down on the meadow from the camp of the enemy, acted like Oregon mist on a chip fire. John heard murmurs and mutterings but no out-and-out flare of hatred.

"You know what the honorable Company says of me?" John went on and he counted off accusations on his fingers. "They say that I supplied American settlers with seed and plows to develop the agriculture of this country at the expense of fur-bearing animals. The Company says I extended credit to settlers when I might have withheld food and plows and forced you from this land. They say—"

"It's your Company we hate," someone called out. "It's Hudson's Bay we'll burn out tonight."

John took a wide stance. "And do you know what the Company says to this plan? They say, 'Come ahead.'"

"Ya-a-a! They don't know nothin' about it."

"That's where you're wrong. It's a trap," John told them. "The Company is an old hand at trapping. Burn Fort Vancouver tonight and you're caught and ripe for skinning, the same as any beaver."

Joe Meek had to help shout them down before they'd let John explain that Captain Gordon was waiting this minute for them to strike the flint that would provide the excuse for him to sail the Queen's Pacific Squadron into the Columbia and turn her cannons loose.

"But you're one of 'em," they yelled.

"What kind of trap is this you're settin' by comin' down here with your big talk?" someone called out. "We ain't takin' your

[265]

word on nothin'. You're as expert at trappin' as the next one. You're one of 'em."

"But he's not, he's not," Joe Meek assured them. "He's up and resigned—jest tonight."

They rallied around John at that and they were harder to quiet down as friends than as enemies. "Come with us then," they demanded. "Lead the party that burns Fort Vancouver! Come on, let's go." They were for hoisting him onto their shoulders.

"Set one torch to Fort Vancouver and you touch off a war," John reminded them. "As I told you, the campaign is all cut and dried."

"We're not afraid to fight them British bastards. One of us is worth ten of them tea-sippin' aristocrats."

"Doc, you're our leader. On to Vancouver!"

"You and your countrymen could beat them eventually. I've no doubt of that," John told them. "A man protecting his homeland fights with God on his side. *Oui, oui*, you could beat them. But you can beat them without getting killed in the bargain. You can beat them without scarring up your farms with cannon shot and dead bodies. Why not beat them by letting them wait at Fort Vancouver and wait through tonight and tomorrow night and next year, if need be? They can't put their big plan in motion until you shove it off with a fire to hang their war on."

"You're still for John Bull." It was a growl near at hand and John looked into the black eyes of a two-shoot gun. The light from the campfire on his right streaked down the twin barrels and picked out a finger crooked around the gun's trigger. Beyond, he could see only shadow—a solid, hulking shadow, immovable as a mountain.

"Johnny." Marguerite's voice came out of the dark as unperturbed as if they stood alone beside their parlor window. "Did you perhaps forget to invite your friends here to come and trade at your new store in Oregon City that you will soon build?" She came slowly across the meadow and stepped between John and the end of that gun. Her hair touched his cheek as she flung her head high on his chest. "Did you forget, too, perhaps," she went on, "to invite our friends to visit us when we get builded our new house beside the Falls of the Willamette?"

The double gun-barrel swung upward and disappeared into the shadow. "You're not still for John Bull?" The growl had fur now but no claws.

Joe Meek bawled out, "You're dead wrong on that John Bull business, Mister Whoever-you-are."

"He could be pretendin' so's to throw us off the scent."

"Doc Long-John hyar's set more wheels a-rollin' than any man in the Oregon Country to git you what you want most," Joe Meek came back. "Stand aside now, thar's all you got to do. Jest don't git in the way of the wheels and, fust thing you know, the boundary line are goin' to be settled, fa'r and squaar."

"And Old Glory wavin'?"

"And Old Glory wavin'," Joe Meek promised.

John stepped forward. "Once the boundary is settled in favor of the United States, I'll be the first man in line to take out my citizen's papers."

Joe Meek gathered his two pistols into one fist and shot his free hand out at John. "You meanin' what you jest said, Doc Long-John?"

"Sure as shootin'," John answered. The shake he gave Mr. Joe would have crushed a lesser man's bones.

Above the rumble and clatter around him as men gathered up their gear and made off for their homes, John heard Jacques's voice. "You ought to read it sometime, *Papa*—that Declaration of Independence. It only preaches what you practice whenever you get the chance."

XXI Joe Meek brought John back with a sock on the shoulder. "Come along, Doc Long-John. We got on our hands two prisoners to bring to trial."

John had forgotten. "Sorry, Mr. Joe, but I'll have to return to Fort Vancouver and wind up my business. If you'd take Marguerite to Oregon City I'd appreciate it, though."

Joe clamped his long fingers around John's arm. "No you don't! You're my only witness ag'in these hyar prisoners. You go with me."

"But at Fort Vancouver there'll be a thousand things to see to that nobody knows about but me. I can't forsake the gentlemen in London by leaving a lot of loose ends."

"Thar'll be time for what you got to do. Let them foforraw critters cool their heels awhile at Fort Vancouver. It won't take you more'n a couple of days to testify ag'in these hyar men. Then back you go to wind things up. Meanwhile, don't tell me you don't relish the picture of all them thar British gunboats stompin' 'round their anchors in the Strait and that George Simpson waitin' thar with his thumbs hung in his pockets for a chanct to di-rect his war."

John and Marguerite went with Mr. Joe. Virginia Meek gave up her feather tick to Marguerite.

Joe Meek called the trial for early the next day and John went to the tannery to testify. The men, it was decided, should be confined in jail for two weeks each because they refused to name the others who took part in the Indian store raid.

John hurried back when the trial was over and took Marguerite for a walk along the main street of Oregon City. The place had grown like a weed patch almost over night.

They passed a tavern and a blacksmith shop and then a tailor's

[*268*]

and John tipped his hat and bowed to all the ladies that they met and all the men stopped him to pass the time of day and ask, "What's the news from Fort Vancouver?"

"Things are quiet," John told them and twisted his ear when he thought of just how quiet things must be at Fort Vancouver with the distinguished gentlemen sitting in the leather chairs and waiting.

"So this then is Father Blanchet's church." Marguerite stopped in the path and pinched up her indigo cotton skirt to lift it from the dust while she looked.

"Would you like to go inside?" John asked. "Soon we will be going to church every Sunday. How our lives will be changed, once we move here to Oregon City!" he exclaimed. "We will be part of an entirely different society."

Marguerite caught his cane and pulled him along in her excitement. "Johnny, I have not stepped my foot inside a real church since first we came to this Oregon Country."

John opened the door and they stood at the back of the bare plank chapel. It smelled of pine gum and mildewed matting. But scarlet draped the altar at the front and suddenly John felt that he and Marguerite had stepped through the door from raw fur country into the land of civilized customs and obligations. He watched Marguerite's hands lift and open. "*Merci*," he heard her murmur. He was thinking, "Now our life together begins on a new plane—a plane of churches and schools and every woman's head high before her neighbors. *Oui*, now is the time."

John found himself picking at the tiny rivet in the top of his cane. When it came out, the wide gold band slipped down the cane's shaft and lay in his palm. His eyes met Marguerite's above it. "Shall we find Father Blanchet?" he asked and closed his fingers on the ring.

When Father Blanchet, in cassock and surplice, had read the words and John had slipped the ring on Marguerite's finger, he saw in her a lifting of the head for which she had waited through the years. Within himself he felt a debt paid off that he had contracted on the day of young Jacques's birth.

"Would you like it to wait here in Oregon City while I finish

[*269*]

up my business at Fort Vancouver?" John asked Marguerite that night. "Soon now, we'll build our house and store here and come up to stay."

"Soon, *oui*, and I stay then. For now, I go with you to Fort Vancouver. I have inside me a feeling that our Eloise will be coming home from California with young Johnny who looks like you."

"Perhaps she will," John answered. "I do hope so."

But when they found Eloise in her old room at Fort Vancouver, she was not the daughter they had sent away. Draped in black, she held her son on her lap and talked to John and Marguerite without emotion.

"Strange things had been going on for years, *Papa*. Runners in the night and guns piled to the ceiling in our bedroom. All Billy would ever say was, 'Governor Simpson's orders.'"

John winced and rubbed his hand across his eyes. "Why didn't you write me this?"

Eloise shook her head. "I couldn't. He read all my letters. He beat me when I even tried to hint to you that something wrong was going on."

"You should have found a way to let me know," John persisted.

"No, no, I had to find a way to stop him, *Papa*," Eloise answered. "I owed it to Jacques to stop Billy and George Simpson's sneaking schemes with guns for renegades and getting the people all mixed up about which government they really wanted in California."

"But you had no chance to stop him, watched as you were."

"I slipped away and went at night to Captain Sutter's fort on the Sacramento, *Papa*. As soon as word got out that Billy was arming men for a revolt against the Mexican rulers, the people of California rose up and formed an independent government."

"They stopped young Rae then without bloodshed." John felt cheered by the news. The people of California would have a chance to choose their flag without submitting to George Simpson's say-so.

Marguerite laid down her knitting and said to Eloise, "As soon as we move to Oregon City, I think perhaps we will go to all

[*270*]

the stores and pick for you a length of the reddest silk for a new dress. And I hear it said in Oregon City that the ladies up Pudding River way wear a style of bonnet, sitting much back from the face and called Kiss-me-quick-before-mama-sees-you. Such a bonnet I should like to see on my daughter's soft brown hair. This black I do not like that you should wear."

"You have not heard, *Maman?* George Simpson had told Billy from the first that all must be kept secret and, of course, the word got out when I went to Captain Sutter. But what George Simpson did not tell Billy was that the guns and lances were all charged to his personal account. He could not pay, of course. He shot himself."

They sat in silence for a moment only. Then Marguerite got up and took her grandson from Eloise's lap. "Young Johnny, you will sleep tonight in the bed of your Uncle Jacques. Who knows? Is it not possible perhaps that you might also wear, someday, his shoes?"

John crossed the room and dropped his hand on Eloise's shoulder. Too bad about William Rae, he thought. The boy had been none too solid to begin with but not evil. He could have been shaped, at first, for good as readily as for violence and intrigue. George Simpson had used the boy. And yet Eloise had stopped Simpson's schemes in California as surely as John himself had stopped them here in Oregon. "At last," John told himself, "George Simpson is not climbing on my family to reach the dizzy heights of his ambition."

Nor did George Simpson seem within reach of his ambition by any means when he stormed into Fort Vancouver to find out why he had not been called upon to declare that Great Britain had been insulted by the burning of the Company fort. Why, he wanted to know, had he not been called upon to sail into the river and issue orders from the deck of the squadron's flagship? What had gone wrong? Why had plans been changed without consulting him? Why was Fort Vancouver not in ashes?

The officers and visiting dignitaries had assembled in John's office. They let George Simpson pace the floor and rant and then run down and fizzle out before they gave him any answers.

John, his chair tipped back against the wall, sat at his desk and waited. He had never felt more calm.

Finally, Captain Gordon kicked aside the brass cuspidor and lumbered to his feet. He hovered above George Simpson and his square jaws waggled when he spoke. "You and your cocksure schemes! So everything was all fixed, was it? So nothing or nobody could stop us? When I think what it's cost the Queen to bring our squadron across and hold us here all this time just because you got steamed up to show what a big bloke you are! Why, I could—" His fists went through the motions of wringing George Simpson's neck.

And then Lieutenant Peel stepped in. Suave as Simpson had ever been, disgust curled the edges of his words. "Mister Simpson, I should like to remind you that knighthood is conferred on the basis of achievement, not on selfish ambition. Had your big schemes been well grounded, you would have won your title, I have no doubt. As it was, a lone man has knocked the feeble props from under your conceit. Now, your presumptions appear in their true light. They are an insult to the Queen and to every decent Briton the world over. You've tried to maneuver nations into paying the price of your kneeling before the Queen. Thank God and thanks to John McLoughlin, we found you out in time."

George Simpson stepped beyond the range of his accusers. He pulled himself as tall as a defiant breath could lift him. "I'll make it yet," he said. The old aloof smile drew his mouth to the side. "You'll see. I'll still be called 'Sir George.'"

"You may." Lieutenant Peel stepped in once more and it was a draw between the two men, John decided, as to which could be more scornful of the other. "You may, indeed. But regardless of any honors you may wangle, you'll be hounded all your life by your greed. There's nothing else inside you. No honor can make you any different from what you are."

John heard a faint knock but, before he could answer, the door swung open.

Marguerite stood there, dressed in a gown of red and white

striped silk. When she came into the room, John saw that she wore the wickedest bustle in the whole of the Oregon Country.

He stepped to her side. "Gentlemen," he said, "my wife."

Lieutenant Peel clicked his heels and bowed and lifted Marguerite's hand to his lips.

Captain Gordon swiped his hairy knuckles across his mouth before he took his turn.

Marguerite stepped forward then and stood before George Simpson.

He hesitated but a moment only before he bowed and he did not falter when Marguerite, turning for the sun to strike her wedding ring, gave him her left hand.

"Bruce will serve tea now," she murmured.

The clatter of iron and the staccato of excited voices in Oregon City's Main Street sent John's household running for rain capes the first Wednesday morning in November.

"War?" Marguerite gasped.

John helped her with the hook beneath her chin. "No, no, I don't think so." He tried to keep his voice calm enough to reassure her.

"But the cannon, Johnny. Why is it that they drag a cannon along the street before our house?"

"I wonder why," he said, pondering and forgetting for the moment that he was not alone. "No, no, it's nothing," he insisted for Marguerite's sake. "I'm sure of it. You'd better stay inside and keep dry. I'll go find out, then hurry back and tell you all about it."

By the time he got into his own India rubber cape and ran out the kitchen passageway beside the Falls, the men had hauled and heaved the awkward old twelve-pounder around his house and to the river bank. There they pried and screwed and shifted to get her mounted on the rocks.

Running up, John blurted, "What's happened? What's going on?"

"Doc Long-John!"

There loomed old Joe Meek in the middle of whatever it was that was taking place.

"What is it, Mr. Joe? Are we at war?"

"At war?" Joe Meek slapped his thigh and guffawed. "That are some now, Doc!" He gave the cannon a friendly pat and came over to jab out his hand at John. "Doc Long-John, it are peace we're at, not war. The boundary line are settled. Soon as ever'-body gits hyar we're goin' to fire the cannon off—twenty-one guns to salute the good old Stars and Stripes."

"Mr. Joe, Mr. Joe, can this be true? The boundary is settled and no bloodshed?"

"True as trappin', Doc. Middle of June, it waar. Word come by the barque *Toulon* by way of the Sandwich Islands to Fort Vancouver yesterday. This child waar aimin' to come for you, soon as gittin' shed of this hyar cannon."

"But where's the line, Mr. Joe?"

"Waal now, we never quite made that 'fifty-four forty' busi-ness stick but that waar a lot of our American big-talk anyhow. Fact of the matter are, we got a sight more'n we expected. The line are set on parallel forty-nine, I understand, with Hudson's Bay property pretected until sech time as the Company can withdraw. We're satisfied and hopin' you are the same."

"Forty-nine—as far north as that," John mused. He'd read in the *Oregon Spectator* only a couple of months ago about the accession of Texas and the editor's claim that this had given new urgency to the Oregon question. "Now," the editor had written, "the want of Oregon, or slicing it away, would put the Union out of shape. It is all wanted to square the American territory." Well, it had been squared, then, and George Simpson must be fit to tie.

"Hyar comes the mayor, boys," Joe Meek called.

"Mr. Joe, hold it up till I get Marguerite. She wouldn't want to miss this, I'll be bound."

"Marguerite! Eloise! Young Johnny! Hurry now," John shouted. "The boundary is settled. We're going to celebrate."

"Hyar's the colors off the *Shark*, Doc Long-John." Joe Meek swung the bundle off his shoulder. "Reckon that thar flagstaff in

[274]

your yard could hold up its head with Stars and Stripes a-flyin'
from her?"

Marguerite and Eloise and young Johnny came running up and
soon the whole of Oregon City was milling beneath John's flagpole.

Everything got tangled and John's fingers turned to thumbs
but when Mr. Joe called out, "Hyar we go!" the cannon thun-
dered and John somehow managed to yank the proper ropes.

The flag rode up the staff and straightened itself and whipped
out above the crowd. John raised his eyes. His flag, it was. The
colors blurred for a moment, then brightened. By the auld
Clootie, this being an American required both hands on the job.
He shifted and gathered up ropes in one fist. Now, he could take
off his hat.

Set in Linotype Janson
Format by Edwin H. Kaplin
Manufactured by The Haddon Craftsmen, Inc.
Published by HARPER & BROTHERS, *New York*